# ROBERT LUDLUM'S™
# THE
# TREADSTONE
# EXILE

## THE BOURNE SERIES

*Robert Ludlum's The Bourne Evolution* (by Brian Freeman)
*Robert Ludlum's The Bourne Nemesis* (by Eric Van Lustbader)
*Robert Ludlum's The Bourne Initiative* (by Eric Van Lustbader)
*Robert Ludlum's The Bourne Enigma* (by Eric Van Lustbader)
*Robert Ludlum's The Bourne Ascendancy* (by Eric Van Lustbader)
*Robert Ludlum's The Bourne Retribution* (by Eric Van Lustbader)
*Robert Ludlum's The Bourne Imperative* (by Eric Van Lustbader)
*Robert Ludlum's The Bourne Dominion* (by Eric Van Lustbader)
*Robert Ludlum's The Bourne Objective* (by Eric Van Lustbader)
*Robert Ludlum's The Bourne Deception* (by Eric Van Lustbader)
*Robert Ludlum's The Bourne Sanction* (by Eric Van Lustbader)
*Robert Ludlum's The Bourne Betrayal* (by Eric Van Lustbader)
*Robert Ludlum's The Bourne Legacy* (by Eric Van Lustbader)
*The Bourne Ultimatum*
*The Bourne Supremacy*
*The Bourne Identity*

## THE COVERT-ONE SERIES

*Robert Ludlum's The Patriot Attack* (by Kyle Mills)
*Robert Ludlum's The Geneva Strategy* (by Jamie Freveletti)
*Robert Ludlum's The Utopia Experiment* (by Kyle Mills)
*Robert Ludlum's The Janus Reprisal* (by Jamie Freveletti)
*Robert Ludlum's The Ares Decision* (by Kyle Mills)
*Robert Ludlum's The Arctic Event* (by James H. Cobb)
*Robert Ludlum's The Moscow Vector* (with Patrick Larkin)
*Robert Ludlum's The Lazarus Vendetta* (with Patrick Larkin)
*Robert Ludlum's The Altman Code* (with Gayle Lynds)
*Robert Ludlum's The Paris Option* (with Gayle Lynds)
*Robert Ludlum's The Cassandra Compact* (with Philip Shelby)
*Robert Ludlum's The Hades Factor* (with Gayle Lynds)

# ROBERT LUDLUM'S™
# THE
# TREADSTONE
# EXILE

## JOSHUA HOOD

HEAD
ℐZEUS

First published in the US in 2021 by G.P. Putnam's Sons, an imprint of
Penguin Random House LLC.
First published in the UK in 2021 by Head of Zeus Ltd.

This is a work of fiction. All characters, organizations,
and events portrayed in this novel are either products of
the author's imagination or are used fictitiously.

9 7 5 3 1 2 4 6 8

A catalogue record for this book is available from
the British Library.

ISBN (HB): 9781789546538
ISBN (XTPB): 9781789546552
ISBN (E): 9781789546569

Printed and bound in Great Britain by
CPI Group (UK) Ltd, Croydon CR0 4YY

Book design by Tiffany Estreicher

Head of Zeus Ltd
5–8 Hardwick Street
London EC1R 4RG

WWW.HEADOFZEUS.COM

ROBERT LUDLUM'S™

# THE
# TREADSTONE
# EXILE

# PROLOGUE

## MAHÉ, SEYCHELLES

It was almost midnight when the Sikorsky S-92 clattered low over Petite Anse bay, the helo's massive fifty-six-foot rotors bending the cocoa palms that stood guard over the Kempinski Seychelles Resort's private beach.

In the back of the helicopter, Andre Cabot sat comfortably ensconced in the Corinthian leather seat, gray eyes playing over the thousand-dollar bottle of eighteen-year-old Yamazaki single malt sitting in the chair beside him.

He'd discovered the aged Japanese whisky the week before while on business in Macau, and while Cabot didn't think it was anything special, his hosts could talk about nothing else.

"You should buy a bottle, take it with you to Mahé," one of them said. "Might put Pritchard in a better mood."

The comment sent the rest of the table into stitches, and while Cabot didn't get the joke, it was obviously at *his* expense.

But he took the hit, forced a smile, and played along. Knowing that he was being watched and that everything he said or did would make its way back to the Seychelles—to Nigel Pritchard.

Cabot had been thinking about the conversation ever since, replaying every detail in his mind. His initial confusion at the laughter, followed by the spark of anger that came when he realized they were laughing at him.

*A month ago, they wouldn't look me in the eye, now they dare disrespect me in public.*

The rage rushed through his blood like a flame up a fuse, but before it could ignite his notoriously vicious temper it was tamped by the same question that was plaguing him now.

*Did the men at the table know something that he did not?*

As the founder and CEO of DarkCloud Cybersecurity, Cabot had made both his name and his fortune by unearthing the secrets the rich and powerful paid millions to keep hidden. He'd hacked governments, rigged elections, and stolen corporate secrets from Fortune 500 companies—all without leaving a trace—and the thought that somewhere out there was a question that he couldn't answer haunted his dreams.

Cabot had made inquiries and used his network of spies, hackers, and snitches to get a sense of what might be going on, but both the streets and the digital ether were silent. No matter how many times he asked the question, the answer was always the same: "No problems here. Business as usual."

But Cabot's gut told him otherwise.

"They're lying," he said.

His words were soft, barely audible over the hum of the engines, but when Cabot looked up, he wasn't surprised to find the wide-shouldered man with the bone-white scar across his throat looking at him.

"They're lying, Beck," he repeated. "I *know* they are."

"What do you want me to do?" the German asked, his damaged vocal cords leaving his voice little more than a gravelly whisper.

"Be ready," he said.

The moment the helicopter touched down, Beck was on his feet, the SIG 226 looking like a toy in his meaty hand. He ducked out of the cabin, slipped to the door with a nimbleness that belied his size, and stepped out onto the tarmac.

When he returned to the cabin a few moments later, his face was dark with anger.

"Problem?" Cabot asked.

"He didn't send a car."

Business, like war, was all about keeping your enemy off balance, and Cabot, seeing the play, instinctively knew what Nigel was trying to pull.

"Call the heliport, have them send the shuttle," he said, moving to the walnut cabinets built into the bulkhead.

"Of course," Beck replied.

While the German made the call, Cabot punched his code into the keypad and waited for the muted *click* of the magnetic lock before opening the panel.

Inside were a pair of safes; one was for storing the cash and other valuables Cabot used to pay off the government officials and customs agents he encountered while conducting business abroad—the other one was for everything else.

He opened the second safe, selected a Glock 42 from the

weapons inside, racked a round into the chamber, and dropped the pistol into his coat pocket. By the time he closed the safe and secured the panel, Beck was waiting, a silver briefcase handcuffed to his wrist.

"Let's get this over with," Cabot said, starting toward the cockpit.

"What about the bottle?" the German asked.

He contemplated leaving it there, but knowing that Nigel would have already been advised that he was bringing it, decided to keep up appearances.

"Bring it," he said.

Compared to the Mercedes-Maybach Nigel usually sent to pick him up, the resort's Cadillac Escalade was a marked step down. But Cabot had more pressing issues on his mind: mainly how much he had riding on this deal. So he settled in for the drive.

They pulled out and drove north on Anse Soleil Road, their destination glinting like a fluorescent jewel in the distance. During the day, the Club Liberté Casino was barely noticeable, the elegant two-story glass-and-stone-fronted building effortlessly eclipsed by the shimmer of the Indian Ocean and the antifreeze-green fronds of the sandragon trees swaying in the salt-laden breeze.

But once the sun went down, and the casino staff removed the protective covers from the Skybeam revolving spotlights mounted to the roof, Club Liberté came to life in a two-million-candle-power blaze of light.

There weren't many left on the island who remembered the casino's humble beginnings, back when it was just a stuffy two-thousand-square-foot pole building where locals went for cheap drinks and to feed their spare change into the nickel slots.

In 2002, Nigel came to town and bought the place for pennies on the dollar. Most people, Cabot included, thought he'd over-paid, but the cagey Englishman proved them wrong, betting that the poker fad sweeping the United States would eventually spread to their far corner of the world.

He was right, and after spending a year strong-arming the rest of the casinos on the island—running them out of business—he unveiled the completely remodeled casino. As the only legal gaming facility left on the island, Club Liberté quickly established itself as the region's premier entertainment venue.

As an avid gambler himself, it was a place Cabot usually enjoyed visiting, but when the Escalade pulled through the gate and followed the cobblestone drive to the main entrance, he felt nothing but dread.

The driver stopped beside the scarlet carpet, where a doorman in a black tuxedo stood waiting.

Before he had a chance to open the door, Beck hopped out, the bulky German making no attempt to hide the pistol on his waist.

He brushed the man aside with a gruff "Tell your boss that Monsieur Cabot is here," and scanned the area. Once the man in the tuxedo scrambled through the main entrance, Beck turned back to the Escalade.

"All clear."

Cabot climbed out and smoothed the front of his graphite-gray W. W. Chan & Sons suit, double-checked the pistol in his pocket, and started for the door. He barely made it to the steps before a man with slicked-back black hair and a tight-fitting Italian-cut suit stepped out to meet him, an accommodating smile spread wide across his face.

"Monsieur Cabot," he began in French, "so very nice to . . ."

He paused, the smile faltering when he saw the Escalade sitting at the curb. *"Oh, merde."*

"My thoughts exactly."

"Please, Monsieur Cabot, the oversight, it was n-not intentional."

"It's fine," he lied. "Now, if you would be so kind, I am late to my meeting."

"Of course," the man nodded. "Mr. Pritchard is waiting in the VIP room."

They stepped inside. Cabot returned the nods of the gray-haired men licking their wounds in the leather club chairs that lined the entryway and pushed through the pair of burnished teak doors before stepping out onto the gaming floor.

It was standing room only, the floor packed with the island's rich and shameless. Gold-chained men and collagen-enhanced women crowded around the tables, chain-smoking while laying thousand-dollar cash bets at the roulette and craps tables.

Cabot followed the man up the carpeted stairs and into a hall, passing a line of rooms before reaching a pair of gold-inlaid doors.

"If the monsieur will permit me," the man said, ducking inside.

Cabot shot his cuff and consulted the Rolex Daytona on his wrist. The minute hand ticked past the top of the hour—the realization that he was late burned hotter than the cigarette smoke that stung his eyes.

Thirty seconds later, the man was back. He held the door open, and with a slight bow announced, "Mr. Pritchard would like you to meet him in the main room."

*About time.*

Cabot passed through the sitting room with its pastel walls, cherry-stained bookshelves, and a pair of cream-colored couches and found himself in a second, larger room with an empty felt-topped card table and a rough-hewn bar where a pair of scantily clad call girls eyed him over flutes of Veuve Clicquot.

He ignored the girls, his focus never leaving the two men seated in the oversized leather armchairs in the center of the room.

"Ah, Bertie, look who finally arrived," Nigel Pritchard said, a sardonic grin stretching across his fleshy face.

*You fat fuck.*

"There were transportation issues," Cabot said.

"Ah, that old Sikorsky of yours finally give up the ghost?"

"No," Cabot said, reining in his temper, "the issue wasn't on *my* end."

"Well, at least you made it."

"Looks like he came bearing gifts as well," the second man said, nodding to the bottle in Beck's hand.

"That must be the famed Yamazaki our friends in Macau were telling me about," he said, eyes lighting up as he hefted his bulk from the chair and tottered across the room.

Nigel had obviously been drinking, and for an instant it appeared the booze had gone to his head and that he was about to snatch the bottle from Beck's hands. His fingers were inches from the neck when something in the German's eyes made him reconsider his actions.

He froze, jerked his hand back like a man who'd seen a snake hiding in the weeds, and stood there nervously licking his lips.

*Not as dumb as you look, eh, Nigel?*

Nigel tore his eyes from the bottle and turned to Cabot with a petulant "Well?"

"Let the dog have it," he told his bodyguard in German.

Beck handed the bottle over and Nigel spent a few seconds studying the label before handing it to one of the hookers at the bar.

"Pour us a drink, love," he said, motioning for Cabot to take the seat across from his.

Cabot lowered himself into the chair, the contemptuous smile of the man seated to his left sending a flash of anger up his spine. He focused every ounce of his considerable will on keeping his face blank, *not* reacting to the obvious bait, but knew he'd failed when Nigel asked, "You remember Bertie, don't you?"

Not trusting his voice, Cabot nodded *yes*.

"How daft of me. Of course you do—he *used* to work for you," Nigel chortled.

"Andre," his former employee nodded.

*Andre, is it? Why, you snot-nosed little fuck.*

The arrival of the booze marked the end of the bullshit, and while Nigel slurped at the whisky, Bertie produced a laptop and set it on the table.

"You have the money?"

Beck was at his side in a flash, unlocking the cuff and placing the case before his boss.

"Five hundred thousand, as agreed," Cabot said, popping the clasps and opening the lid, revealing a stack of bearer bonds.

Bertie nodded, typed a passcode, hit the enter key, and spun the laptop toward Cabot, who pulled a pair of gold reading glasses from his pocket.

*This is it.*

He slid the glasses over his eyes, leaned forward, and grabbed the laptop. He pulled it into his lap and inspected the files, heart thumping in his chest as he scrolled through the diagrams and blueprints, noting the marked security positions and locations of the mainframe computers, everything he needed to pull off the job that would save his company—save his *life*.

He was almost to the end of the document, the elation and relief welling inside of him until he thought that he might burst, and then he reached the last page and deflated like a balloon.

*The codes, where the hell are the codes?*

Cabot sat there staring at the screen, momentarily confused by the missing data, then he looked up, found Nigel staring at him over the rim of the half-empty lowball.

"We had a deal," he hissed.

"Yes, well, that was *before* you bolloxed the Uganda affair."

"What are you talking about?" he demanded.

"Do you believe this, Bertie, he *actually* thought that he could keep it a secret," Nigel hooted, his jowls bouncing in time with his laughter. "Thought no one would find out that he was spying for the Ugandan government, helping them rig the election."

"Or that while the French government is working to seize all of DarkCloud's assets," Bertie sneered, "they have banned its CEO from traveling to Africa."

"How much?" Cabot asked, cutting straight to the point.

"An additional five hundred thousand," Nigel said, wiping the tears from his eyes, "and considering your current financial woes, I'd suggest taking the deal before the price goes up."

"You will wire the money to Nigel's Cayman account," Bertie began, "and when I get confirmation—"

But Cabot had heard enough.

He jumped to his feet, yanked the Glock from his pocket, and centering the sights on Bertie's forehead said, "I'd rather pay you now."

The pistol bucked in his hand, Cabot turning as the bullet snapped the man's head back and he pumped two rounds into Nigel's gut.

"Shut them the fuck up," he yelled in German. The command was barely out of his mouth before he heard the wet smack of flesh on flesh and the whimper of one of the women at the bar.

"Quiet now, girls, or I'll slit those pretty throats," Beck warned.

In the chair, Nigel looked down at the spread of crimson across his shirt, then up at Cabot. "What . . . what have you done?" he asked, eyes wide with disbelief.

Cabot chopped the Glock across the man's mouth, the blow knocking him out of his seat, sending a spray of blood and shattered teeth across the room. Before the fat man hit the ground, Cabot had him by the front of his shirt.

"Where are the codes?" Cabot demanded, pressing the barrel of the Glock into his face. "Tell me and you die fast—lie to me and I'll have Beck peel off your skin with a shard of glass."

"Gra . . . Grand-Bassam."

"Where in Grand-Bassam, who has them?"

His reply was so faint that Cabot had to lean in to hear it. Only after Nigel had repeated it again and he was sure the Englishman was telling the truth did he let go of the man's shirt and press the Glock against his chest.

"Not so smug now, are you, fat man?" he asked, before pulling the trigger.

**1**

CEUTA, SPAIN

I t was late afternoon and hot as hell when Carlito Rocha eased
the Yamaha YZ125 to a halt on the hill overlooking the Calle
Real. An hour before, the block was alive, the street packed
with cars and the cobblestone sidewalks that bordered the glass
boutiques awash with shoppers.

But now it was siesta, and the street lay silent and still. The
only sound: the gentle *put-put* of the dirt bike's two-stroke engine
as Carlito motored down the hill and turned into the alley at the
end of the block.

He stopped next to a green dumpster, backed the bike out
of sight, and deployed the kickstand with the heel of his ratty
tennis shoes. He made sure the front tire was pointed at the street.
He thought about leaving the engine running in case someone

called the *policía,* in which case he'd need to make a quick get-away.

*No, someone will steal it,* he thought.

Carlito pulled the key from the ignition and climbed off the bike. He wiped the sweat from his forehead and tightened the straps of his backpack before starting toward the metal door twenty feet in front of him, carefully avoiding the broken beer bottles and scattered trash that lined his path. He was almost to the door when something stopped him in his tracks.

*What the hell is it?*

He didn't know, but something was wrong, and he was instantly on guard. Eyes ticking back the way he'd come, searching the mouth of the alley for a threat that wasn't there.

Carlito found himself hesitating, thinking back to the plan he'd made a week ago. Wondering why in the hell he'd *ever* thought it was a good idea to leave the Barrio del Príncipe—the lawless fourteen-thousand-square-meter slum that he knew better than the back of his hand—and come north to the Barrio de Borizu.

He knew the answer was the same then as it was now. He'd come north *after* the economic collapse of 2008 that had precipitated his family's move from their two-story house near the ocean to the squalid apartment in the barrio. After his father used what little money they had left to drink himself to death, Carlito had become the man of the house, leaving *him* responsible for feeding his mother and young sisters.

He'd tried to do the right thing, get a job, but with the Ceuta economy in shambles there was no work. It was a situation that left him with only two choices: starve or steal.

And Carlito was done being hungry.

So he decided to go north and try his hand breaking into the hotels close to the marina where the *guiris*—the rich tourists—stayed.

He thought back to his mother and sisters sitting at home, starving in that piece-of-shit apartment. *They are counting on you, coward,* he thought.

Carlito tugged the gray ski mask from his back pocket and pulled it over his curly brown hair. The mask was filthy, the fabric reeking of sweat and exhaust, but he ignored it. He grabbed the scarred crowbar from his pack and turned back to the door.

In one practiced motion, he drove the tip into the seam an inch above the lock and yanked on the handle. The door flexed and the bolt grated against the frame but refused to give.

"C'mon, you bitch," he cursed, bracing his foot against the wall.

He pushed off, leaning back, pulling until his biceps shook and the sweat rolled down his face. He was panting now, mouth moving in a silent prayer, begging whatever god was listening that the door would open before he ran out of strength.

Then the lock tore free of the frame and the door swung open, throwing Carlito off balance.

He stumbled backward, losing his grip on the crowbar, the clatter of the metal off the concrete sending ice up his spine.

*Oh, shit.*

He scooped the crowbar off the ground, heart hammering in his chest when he stuffed it into the pack, the open doorway before him looming dark as the grave. Every instinct screaming at him to run. *Get back to the bike and get the hell out of the alley.*

But in the end, it was the hollow growl in his stomach and the thought of his family back in that wretched apartment that won out.

Carlito rooted around the bottom of the pack, brushing over the tools of his trade, the rusted hammer and dull bolt cutters, before closing around the grip of the .44 Magnum he'd stolen the week before.

The heft of the heavy revolver in his fist, the rattle of the massive bullets in the chamber, restored his confidence, reminding Carlito that no matter what was waiting for him inside, *he* was the one with the gun.

*The motherfucker in charge,* he thought, stepping inside.

When Adam Hayes arrived at the Hostal La Perla, he hadn't killed anyone in one hundred and fifty-two days. It wasn't the kind of achievement you gloated about, not even in a lawless town like Ceuta, but it was a streak he wanted to keep alive. Which is why he was standing in the street, blue eyes scrutinizing La Perla's weathered yellow façade and wondering if the hostel was worth the twenty-five euros advertised on the faded marquee.

*It's only for one night.*

With that thought in mind, he started toward the front door.

The "lobby" was on par with the exterior: four bare concrete walls and a peeling linoleum floor—the only furniture a pair of worn couches and a scarred wooden table covered in faded travel magazines.

But Hayes didn't see any rats, which meant it was clean enough. More importantly, the lobby was free of the scumbags he would have encountered if he'd gone to *any* of the off-the-grid hotels he'd frequented in his past life.

Places that catered to murderers, pimps, and human traffickers—the kind of trash that made Hayes's trigger finger itch—threatened to break his streak.

He moved to the front desk, where the night manager sat, eyes glued to the television perched in the corner.

"Yes?" he asked, eyes never leaving the TV.

"A room," Hayes answered in accentless Spanish. "One on the bottom floor, near the back if you have it."

"Yes, yes, whatever you want," the manager said.

The manager grabbed the twenty-five euros Hayes placed on the desk without looking up. His hand darted below the desk and returned with a key attached to a faded square of plastic.

"Room 107," he said, still glued to the TV. "It's around back, next to the toilets."

*"Gracias."*

Hayes took the key and followed the burnt rope smell of marijuana into a hallway lit by a pair of bare bulbs. He was on autopilot now, the thousands of hours spent working the Treadstone kill houses back in the States taking over. Freeing his mind and body to work independently of conscious thought. His eyes locked on an open door, muscle memory taking over as he approached, pace slowing, hand dropping to the pistol holstered at his waist, fingers closing around the grip.

But instead of an assassin waiting with a gun, Hayes found a mass of unwashed backpackers passing a joint.

"Want a hit?" one of the kids asked in French.

"Thanks, but I'm good."

He continued down the hall, pausing at the emergency exit to check the deadbolt, make sure it was secure before stopping in front of room 107. He unlocked the door; any thought that his days of staying in run-down hotels were over when he left Treadstone twenty-four months earlier vanished at the sight of the chipped Formica table and the ancient air conditioner hanging over the sagging bed.

*It's only for one night.*

That was three days ago.

The A/C had given out the first night, and it was stifling in the room. Too hot to sleep, or think, or do *anything* other than sit there and sweat.

But Hayes was well versed in the art of suffering. It was a skill he'd mastered during his time in Treadstone—the CIA's Special Access Program that had plucked him out of the military and turned him into a government-sanctioned assassin.

He sat at the table, the sand linen button-down clinging to his back like a sheet of Saran Wrap as he dropped the magazine from the STI Staccato XC, racked the round out of the pipe, and began breaking down the pistol for the third time that day.

He took his time, wiping a rag over the Trijicon miniature reflex sight mounted in front of the rear sight before removing the slide. Hayes had just set the guide rod and spring on the oil-soaked shirt he'd laid across the table when his cell finally chirped to life.

*About damn time.*

"*Da?*" he answered, putting the phone on speaker.

"Marina Hércules," the voice replied in Russian. "Do you know where that is?"

Hayes might have been stuck in the room for the past three days, but he hadn't been idle. Besides checking his gear and cleaning the pistol, he'd memorized the travel map he'd picked up during one of his forays out for food, and while his fingers flew over the pistol, Hayes brought it up in his mind.

"Yes, I know where it is."

"Good, be at the Sky Bar in one hour, and come alone."

Hayes ended the call, slammed the magazine into the now reassembled pistol, racked a round into the chamber, and got to his feet. He stuffed the STI into its holster and moved to the bed, where his bag lay waiting.

His time as a Green Beret in Afghanistan had taught him how to live out of a rucksack; how to pack light, which is why the only comfort items in his bag were an extra shirt, a pair of pants, one small toiletry bag, and four pairs of socks.

Everything else either went bang or boom.

Hayes stripped off his shirt, strapped a level III Kevlar vest to his chest, and shoved an extra magazine of 9-millimeter hollow points into the pouch on his belt. After belting the travel wallet with his passport and emergency cash across his stomach, he pulled on his shirt. He stuffed the wad of euros into his right pocket and the spring-loaded Microtech Troodon knife into his left, shouldered the pack, and started for the door.

Hayes stepped out into the hall and after locking the door behind him, started toward the office. He was two feet from the emergency exit when the door flew open. The blaze of sunlight that rolled into the dark hallway hit Hayes in the face. It exploded like a flashbang, leaving him blind.

His instincts took over and he stepped to the left, shoulder searching for the wall, right hand yanking the pistol from its holster. He blinked the stars from his eyes and was seeking a target when a masked figure stepped into the hall, the pistol in his hand aimed at Hayes's face.

# 2

Hayes stared at the man, oddly calm despite the barrel of the .44 Magnum yawning like a tunnel in front of his eyes. He was aware of every detail, the weight of the 9-millimeter in his hand, the press of his finger against the trigger, and the voice in his head screaming like a banshee.

*KILL HIM. KILL HIM NOW.*

Hayes understood that neither the voice nor the extreme calm that came over him in times like these was natural. They were synthetic emotions, by-products of the mind job the Treadstone scientists had done when they transformed him from a Green Beret to a government-sanctioned assassin.

An apex predator trained to hunt and kill without the slightest hesitation.

But he was done killing and the fact that the man was still breathing was a testament to how far he'd come.

Hayes silenced the voice—pushed it back into its box until it was nothing more than an annoying hum—and then focused all his attention on the man with the pistol. He wasn't sure if it was the fear in the man's eyes or the tremble of the pistol in his hand, but for whatever reason, he found himself hesitating.

Searching for a reason *not* to kill the man.

He took his finger off the trigger and lowered the 1911, praying he wasn't making the biggest mistake of his life.

"Take it easy," he said in Spanish.

"M-money . . . g-give me your money."

The figure's voice was rough around the edges but not deep, and Hayes realized that it wasn't a man in front of him, but a teenager.

*Yeah, I'm definitely not killing a kid.*

"What's your name?" he asked, returning the pistol to the holster.

"What?"

"Your name."

"C-Carlito," he stuttered.

"Listen, Carlito, why don't you . . ."

"No, you listen. Give me your money, or I'll k-kill you."

They were tough words, but Hayes wasn't buying it.

"It's a hell of a thing to kill a man," he said, taking a step forward.

"Ba . . . back up."

Hayes ignored him, took another step, closing the distance until he was inches from the pistol. Close enough to see Carlito's index finger whiten as he increased the tension on the trigger.

"Just take it easy," he said.

Still holding the room key in his hand, Hayes lifted his arms to his chest and held them palms out—hyperaware of the pistol pointed at his face. He was determined to end the situation without violence, but when he heard the *click* of the trigger spring engage the hammer, Hayes wasn't sure if that was a possibility.

While he wasn't sure if the boy was preparing to shoot him or was simply unaware of how much pressure he was exerting on the trigger, Hayes realized it didn't matter. Especially considering that either option ended with him taking a bullet to the face.

*Had about enough of this silly game.*

His hands were almost level with Carlito's eyes when Hayes opened his fingers and let the room key drop from his hand.

The light tumbling in through the open door glinted off the key as it fell. The unexpected spark of sun on brass caught Carlito's attention. Hayes watched his eyes, waited for the shift in focus he knew would come—and the moment the boy's eyes ticked down to the falling key, he struck.

He grabbed the barrel with his left hand and the cylinder with his right. His fingers closed around the hammer, locking it down before torquing the pistol from the boy's hand.

In the blink of an eye it was over. Hayes's fingers were wrapped around the grip of the revolver, the barrel jammed into Carlito's forehead.

"D-don't kill me," the boy begged.

Hayes lowered the pistol and dropped the hammer before stuffing the revolver into his waistband. "I don't kill kids," he said, pulling the wad of cash from his pocket.

Carlito looked at the fistful of euros, then up at his face, the confusion in his eyes evident.

"I-I don't understand."

"Don't overthink it, kid, just take the money," Hayes said, slapping the cash into his palm. "Now get the hell out of here."

Carlito stuffed the cash into his pocket, turning to the door as Hayes bent down and retrieved his key.

"Oh, and kid," he called after him. "Do yourself a favor. Stop pointing guns at strangers."

Twenty minutes later, Hayes was sitting in La Habana Café, a double vodka tonic sweating on the cocaine-white tablecloth before him. The money he'd given Carlito was supposed to have lasted him the rest of the month, and the gesture, while noble, had put a serious dent in his operating funds.

*You're an idiot,* the voice told him.

*Maybe so,* he thought, lifting the drink from the table and taking a sip, *but I'd rather be broke than have another body on my conscience.*

The bitter mix of lime and melted ice offered a brief respite from the sweltering heat, but more important, the double shot of vodka calmed his frayed nerves. He wanted another one but resisted the urge, knowing that he'd need a clear head for the task at hand.

Hayes turned his attention to the mouth of the harbor and the Westport tri-deck streaming past the seawall. The sight of the luxury yacht was a sign of how much the city had changed since the last time he'd been here.

He sucked on the ice, admiring the captain's skills as he worked the throttles and gracefully maneuvered the ungainly yacht into the harbor. Hayes was enjoying the show until he noticed the woman with the red hair standing on the sundeck, the young boy in her arms sending his mind racing back to the States.

Back to his wife, Annabelle, and his three-year-old son, Jack, and the promise he'd made when he left Treadstone. How he told them he would do *whatever* it took to break free of the violence and rage that came from the behavior modification the docs had used to turn him into an assassin.

He'd done everything in his power to keep that promise, going so far as to pack everything he owned into the back of his old Chevy and driving out to Washington State for an eighteen-month exile. He'd even swallowed his pride and started working with a shrink in Tacoma, taking the meds she prescribed, believing her when she told him that he was "making wonderful progress."

But in the end, he knew it was only a matter of time before his past caught up with him, forced him into a situation where the only way out was to do what he did best—kill. Which is exactly what happened.

Hayes had known there would be consequences for his actions—figured there was a good chance Levi Shaw, the director of Treadstone, would send him to some dark corner of the world, lock him into a black site, and throw away the key.

But never in his wildest dreams did he imagine they'd kick him out of the country—stamp his passport with PNG.

Persona non grata.

*Not fucking welcome*, he thought.

The thought of leaving the United States had been a hard pill to swallow, but it was having to leave his wife and three-year-old son that had almost killed him. But it was either that or spend the rest of his short life looking over his shoulder, waiting for the day when the government sent someone to put a bullet in the back of his skull.

Hayes untangled himself from the past with a shake of his head and took a moment to clear his mind before turning his attention west.

With its white stucco façade and crimson awning, the Sky Bar was hard to miss. But with the rays of the dying sun glinting off the emerald blue of the sea, Hayes was having a hard time identifying the people who ducked through the front door, and if it hadn't been for the loud Hawaiian shirt his contact was wearing, he might have missed him.

Hayes used the napkin to wipe the prints off the glass, grabbed his bag, and got to his feet. He moved to the door, where he paused to study the trickle of sunburned faces that streamed past him, absorbing their pace and posture, willing himself to relax.

The transformation was subtle, a softening of the tension lines at the edge of his blue eyes and a relaxed sag of his shoulders, but they were effective, and when Hayes stepped out onto the cobblestones, he was just another vacationer out for a late afternoon stroll.

He followed the street west, but while his body was at ease, his eyes never stopped moving. They probed every doorway and alley. He used the mirrors of the cars parked on the street and the glass-fronted shops to check his backtrail, and when he was sure that he was clear, ducked into the alley on the north of Sky Bar.

He stashed the bag behind a stack of empty beer crates piled next to the service door and tried the knob.

Locked.

But Hayes had come prepared.

He pulled a nylon case from his back pocket and crouched in front of the knob to get a better look into the keyway.

*What are we working with here—single cylinder deadbolt? Too easy.*

Using a tension wrench to apply pressure to the cylinder, Hayes stuck the pick into the lock and began manipulating the pins. Three years ago, and he'd have had the door opened before the owner could get his keys out of his pocket.

But lockpicking was a perishable skill and Hayes was out of practice.

*C'mon, you son of a bitch.*

The seconds seemed to stretch into hours and realizing how exposed he was to the people walking past the alleyway, Hayes was about to say to hell with it and boot the door, when the pins clicked into place and the knob turned.

*Thank God,* he thought, stepping inside.

He followed the service stairs up to the second floor and stepped out into the kitchen. Ignoring the curious looks from the cooks and dishwashers, Hayes crossed to the stainless-steel door and using the scarred plexiglass window looked out into the dining room.

It was early for dinner, and near the front door the raven-haired hostess stood bored behind her mahogany podium. Out on the patio a handful of older patrons picked at salads and sipped wine while watching the sun dip below the horizon.

But most of the action was at the bar, and that's where Hayes found his contact, Vladimir Drugov, sitting with his back to the hall. His gaudy floral shirt stretched over his bulging midsection; rheumy gray eyes locked on the half-empty bottle of vodka before him.

Hayes eased through the door, waiting until Vlad had the

glass to his mouth before slipping up behind him and jamming his index finger into the back of the man's skull.

"*Ne dvigaysya.*" Don't move.

Vlad jerked in his chair, booze sloshing down the front of his shirt.

"What the hell is wrong with you?" he demanded in Russian. "Scaring me like that. I might have had a heart attack."

Hayes flashed a smile he didn't feel and took a seat, watched as Vlad dabbed at the front of his shirt with a napkin.

"When I was stationed in Syria, there was this annoying little *koshechka*—a cat that hung around the safe house. It was a pest, always showing up when it wanted to, scaring the hell out of people."

"What did you do? Kill it?"

Vlad shot him a hard look. "No, I didn't *kill* it," he scowled. "I put a bell around its neck."

"A bell?"

"So, I could *hear* it coming."

"Never took you for a cat lover."

"The cat was annoying, like you," Vlad said, reaching for the bottle, "but being annoyed is better than being alone? Yes?"

Hayes stared, watched as he lifted the bottle to his lips and took a long pull.

"You know what's annoying, Vlad? Sitting in your room for three days while your contact is out fucking off."

The Russian came up for air, wiped the back of his hand across his mouth, and shot Hayes a frown.

"I—I, uh . . ."

Hayes held up his hand, cutting him off, not interested in his excuses.

"All I want to know is if you made contact."

"I don't understand you, putting yourself at risk for—"

"Where is the meet?" Hayes interrupted. "That's all I need to know."

Vlad was not used to being interrupted, and his face reddened, the anger in his eyes sharp as the blade he carried at his waist.

Of all the Russians Hayes had met, Vlad was the most mellow. Or he had been *before* he got back on the booze. He wasn't sure what had knocked him off the wagon, but in the last month he'd noticed that Vlad was drinking more and sleeping less. The unhealthy combination added a hair trigger to the Russian's volatile temper.

"Mogador."

"Morocco, that's Luca's territory." Hayes grimaced.

"Is that a problem?" the Russian asked.

Hayes frowned and glanced out the window, where a black powerboat was speeding toward the marina, the guttural roar of the boat's engines rolling loud across the emerald-blue water.

"When?" he asked.

"Eight hours."

"Are you serious?" he asked, turning his attention back to the Russian.

"*Da,*" Vlad said, pulling a phone from his pocket and setting it on the table. "They will call you."

"Then I better get going," Hayes said, grabbing the phone and getting to his feet.

"It's a waste of time," the Russian said, reaching for the bottle of vodka.

Hayes stuffed the phone into his back pocket, leaned over, and snatched the bottle off the table before Vlad's fingers could close around the neck.

"What the fuck?" he demanded.

"You're done drinking."

Vlad jumped to his feet, his face scarlet, the knife snapping open in his hand.

"And who are you to tell me anything?" he demanded.

Hayes glanced down at the blade, felt the heat in his guts unlimber, his eyes flashing hard as he turned to face the Russian.

"I'm the one telling you how it is," he said.

There was murder in Vlad's eyes, and he stepped around the table, his lips stretched tight against his teeth.

His time at Treadstone had taught Hayes the importance of blending in, and to avoid *any* situation that would draw attention to themselves and thereby compromise their mission. But all it took was one look at the Russian's face and he knew that wasn't a possibility.

*Have it your way.*

Hayes stepped in, clamped his right hand around Vlad's wrist, and twisted the knife down as he pulled the Russian in close. His left hand was already screaming up from his waist, thumb and forefinger splayed, aimed at his throat.

He hit him hard, but with a practiced control that made sure the wet *pop* of the blow was barely audible over the voices in the bar.

Hayes had half a mind to put the Russian down right then and there, but he resisted the urge and cast a quick glance around the bar.

So far, the altercation had gone unnoticed, but Hayes had been here before and knew it wouldn't last. Knew he couldn't hold out against the violence rolling through his veins like lava before it consumed him. Before he gave in to the voice, pulled the pistol from his hip, and put a bullet through the center of the Russian's forehead.

Summoning the last bit of self-control, Hayes ducked under Vlad's arm and grabbed the back of his belt. He heaved him to his feet and half carried, half dragged him to the bathroom.

By the time he made it to the first stall, Hayes's heart was beating like an AK on full auto, his breath coming in deep, ragged gasps. He dumped the Russian unceremoniously onto the shitter, his only thought getting the hell out of the bathroom before he lost control.

Vlad staggered backward, the thump of his body against the wall bringing him back to the land of the living.

The Russian looked up, hand curled protectively around his neck, eyes blinking like a man coming out of a trance.

"I-I don't . . ." he began in a raspy voice.

But Hayes wasn't listening.

He pushed off the wall, the collar of his shirt tight as a noose around his throat.

*I can't breathe.*

He clawed at the button, his vision tunneling around the edges as he staggered to the sink. He turned on the faucet and splashed a handful of cold water over his face.

*Get ahold of yourself.*

When his mind had cleared, Hayes turned off the water, dried his face with a handful of paper towels, and was crossing to the door when Vlad broke his silence.

"You need me!" he shouted.

Any other time, the fact that he was leaving the Russian with his life would have been more than enough for Hayes to walk out with his conscience intact.

But this time it was different.

He'd made promises—given his word to a doctor back in Burkina Faso—and there was no way in hell Vlad was going to turn him into a liar.

*Dammit.*

He turned to the Russian, the voice in his head screaming like a drill sergeant.

*You're fucking up. The man's a rabid dog. An animal. Do the world a favor and put a bullet in his head before it's too late.*

"I want you to sober up," he said.

"Yes, yes, of course."

"I want you to go to the airfield, get the plane fueled up, and *wait* for me there—you got that?"

"Yes."

"And Vlad, the next time you pull a blade on me, I'll kill you."

# 3

T he Lincoln Town Car pulled up outside the Congressional
Visitors Center and Treadstone Director Levi Shaw climbed
out. He flashed his ID card to the security officer at the door
and dropped his battered attaché case onto the X-ray machine.
After emptying his pockets, he walked through the metal detector
and started toward the elevator, where a pair of government-
issued pit bulls in matching blue suits stood waiting.

"Morning, Tommy," he said, noting the hint of a smile at the
corner of the taller man's lips.

"Director Shaw," the man nodded, following him in and in-
serting his ID card into the reader.

The light blinked green and the doors hissed closed; Tommy
punched the down button before keying up on his radio.

"On our way."

"Just so you know," Shaw said, reaching into his pocket and retrieving a hundred-dollar bill, "that last call was *bullshit*."

"He was out by a mile," Tommy grinned, plucking the bill from his hand and holding it up to the light.

"Seriously?" he asked.

"Never know with you Agency boys."

"Now you're hurting my feelings," Shaw said.

Tommy shrugged and, satisfied that the bill was legit, stuffed it into his pocket.

"So, what's going on?" Shaw asked, face turning serious.

Tommy reached for the radio on his hip and rotated the switch, waiting until it clicked and the red power light went off before answering.

"I don't know what you did, but the council is pissed."

"Details, Tommy."

"It's about your boy, that's all I know."

*Fuck.*

"Thanks, I owe you one."

"Least I can do, sir," he said, turning the radio back on for a second before the elevator settled on its bumper.

The doors hissed open and Shaw followed his minder down the hall, patent leather shoes squeaking off the freshly waxed floor.

To most people it was just another government basement, its bureaucratic beige walls and line of unmarked doors barely worth noticing. But to Shaw it was a reminder of how far he'd come in the last six months. A monument to his unexpected rise from the National Intelligence Program's administrative graveyard buried deep in the bowels of the Pentagon. The purgatorial pit where

Operation Treadstone had been sent to linger until its source funding ran out and it died.

Having his life's work put to such a slow and painful death had been a hard pill to swallow, but Shaw had come to grips with his fate. Prepared himself for the inevitable moment when the program slipped quietly into nonexistence. But at the final hour, Treadstone was given a reprieve. Saved from the brink of death, Shaw found himself once again standing on center stage.

But that was in the past—right now the only thing that mattered was what lay on the other side of the solid steel door at the end of the hall.

*Get your head in the game,* Shaw told himself as they rounded the corner, stepping into a short hall with a single door at the end.

At first glance it was just another door, the only feature that hinted at its purpose—the blood-red placard in the center with RESTRICTED ACCESS printed in one-inch letters. But the illusion faded after Tommy swiped his card over the reader. Once the magnetic lock disengaged with a tiny click, the thickness of both the frame and the door itself proved that this was *not* just another office.

A stern-faced man in black BDUs stood next to the X-ray machine, a second seated inside a bulletproof cube. Both were armed, but unlike the pristine pistols that glinted in the holsters of the security guards upstairs, the SIGs on their hips were battle-worn, the textured grips abraded by years of use.

"Good morning, Director," the man at the X-ray machine said. "Please place your bag on the belt and empty your pockets in the tray."

Shaw followed the man's directions, repeating the same steps he had on entering the building. But this time, instead of walking through a magnetometer he was directed to a full-body scanner and advised to place his hands on his head.

"He's good," the man inside the cube said.

By the time Shaw stepped through, the man in the BDUs had already placed everything by his attaché case into a black bag, zipped it up, and stuffed it into a locker.

Shaw clipped the badge to his lapel, grabbed his case from the belt, and stepped to the mahogany door to his front. He took a deep breath, mentally preparing himself for whatever lay on the other side, and then grabbed the handle.

Compared to the austere antechamber, the interior of the Senate Intelligence Committee SCIF—or Sensitive Compartmented Information Facility—looked like any other meeting room in the building. Same mahogany wainscoted walls, burgundy carpet, and horseshoe table at the front of the room.

Shaw made his way to the solitary table in the center of the room and took a seat. He placed his attaché case on the floor and was turning his attention to the men seated before him when Senator Landon Miles rapped the gavel against the sounding block and called the Senate Intelligence Committee to order.

"Director Shaw, there are three reasons you have been called before this committee today. The first is the memo you submitted at the beginning of the month regarding the Gen 4 program. Do you recall that memo?"

"Yes, sir, I have a copy here," Shaw answered, pulling a stack of files from his attaché case and placing them on the table.

"Now, correct me if I'm wrong, but six months ago you advised this committee that by the end of the year the Gen 4s would be operational," Miles said, pausing his attack to consult his notes. "I believe your exact words were, 'They will be ready to kick ass and take names.' Do you remember saying that?"

"Yes, sir."

"But according to your latest timeline you now require an additional six months. Why is that?"

"Well, Senator, it's not like we are making license plates."

"Excuse me?"

*Dammit, c'mon, Levi, get your head out of your ass.*

"My apologies, Senator, what I meant to say was that turning a man into a weapon takes time, especially taking into account certain abnormalities we found with the Gen 3s."

"You're talking about Adam Hayes. Am I correct?"

All it took was one look at the senator's face, the triumphant jut of his jaw, and Shaw knew that he'd screwed up. Let his focus slip just long enough to walk right into the chairman's trap.

*Got to get ahead of him, redirect the conversation.*

But before Shaw had a chance, Senator Miles leaned forward in his chair, his eyes hungry as a starved wolf. "Since you brought it up, Director Shaw, I don't think my colleagues would object if we put a pin in that first question and cut to the *real* reason I called you here this morning."

Shaw reached instinctively for the bottle of water sitting next to his microphone, mentally preparing himself for the question he knew was coming.

"I would also like it clearly noted in the record that this is the *last* time I am going to ask you this question—do you understand that, Director Shaw?"

"Yes, sir," Shaw replied, twisting the cap free and taking a drink.

"Good, now, for the last time, where in the hell is Adam Hayes?" Miles asked, his voice cold as a knife.

Shaw swallowed the mouthful of water and was returning the bottle to its place when his mind drifted back to the last time he saw Adam Hayes. The memory was crystal clear, every emotion, every angry word etched painfully in his mind.

He hadn't wanted it to go down the way it had, but Hayes had left him with little choice.

*"Either you come in, or I will send a team to bring you in," he'd told him over the phone.*

*"Are you threatening me, Levi?"*

*"No, Adam, we are way past that point."*

*"Somewhere public, where I can see you and you can see me."*

*"The bridge at Rock Creek, two hours."*

*"I'll be there."*

*Shaw had arrived in an hour and sat on the bench at the west side of the bridge while a General Atomics MQ-9 Reaper circled silently twenty-five thousand feet above. At $15.9 million, the Reaper was the most advanced surveillance platform in the government's arsenal. With its sophisticated ground targeting systems and APY-8 Lynx II radar the UAV was the perfect blend of technology and lethality.*

*Ten minutes later the operator reported in, his voice clear through the microcommunication bud pressed into Shaw's ear.*

*"This is Viper two-one, we've finished our sweep, no contact with target."*

*With the area clear, Shaw was beginning to think that Hayes had somehow detected the surveillance—knew that he was being watched and had blown off the meet.*

*But how?*

*"Because that's what you trained him to do," he muttered.*

*Shaw got to his feet and was preparing to leave when he saw him standing alone on the far side of the bridge.*

*"What's this all about, Levi?"*

*"Are you serious?" he demanded. "Adam, you killed a United States senator in broad fucking daylight. Did you really think there weren't going to be any consequences?"*

*"I did what you trained me to do," Hayes said, voice flat, eyes cold and lifeless as a shark's. "I did what you and everyone else up on the Hill were too scared to do."*

*"You've got two options. You come back and go to work or . . ."*

*"Or what?"*

Senator Miles's voice shattered the memory and yanked him back to the here and now. "Director Shaw, do you need me to repeat the question?"

Shaw took a deep breath and cleared his mind, set the bottle on the table, and looked up at Senator Miles, his face unreadable.

"I have no idea, Senator," he lied.

# 4

CEUTA, SPAIN

**S**tealing a boat hadn't been on Hayes's to-do list when he woke up that morning, but plans changed, and if there was one surety in this line of work it was that survivability and flexibility often went hand in hand.

By the time Hayes made it down to the alley and retrieved his bag, the sun had dropped below the horizon and the shadows were advancing across the water like a skirmish line. He shouldered the pack and started back the way he'd come, his mind on the black speedboat he'd seen from the window.

But the plan crumbled when he stopped at the mouth of the alley and stared, disbelieving, at the street.

On his way over, the Avenue Juan de Borbón had been almost empty, the bars and nightclubs that lined it locked up tight. But with the sun on its way down that had changed. Now the street was alive, the neon signage from the bars bouncing off the stucco walls, illuminating the sea of flesh that writhed and danced in time with the music pouring from the clubs.

*Well, shit.*

Hayes stepped off the curb and turned to the side, trying to shoulder his way to the edge where the crowd thinned out, but it was no use. He was hemmed in, blinded by the flashing lights and thumping bass from the clubs and unable to break free of the sea of flesh carrying him down the street.

The panic attack started in the pit of his stomach, a cold twinge that raced up his spine and into his ears, where it hissed like static from a busted TV.

*Not now,* he begged, fighting the urge to lash out at the bodies pressing against him and the hands clawing at his skin.

He kept his head down and his hand clamped over his pistol, twisting and shouldering his way through the crowd, fighting his way to the edge.

Then he broke through and found himself standing alone, staring at the white halo of the stadium lights beating down on the marina a hundred yards ahead.

*Almost there,* the voice taunted.

"Fuck off," Hayes said, wiping the sweat from his forehead.

Growing up in Tennessee, Hayes's knowledge of boats was limited to fishing trips with his dad in Florida and the riverine training he'd received in Special Forces. But you didn't need to be Magellan to figure out that if renting a twenty-foot Yamaha center console cost five hundred dollars a day, owning one of these yachts cost a hell of a lot more.

He guessed that there were at least a hundred million dollars'

worth of boats floating in the marina. Which is why he was surprised that the only people keeping him from walking down the
pier and stealing whichever one he wanted were the doughy security guard sleeping in the air-conditioned shack and the single
attendant fueling a Hacker Runabout from the gas pump on the
edge of the pier.

But Hayes wasn't buying it.

Mainly because he'd seen what lay beneath the town's warm
and sandy façade. Knew that the majority of the yachts bobbing
in the marina didn't belong to the rich tourists, but to the smug-
glers and drug runners who used Ceuta as a base of operations.
People of means, guarded by serious men trained to shoot first
and ask questions later. A fact that promised that somewhere
down there, hiding in the shadows, were men with guns.

*Only one way to find out.*

Hayes skirted the marina, searching the slips until he located
the black speedboat bobbing next to the Westport tri-deck he'd
seen earlier. He was close enough now to read the name off the
bow—*The Mako*—and recognize the model. It was an Outerlim-
its SV43—one of the fiberglass rocket ships drug runners used to
outrun the Guardia Civil ships that patrolled the area.

It was the perfect boat for the job at hand, but first Hayes had
to knock out the lights.

He found the junction box on the northwest side of the marina, a brushed metal square attached to a utility pole three feet
from the guard shack. In a perfect world, one where Hayes had
the time and resources to come up with a plan that didn't involve
him going to jail or getting shot, he would have requested a wiring diagram. Used it to find the upstream source of the thick
black power cable that went into the side of the junction box.

Once he located it, an explosive charge with a time delay would have allowed him to kill the power at his leisure.

But now all he had was a ticking clock and the gear in his pack.

He opened the front pocket and pulled out a magnesium road flare, a miniball fragmentation grenade, and a roll of duct tape.

Hayes stripped a length of tape from the roll, ripped it free, and stuck it to the front of his pants. He zipped the bag, stuffed the flare into his back pocket, and, holding the grenade, stepped out of the shadows.

Staying low, he eased onto the pier, footsteps silent as he slipped past the guard shack. At the junction box, he secured the grenade to the electrical cable with the strip of tape.

*This is a terrible idea,* the voice said.

As Hayes pulled the pin from the frag, he realized that, for once, he agreed with the voice.

*Too late now.*

He moved toward the Hacker Runabout, knowing he had about five seconds before the minifrag went off and all hell broke loose.

The attendant heard him coming and glanced up, a bored look on his face as he continued refueling the boat.

"There's a fire," Hayes said, tugging the road flare from his back pocket.

"What? Where?" the man asked.

"Right here," he answered, scraping the nose of the flare across the abrasive striker.

The flare came to life in a sputtering rush of smoke and magnesium, the attendant's features changing from boredom to alarm when Hayes dropped the flare atop the life jacket in the stern of the boat.

"If I were you, I'd get the hell out of here," he said.

The man nodded, and leaving the nozzle in the Hacker ran toward the guard shack, screaming at the top of his lungs.

Hayes pushed himself into a jog and had just clattered aboard the *Mako* when the minifrag detonated and the marina went dark. He ducked behind the wheel, tore open his bag, and fumbled around inside until he found the crap pair of Russian night-vision goggles he'd borrowed from Vlad.

With a twist of the switch he activated the goggles and night-shifted to an emerald-green twilight. Compared to the PVS-23s or the GPNVG-18s the SEALs were using, the Russian-made night vision was junk, but he could see and that was all that mattered.

After casting off the lines, he ducked into the cockpit and was about to use the knife to snap the ignition lock when Hayes saw the key dangling from the dash.

*It's about time I caught a break.*

He twisted the key to the *on* position and the gauges flickered to life, filling the cockpit with a pale yellow glow. Hayes was checking the fuel level when he heard the crackle of static from the Westport tri-deck, followed by an angry voice.

"Alexander, what the hell is going on out there?" the voice demanded in French.

Hayes followed the voice to the sundeck and found a man standing at the rail, the unmistakable outline of a submachine gun hanging from the sling around his neck.

*Told you this was a bad idea,* the voice said.

The man lifted the submachine gun to his shoulder, the bone-white glare of the LED weapon light mounted to the fore-end cutting through the darkness like a knife.

"Some kind of explosion, boss," the man replied, "looks like a boat is on fire."

"Get everyone on deck, *now!*" the voice screamed over the radio.

Hayes ducked beneath the dash, adjusted the brightness of the gauge lights, and then hit the power button on the Simrad HALO surface radar. During the day he wouldn't need the GPS or the navigation computer to clear the marina, but at night it was a different story. And Hayes knew that even *with* the night vision, trying to get the *Mako* out to sea without the nav computer was a great way to end up as a grease stain on the rocks.

*Safety first.*

He wasn't sure if the *Mako*'s owner was blind or if the universe just hated him, but when the Simrad's LCD screen blinked to life, the brightness setting was maxed out. The screen lit up the cockpit like a searchlight, and Hayes was trying to turn it down when the light caught the attention of one of the men on the tri-deck.

"There, in the water," he shouted, the blaze of white from the weapon light attached to his submachine gun hitting Hayes in the face, flaring his night vision, leaving him blind and exposed to the peal of gunfire that followed.

# 5

CEUTA, SPAIN

Hayes was blind and pinned down, the spray of lead from the yacht buzzing over his head like a swarm of angry hornets before slamming into the captain's chair. The 9-millimeter rounds shredded the seat, filling the cockpit with a confetti of vinyl and bits of insulation.

Hayes slapped the now-useless night-vision goggles up and out of the way and ignored the snap and crack of the rounds past his head. He inched forward, groping in the darkness like a child playing a lethal game of blindman's bluff, desperate to find the dashboard.

His hand brushed the wheel and Hayes adjusted left, fingers fumbling over the switches and buttons that dotted the control panel.

*But where the fuck is the key?*

Then he found it and the *Mako* was alive, her twin Mercury 1350s rumbling like a primeval beast, the vibrations from the engines rolling up Hayes's spine.

"Oh, hell yes," he said, shoving the throttles forward.

The *Mako* leapt from her slip like a stone from a sling, the sudden acceleration sending Hayes tumbling backward, the wheel spinning free as she raced into the night. He scrambled to his feet, knowing he had to get the *Mako* under control or he'd never make it out of the marina alive.

Keeping his head low, Hayes reached up and grabbed the wheel, a quick glance at the LCD showing the nav computer still trying to sync with the satellites.

As the *Mako* accelerated, the bow lifted free of the water, and without the aid of the nav computer, Hayes was blind to what lay ahead. His internal compass told him that he was heading north, but as a pilot, he knew better than to trust his instincts in the darkness.

"Looks like I'm going to have to do this the old-fashioned way," Hayes said, slapping the night vision over his eyes.

Still under fire, he climbed to his feet and grabbed the wheel, ignoring the snap of the bullets over his head. He needed to see what lay ahead, which was impossible with the bow pointing skyward. By adjusting the trim tabs he got the nose down in time to see the pylon sticking out of the water ten feet ahead.

With the *Mako*'s engines running wide open and the tachometer sweeping toward five thousand RPMs, there was little time to think, so Hayes desperately yanked the wheel hard to the left.

The powerboat sidestepped the obstruction like a running back dodging an open-field tackle, swinging the nose wide, away from the mouth of the marina and toward the massive seawall on the south side.

A second burst of rifle fire buzzed past his head, but Hayes ignored it. His only concern was getting the *Mako* back on course. He inched the wheel back to port, knowing that at this speed even the slightest miscalculation could be deadly, but the *Mako* handled like it was on rails, swinging smoothly back on course. Hayes hazarded a quick glance over his shoulder where a second shooter was now engaging him from the aft deck of the yacht. He raised the barrel of his MP5 skyward to compensate for the submachine gun's limited range.

The bullets fell short and Hayes watched them slap harmlessly in his wake, but any reassurance that came from being out of the shooter's range evaporated when he saw additional gunmen launching a pair of two-person Jet Skis from the back of the yacht.

*You've got to be kidding me.*

In open water, the Jet Skis' small engines didn't stand a chance against the *Mako*'s twin Mercurys, but to take advantage of the powerboat's speed, Hayes had to clear the surf zone, get past the six-foot breakers slamming across the mouth of the harbor without being swamped or smashing into the jetties.

The safest choice was to slow down, wait for a lull in the surf, and *then* use the *Mako*'s power to get the hell out of Dodge. But Hayes knew from the hissing snap of lead past his head that if he wanted to get out of Ceuta with the same number of holes he'd arrived with, he had to go now.

"Let's do this," he said, shoving the throttles to their stops.

The *Mako* blasted from the marina like a fiberglass bullet, and in the cockpit all Hayes could do was hold it steady, watching as the swell reared up like a white-maned stallion. There was a moment, a split second, when he thought that his luck had changed, that somehow he'd timed it just right and all he had to do was punch the *Mako* through the back of the wave and go about his business.

Which is exactly what *would* have happened if the swell had stayed upright, but at the last moment the wave seemed to trip and then it was falling headlong before the *Mako*, its once-majestic peak now a raging ramp of white water.

One second the powerboat was planing smoothly across the water and in the next instant, it was airborne. Hayes was helpless to do anything but hold on as the *Mako* soared clear of the waves.

For a moment Hayes was weightless, free of both land and sea. But then gravity took over and he was falling, stomach rushing into his throat as the *Mako* nosed over, plunging like a lawn dart toward the glassy water below.

*Oh, yeah, this is going to hurt.*

The *Mako* hit hard and bounced skyward, skipping across the surface like a stone, the impact slamming Hayes into the wheel.

There was no pain, just a flash of white followed by the copper taste of blood and the flicker of black at the edge of his vision. He tried to get to his feet but the *Mako* was spinning, its centripetal force pinning him to the bulkhead while the water being sucked into the intakes killed the engines.

Finally, the *Mako* came to rest, the silence that followed the roar of her twin Mercs deafening as Hayes shook off the blow. He crawled to the front of the boat and tried the key.

The starter clicked but failed to turn over and Hayes adjusted the choke.

"C'mon, c'mon," he begged. But the *Mako* was dead in the water.

Hayes was heading aft when the *wheeeeem* of a small engine stopped him in his tracks.

*There is no way.*

He followed the sound to its source in time to see the first two-person Jet Ski arcing over a wave, flame already spitting from the muzzle of the machine pistol in the passenger's hand.

The first burst was short and when Hayes saw the bullets splash harmlessly into the water thirty yards short of the disabled powerboat, he felt a glimmer of hope.

*I've got time.*

He dropped to a knee and reached down for the fuel line, the overwhelming odor of raw gas emanating from the engine scalding his eyes—confirming his worst fears.

*Only way to get this thing running is to pull the spark plugs, clear the excess fuel from the cylinders.*

Hayes glanced up at the rapidly approaching Jet Ski, knowing that he was out of time.

*Fight or die,* the voice warned.

Hayes jumped to his feet and raced back to the captain's chair for his assault pack, wishing there was another way as he un-zipped the large pocket. Grabbed the pistol grip of the six-and-a-half-inch Serbu "Super Shorty" shotgun.

*Fight or die,* the voice repeated.

"Shit," he yelled, pulling the Serbu from the pack.

The Jet Ski arced closer, the machine pistol rattling in the pas-senger's hand, the bullets kicking up a line of miniature geysers as they raced inevitably toward the *Mako.*

Hayes racked a 12-gauge shell into the action and brought the shotgun to bear. He centered the bead on the driver's chest and disengaged the safety, but held his fire. Waited until the bullets were slapping so close to the *Mako* that he could feel the spray of water on his skin. See the determination on the shooter's face as he lined up the kill shot. Only then did Hayes pull the trigger.

The shotgun roared like a howitzer, the spray of double-aught buck slamming into his target's chest like a freight train—blowing both men off the Jet Ski.

Hayes racked the pump and waited for the second pair of attackers. He caught them as they were cresting a swell four feet away and dumped them with another blast from the shotgun.

Then he was alone and instead of the relief that usually came with winning a gunfight, all Hayes felt when he looked down at the smoking shotgun was disgust.

"Five months, down the FUCKING drain," he snarled, flinging the shotgun into the sea.

*Better them than you,* the voice answered.

But as Hayes grabbed the toolkit from beneath the wheel and returned aft to begin work on the engines, he found there was no solace in the words—only regret.

# 6

## CEUTA, SPAIN

The second Hayes left the bathroom, Vlad was on his feet, stumbling on rubber legs to the door. His hands shook as he pawed at the lock. The stale stench of old vodka and new fear that seeped from his pores sent his guts heaving into his throat.

Vlad retched, but stayed focused on the task at hand, knowing that *if* Hayes changed his mind and decided to come back and kill him, he'd have to boot the door off the hinges to get in.

There was a part of him that knew it was a fool's errand, knew that it would take more than a flimsy door and the three-dollar latch to keep a man like Hayes out, but it was all he had.

The metallic snap of the latch sliding into place echoed off the walls and the Russian lurched to the trash can in the corner and vomited until he tasted bile.

After twelve years in the GRU—the Russian Intelligence Directorate—Vlad was no stranger to violence. He'd joined the military at eighteen and spent the first five years with the 45th Spetsnaz Airborne Brigade, gaining valuable combat experience in Chechnya and the Caucasus. But it wasn't until Vlad was selected to join Directorate V that he learned the art of *mokroye delo*—wet work.

During his time with Directorate V he'd gone up against Mossad hit teams in Libya, French DGSE in Marseilles, even a member of the CIA's Ground Branch in Iraq—and always came out without a scratch.

But as Vlad sagged against the wall, the cold tile against his fevered skin welcome as a lover's touch, he realized that despite all the men he'd gone up against, none of them compared to Adam Hayes.

When he trusted his legs to hold him, Vlad got to his feet and went to the sink. He turned on the water, rinsed the vomit out of his mouth, and washed his face, making himself as presentable as possible before stepping out of the bathroom.

Keeping his head down, Vlad crossed the bar and stepped out the front door, pausing to shake a Prima from the pack in his breast pocket. He stuck the cigarette between his lips and lit it using a battered Zippo. The acrid burn of the Russian tobacco and the rush of nicotine into his blood settled his nerves.

The altercation with Hayes played in his mind on an endless loop. Vlad saw himself get to his feet, heard the click of the blade snapping open in his hand. He moved around the table, heart pumping in his chest, the only thought on his mind burying the knife in the American's gut.

But before the blade could find flesh, Hayes had him by the wrist, and then he was twisting the knife away, pulling him close.

Vlad never saw the blow that put him down, which shocked him because he'd been eye to eye with the American, close enough to feel his breath on his face, hear the snap of his shirt as his hand shot up from his waist.

His mind bounced back to the hand-to-hand training he'd received with the Spetsnaz at the Defense Ministry's Military Academy, and the rawboned sergeant who'd taught them to kill with the knife.

*"One and a half seconds. That is how much time it takes a man standing twenty-one feet away to get close enough to bury a blade in your gut."*

By the time he was done with the course, Vlad was doing it in half that.

*Then how is he still alive?*

The fact was, he didn't know.

But it wasn't for lack of trying.

The first time he met the American, Vlad had thought he'd finally found his mark, a way to get out of the trouble he was in. He had to give it to Hayes: The man hid it well, with his wide-eyed optimistic talk about helping the poor people of Africa. But slowly Vlad began to see through it. He saw the way Hayes's eyes never stopped moving. How he would always sit with his back to the wall. The man had training. The signs were subtle and while they wouldn't have registered with ninety-nine percent of the world's population, Vlad picked them up in stereo, and immediately set out to find out all he could about the bearded American.

But despite his extensive intelligence network he could find nothing.

Now he didn't care, and as he turned onto Avenue Playas del Duque, the only thought on his mind was getting the hell out of Ceuta, putting as much distance between him and Hayes as possible.

*I need a car.*

Staying in the shadows, Vlad scanned the street, looking for something that wouldn't draw attention, like a Citroën or a Toyota, but after ten minutes of searching he realized he'd have better luck finding a virgin on prom night than an economy car near the marina. So he settled on a midnight-blue Audi RS 5.

The door was unlocked, and he slipped inside. Vlad used his knife to snap the plastic covering free of the steering column. After exposing the wiring harness, he sorted through the birds' nests of wires until he found the battery wire and the ignition wire.

He stripped the insulation free, and using his shirt as an insulator, twisted the two wires together, jumping when the radio blared to life.

*Shit.*

Vlad hastily turned the stereo off, giving the street a quick scan before getting back to work. He ducked down, muttering in Russian as he searched for the starter wire.

"C'mon, c'mon."

Finally, he found it, and after stripping off the yellow insulation, touched it to the power wire. Once the engine hummed to life, Vlad cut a U-turn, and stomped the accelerator to the floor.

The car shot forward like a sprinter from the blocks, the 2.9L

V6 growling beneath the hood as the needle swept past sixty miles an hour. He lit a second cigarette off the butt of the first and thought back to his time in the GRU—the day he realized that there was only so much damage a body could take, so many times a bone could be broken and reset before you lost a step.

*And then what?*

As far as Vlad knew there were no retirement homes for broken spies—only desk jobs, disability stipends, and a piece-of-shit gold watch when the government decided it was time for you to pull the pin.

If there was anything he'd learned during his time abroad it was that he'd never be poor. There were too many men willing to pay top dollar for someone with his skill set.

So he left the institutional-gray walls of the FSB for the glitz and glamour of the "west." He eventually ended up in Malta, where he set up shop as a gun for hire.

And there was no shortage of takers.

The money was great and in the span of a year Vlad had made more than he had during his ten as a civil servant. His five-year plan was to save up enough and get out. Retire and buy a place on the beach, somewhere warm to die—and he was almost there.

But then he'd gone to work for Cabot and everything had gone to shit.

He stopped at the intersection, eyes drawn to the blue sign on the side of the road, and for the first time in his life he considered running.

*What to do?* he thought, glancing up at the rearview mirror, an idea floating at the back of his mind as he studied the rust-colored bruise on his throat.

*The plane, if I could steal the plane, I might be able to . . .*

In an instant he knew what to do.

He pulled to the side of the road, grabbed his phone from his pocket, and dialed the number.

"Hello?" a voice answered in French.

"I need to talk to Monsieur Cabot."

# 7

## MAYOTTE

A ndre Cabot sat at the conference table in Mayotte, the tiny island off the coast of Madagascar that was all that was left of France's once vast colonial empire. He'd been sitting at the table for the past three hours. Listening to his lawyer and the bureaucrat from Paris squabble over the nuances of international law, his head was beginning to ache.

*Dear God, will they ever shut up?*

"So, as I was saying, since relocating your headquarters to Mayotte, all business conducted by DarkCloud is now governed by French law."

Andre Cabot got to his feet and crossed to the cherrywood humidor perched on the edge of his desk. He opened the lid and selected a Cohiba Lancero, remembering how he'd come to Mayotte to get away—to start over.

But despite being separated from Paris by two oceans, one continent, and five thousand miles, all it took was one look at the bureaucrat sitting at the end of the table to realize that he hadn't run far enough.

Back at the table, he fished the 18-karat gold Dunhill Apex from his pocket, thumbed the striker, and twirled the end of the cigar above the flame. When it was lit, he snapped the lid closed and studied the lighter.

Cabot had purchased it in London, because he liked the timeless quality, the craftmanship, and the way it felt in his hand. It had cost him three grand and had been worth every penny.

The same could *not* be said for the $1,500-an-hour lawyer sitting across from the French bureaucrat. The one who was supposed to be getting him out of this shit.

"The law is quite clear on the matter," the man said, glancing up at Cabot as he walked over, "which means besides the travel restrictions already imposed by the court, the government is filing the necessary motions to freeze all of DarkCloud's assets."

"Now, you listen here," the lawyer scowled, "if you think for one minute that Mr. Cabot is going to let some third-world puppet court dictate where he can and *cannot* go, then you are out of your mind."

"Be that as it may, Monsieur Cabot is a French citizen and as such is required to abide by French laws."

Cabot puffed on the cigar, letting the smoke eddy in his mouth as he studied the lawyer, trying to remember the man's name.

*It's one of those stupid Ivy League names, like Chip, or Skip . . .*

He tried to remember but he had so many lawyers representing him, so many hotshots strutting around like cocks of the walk with their trust-fund names and their $1,500-an-hour rates—and none of them worth a shit.

"Well then, we will file the necessary motions . . . and . . ."

*I'm surrounded by fucking idiots.*

"You," he said, slapping his hand on the table and pointing at the lawyer.

"Yes, Mr. Cabot?"

"Get the fuck out."

"But I . . . I . . ."

"Now!" he snapped.

The man's face fell. He got to his feet, pulled his shoulders back, and marched across the office. Cabot skirted the recently occupied chair and took his seat, waiting until he heard the click of the door before blowing the mouthful of smoke across the table.

"How much?" he asked.

"M-Monsieur C-Cabot," the man coughed. "I-I don't know what you mean!"

"You think this is my first time playing this game? Or the first time Paris has sent someone to shake me down?" he asked, voice cold as ice.

"No," the man answered, dropping the act, "I do *not*."

"Then let's cut the foreplay, shall we? Name your price."

"Price?" the man asked, getting to his feet and retracing the steps Cabot had taken earlier to the box on the edge of the table. "You wish to buy your way out of this? With what, this box?" he asked, bending at the waist and reading the inscription off the brass plate.

"'May this ornament suffice as a token of gratitude from a thankful nation.'"

"Yes, that is what it says," Cabot said, getting to his feet, the cigar in his hand shaking with rage as he walked over to the man.

"No date?" The man frowned. "No years of service, no *vraiment désolé*—very sorry—that your wife left you? That you were thrown out on some trumped-up charges so men in Paris could save face?"

Cabot took a deep puff, his eyes hot as the ember at the end of the cigar. "Who sent you?" he asked, blowing the mouthful of smoke into the man's face.

The man coughed and stepped back, the smile falling from his face.

"Someone who doesn't appreciate your meddling in their African affairs."

"So, that is what this is about—money?"

"No, Monsieur Cabot, money is what we carry in our pockets. What we are talking about is power and the hundreds of millions of dollars it costs to keep it," the man said, turning to the door. "But trust me, Andre, you will find out all about it very soon."

When he was gone, Cabot lifted the box off the table and slammed it into the wall before rounding the desk and yanking open the drawer, revealing a silver Walther PPK.

He stared down at the pistol, debating whether he should pick it up, rush out into the lobby, and put a bullet in the man's head, when there was a polite knock at the door.

"What?" he shouted, looking up to see Beck step inside his office, holding out a satphone.

"*Qui est-ce?*" Who is it?

"Vlad," the man answered, making no attempt to mask his disdain. "He says he has a solution for getting someone into Grand-Bassam."

Cabot took the phone and pressed it to his ear, suddenly calm despite the rage that had consumed him moments earlier.

"Yes?"

"Do you still need a pilot?"

"Why, do you suddenly have a plane?"

"Yes, and plenty of room for cargo."

"And what is it going to cost me?" Cabot asked.

"My marker."

Cabot had learned long ago that there was no such thing as data protection. If information was recorded, either physically or stored on a drive, it could be hacked or stolen. Which was why unlike most men in his line of work, he committed everything to memory.

He paused before answering, pictured Vlad's file in his mind. The Russian owed him a little less than a million U.S. dollars.

Most men in Cabot's position wouldn't have bothered with such a paltry sum, and instead of trying to collect the money would have killed the Russian.

But not Cabot.

For him, the money was secondary; what mattered was the *respect*. Breaking and bending men like Vlad to his will. His strategy was straight out of Clausewitz's *On War*—first Cabot bought up all the man's outstanding debts and then put the word out on the street that no one was to do business with the Russian, knowing that it was only a matter of time before the financial isolation brought him back on bended knee.

"Agreed," Cabot said. "How soon can you begin?"

"Tomorrow afternoon."

"Very well, but Vlad, this is your last chance. If you fail, I will kill everyone you have ever loved. Do I make myself clear?"

"Yes," the Russian said. "Crystal clear."

"It seems our luck is beginning to change," he said, hanging up the phone.

"So, Vlad has a plane," Beck shrugged. "*You* still cannot fly."

"No, but Zoe can," Cabot said.

"Your daughter?"

"Go to the house, tell her to start packing."

"And what about you?"

"I have some favors to call in," Cabot said, turning to his desk.

# 8

## CEUTA, SPAIN

Three hours later, the navigation computer alerted him that he was a mile from his destination. He killed the engines, dug the earplugs from his ears, and flipped the night-vision goggles up. After the continuous roar of the *Mako*'s engines, the silence was deafening.

Hayes was soaking wet, his face raw from the abrasive spray of the salt water, and his head ached from the night-vision goggles against his skull. But he'd been here before. Alone and beat to hell. His muscles aching, eyes burning from lack of sleep. Every fiber of his being begging him to stop before it was too late.

He thought back to the army, trying to remember the phrase they used to throw around when anyone got tired: *You can rest when you're dead.*

*What a bunch of bullshit,* he thought, lowering his night vision and turning his attention to the tangle of marshland off the port bow.

From the cockpit, the cove appeared deserted, the only sign of life the tangle of reeds that choked the bank swaying in the wind. Even with the night vision, Hayes was unable to pierce the dense undergrowth or see anything past the dilapidated dock that bobbed near the beach.

He double-checked the coordinates.

*This is the right place.*

He dug the flashlight from his pocket and pointed it at the dock. He strobed the pressure pad—two long, one short, just as he'd been told—and waited.

The seconds ticked by, the thick marsh air weighing oppressively against his skin, the only sound the buzz of the mosquitoes around his ears.

Besides his ability to withstand pain and privation, Hayes's time in Treadstone had given him a unique insight into the worlds that populated the gray zone—the shadowy world inhabited by the ghosts of cast-off countries.

Most of what he'd learned of Luca Harrak was rumor—hushed words traded over a round of drinks in one shithole bar or another.

The warnings came in whispered Russian, French, or Arabic—the language didn't matter; the words were always the same—"a savage who'd sell his mother if the price was right."

But Hayes had been in the game long enough to realize most of it was bullshit. Ghost stories told by rough men at the end of their serviceability. A way for them to remember the "bad old days" when they mattered.

The only thing he knew for certain was that to Luca punctuality mattered—not as a virtue but because the smuggler had learned that it was harder to hit a moving target. Hayes glanced at the Sangin Neptune strapped to his wrist. The Day-Glo hands told him that he was thirty minutes late.

*Shit. Had they gone?*

The answer came from the shadows, an armed man stepping out of the foliage that lined the bank, a cigarette dangling from his lips. He strolled leisurely to the edge of the dock, pausing to take a final drag of the smoke before flicking it into a barrel.

The contents ignited with a rush of flame that looked yellow through the night vision and Hayes watched the man wave him toward the shore.

He started the engine, the voice in his head screaming at him as he guided the boat toward the channel.

*Are you crazy? Do not go in there.*

But Hayes had come too far, gone through too much to turn back now.

By the time he made it to the back of the cove and nosed the boat to land, a second man stood on the dock, a coil of rope in his hand.

"You're late," he said, tossing the line.

"Traffic," Hayes answered.

He tied off the boat, grabbed his bag, and stepped out—the stability of the dock beneath his feet unsettling after the pitch and roll of the open sea.

"This way," the man said.

Hayes nodded and let his guide step off, but instead of following turned to the second man.

"After you," he said, not liking the idea of an armed stranger on his backtrail.

But the man wasn't having it.

"No," the man said, shaking his head. "You go."

When he still didn't budge, the gunman unslung the AK-47 and leveled the muzzle at Hayes's chest. He laid his thumb across the selector and flicked the catch from safe to fire.

The smuggler was less than a foot away, close enough for Hayes to smell the tobacco on his breath, watch his finger slip into the trigger guard when he said, "You go, *now*."

Hayes was thinking about tearing the rifle from the man's hands and beating him with it when the voice in his head chimed in.

*No. You kill him, and all of this is for nothing. Just let it go.*

But it was easier said than done. The altercation with Vlad had flipped a switch and now his mind was locked on *destroy*, and breaking free of the cycle was going to take a hell of a lot more than the calming exercises he'd learned from the shrink in Tacoma.

He ripped himself away, ignoring the smug smile that spread across the man's face as Hayes turned and followed his guide.

The man led him down a scratch of a trail that cut through the underbrush, then took a hard left before ending at an ancient wood-planked footbridge.

*You've got to be kidding me.*

He stopped, desperate for another route across, but a quick glance showed nothing but marshland on all sides.

Sensing his hesitation, the guide flashed a toothy smile and stepped onto the first plank. Beneath his weight, the aged wood and the rusted chain screeched like a dying animal, but instead of being concerned, the man flashed a wide smile.

"It is perfectly safe," the man said.

"For you, maybe," Hayes said, staring at the rail-thin guide. "What do you weigh, sixty-five kilos?"

"Sixty," the man grinned, "but it will hold."

*Sixty kilos, that's, what, a hundred and thirty pounds? Shit, I weighed more than that in high school.*

He scanned the bank, desperate for another way across, when the man at his back prodded him forward with an AK barrel to the kidney.

Hayes gritted his teeth, bit back on the anger, and glanced back at the man.

"You and I are going to have a serious problem if you do that shit again," he said.

The man didn't bother with a reply. Instead, he stepped forward, the rifle at the ready, leaving Hayes with two choices. He could make a play for the rifle, kill both men, and hope he could get back to the boat and the hell out of the area before more men showed up. Or he could stop being a little bitch and cross the bridge.

He turned and stepped onto the first plank and started across.

According to Vlad, the island was a major smuggling depot, a vital hub for Luca's operation, but as he neared the end of the bridge, Hayes had yet to see any sign of life. In his mind there were two options: Either Vlad was telling the truth and the fabled smuggler hideout was so well camouflaged that it was invisible to even his well-trained eye, or . . . that sneaky Cossack had set him up. Paid the two assholes with the AKs to take him out in the woods and put a bullet in his skull so he could have the plane.

Either way, it was too late to turn back.

**9**

## MOGADOR

He stepped off the bridge, walked over to where the guide stood beside a tree, a fresh cigarette clutched between his lips.

The man nodded down the hill, at the cluster of buildings in the low ground. "The boss is waiting in the bar," he said, pointing to the building in the middle. "You knock first, yes?"

"Sure."

It was hot at the top of the hill. The air was thick with moisture and mosquitoes that swarmed around his head and neck and Hayes was sweating. But halfway down the slope the temperature began to change. The oppressive heat and humidity were banished by a cool, salt-laden breeze that blew in from the east.

There was movement a hundred yards to his right, voices and the distant sound of machinery. *What is that? A forklift?*

He left the path, moved laterally along the slope through the trees until he had a clear view of a second harbor nestled in the dead space behind the building.

*Yet another reason you don't go off on half-cocked plans,* the voice in his head chided.

"Yeah, *thanks*," he said.

Hayes reached the flats, the dirt path giving way to gravel, the voices and laughter louder now as he approached the bar. He stopped at the door, the interior falling silent as a grave at the sound of his knock. There was a scratch of a chair across the floor followed by heavy footfalls walking in his direction.

*Here we go.*

Hayes looked down in an attempt to save his dilated pupils from the wash of light he knew would come when the door was pulled open from the inside. But it never came.

*What the hell?*

The reason was evident when he looked up, found a giant of a man—in a black tank top—his thick biceps and wide shoulders blocking out the light.

"What do you want?" the man demanded in French.

"I'm here for the gangbang," Hayes answered, leaning past the man to get a look inside.

The bar was a small rectangle of a room with a bare floor, five scuffed wood tables, and a half moon of a bar on the far side. Hayes took in the men at the tables to his right and dismissed them but couldn't see the rest of the room until the man took a step back and motioned him to enter.

He stepped inside and immediately shifted to the left, eyes darting to the back table where a man sat reading a copy of *Le Monde* and ignoring the three radios squawking on the table.

Hayes was on his way over when the man in the black tank

top intercepted him with an open palm to the chest. "Hands on the wall," the man ordered.

"Not happening," he said.

The man's lips curled into what he thought was a smile, displaying a mouthful of gold teeth. "What did you say, little man?"

"I said, fuck off before I knock those pretty teeth down your throat."

The smile crumbled from the man's face and he stepped forward, his hands curling into fists at his sides.

"Closest hospital is what, two hours away?" Hayes asked, without taking his eyes off the doorman before him.

Luca Harrak folded the newspaper in half and set it on the table, but instead of looking up, turned his attention to his fingernails. He studied his manicure for a few seconds and when he finally spoke, his voice was calm, seemingly indifferent to the impending violence before him.

"About that," he said, looking up. "Why do you ask?"

"Because unless you have an orthopedic surgeon behind the bar, you might want to put your dog on a leash."

"Emil, let him pass."

The man grudgingly stepped aside, and Hayes made his way to the table, took a seat, and studied the man before him.

Luca Harrak was in his early forties and well dressed. The Saint Laurent suit, eggshell-white button-down, and slicked-back hair made him look more like an accountant than the head of the largest smuggling ring in the North Atlantic.

But Hayes wasn't fooled.

"You are late," Harrak said, his hand coming to rest on the black case sitting on the table.

"Yeah, but I'm here now."

Luca popped the clasps that secured the Pelican case and opened the lid, revealing three stacks of white cartons with ERYTHROMYCIN 250MG written in black letters.

"May I?" he asked, waiting for Luca's nod before grabbing two of the boxes from the case, opening them, and studying the pink pills inside the blister packs.

Hayes checked over the packaging, made sure the seals were intact while Luca spoke.

"In my line of work, I have been asked to acquire *many* things. Drugs, guns, even people," he shrugged. "But never antibiotics. Turns out they are rather hard to find."

*Sucks for you.*

He got to his feet, pulled a sodden envelope from his back pocket, and handed it to Luca.

"Yes, *very* hard to find," the man said, opening the flap and thumbing the bills inside.

The menace in the man's voice told Hayes it was time to go, and he hurriedly tossed the pills back into the case and shut the lid. He was reaching for the latches, ready to thumb them back into place and get the hell out, when Luca slammed his hand flat on the lid.

"Did you hear what I just said?" he demanded.

"Yeah, I heard ya," Hayes answered. "But we had a deal—a deal that ended the second I handed you ten thousand euros."

"That was the price an hour ago, but . . ."

"But what?" Hayes asked.

"But you were late."

"You're breaking my heart."

"Be that as it may, if you want the merchandise, it will cost an *additional* five thousand euros."

"You're shitting me, right?"

Luca clicked his tongue behind his teeth, eyebrows and shoulders lifting into a prototypical Gallic shrug.

"What the hell is that supposed to mean?" Hayes asked, aping the gesture.

The moment his hands were off the case, Luca tugged it back to his side of the table and lowered himself into his chair with an exaggerated sigh.

"Pay or leave," he said, unbuttoning his jacket and leaning back in his chair. "The choice is yours, but either way, you are wasting my fucking time."

In an instant, the atmosphere in the bar dropped from chilly to downright inhospitable and all talk ceased, the only sound the scrape of Emil's chair against the floor as he got to his feet and walked to the table, coming to a halt behind his boss, fingers tapping the butt of the pistol at his waist.

The pistol was a Norinco NP-20, a Chinese knockoff of the Heckler & Koch P7. The pistol was a favorite in places like Morocco because they took a beating, and with a street value of fifty bucks cost a hell of a lot less than the German-made H&K.

While he generally believed in the old adage that you get what you pay for, he'd been around the block enough times to know that the 9-millimeter fired from the chamber of a fifty-dollar piece of shit would kill him just as fast as one from the custom STI on his hip.

"Well?" Luca asked.

Any other time Hayes would have paid the man, but after the boy in Ceuta, he was flat broke, and he'd come too far to leave empty-handed.

Which left only one option.

Hayes stepped away from the table, a shot of adrenaline rolling through his veins, widening his vision until he saw the entire room. His hand dropped to his side and he stood there, calm and relaxed, seeing everything but focusing on nothing.

"That's not going to work for me," he said, voice sharp as a straight razor.

The silence fell heavy over the bar. The blood hissing in his ears like static, Hayes took in the room. Aware of Emil's hand cheating toward the pistol on his waist, the bartender reaching below the counter, and, finally, the bald smuggler near the door shifting so he could reach the pistol Hayes assumed was tucked into the small of his back.

Hayes worked the lethal calculus in his head. *Big man first, then old Hooknose behind the bar, and then Baldy. Four seconds, five max? Is it enough?*

A gunfight was all about angles, space, and timing. Hayes had been in enough to realize that he was holding the short end of the stick. There was no doubt in his mind that he could dump one or two of the men before they got their pistols into action, but not all four.

He didn't like the odds and would have bowed out if he could have, but the men in the bar were all gas and no brake, which didn't leave Hayes many options.

"No one has to die," Hayes said, "just give me what I came for and I'll be out of your hair."

"I'm afraid that is impossible," Luca said.

"This isn't going to go the way you think it is."

"You Americans, so John Wayne, so *Gunfight at the K.O. Corral.*"

"That's the O.K. Corral, and you've been watching too many Westerns."

"Perhaps, but, since I am a sporting man, what do you say I count to three and yell *draw* like they do in the Westerns? Would that be fair, Emil?" he asked, looking up.

"Yes," the man grinned.

"And you?" he asked, turning to Hayes.

"You can count to a thousand for all I care. But if I were you, I wouldn't be sitting in that chair when the shooting starts."

Luca's face went white, the realization of his position in the line of fire sending a bead of sweat down his forehead. His hands snaked out for the arms of the chair and he cleared his throat, his voice weak when he spoke.

"If you gentlemen will allow me to get out of the way," he began.

"Sure, take all the time you need," Hayes said, already reaching for the STI.

The towering Frenchman saw the move and was reaching for his pistol when he realized that with his boss standing in front of him, there was no way he could draw and fire without hitting him.

He cursed and moved to shove his boss out of the way, but it was too late.

# 10

General Joseph Dábo was sitting at the breakfast table with his wife, half listening while she went on about the drapes she was planning on buying for the living room.

"At first I thought beige would match the décor," she said, flashing the smile that came anytime she was talking about spending his money.

"Hmm," he said, absently taking a battered cigarette case from the chest pocket of his BDUs.

"But I was wrong."

"Wait, what?" he asked, plucking a Gauloises from the case.

"I said I was wrong about the drapes matching."

"A Soro . . . admitting they were wrong? Now *that's* something you don't hear every day," he grinned, snapping the case shut.

"I thought you were quitting. Does Laurence know?"

"No," he said, getting to his feet and moving around the table, his six-foot-three frame dwarfing his diminutive wife as he bent to kiss her forehead. "And don't you go telling him, either."

"And why is that?" she asked, a coy, mischievous sparkle in her almond eyes. "You worried he will sack you again?"

"President Soro, fire me?" Dábo laughed. "He wouldn't dare."

"Because you control the Republican Guard?"

"No, because I told your brother the next time he fired me, I'd send you back to live with him," he grinned, ducking out of the kitchen before his wife could throw something at him.

Dábo was still smiling when he stepped out the front door and returned the salute of the two guards posted on the porch on his way to the up-armored Mercedes G-Class waiting at the bottom of the stairs. He climbed into the backseat, nodded to the driver, and leaned back, the custom Corinthian leather seat conforming to his frame.

The Mercedes glided away from the curb and Dábo pulled a pair of gold-rimmed Versace aviators from his pocket, slipped them over his intelligent eyes, and turned his gaze to the window.

The view took him back to 1999 when he was just another illiterate son of a farmer from Doropo hoping to make it in Abidjan. If someone had told him, back then, that one day he would be living in a three-thousand-square-foot villa in Cocody, the upscale enclave that housed Ivorian cultural elite, prominent expats, and foreign embassies, it would have seemed impossible. He'd come to the capital not to make it rich, but because he wanted to be a pilot. Unfortunately, the army had other ideas, sending him to the motor pool instead of flight school.

Being a mechanic was boring work, but he didn't mind; after

all, he was getting paid. But that changed in 2002 when troops from the northern provinces staged an armed uprising and stormed the capital.

Sensing an opportunity, Dábo resigned from the army and joined the rebels, who were now calling themselves the Ivorian Popular Front, or FPI.

While there was fighting all over the country, the rebels' main goal was to take the capital. During the first few months of close and brutal fighting, Dábo showed natural aptitude for the ruthlessness and tenacity that would earn him the attention of Laurence Soro—the leader of the FPI.

By the end of the year, Dábo was promoted to captain and six months later he was made an area commander. Soon he established himself as one of Soro's most able commanders, a role he ultimately used to bring his now brother-in-law to power.

Which was how at the young age of thirty-seven General Joseph Dábo became commander of the Republican Guard, a position that made him the second most powerful man in the country, but it also put a target on his back—especially among the groups that had broken off from the FPI and continued to fight Soro's government from their strongholds in the north.

It was this continued hostility and the rebels' willingness to try and kill Dábo at home that explained the blast-resistant gate at the bottom of the hill. The driver came to a halt next to a pair of concrete pillboxes and two soldiers stepped out. One of the men flashed a salute, then hustled to open the gate while the machine gunners on the roof swiveled the barrels of the belt-fed PKMs toward the street, ready and willing to kill *anyone* stupid enough to try and enter the compound.

The gate slid open on well-oiled rollers and the driver was

pulling onto the street when Dábo's satellite phone chirped to life. He pulled it out, ready to ignore the call until he saw the number on the screen.

*Cabot, Jesus, why is he calling me?* he wondered before answering.

"Yes, sir?"

As usual, Cabot cut right to the point.

"The airfield in Korhogo, I need it opened."

Since President Soro had taken power, he'd authorized Dábo to use the Republican Guard to stamp out the opposition, but his brutal methods had garnered unwanted attention and the general had been told to stand down. In fact, the president had been adamant that no additional incursions would be made without his *direct* authorization.

"General, are you there?" Cabot asked.

"Y-yes . . ." Dábo stammered, "but you know the president's orders."

More than anyone else who he'd met during his journey from lowly private to commander of the Republican Guard, Dábo was in Cabot's debt—the man had literally saved his life.

Even now he could remember every detail of that day, the convoy leaving the presidential palace and turning onto Boulevard Clozel, driving south, through the rain, toward the Heden Golf Hotel—and then the ambush.

The IED blew his truck off the road, killing the driver and mangling the armored Mercedes. He could still remember the caustic burn of the smoke in his lungs, the flames licking at his clothes.

By the time he got out, crawled free of the burning truck, Dábo had second-degree burns on half of his body and his left arm was broken. He managed to roll into a ditch, the rainwater extinguishing the fire as the attackers raked the area with machine gun fire.

He killed three of them with his pistol, saving the last bullet for himself, when Cabot and his squad of French paratroopers arrived and saved his life.

Dábo owed the man, that much went without saying, but this . . . *this was impossible.*

"General, are you there?"

"Yes . . . but Korhogo is—"

"Surrounded, cut off, yes I know. Why do you think I'm calling you?"

# 11

## MOGADOR

One second Hayes was standing there, his hands empty, and in the next instant the STI was out of its holster and rotating on target. He fired a single shot, the bullet catching Luca in his hip, spinning him to the ground, and then Hayes pushed the pistol up into a two-handed grip, the reticle locked on Emil's forehead.

*Too slow, motherfucker.*

He pulled the trigger. The 9-millimeter bucked in his hand, the bullet snapping the man's head back, as Hayes turned. He dropped to a knee and vented the bartender with a double tap to the chest.

Near the door, one of the men had a pistol out and was pulling the trigger as fast as he could. Flame spit from the barrel as he sent a rapid string of shots toward Hayes.

The first round hit the floor, tearing a gouge in the wood, and the second zipped high over his head, but Hayes kept his composure, lined up the shot, and ended the man with a hollow point through the eyeball. Then he was on his feet, diving over the top of the bar, bullets slamming into the bottles on the back wall, glass and booze spraying down on him.

The bartender lay on his back, the contents of his skull splattered across the kegs of beer, eyes staring sightless at the ceiling, a shotgun lying across his chest.

*Hello, beautiful,* Hayes thought, ignoring the shots punching through the front of the bar.

He shoved the pistol into its holster and was leaning forward to retrieve the shotgun from the dead man's chest. His hands were closing around the weapon when a bullet ricocheted off one of the kegs below the bar and slammed into his side.

The impact blasted the breath from his lungs and shoved him sideways across the floor. Hayes landed on his back, the pain white-hot and all-consuming. His mouth yawned in a silent scream, his lungs begging for air as a second bullet slapped into the wall inches from his face.

*Move or die,* the voice commanded.

Hayes kicked at the ground, trying to scramble out of the line of fire, but the floor was slick with booze and the bartender's blood. A second hail of lead came punching through the wood and he knew that the second shooter had followed his partner's example and adjusted his aim.

He was stuck, the floor too slick to get out of the line of fire. His only option was to roll onto his side, bring the shotgun up to his shoulder, and center the barrel on the light streaming through the growing cluster of bullet holes.

Hayes pulled the trigger and the shotgun roared like a howitzer, the stock recoiling hard into his shoulder. The first blast of double-aught buck blew a hole the size of a dinner plate through the wood, but he still couldn't see his attackers. As he fired a second shot, he managed a shaky breath.

He hacked on a lungful of gun smoke, the pain from his bruised ribs and the battery acid burn of the sweat in his eyes adding to his discomfort as he turned his full attention to kill his attackers.

The shotgun blast had punched a ragged hole through the front of the bar, and lying on his back, Hayes could see a pair of legs on the other side. Pushing everything away, he lined up the bead on the man's thigh, waited for it to steady, and pulled the trigger.

The buckshot slammed into the shooter's thigh at thirteen hundred feet per second and cut through the flesh and bone like a blade through butter.

Hayes dumped the shotgun, rolled onto his stomach, and low-crawled to the end of the bar. He jerked the pistol from the holster and forced himself up into a crouch, ignoring the dying screams of the man he'd left splayed out on the floor.

The remaining smuggler stood vapor-locked in the center of the room, the pistol in his hand forgotten as he gaped at his dying partner.

Quickly Hayes vaulted the bar, the slap of his shoes against the floor nudging the man back to reality.

"I'll kill you," the smuggler screamed, not realizing the pistol was empty until he pulled the trigger and heard the click of the hammer on the chamber.

Hayes stayed on target, knowing that the smuggler had tried

to kill him and that he had every right to return the favor. "You just won the lottery, pal," he said, lowering the pistol.

"You—you're going to shoot me in the back," the man said, his face white as bone.

"Not my style," he said.

When the smuggler was gone, Hayes scanned the room, making sure all the threats were down before bringing the pistol in. He dropped the magazine and shoved a fresh one home, the simple act of holding the thirty-four-ounce pistol in front of his face sending lightning bolts of pain radiating from his damaged ribs. By the time he holstered up, Hayes was sweating.

He ripped his shirt open and ran his hand down the outside of his vest, fingers finding the indentation where the bullet had hit three inches below his armpit. He'd been lucky and knew that if the shooters' aim had just been a little higher he'd be breathing blood bubbles right now.

But damn, did it hurt.

Hayes shuffled to the table, popped the lid of the Pelican case, and was grabbing the stack of pills when the radio hissed to life.

"Emil . . . Emil, do you copy?"

When there was no answer, the voice said, "Post one, head down to the bar and check it out."

"On our way," a man answered. His breathless voice telling Hayes that he was running.

*That's my cue.*

Hayes stuffed the pills and the envelope of cash into the bag. Knowing that he needed to do something to disrupt their communications, he grabbed the radio. He scanned the surface of the table, looking for a rubber band or anything else he could use to hold down the transmit key and jam the frequency, so none of the men outside could use their radios. A cursory search proved fruit-less.

Then Hayes's eyes drifted to the dead bodyguard splayed out on the ground. He came around the table and dropped to a knee beside Emil.

"Hey, man, can you give me a hand here?" he asked, placing the radio into the man's hand and closing his stiffening fingers around the transmit button.

The hiss of static from the speaker told him the radio was transmitting and Hayes moved to the door. He killed the lights, tugged the night vision over his eyes, and stepped outside.

He thought about making a play for the *Mako*, but knew it was pointless, since the powerboat was not only under guard, but damn near out of gas.

*But whoever is coming up from the docks doesn't know that.*

Hayes burst from cover and, staying low, raced back the way he'd come. He made it to the path and spent a few seconds scrap-ing his feet on the ground, leaving an obvious trail that he hoped the men coming from the docks would follow toward the scrub on the left side of the path.

He dove for cover behind a tree and was catching his breath when he saw the line of bodies running up from the east.

*Here they come.*

He figured they would start at the bar, check the interior, and then, *if* he was lucky, head north where the *Mako* was docked. If he was *super* lucky, they would see the tracks he'd made, assume he was an idiot, and haul ass up the hill.

It wasn't the most solid plan, but he'd lived through worse. Hayes was craning his neck to the south, trying to get a clear look at the dock, when he heard a sound that sent ice rushing through his veins.

He snapped his head back toward the men running to the bar, fifty feet to his front. They were closing fast, and he could hear their angry chatter and see the assortment of eastern bloc hardware they were toting.

But while Hayes wasn't worried about the exotic array of Kalashnikovs in the men's hands, the same could not be said of the beast straining against the length of chain that ran from its collar to the handler's waist.

*What the hell is that, a bear?*

With the branches and tall grass blocking his view, Hayes was able to get only brief glimpses of the animal, but what he saw made no logical sense. His first thought was that it was some kind of visual distortion, his brain trying to help out his eyes by boosting the magnification of what he was seeing through the night vision. But he rejected the thought when he realized the phenomenon didn't carry over to the men.

*Maybe they breed fighting dogs and one of those dudes got a lion drunk and got it to mate with a St. Bernard or something.*

Hayes was forced to wait an agonizing couple of minutes before the men were close enough to get a clear view of the animal.

*It's a freaking Boerboel.*

In most cases the fact that he was dealing with a dog and *not* some failed genetic experiment would have brought a modicum of relief. But knowing what he did about the Boerboel—that the males weighed close to two hundred pounds and had a bite pressure of more than 850 psi—Hayes wished he had a bigger gun.

And if the beast's size wasn't a big enough challenge, he realized that he had another problem when he felt the tickle of wind dance across his back, then dive down the incline toward the men.

Before the breeze, the Boerboel seemed almost passive, perfectly content to drag his handler through the undergrowth. Up to that point Hayes's plan of lying still and waiting for the men to pass had seemed feasible. But the moment he felt the breeze, he realized the dog's size was the least of his worries.

According to a study Hayes had read, the average human had six million scent receptors and was able to detect up to a trillion different odors. Both were big numbers, but even with the men standing downwind of him, he wasn't worried about them catching his scent. Mainly because, like him, evolution had programmed his pursuers to process their environment *visually*.

The Boerboel, on the other hand, had come into the world blind and deaf and like all puppies had learned to process its environment *not* with its eyes, but with its nose and its up to *three hundred million* scent receptors. So it was no surprise when, seconds after sniffing the air, the Boerboel froze, its massive head snapping left, a mohawk of fur running up its back as its eyes locked on to Hayes's hiding place.

*Annnd . . . dammit.*

The second the Boerboel turned in his direction, he had the reticle of the STI centered on the animal's chest and his finger hovering over the trigger.

*For God's sake, shoot the dog,* the voice urged.

While twenty yards was a long pistol shot for some, Hayes knew at this range he could shoot the wings off a gnat, but still he held his fire. Not because he had any ethical problems with shooting a dog but because he honestly wasn't sure if the 9-millimeter had the ass to bring it down.

*Better to go with what you know.*

Hayes shifted targets, transitioned from the Boerboel to the handler, who was in the process of unclipping the chain from his waist when Hayes fired.

The 9-millimeter Corbon Pow'R Ball left the barrel at fourteen hundred feet per second and punched through the man's skull, before mushrooming inside his cranial vault.

It was lights out—instant death.

The handler's comrades spun in the direction of the shot, but before they could open fire, Hayes dumped the rest of the magazine, firing so fast that the STI sounded like it was on full auto, trying to keep their heads down long enough to unass his position.

But the men were well trained and reacted to the incoming hail of bullets by dropping prone and hosing the tree line with a wall of lead. The bullets came snapping through the brush, one of the rounds slamming into a tree two inches above Hayes's head.

He rolled out of the line of fire, snagged a fresh mag from the magazine pouch clipped to his belt, and slammed it into the pistol. Then he was on his feet, bent at the waist, twisting and dodging through the trees, sprinting for higher ground, knowing from the hail of lead impacting all around him that he wasn't going to make it.

Hayes changed directions, threw himself off the edge and down the hillside. He tumbled head over heels, the scrub brush slapping his face, tearing the night vision from his head.

By the time he reached the bottom he was cut to shit—his mouth filled with dirt and bits of leaves and bark. But he was alive and knew that if he wanted to stay that way he needed to find some cover—fast.

He hobbled into the low ground and ducked behind a boulder

and was checking his pack, making sure that he hadn't lost the pills, when he heard his pursuers crashing through the undergrowth behind him.

Hayes brought his pistol to bear and was squinting through the darkness, ready to engage the first target of opportunity, when he heard the guttural bark of the Boerboel.

*You've got to be shitting me.*

But there was no mistaking the hulking silhouette that burst out of the trees or the lifeless bounce of the figure dragging behind it.

*Run.*

Hayes shot to his feet and, throwing caution to the wind, raced toward the dock, figuring that he had a better chance of outrunning the dog than a bullet. He ran as hard as he could, taking long, loping strides, but Hayes had never been a sprinter and knew that if it weren't for the added deadweight of the handler, the Boerboel would have easily run him down.

He hit the gangway at a full sprint, eyes locked on a rusted twenty-six-foot trawler pulling out of its slip. Hayes had no way of knowing how many men were on board, or if they were armed and, honestly, at this point, he didn't give a shit.

The only thing that mattered was getting away from the hellhound snapping at his heels.

He was halfway to the T intersection at the end of the dock when the captain swung the bow, aiming for the buoy that marked the channel mouth.

Hayes was almost to the end, the dog so close he could feel its hot breath on the back of his legs. All that was left was a hard right turn and a dash to the crates stacked at the far edge of the pier and he was free.

*Might want to slow down for that turn,* the voice suggested.

Hayes hazarded a glance over his shoulder, saw the beast preparing for a lunge, and knew there was no way in hell he was slowing down. Instead he reached out, hooked the last pylon with his hand, and, using it as a pivot, swung his body into the turn.

The dog tried to stop, but the wooden planks were slick, and that plus the weight of its dead handler slingshotting past it while it skittered to a halt sent it flying into the water with a colossal splash.

With the dog off his ass and running parallel to the trawler, Hayes focused everything on his makeshift springboard at the end of the dock. He poured on a last burst of speed, praying that the captain kept the boat close to the docks, and then he was clambering up the crates, flinging himself into the air.

# 12

I t was almost noon when Shaw emerged from the Congressional Visitors Center, the unfamiliar navy-blue tie tight as a garrote around his throat. He clawed at the knot and after tearing the tie free, unbuttoned his collar and started down the stairs.

The four hours he'd spent before the committee had taken their toll and Shaw was exhausted—his body stiff from the uncomfortable chair, his mind wrung out like a dish towel after the verbal judo session with Senator Miles.

He reached the bottom of the stairs, his driver, Luke Carter, already hustling around the car and opening his door.

"How was it?" he asked.

"Boring," Shaw lied, shoving the tie into his pocket and handing over his attaché case.

"That's good, right?"

"Listen, kid, why don't you head back to the office? I think I'm going to take a walk, maybe grab some lunch while I'm at it."

"You want me to come with you, sir?"

"No, head back to the office. I'll give you a buzz when I'm done."

"Yes, sir," Luke said.

Shaw watched the Town Car pull out and waited until it was out of sight before turning east, toward the National Mall.

It was a shit day for a walk, the sky over Capitol Hill was sullen gray, the winter wind that blew in from the east sharp as a blade across his bare skin. But he was too busy thinking about his next move to care.

That Senator Miles was out for blood was no surprise; he'd been wanting his pound of flesh from Hayes since the moment he became chairman. And while Shaw had done everything he could to protect his star recruit, he was slowly beginning to realize that all he had accomplished was to put his *own* neck on the chopping block.

He skirted the White House, hands shoved in his pockets as he started across Lafayette Square, the senator's parting words echoing in his mind.

*"If you don't give me Hayes, I promise you, this committee will find someone who will."*

Shaw stopped at the intersection of H and 16th, the sight of the Hay-Adams hotel making him realize how badly he could use a drink.

He glanced at his watch, saw that it was a quarter to one, and then thought about the work waiting for him back at the office.

*The hell with it.*

Shaw started across the street, angling for the front door, confident with the knowledge that he wouldn't be the only one at the hotel enjoying a midday cocktail.

The Hay-Adams was more than a Washington icon—it was an institution, the meeting place of choice for ranking senators, senior aides, and political dilettantes to plot and scheme over trays of East Coast oysters or plates of Dover sole.

Shaw stepped inside, the warm air of the lobby thawing his face as he crossed to the stairs leading down to the aptly named Off the Record. He hit the landing, cold hands still in his pockets, the only thing on his mind the lowball of Blanton's waiting for him inside—so close that he could taste it.

He was almost there when a whisper of fabric followed by the scrape of a shoe against tile sent the hairs on the back of his neck standing on end. Shaw turned, alerted by the premonition of danger, hand darting to his sleeve and the carbon fiber blade hidden inside.

Shaw jerked the blade free and whirled to face the threat, muscles taut as a bow at full draw, ready and willing to kill when he saw his would-be attacker's face.

"Easy, killer," the man said, hands held palms open in front of his chest.

"Mike?" Shaw asked, the tension easing from his muscles. "What the hell are *you* doing out here?"

"Figured if even half of what I heard about this morning's hearings were true that you'd be needing a drink."

"And you decided to greet me by waiting out here in the shadows?"

"Old habits," he shrugged.

"Good way to get yourself killed," Shaw said, returning the blade to its sheath while he studied the man.

As the deputy director of operations, Mike Carpenter wasn't just the CIA's chief spy, he was also the Agency's heir apparent, the man tapped to take over for the director when she left at the end of the year, a role that made him the second most powerful man at the Agency.

"You following me, Mike?"

"Nope, just in the area."

"Is that a fact?" Shaw asked.

"Yep. Now, how about that drink?"

"Lead the way," Shaw said.

Carpenter nodded and headed for the entrance, where the host stood waiting.

"Good afternoon, gentlemen," he said. "If you will follow me, I have a private room already set up."

*In the neighborhood, my ass.*

"What would you gentlemen like?" the host asked, after seating them.

"Blanton's Single Barrel," Carpenter said.

"Make it two," Shaw said.

"Right away, gentlemen."

Shaw waited until the man was gone and then pulled a black box the size of a deck of cards from his jacket pocket.

"An RF scanner? Seriously?" Carpenter asked, a hint of a smile twisting the corner of his lips as Shaw wanded the room. "Where's the trust, Levi?"

Satisfied that the room wasn't bugged, Shaw adjusted his chair so he could keep one eye on the door and the other on Carpenter.

"Trust, Mike?" he sneered. "You've got to *earn* trust."

The two men had history, not the good kind, but Shaw was too well trained to ask why he was here. So he sat and studied the room in silence, searching the crown molding around the ceiling and the joints of the walls, anywhere the cagey cold warrior could have hidden a camera or some other device the scanner hadn't picked up.

"It's clean," Carpenter said.

*Yeah, okay,* he thought.

The waiter returned with the drinks, placed them on the table, and after asking if they wanted a menu and receiving a curt "no" from Carpenter, stepped out and shut the door behind him.

Shaw took a sip of the whisky, savoring the heat of the rye and the mellow caramel finish, and nodded in approval. He returned the glass to the table and turned his full attention to Carpenter, who cut right to the chase.

"Miles isn't playing around. He wants Hayes."

"Tell me something I *don't* know," Shaw said.

"Okay, he knows about the deal, knows you gave him six months to make a decision."

*Shit. How?*

"Not relevant," Carpenter said, reading his mind. "What is relevant is that right now you are in the way."

"So, Miles sent you here thinking I'd tell you where Hayes was for old times' sake? C'mon, Mike, you know me better than that."

"Listen, Levi, I get it," Carpenter said, leaning across the table, his eyes deadly serious. "Hell, part of me even respects what you did, but it's time to pick a side. Not tonight, not tomorrow, but right now."

*Dammit.*

If it had been any of the other directors who ruled the CIA from the seventh floor sitting before him, Shaw would have told them to fuck off and never lost a wink of sleep. But Mike Carpenter hadn't risen to the number two man at the Agency because he was a bureaucrat. No, the only papers he'd ever pushed were the toe tags he'd handed out wholesale during the past twenty years of the war on terror.

"He won't come in easy."

"Why do you think I'm here?" Carpenter asked, leaning back in his chair.

*Fuck.*

"When is his next check-in?" Carpenter asked.

"Twenty-four hours," Shaw lied.

"Fine. If he's not back stateside in forty-eight, it's game over, understood?"

"Yeah, I got it."

"Good," Carpenter said, getting to his feet.

He dropped a few bills on the table and started for the door, pausing just short of the knob. He turned back to the table.

"And Levi, one more thing."

"What's that?"

"Don't go anywhere."

# 13

MOGADOR

Hayes knew the moment he launched himself from the dock that he'd shorted the jump. Knew that instead of landing gracefully onto the deck, he was going to hit the side.

*Shit.*

His chest slammed into the hull, the impact blasting the air from his lungs and tearing the pistol from his hand. The STI went cartwheeling through the air and Hayes reached up for the gunwale, kicking his legs, desperate to find a toehold.

But the hull was slick, and he couldn't get a grip. He was falling, grip weakening, boots sliding closer toward the dishwater-gray surface of the sea.

*Get your ass up there,* the voice ordered.

Summoning the last of his strength, Hayes managed to hoist

his armpits over the edge, relieving the pressure on his slipping grip and, once secure, kicking his leg over the edge. Hooking the lip with his toe, he hoisted himself up and over.

He crashed onto the deck, rolled onto his back, and was trying to catch his breath when there was an angry shout from the pilot-house.

"Who the fuck is that?"

Hayes staggered to his feet, spied the STI wedged underneath a crate on the far side of the deck. But before he had a chance to recover it, four angry sailors were blocking his path.

*Can this day get any worse?*

"Captain, it's him," one of the men shouted in Arabic. "The one they are looking for."

"Kill him," came the reply.

"Guys, can we talk about this?" Hayes asked.

"Afraid not," the man said, pulling a wicked-looking blade from the small of his back.

The rest of the sailors were quick to arm themselves with whatever was lying around on the deck—junkyard weapons—a lead pipe, a length of chair, and something that looked like a small harpoon.

"Look, I've got this anger thing that I'm working on," Hayes said, hands open in front of him, "and I'm *really* trying to make it through the rest of the day without killing anyone else . . ."

But the man with the knife wasn't interested in talking and slashed at his head, forcing Hayes to where the man with the section of lead pipe stood waiting.

*Well, I tried.*

While Hayes was fully capable of killing with a knife or a garrote, he'd been trained to avoid getting too close to his target. Putting himself into a position where he could be identified—or worse, shot. In his world, a fair fight was to be avoided at all cost. Which was why Hayes spent so much time and energy stalking his prey—analyzing his target's every move.

Always waiting. Always watching.

Until it was time to take that *one* perfect shot.

But a street fight was an entirely different story and, outnumbered four to one, Hayes knew that the only way he was going to survive was by inflicting the maximum amount of damage in the minimum amount of time.

The man with the knife tried to stick him in the side, but Hayes landed a hard ridge hand to his throat that dropped him to his knees. Before the man with the harpoon had a chance to strike, Hayes rolled across the deck, snatching the STI from beneath the crate.

He came up in a crouch, snapped the pistol onto target, and just like a day on the range, engaged the targets from left to right.

By the time the last expended shell hit the deck, the men were all dead.

"So, what do you say there, Cap'n?" he said, turning the pistol on the openmouthed man standing in the pilothouse. "Feel like a swim?"


An hour later Hayes cut the engines, grabbed his bag, and stepped out onto the deck. To say the meeting with Luca had *not* gone according to plan was the understatement of the year. Hayes might have come out on top, but he hadn't walked away unscathed.

He was wet, tired, and generally beat to shit—and definitely *not* looking forward to swimming to shore.

Hayes had ditched the bodies at sea—weighed them down with lengths of chain—and would have piloted the boat all the way to shore if it hadn't been for the quarter ton of raw hash he'd found in the hold.

*Still screwing me, aren't ya, Luca?*

He moved to the rear of the boat and stood there staring out into the darkness.

Without the night vision, Hayes couldn't see the coast, but he could smell it—the nauseating mix of unwashed bodies and meat roasting over an open flame. So close that he could almost feel the hot shower and the cot waiting for him at the airfield five miles away.

But first he had to get there.

Hayes opened the pack and double-checked the ziplock bag he'd put the pills in, made sure they were airtight before taking off his boots and stuffing them inside. He grabbed a Petzl headlamp, shouldered the pack, and snapped the sternum strap across his chest on his way aft. At the transom he looked over the side—the water shimmering like motor oil in the headlamp's red glow.

Hayes had been fading fast during the last leg of the trip, and even with the windows of the pilothouse open he'd fought to stay awake. But he knew that was about to change.

*Might as well get it over with,* he thought.

Even though it was summer in Morocco, the North Atlantic was frigid, the ice-cold water cascading over his body instantly taking his breath away. Hayes bobbed to the surface, his pack filling with water—trying to drag him under as he kicked off. The distant sliver of the shore was suddenly impossibly far.

Dumping the assault pack wasn't an option, so he turned onto his back, hoping what air hadn't been pushed out of the pack would keep him buoyant as he forced himself into a backstroke.

Free will, the ability to quit, wasn't a Treadstone trait, which was why it was one of the first things they'd removed at the behavior modification laboratory. Only problem was, just like any high-performance machines, Treadstone operators required the occasional tune-up to keep them running at peak performance.

"Retreading" is what the docs called it, and Hayes hadn't had one in almost three years, which meant that while he got to keep all the shitty side effects—the anger, nightmares, and brain-splitting migraines—his once razor-sharp edge was starting to dull.

*Bet you'd sell your soul for a chem right now,* the voice said.

Since the first recorded history of organized warfare in the fifth century BC, man has sought better weapons—sharper swords, stronger metals, faster horses—*anything* to give them an edge in battle, only to learn that in the end, the difference between the living and the dying had less to do with the weapon and more to do with the man wielding it.

It was this knowledge more than anything else that drove the Treadstone doctors in their pursuit of the perfect soldier. An assassin who could kill without thought or fear. A man or woman who could outlast, outthink, outfight anyone in the world.

But there was only so far the human body could go, and no amount of motivation could take the icy chill out of the water or replace the calories Hayes had already burned.

*Think about something else—anything else.*

Hayes forced the pain and the bullshit that had run roughshod over his day from the front of his mind until there was nothing but blank space, an endless black canvas. His mind drifted like a dog let off its leash, wandering back and forth before returning to the reason Hayes was in this mess in the first place—the promise that he'd made to Dr. Karen Miles three weeks prior.

He'd been inside World Aid's dilapidated hangar at Essaouira breaking down a fuel pump when Dr. Miles walked in, a grim frown in the place of her usual perky smile.

"Adam, I need . . ." she began.

"What's wrong?"

"It—it's easier if I show you," she said.

He followed her to her office, the plywood hutch in the back of the hangar, and watched as she opened the laptop on her desk.

"This is from Camp Four in Bobo-Dioulasso," she said, keying up the video.

After tours in Iraq and Afghanistan, Hayes had seen his share of misery, but nothing prepared him for the video he saw in that hangar. The white-shrouded bodies lying shoulder to shoulder in the trench and the hopeless eyes of the women and tear-stained faces of the children standing above, looking down at their loved ones.

"Wh-what the hell is this?" he choked.

"Cholera," she said, "easily treated with the proper medication, but with Camp Four besieged . . ."

Hayes had heard the rumors about the militants operating in the area, surrounding the camps, refusing to let the aid workers in unless they paid an exorbitant toll. Some of the aid groups had called their bluff, tried to sneak past their blockade. As far as Hayes knew, none of them had ever made it back.

"Tell me the medicine they need, and I'll find it and fly it in myself."

*Why in the hell did I say that?*

Hayes was still trying to find the answer when his knees scraped the ground. He was spent, his legs shaking like a bowl of Jell-O, screaming against the weight of the water-filled pack that threatened to pull him back into the sea. He grunted to his feet and sloshed to shore, eyes locked on the canted palm tree peeking over the top of the sand dune ahead.

Hayes staggered across the beach, the shifting sand causing his legs to cramp.

*Maybe you should stop. Take a breather,* the voice suggested.

It was tempting, and while he could certainly use the break, Hayes was afraid that if he collapsed into the sand, he might not be able to get up.

*Better to keep moving.*

Leaning forward like a man walking against the wind, Hayes started across the beach, his eyes locked on the tree fifty yards to his front. But in his condition, it might as well have been a mile.

*Just keep moving. One foot in front of the next,* he urged.

By the time he made it to the sand dune he was running on fumes. He dropped to his knees and punched his hands into the sand, using them like hooks to claw his way to the top, and then he was at the apex, the sight of the dilapidated shack on the other side feeling like Christmas morning. Hayes dug his toes into the sand and, summoning the last of his strength, inched his upper body over the lip of the dune, farther and farther until gravity took over. He tumbled down the back side of the dune, closed his eyes and mouth against the rush of sand that pelted his face.

When he reached the bottom, every inch of his skin was

covered in sand. He got to his feet, shook off like a dog fresh from a pond, and started for the door, legs bowed wide to lessen the sandpaper scrape of the grit between them.

*Thank God I don't wear underwear.*

The shack wasn't much to look at—a fifteen-by-twenty-foot rectangle of weather-beaten wood one of the local fishermen had once used to store his boats. While he was sure no one would ever know that he was using it as a stash spot, the idea of being a squatter didn't sit well, so he had spent a few days tracking down the owner and offered to rent it from him.

*Always have a way out.* It was the first rule they had taught him at Treadstone—one that had saved his life more times than he could count. Which was why even though he wasn't operational he kept his bags packed and guns clean—made sure he had the means to drop everything and hit the road at a moment's notice.

Hayes stopped at the door and bent down to check the two quarters he'd stuffed into the crack—the primitive anti-intrusion device that would have alerted him if anyone had been inside. When he saw that they were there, he grabbed the lock, spun in his combination, and stepped inside, closing the door behind him and lighting the ancient Coleman lantern on the table.

The sallow light illuminated a spartan interior: a battered Land Rover in the center, a stack of bottled water, three cases of MREs, and a metal cabinet in the back corner. Hayes stripped out of his clothes and retrieved a small bucket from the cabinet, which he filled with five bottles of water. He stuffed the empties and the filthy clothes into a trash bag, took a shop rag over to the bucket of water, and did his best to clean up.

When he'd gotten as much of the grime off as possible, Hayes toweled off and dressed in a black T-shirt, jeans, and a pair of boots. He retrieved a medium-sized drybag from the bottom of the cabinet, untied the drawstring, and pulled out a backpacker's stove.

The MSR DragonFly didn't look like much, but Hayes had fallen in love with the miniature stove not because it was the most powerful on the market, but because, according to the manufacturer, you could pour *anything* remotely flammable into the fuel bottle and the MSR would burn it.

Hayes had bought the stove simply because he wanted to refute MSR's claim, and since purchasing it he'd used everything from rubbing alcohol to diesel fuel and the little stove had never let him down. He filled the fuel bottle from a can of white gas and used the integral pump to pressurize it before connecting the bottle to the small burner and lighting the wick. After adjusting the air flow so the flame burned evenly, Hayes went back to the cabinet, retrieved an enamel mug, added two scoops of instant coffee from a pack, filled the mug with water, and set it atop the burner.

He watched the flame lick the bottom of the mug, the flicker of orange reminding him of how he'd ended up in Morocco.

Hayes hadn't come to Africa with the intention of becoming a humanitarian. He came because he needed a plane and knew that Africa was his only chance of finding one that would accommodate his limited budget. He started in South Africa, bought the old Land Rover, and headed north through the maze of conflict zones and failed states in search of his prize. He spent the next two weeks dodging bullets and mortars, searching the shot-up airfields and military scrapyards during the day and sleeping in the truck at night; his only goal was to find *anything* remotely airworthy. He was about to give it up when he heard of a military arms bazaar being held in Monrovia, Liberia.

According to his source, the bazaar was run by a South African soldier of fortune named Pieter van Wyk, and while it was mostly geared toward third world warlords with dreams of mounting a coup, it was Hayes's last shot.

The plane was a Vietnam-era C-123 Provider and not only was it the oldest plane on the tarmac, it was easily in the worst shape. But Hayes saw through the rust, the fogged windows, and dry-rotted rubber seals—seeing the plane not for what it *was*, but for what it had been.

"Hello, beautiful," he said, ducking under the wing and running his hand over the skin.

*Thought you were here for a plane, not a project,* the voice chided.

But Hayes was in love and after spending an hour checking the plane out from top to bottom, compiling a list of broken hoses, dry-rotted seals, and busted engine parts, he spent another hour scrounging through the yards of parts on the other side of the field before making an offer.

"Deal, but just so you know, van Wyk only paid off the cops for forty-eight hours, so if you and that heap aren't gone in the air by then, it's off to jail with ya."

*Now you tell me.*

It wasn't easy, but twenty-three hours of work later, he managed to get the engines started and limp the plane north, stopping at every airfield along the way to fix busted hoses, but by the time he reached Essaouira, it was obvious she wasn't going any farther.

Hayes knew he could get the plane back into shape, but he needed the tools, equipment, and hangar space to make the repairs; the only problem was he didn't have the cash to pay for them.

He was trying to work a deal with one of the mechanics when a pinched-face man with mischievous blue eyes came strolling over.

"You a pilot?" he asked, his British accent on full display as he mopped his bald pate with a grimy handkerchief.

"That's right," Hayes answered.

"Dr. Thomas Watson," the man said, sticking out his hand. "I am the director of World Aid."

"World Aid?"

"That's right, we're an NGO, like Doctors Without Borders, but without the flashy name or the accompanying money."

"Huh," Hayes said noncommittally.

"But while we don't have mounds of cash lying around, we aren't without resources," Dr. Watson added, seeing that he was losing Hayes's interest.

"Like what?"

"Like that," he answered, nodding to a dilapidated hangar with a white-and-blue globe hanging over the door. "Fully stocked facility, one you would have access to if you were to come fly for us."

"That's it, just fly?"

"We even pay for the fuel."

Sitting there inside the shack, the now-empty mug before him, Hayes's mind shifted tack again, this time to his wife and son. How he'd love to show them Africa. Maybe rent a little cabin in Kenya, spend the days showing little Jack the real-life versions of the toys he loved to play with. And the nights making love to his wife.

*Dreams like that will kill you faster than a bullet,* the voice chided.

"What the hell do you know?" Hayes asked aloud.

*Enough to know that even in Africa, a leopard can't change its spots. You're a killer, Adam, and that's all you are ever going to be.*

# 14

## ESSAOUIRA, MOROCCO

The plane was loaded and ready, but instead of sitting behind the controls, Hayes was standing inside the sun-faded phone booth at the corner of the hangar. He held the phone to his ear and typed in the number, eyes drifting to the ceiling, where hornets were busily constructing a nest.

"Just making a call—no need for anyone to get excited," he said.

Usually, his wife was quick to pick up the phone but when she hadn't answered by the fifth ring, Hayes glanced at his watch. Realizing, too late, that it was three a.m. back in the States.

*Adam, you stupid ass.*

He was about to hang up when there was a click on the other end, followed by his wife's sleep-laden voice.

"H-hello . . ."

"Shit, baby, I'm sorry . . . I didn't realize—"

"*No*, it's fine . . ." She yawned. "I was, well, *we* were botɴ hoping you were going to call today."

"Yeah, I got in pretty late last night, and . . ."

Hayes trailed off, eyes dropping to the ground, suddenly unsure what to say. He kicked at the rocks that lay inside the phone booth, sent them skipping across the tarmac.

*Dammit, it shouldn't be this hard to talk to your wife.*

As usual, Annabelle was there to save him.

"Last night when you didn't call, I was a little bummed out. You know what your son said to me?"

"I can't *even* imagine," Hayes said, a grin starting at the corner of his mouth.

"He said, 'Don't be sad, Mommy—Daddy's busy helping those sick people.'"

"That boy is smart as a whip—he must have got that from you," he laughed. "He's not giving you any trouble, is he?"

"Nope. But he misses you . . . we both do."

"I know, baby . . ."

There was so much that he wanted to say. So much that he wanted to tell her, but the emotion that came from hearing her voice and the thought of their son expanded inside his chest like a balloon.

"I miss you guys, too. More than I'll ever be able to tell you."

"I know," she said.

"Do you?"

There was a momentary pause between his question and her answer, a hiccup in the conversation caused by the signal having to be bounced from Africa to the States and back again. It was less than a second, not even long enough to take a full breath, but it was enough to send his mind back to the previous summer.

Back when they were on the verge of a divorce, even this stilted conversation wouldn't have been possible.

"Yes, I do. You're my husband, and I love you . . . I just wish you were home."

"Me, too."

"H-have you thought about it . . . about what you are going to do?"

"Sometimes it feels like that's all I think about," he said.

"Well, whatever you decide, we support you. Now, let me get back to sleep. Jack and I have an early morning at the zoo."

"You guys have fun. Be safe and tell the little man I love him."

He waited until she'd hung up, used his index finger to hang up, double-checked the hornets, and then dialed the number Shaw had given him.

This time the line connected after the first ring, but instead of a person, Hayes got a recorded message in Cantonese.

"Thank you for calling Sterling Mercantile and Trust," it said. "If you know your account, please enter it at any time."

He typed in his twelve-digit PIN, and a moment later, Shaw's voice came over the line.

"Hayes, my boy, how's the dark continent treating you?"

"It's fucking hot, Levi."

"You're breaking my heart," Shaw replied. "Any other man in your shoes would be lying in the sand drinking something with an umbrella in it, but not Adam Hayes."

*Here we go with this shit again.*

"The sand is overrated."

"Yeah, I imagine it wouldn't be much fun lugging that cross

of yours around. When are you going to stop playing Mother Teresa and come back—do what God put you on this earth to do?"

"God didn't make me this way, you and that psycho Dr. Saddler did this to me."

"Son, you were a killer when I recruited you; all we ever did was make you better at it."

"Look, as much fun as I'm having listening to your bullshit, I've got things to do."

"Fine, where are you going this time? The Congo, Uganda, or some other third world hellhole no one gives a shit about?"

Hayes squeezed the receiver until his knuckles popped and was about to slam the phone into the wall when he remembered the hornets.

*Just take a breath, tell the old man where you're going, and get off the phone.*

"Burkina Faso," he said.

"Where in Burkina Faso?" Shaw replied.

"Bobo-Dioulasso."

Then there was silence.

The calls were part of the amnesty agreement he'd made a day after Levi Shaw was reaffirmed as the director of Operation Treadstone. Hayes had hoped they would get easier, but so far, it hadn't happened.

"Adam," Shaw said, his voice suddenly tired, "there is something I need to tell you."

# 15

## GEORGETOWN, WASHINGTON, D.C.

From the street, there was nothing untoward about 2908 North Street NW—nothing that separated the two-story red-brick row house from the rest of the eighteenth-century Federals that lined Georgetown's exclusive East Village. In fact, with its freshly painted window boxes, snow-covered cornice, and the pair of wrought-iron greyhounds flanking the fire-engine-red door, the house looked downright suburban.

But it was all a lie, carefully constructed urban camouflage orchestrated by the man in the office on the second floor.

Director Levi Shaw had spent most of the night mulling over his meeting with Carpenter, finally giving up on sleep around four-fifteen and heading into the office. After putting on a pot of coffee, he'd built a fire in the old-world fireplace and waited until the shadows of the flames were dancing merrily across the floor-to-ceiling bookshelves lining the cherrywood-paneled walls before filling his stained CIA mug to the brim.

Properly armed, he took a seat behind his massive oak desk and, while waiting for the coffee to cool, turned his attention to the blast-resistant window and the snowfall outside.

*What the hell am I going to do about Hayes?*

Twenty minutes later, Shaw was on his second cup and still no closer to an answer when Hayes called in.

*Might as well get it over with.*

"Adam, there is something I need to tell you."

"What now, Levi?" Hayes answered, his voice ice-cold, void of any emotion.

In many ways, Shaw knew Adam Hayes better than the man knew himself, which wasn't surprising, considering the fact that he'd not only recruited him but personally oversaw every aspect of his training.

During his tenure as director, Shaw had spent hours combing through the DoD databases searching for men with specific skill sets, certain psychological traits, and while he'd recruited hundreds of men, he'd never met *anyone* like Hayes.

"They want you back," he said.

"I still have thirty days left."

"Not anymore," Shaw said.

"What the hell happened?"

Shaw filled him in, told him about being called before the Senate Intelligence Committee, his sparring match with Senator Miles, and his subsequent "meeting" with Carpenter.

"Mike Carpenter?" he asked. "What the hell does the deputy director have to do with any of this?"

"Listen, son, things are happening around here. Things I can't control . . ."

"Care to elaborate, old man?"

"Open your eyes, son. We are at war, and right now, Miles and Carpenter think you are the enemy."

"What else is new?"

"This time, they are not playing around. If I can't get you to come in on your own, Carpenter will send a team to hunt you down, and if you are lucky, they will put a bullet in the back of your head."

"Why the hell do they care?"

"Because you are a killer, son, and like it or not, that's all they are ever going to let you be."

"You got a pen?" Hayes asked.

"A pen? Yeah, I've got a pen," Shaw frowned. "What for?"

"Because I've got a message for that dumb son of a bitch, and I want to make sure you get it right. You ready to copy?" Hayes asked.

"Yeah, go ahead."

"Tell Carpenter that whoever comes after me better bring their own postage."

"Postage . . . what for?"

"Because whoever he sends over here is coming back in a box."

"Adam, for once in your life can you please listen to—"

"I'll catch you later, Levi," Hayes said, and then the line went dead.

Two hundred miles west, in West Virginia, Skyler Harris was at the tail end of a ten-hour shift when she cracked a fresh Red Bull in preparation for the task at hand.

"Freaking dailies, what a joke," she muttered, before taking a long gulp.

Skyler had been working at Site Tango for three years and was tired of pulling the graveyard shift in the CIA's Signals Intercept and Analysis Lab. She'd already put in three requests for transfer to the day shift, but each time her supervisor's response was the same.

"You know how it works around here," he patiently explained, "all moves are based off seniority, and since you're just a GS-11 . . ."

"I'm stuck," she finished for him.

"It sucks, but that's the way it is," he shrugged.

"C'mon, Carl, there *has* to be a way," she'd pleaded.

"You can do it the old-fashioned way—mine the *dailies*, try to find something that will impress the bosses upstairs."

"Be serious, Carl, *nobody* looks at the dailies," she said. "They're garbage."

"You know what they say, one man's trash—"

"Yeah, yeah."

Back at her workstation, Skyler waited until she felt the flutter of the Red Bull taking effect, and after pulling on a pair of Bose headphones opened the task bar. She double-clicked the icon, typed today's date into the search bar, and hit the enter key.

*Here we go again.*

The dailies were the slush pile of the intercept community—steaming piles of raw intel and uncategorized audio intercepts that the spy satellites dumped onto Site Tango's servers every morning, where they sat until a system administrator decided they were taking up too much space and finally deleted them.

Skyler opened the most recent file, grabbed the half-filled legal pad and a pen from the holder, and hit the play button. The audio started with a rush of static; she was reaching for the volume knob when she heard a voice.

She closed her eyes, focused her attention on the voice, ready to record anything of note, but the audio was so distorted she couldn't understand what the man was saying. Then it went silent.

*Great start,* she thought, hitting the delete button and moving on.

The next hour and fifty minutes was more of the same, and with ten minutes left on her shift, Skyler was tempted to call it a day.

*Just one more.*

She hit the play button and was about to close the pad and return to the pen to its holder when she heard it.

*"Mike Carpenter?"* he asked. *"What the hell does the deputy director have to do with any of this?"*

*"Listen, son, things are happening around here. Things I can't control . . ."*

*"Care to elaborate, old man?"*

*"Open your eyes, son. We are at war, and right now, Miles and Carpenter think you are the enemy."*

"Holy shit," Skyler said, reaching for the phone.

# 16

## ESSAOUIRA, MOROCCO

Hayes slammed the phone into the cradle and crossed to the plane where Vlad stood at the ramp, the red-and-black box of Prima cigarettes in his hand. He stuck one between his lips, scratched a match against the skin of the plane, and lit the smoke before looking up and hitting Hayes with a sardonic smile.

"Problems?" he asked.

*Just one,* Hayes thought, stopping in front of the man. "Do you ever buy cigarettes that *don't* smell like a barrel of assholes?"

"That's fine Russian tobacco you are talking about."

"Why don't you take your fine Russian tobacco up to the cockpit so we can get the hell out of here?" he demanded.

"*Mudak,*" Vlad muttered before turning on his heel and stomping off. *Asshole.*

Once he was gone, Hayes turned his attention back to the plane, and started his preflight checks. He methodically inspected the control surfaces, checking the tail rudder, flaps, ailerons. By the time he made it to the cockpit and dropped into the pilot's chair, his mood had regulated—the morning's aggravations fading beneath the smell of jet fuel, burnt oil, and canvas that permeated the cockpit.

He pulled the headset over his ears while his copilot sat stoically, a fresh smoke clutched between his lips, content to let Hayes handle the preflight.

Vlad tuned the radio to 118.25, waiting until Hayes stopped at the edge of the runway before contacting the tower in French.

"Mogador Tower, this is Pilgrim three-niner x-ray holding short of runway sixteen."

"Pilgrim three-niner x-ray, you are cleared for takeoff runway sixteen at one-five-seven degrees."

Hayes taxied to the end of the strip and went through the takeoff checklist in his head—locking the rear wheel straight and opening the cowl flaps.

He depressed the brakes, held them down while increasing the throttles, eyes glued to the RPM gauge. The plane inched forward, struggling against the brakes like a greyhound tugging at the leash, but he held her in place waiting for the RPMs to rise.

*Here we go.*

He let off the brakes and the C-123 lumbered down the runway, Hayes watching the airspeed indicator. He waited for the needle to pass ninety knots before pulling back on the yoke. And then they were airborne, the twin radials roaring like a swamp fan as the plane cut through the tendrils of clouds that hung like strips of cotton over the airfield.

Hayes retracted the landing gear, and after leveling out at ten thousand feet Vlad gave him his heading.

"Come south to one-six-one degrees."

Hayes made the course correction and was about to ask Vlad what their flight time was but, not really wanting to hear the Russian's mouth, decided to check it himself. He waited until he was at altitude, and, after activating the autopilot, glanced at the rack between the throttles where they kept the flight plan and navigation charts and found it empty.

"Where's the chart?" he demanded.

"It's in my bag," Vlad answered, without looking at him.

"You think maybe you can get it out, you know, in case I want to do something stupid like know where in the hell I'm going?"

The Russian *tsk*ed his tongue against his teeth, and with an exaggerated sigh reached down and plucked the map from the flight bag on the ground.

"Happy now?" he asked, tossing it onto the dash.

*This fucker.*

He retrieved the chart and opened it to the correct quadrant, studying the route Vlad had penciled on the paper. The day's flight consisted of three airdrops; the first two were straightforward—a new well pump for the camp at Damba and a resupply of fuel and water for Ouagadougou.

Hayes wasn't worried about either of those because the fighting had died down in the north, but the medical drop to Bobo-D was a different story.

They flew in silence, the only words spoken a brusque "come south to heading one-six-eight degrees" when they crossed into Algeria, and a second course correction that put them on a heading to Damba.

At fifty miles Hayes saw the coffee stain of a camp on the horizon and keyed up the radio.

"Camp Two, this is Pilgrim Resupply, how copy?"

"Pilgrim, this is Camp Two, we have you in sight. Recommended you maintain your current heading, drop zone is being marked in purple smoke."

"That's a good copy," Hayes said, watching to see if Vlad was going to get up and head back to the cargo area for the drop.

*Guess him doing his job would be too much to ask.*

Hayes turned the controls over to the Russian, unstrapped from the seat, and climbed down the steps into the cargo hold. He grabbed one of the parachutes from the bulkhead, a surplus T-10 Delta, the bite of the leg's straps around his thighs combined with the burnt jet fuel smell that inundated the cargo hold sending his mind back to the Military Entrance Processing Station (or MEPS) in Tennessee and the day he decided to join the army.

*Hayes was nineteen and in college on the morning of September 11, and unlike so many of the boys he'd grown up with in Tennessee, his decision to join the military wasn't decided on that fateful day. In retrospect he wasn't sure why he hadn't been swept up in the patriotic fervor that followed the terrorist attacks—how he'd been able to see the names of the dead on the television, read about the casualties in the papers and not be stirred to do his part.*

*Perhaps it was the fact that he didn't know anyone who died in the Towers or maybe it was that he was too selfish, too absorbed—by his relationship with Annabelle and the thought of getting a high-paying finance job when he graduated—to care.*

*But that changed when he came home for Christmas break*

and learned that two of the boys from the old neighborhood had been killed in Iraq and two more in Afghanistan. Hayes had gone out to the local veterans' cemetery and spent an hour locating their graves. He was not sure why he was there, but there was no denying how he felt seeing those alabaster tombstones with the names of his friends etched on the marble.

Of course, Annabelle hadn't been happy when graduation came and instead of the finance jobs Hayes had been offered, he told her he was joining the military.

"Why?" she asked.

Hayes tried to explain, but realized he only had pieces of the answer.

"There's a war on."

"So?"

"Doesn't it bother you?" he asked.

"Is this about your friends?"

Hayes didn't have an answer, but he instinctively knew that if he didn't do his part, he would forever regret it.

Thanks to his degree, he had the opportunity to go in the military as an officer, but the day he showed up at MEPS to take the necessary tests, Hayes still didn't know what branch he wanted to join. After being checked out by the doctors, he was sent into the lobby where recruiters from each branch of service had their own office and the first thing he saw was the poster of the Marine Corps officer in his dress blues—the same uniform Annabelle drooled over every time she saw it.

The thought of his girlfriend and how pissed she'd been when he told her that he'd decided to join the military made him sick to his stomach, and he wondered for the tenth time that day if he was screwing up.

*He brushed it away and turned his attention back to the poster—wondering if the thought of him one day wearing those dress blues might make her cut him a little slack.*

*Probably not. But it couldn't hurt.*

*But that was as close as he ever got, because on the way to the Marine recruiter's door he glanced inside the Army office, paused when he saw the thick-necked captain sitting behind a battleship-gray desk, a stack of combat and special skills badges sewn above his* US ARMY *name tape.*

*"Can I help you, son?" he asked.*

*Usually Hayes would have kept walking, but there was something in the man's eyes, the challenge in his voice, that held him there. Made him feel somehow inferior. He wasn't sure if that was the right word, but whatever it was, it pissed Hayes off, and instead of telling him "No, thank you," and continuing on, he heard himself asking, "Where'd you get that scar?"*

*"Which one?" the captain asked, leaning back in his chair.*

*Hayes nodded toward the angry red line that stretched from his ear down to his jaw before disappearing beneath his uniform top.*

*"On your face."*

*"Little shithole called Fallujah."*

*"What were you doing there?"*

*"What paratroopers are trained to do—put foot to ass for the US of A."*

*In that moment he forgot all about the Marines.*

*Five months later, Hayes was walking out of the pack shed at Lawson Army Airfield in Fort Benning, Georgia, a freshly minted second lieutenant—the only thing standing between him and a posting at the 82nd Airborne five jumps from a high-performance aircraft.*

*"On your feet, chalk two," one of the airborne instructors yelled.*

*Hayes got to his feet and shuffled toward the door, the straps from the T-10 Delta digging into his thighs, his stomach in knots at the sight of the C-130s idling on the tarmac.*

*He was almost to the door when a second instructor, sensing his apprehension, stepped into his face. "Just remember, young lieutenant," the man yelled over the roar of the C-130's engines, "paratroopers don't die, we go to hell to regroup."*

These guys are fucking crazy.

*But it was too late to turn back, too late to do anything but follow his chalk out the door and up the ramp of a C-130—the prop blast on his face hot as an oven.*

But that felt like a lifetime ago. Now, inside the Provider's cargo area, Hayes secured the chest harness and started aft, each step sure and measured despite the rise and fall of the plane beneath his feet. He unlocked the brakes of the first pallet and, using the rollers bolted to the floor, scooted it toward the ramp. Once in position, Hayes threw the brake and double-checked the webbing stretched tight over the pump motor and the deployment chute on the top. When he was sure that everything was secure, he snapped his static line into the metal cable that ran the length of the plane and reached up for the ramp control panel and pulled the lever down.

The latch disengaged with a metallic *thunk* and the hydraulics whined. A rectangle of blue sky appeared as the ramp yawned open. Hayes felt the humid rush of the African air fill the cargo hold, the humidity so thick he felt that he could take a bite of it.

He made sure the ramp was locked and the rollers clear before moving to the back side of the pallet, Vlad giving him the "one minute" call over the radio.

At the "thirty seconds" call, Hayes popped the brake and retrieved the orange drogue chute that was attached to the pallet by a yellow cord. He snapped the retaining band free from the beach ball–sized chute and, holding it closed in his hand, moved back to the edge of the ramp where he stood, wind clawing at his clothes, the roar of the engines deafening despite the headset over his ears—eyes locked on the amber light attached to the strut.

He waited as the light turned green and then he tossed the drogue chute from the plane.

The chute caught air and the yellow line jerked tight, pulling the main chute from the pack tray. The chute snaked free of the Provider and blossomed in the slipstream, the sudden resistance yanking the pallet from the back of the plane.

"Cargo away!" he shouted into the radio, staying on the ramp long enough to watch the pallet float gracefully toward the waiting trucks before slapping the plunger and heading forward.

The flight time to the second drop was less than fifteen minutes, so Hayes didn't bother taking off the chute. He moved back to the cockpit and stood there, eyes locked on the map in its holder. There was something about Vlad's flight plan that wasn't sitting right, that kept itching at the back of his mind like a splinter beneath the skin.

*But what the hell was it?*

The resupply drop at Ouagadougou went off without a hitch,

and Hayes was back in the cockpit, staring out the windscreen when Vlad banked toward Camp Four.

For the most part, northern Burkina Faso was arid and perfectly flat thanks to centuries of erosion, but as they flew south, the terrain began to shift, the scrubby lowlands giving way to sandstone massifs, brushy shea trees, and picturesque stretches of lime-green savannah.

From fifteen thousand feet it was beautiful country, but Hayes wasn't fooled, because he'd been on the ground. He'd seen firsthand the hell on earth the rebels from Mali had created. How they'd load up in their dusty Toyota pickups and speed into a village, machine-gun the men before dismounting to rape the women. The thought of it made him sick with rage, but he forced himself to clear his mind and turn his attention to the task at hand.

Mainly getting Vlad's head in the game.

Besides having to worry about getting shot out of the air, Hayes knew that if he dropped the bundle anywhere but *inside* the camp walls the sick and dying would never get it.

He wasn't worried about getting the bundle on target, but what had him concerned was that the success or failure of the drop depended entirely on Vlad following his instructions, and while the moody Russian was difficult to predict in the *best* of times, the fact that he was still pissed off made it all but impossible to know what the man would do.

*Just tell him you're sorry,* the voice suggested.

It was the last thing Hayes wanted to do. In fact, throughout most of the flight it had taken a considerable amount of willpower not to throw the man out of the plane. But after all Hayes had gone through to get this far, he couldn't risk the Russian screwing things up just out of spite.

"Listen, I know you are still pissed about last night, but I need you to get over it."

The Russian ignored him, and Hayes realized he was going to have to try harder.

"What I'm trying to say is that . . . I'm . . . I'm . . . " He stopped, the words like ash in his mouth.

"You're what?" Vlad demanded, eyes cold and enshrouded in smoke from the cigarette dangling between his lips.

"I'm trying to apologize for what happened back at the Sky Bar."

"I tell you what," the Russian began, "there is a package waiting in Korhogo . . ."

"Nothing illegal, or anything that would break your precious code," Vlad added hastily, "but it would allow me to pay back some of the money that I owe."

*He brings this up now? Before the drop?*

"How about we focus on the drop and *then* talk about this Korhogo thing?"

"Fine, whatever," Vlad said.

Hayes left the cockpit armed with the realization that no matter what he did, it would never be enough to please the Russian.

"The hell with him," he said, focusing on the task at hand. Unlike the other two drops, where they'd used a pallet, this time he'd chosen a speedball—a double-reinforced canvas drop bag that looked like an overstuffed football. He snapped the static line to the cable and inched the bundle to the end of the ramp.

He set the bag down and glanced back to the cockpit, the lemon-yellow glare of the sun through the bug-spattered windscreen starring his vision.

*Damn, that's bright.*

They were halfway up the valley and closing in fast on the rows of off-white tents shimmering like a beacon in the center of the postage stamp of bare earth.

"We're going to make it," Vlad said in disbelief.

"Just hold her steady," Hayes said, about to turn back to the ramp when the ground exploded with the flicker of hundreds of muzzle flashes.

# 17

General Dábo stood next to his up-armored Mercedes SUV, casually smoking a cigarette, the clatter of the distant helos sending a charge through his blood.

*Where are you?*

He scanned the sky from left to right, almost missing the pair of Mi-24 Hinds coming in low on the horizon, the rocket pods that hung from their stubby wings giving them the look of lethal dragonflies. The sight of the gunships took him back to the cinema in Abidjan and the showing of *Rambo III*. It was his first movie, and seeing the helicopters in action had been the defining moment in his life. The reason he'd come to the capital and joined the army in the first place.

He watched the lead Hind drop toward the field, its mate

settling into an orbit high overhead, the door gunners sweeping for targets. The roar of the helo's turbines when it settled on the ground sent Dábo's eyes east to the blood-red tiles of the presidential palace.

*Too late to turn back now.*

He flicked the cigarette into the grass and grabbed the AK-47 from the young captain.

"You ready?" he asked.

"Yes, sir."

Dábo nodded, slinging the rifle across his chest and starting toward the helo, the young captain tight on his tail.

Holding the AK and maroon beret, the general ducked under the blades, the rotor wash from turbines clawing at his camo BDUs. The Russian-made gunship was a massive bird and usually the six-foot-three general wouldn't have had a problem finding a spot to sit. But with the troop compartment already packed with the squad of soldiers and their weapons of war, it was a tight fit.

But rank had its privileges, and without having to say a word, one of the sergeants got to his feet and Dábo dropped into the seat. He set the AK between his knees, barrel pointed to the floor, and grabbed the headphones from the hook. By the time he stretched them over his head, the pilot had already bumped the throttles and the twin TV3-117 turboshafts screamed as the gunship rolled forward—gathering speed before leaping skyward.

"Sir, where are we going?" the pilot asked over the internal net.

Dábo smiled and turned his attention to the troop commander sitting on the bench across from him, the same question written across the man's face.

Out of all the units in the Ivorian military, the Republican

Guard was the elite of the elite. It had the most funding, the best training, and was designed to operate as an autonomous unit. If Dábo had been in command of a traditional unit, he would have had to get orders cut, request fuel, and wait for chain of command's approval.

But as the commander of the Republican Guard, all he had to do was pick up the phone.

"The president wants us to take Korhogo," he lied.

"It's about time," Captain Koffi said.

Dábo smiled at the young officer's exuberance, reassured that he'd picked the right man.

"This is going to be a quick and dirty hit. Our objective is the airfield and our goal is to take and hold it long enough for an aircraft to land and take off. Do you understand?"

The captain nodded, and if he had any questions wisely kept them to himself.

"Good. Now brief your men."

It was three hundred miles to Korhogo, and the Hinds had to land at a forward arming and refueling point—or FARP—at Kiémou to take on fuel. Waiting for them on the ground was a matte-black Mi-17, a squad of heavily armed mercenaries forming a defensive perimeter around the unarmed helicopter.

While the gunships took on fuel, Dábo climbed out and walked over to the Mi-17, one of the bearded mercs leading him to the bottom of the ramp.

"Wait here. Keep your eyes to the ground," the man ordered, finger never straying from the trigger of the Vektor R4 assault rifle in his hands.

Dábo listened to the first command, stopping where the man told him to, but despite his best intentions, his curiosity got the better of him and he hazarded a quick glance up the ramp. The interior of the cargo hold was dimly lit, but he was able to make out two figures. The first was an auburn-haired woman in a black dress, her bare legs backlit by a trickle of light through the window.

But it was the second figure, the younger woman, that held his attention.

*That face, I've seen it before, but where?*

He tried to get a better look but before he had a chance the woman was walking toward him with a black duffel in her hand.

"General Dábo," the woman said in French. "I am Theresa Mallory, Monsieur Cabot's representative."

"And who is that?" he asked, nodding toward the figure inside the helo.

"That is none of your concern."

"This is my country, which makes what happens here my concern," he hissed. "So, I will ask you again, who is that?"

"I think this should be enough to make up for any inconvenience," she said, unzipping the duffel, and dropped it at his feet.

He looked down at the bag. Banded stacks of U.S. hundred-dollar bills spilled out on the tarmac.

He nodded. "Yes, I believe you are right."

"Good. Now to business," the woman said, handing him a manila envelope. "Inside you will find the satellite imagery you requested and the inbound flight information. My understanding is that the aircraft is due to arrive in two hours."

"Two *hours*?" Dábo demanded. "It will take twenty minutes to fuel the helicopters and another thirty minutes of flight time just to get to the airfield."

"According to Monsieur Cabot, you are a capable and resourceful man—I'm sure you will be able to figure it out."

"Is there anything else?" he asked, picking up the duffel.

"No, as soon as you are fueled and my men have the tactical frequency you will be using, we can get this show on the road."

Dábo nodded, already feeling the clock ticking down in his head when he started back to the gunships.

The moment the general was out of earshot, Theresa Mallory turned to the bearded mercenary. "Du Brun, a word," she said, starting up the ramp.

At the top of the ramp she stopped at the bench seat and removed her sunglasses.

"Yes, ma'am?" the man said.

Theresa dropped the sunglasses on the seat and reached into her bag, fingers closing around the grip of the Walther PPK.

"Yes, ma'am?"

In a flash she jerked the pistol out and whirled on the bearded mercenary, chopping the suppressor hard across his face.

The blow sent the man to his knee and Theresa jammed the suppressor into the center of his forehead, her voice like ice when she spoke.

"I ought to shoot you right here."

"Wh-what did I do?" the man asked, ignoring the rivulet of blood running down his face.

"What was the one thing you were told?" she demanded.

"No one sees the girl."

"And if you failed?"

"Please, Theresa . . . I . . ."

"Sorry, luv," she said, pulling the trigger.

The Walther spat, and the bullet snapped the man's head back, Theresa stepping out of the way as the body tumbled forward.

*Bloody idiot,* she thought, stepping to the troop door.

"Wikus, you are in charge. Get someone to clean this up and get ready to leave."

"Yes, ma'am."

Theresa returned the pistol to her bag, exchanged it for a satellite phone, and dialed.

"Yes?" a voice answered in French.

"Monsieur Cabot, we may have a slight problem."

"You know how I feel about problems."

"Yes, sir, I do."

"Well, what is it?"

"The general, he saw the package."

There was a pause, and for a moment Theresa thought he'd hung up.

"Did he recognize her?"

"No, I don't thi—"

"You don't know?"

She wanted to tell him that Dábo had not recognized the other woman, but she wasn't sure and knew better than to lie.

"No, sir, I do not know for sure."

"Well, that *is* a problem," Cabot said, and then the line went dead.

# 18

## BOBO-DIOULASSO

One second the sky in front of the Provider was clear and blue and in the next instant, tracers were coiling up toward the windscreen like red whips. The bullets punched through the bottom of the aircraft, blowing fist-sized holes through the cargo hold.

"Hold her steady!" Hayes yelled, turning back to the ramp.

The ground fire had picked up, and all he could do was watch as the tracers blinked like fireflies on a summer evening.

*Just kick it out,* the voice urged.

But that wasn't an option. Hayes had come too far, risked too much to take the easy road now, and held fast—knowing that there were more lives than just his at stake.

Holding on to the edge of the ramp, he leaned out into the

slipstream, squinted against the burning mix of wind and engine exhaust that clouded his vision. The camp was coming up fast, and Hayes ducked back inside.

He wiped the tears from his eyes and grabbed the bundle, ready to throw it out, when Vlad screamed over the radio, talking so fast in Russian the only words Hayes made out were "RPG" and "pulling up."

In the cockpit, Vlad jammed the throttles forward and yanked back on the yoke, sending the Provider's nose skyward. The sudden change in the aircraft's attitude threw Hayes off balance, and he stumbled forward.

He reached out to snag a strut but missed, and then he was tumbling forward, falling hard across the bundle, the sudden push of his body sending it shooting across the rollers—toward the gaping maw of the open cargo hatch.

Hayes kicked his legs behind him, desperately trying to hook his foot around anything that would keep him inside the plane, but there was nothing there. The bundle hit the lip of the ramp, bounced into the air, and launched him from the back of the aircraft.

Twisting in midair, he grabbed the bundle's handle with his left hand and the static line with his right. By now Vlad had the Provider in a near-vertical climb, and when Hayes jerked to a halt, the deadweight of the bundle threatened to pull his shoulder from its socket.

While the static line was strong enough to hold him, the quarter-inch nylon was too thin for a proper handhold, and the scalding of his palm told Hayes that he was slipping.

*Drop it, drop it now!* the voice screamed.

But Hayes held on, ignoring the static line slicing into his left palm and the tug of the bundle that threatened to rip his right arm from the shoulder joint. He waited until he saw the camp below, and only when he was sure the bundle would hit its target did he let it go.

The bundle tumbled from his grasp, its static line snapping taut, ripping the parachute from the pack tray. It caught air. The silk dome inflated with a *whump* and the bundle slowly dropped gracefully into the center of the camp.

While the camp's occupants rushed to claim the bundle, one thousand feet above them, Hayes was trying to save his own life—frantically trying to climb back inside the plane.

The ramp was less than four feet above his head, but even with the surge of adrenaline rushing through his veins and two hands on the static line, Hayes knew the odds of making it to safety were not in his favor.

He started up the static line, climbing hand over hand, ignoring the bullets snapping past his head, the rush of the wind buffeting his body.

"Get your fat ass up there," he yelled at himself.

By the time he reached up and grabbed ahold of the ramp, his forearms were on fire and his clothes soaked with sweat. His shoulders and lats screamed as he pulled himself onto the ramp and squirmed his way into the cargo hold.

Once inside the aircraft, Hayes crawled to the bulkhead and slapped the plunger, his mangled hands leaving a crimson streak on the button. The ramp closed behind him and he collapsed to the floor, chest heaving, throat burning from breathing in the acrid exhaust.

He was worn out and his body screamed for rest, but Hayes

knew he had to get to the cockpit. Had to get the plane back on the deck before Vlad got them both blasted out of the sky.

Shrugging out of the chute, he climbed to his feet and was staggering toward the cockpit stairs when a 14-millimeter shell hit the belly of the Provider and detonated.

The explosion opened up a section of the floor like a can opener, blasted Hayes off his feet, and bounced him off the bulkhead. The impact left him dazed and wobbly, but the sight of the flames spreading across the floor launched him into action.

Hayes staggered through the smoke and yanked the fire extinguisher off the wall. He ripped the pin free, aimed the hose at the flames, and mashed down on the handle. While he worked the retardant across the flames, Hayes yelled at Vlad over the radio.

"Get the fucking nose down!" he screamed.

Silence.

Hayes ditched the empty extinguisher and climbed up the stairs and into the cockpit.

"What the hell are you doing?" he demanded. "Get us down!"

But Vlad was vapor-locked, his eyes vacant, hands bone white on the controls, brain so overcome by the overwhelming fear that came in the face of imminent death that it had shut down.

*He's done,* the voice said. *Take over.*

But before he could drop behind the controls, the flash of the sun off metal drew his attention, the disbelief of what he saw freezing him in place.

Ever since Muammar Gaddafi was overthrown in 2011, there had been reports, whispers really, that black-market profiteers had gained access to the Libyan dictator's arsenal and absconded with crates of Iglas—Russian man-portable surface-to-air missiles.

Western intelligence agencies spent nine months searching for the weapons, and when the intel was compiled in late 2012, they gave Hayes a list with six names.

He spent the next six months hunting his targets, and by the time he crossed the last name off the list, he'd personally recovered and destroyed four cases of the missiles. When he returned to the States, Director Shaw told him that the rest of the stolen ordnance had been recovered.

*Guess he was wrong,* the voice said.

It was the understatement of the year, and Hayes realized he had two choices: He could play the blame game or deal with the surface-to-air missile rushing toward the starboard engine.

He dropped to a knee and reached into the space behind Vlad's seat, where the plane's emergency equipment was stored. In one quick motion, he jerked the pyrotechnic pistol from its mount on the floor, grabbed a flare, and got to his feet.

Hayes stepped out of the cockpit, cracked open the pyrotechnic pistol, and shoved a flare into the breach on his way to the emergency escape window on the starboard side of the hold. He ignored the black-and-yellow caution tape that bordered the window and the CAUTION: DO NOT OPEN IN FLIGHT warning stenciled above it. He yanked up on the release and pulled the window open.

The window wasn't much wider than his shoulders, and the first hurdle was wedging his upper body through the opening, a difficulty compounded by the rush of air across the fuselage that kept trying to shove him back into the plane.

With the Igla closing in on the Provider at Mach 1.9, Hayes knew any delay could prove deadly, and he ignored the metal scrape of the window frame, kicking and twisting his torso out of the aircraft.

Then he was through, upper body hanging free of the aircraft, the rush of the slipstream tearing his eyes, making him feel like a hood ornament on a freight train.

Unlike earlier models, the Igla was designed to attack its targets head-on, and once the IR sensors in the nose had a lock, the guidance system would steer it onto target. When Hayes had first seen the missile in the cockpit, it was flying on a relatively flat arc, but now that the seeker had a lock, the missile was maneuvering— the contrail doglegging hard to hit the engine from the front.

Hayes raised the pyrotechnic gun toward the oncoming missile and adjusted his aim, so the barrel was pointing a good four inches above the target. His goal was to use the heat from the flare to trick the seeker head off target—get it to change course, thinking there was a closer target.

However, to pull it off, his timing had to be perfect.

If he fired too soon, the sensors would have time to reacquire the Provider—too late, and it would race right past it.

So he waited until he estimated the missile was two hundred yards out, and then he pulled the trigger.

Compared to the Igla's solid-state rocket motor, the flare's propellant that launched the magnesium projectile toward the oncoming warhead was woefully underpowered, and Hayes worried that it wouldn't even get there.

"C'mon . . . c'mon," he begged.

Finally, the projectile reached its target, the place in the sky five feet above the onrushing warhead. It had been in the air for less than a second and the flaming ball of magnesium was burning white hot—and just as Hayes had hoped, the sudden heat source so close to the warhead proved irresistible to the IR sensors.

With the sensor locked on to the new target, the guidance system took over and made the necessary adjustment to the tail fins, sending the warhead climbing skyward—away from Hayes and the Provider.

"Hell, yes!" Hayes screamed, pounding his fist against the skin of the aircraft in triumph.

But his relief was short-lived, and in the next instant turned to dread.

Just as Hayes had feared, the Igla was too fast, and after blasting past the flare and finding nothing but cool air on the other side, the sensors began searching for a new target, sending the contrail doglegging back toward the aircraft.

Hayes pulled himself back into the cargo hold, dumped the flare gun, and went racing to the cockpit. He dove through the opening, screamed a warning to Vlad, and was trying to pull him from the seat—get him away from the window—when the Igla's proximity switch detonated the warhead four yards short of the engine cowling.

The over-pressure slapped the plane, the shock wave punching through the copilot window. The spray of razor-sharp glass and slivers of metal hit Vlad in the side of the face and he slumped against the controls, dead as a hammer.

The Provider pitched forward, its nose dropping back toward the earth. Hayes wiped the blood from his eyes and scrambled into his seat. He grabbed the yoke and tried to pull the plane out of the dive, but with Vlad's deadweight wedging the controls forward, it was impossible.

"Sorry, buddy," he said, reaching over, unhooking the Russian's harness and pulling him off the yoke.

For a moment Vlad stayed upright, but without the harness or active muscles to hold him in place, his body listed, before crashing to the floor.

Hayes had read the Provider's flight manual from cover to cover, so sitting behind the yoke, the instrument panel flashing like a Christmas tree, he finally understood why the first line of "Section V: Operating Limitations" clearly stated, "the minimum number of crew required to safely operate the Provider in a nontactical situation is a pilot and copilot."

It was a rule he'd broken before when he soloed from Monrovia to Morocco, so he knew it was possible to operate the aircraft with only one pilot *under normal conditions*—but these were anything but normal conditions.

He looked down at the control panel, trying to get a sense of how bad the Provider had been hurt, but the gauges and lights were too obscured by brain tissue and blood to see clearly. He used his sleeve to wipe the gore from the control panel, the blinking of red warning lights and bouncing needles on the now-visible gauges overwhelming.

"Just take it one problem at a time," he told himself.

Taking a deep breath, he glanced at the altimeter. They were at thirty-five hundred feet and he knew the first order of business was to get the stricken bird on the deck before it took any more damage.

He pushed the yoke forward and to the left, trying to put the Provider into a banking dive, but the aircraft responded like a barge with a stuck rudder—the shake of the yoke in his hands and her sluggish response told Hayes that the control surfaces were shot to shit. He leaned forward, craning to get a look at the left wing where the sight of the bullet-riddled aileron confirmed his suspicion.

"C'mon, girl," he begged, kicking the rudder pedals left and shoving the throttles to their stops.

Finally the Provider responded, and he twisted her into a screaming dive, jaw set as he plummeted through the spiderweb of tracer fire. But the rebels had him dialed in and opened up with everything they had, the bullets against the aircraft sounding like hail on a tin roof.

Hayes gritted his teeth and watched the altimeter spooling down—*two thousand feet, fifteen hundred, a thousand*—when a final burst found the port wing, the bullets shredding the engine cowling.

The port engine stuttered and backfired like a shotgun, a flash of orange, followed by the bright-red blink of the fuel gauge, oil pressure, and hydraulic warning lights on the panel.

He was reducing the power when the master fire light blinked red on the upper-left-hand corner of the copilot's instrument panel. Hayes looked out the window to find the port engine smoking like a diesel train.

*Shut it down.*

It was the right call.

The only problem was he wasn't sure if he could make it over the sandstone cliffs guarding the end of the valley five miles to his front with only one engine.

# 19

## LANGLEY, VIRGINIA

I t was seven p.m. at Langley, and Carpenter was exhausted, his stomach churning from one too many cups of coffee. He logged off his computer, and after removing his ID card from the reader, opened the top drawer and retrieved the roll of Tums he'd bought earlier in the week. There were two left. He popped them into his mouth and got to his feet.

As a younger officer, the long days and short nights hadn't fazed him. Like a toddler, he viewed things like sleeping and eating as a distraction, something that kept him from the work at hand.

But his days of being able to survive on vending machine food and four hours of sleep were long gone. These days all he had to do was look at a carton of takeout and he'd be up all night with heartburn.

*Getting old is a bitch,* he thought as he looped the lanyard connected to the ID card over his head.

Carpenter crunched on the antacids on his way to the door, grimacing at the chalky aftertaste they left at the back of his throat, and grabbed his coat from the rack. He was looking forward to a quiet ride home and maybe a beer or two before bed, but when he stepped out into the anteroom and saw the illuminated lamp at the corner of his secretary's desk, he knew it wasn't happening.

At its core, the CIA was a giant bureaucracy, a clandestine corporation run by pencil pushers—nonoperational administrative types who were more concerned with improving productivity than national security. While Carpenter and those under him were busy trying to keep the free world from imploding, the people above him were busy issuing memos reminding everyone to use the correct color coding for internal files and memos. The idea was to allow men like Carpenter to separate the important from the nonessential, but all it did was create more work.

He cursed under his breath, annoyed because he had to sort through the blue-and-white low-priority files to get to the reds.

"Damn folders," he said, as he stuffed them into the outside pocket of his briefcase.

When he had everything he needed, Carpenter stepped out into the lobby and crossed to the express elevator that took him down to the parking garage, where his driver was waiting in a black-on-black Suburban.

"Rough night, chief?" he asked.

"Is there any other kind?" Carpenter answered, retrieving his AirPods from his jacket pocket.

He pressed the wireless headphones into his ears, unlocked his phone, and scrolled through the apps until he came to a white tile with an orange ball in the center. Carpenter launched the app and waited for it to load, remembering how skeptical he'd been when his wife, Erin, first introduced him to it.

The life of an Agency wife wasn't for the weak or faint of heart. It took a special woman to put up with all the bullshit—the travel, long hours spent at the office, and even longer months away when Carpenter was deployed overseas, which was why most of his coworkers were on their second or third marriage.

But Carpenter had gotten lucky when he met Erin, which was why he pampered her and put up with the endless string of fad diets and hobbies she dragged him into. The latest was yoga, so he wasn't surprised when she started talking about meditation.

"An app for guided meditation. You're serious?" he asked.

"It helps with stress and sleep. You will love it, I promise," she beamed.

She was right.

Carpenter hit the play button and settled back in his seat, listening while the soothing voice instructed him to "close your eyes and take a cleansing breath." He was just settling into the meditation, allowing the stresses of the day to "drift past your conscious mind like clouds in the sky" when the voice was interrupted by the ding of his phone.

He cracked an eyelid and glanced down at the screen, any chances of achieving Zen vanishing when he read the text.

**Found something you are going to want to see.**

**On my way home, can it wait?** he replied.

**No. Come to Site Tango ASAP!!!**

**This better be GOOD!** he typed back.

**Better than Christmas morning.**

"Change of plans," Carpenter said, fingers flying over the keys.

"What's up, chief?" his driver asked, glancing up at the rearview.

"South Capitol Street Heliport," he said.

"Yes, sir."

Carpenter called his wife and told her that he wasn't going to make it home for dinner. He returned the phone to his pocket, the last line of the text still sending a lightning bolt of exhilaration up his spine.

*Better than Christmas morning.* The code to drop everything and get here as fast as possible. But what had she found?

The Airbus H155 was sitting on the pad, rotors already turning and burning when the Suburban arrived at the heliport. The driver badged through the gate and pulled up beside the helo, tires still rolling when Carpenter threw open the door and hustled aboard.

"Let's roll."

"Roger that," the pilot said, advancing the throttles.

The torque of the rotors squatted the helo on its wheels, the whine of the turbines barely audible thanks to the Bose noise-canceling stereo system built into the cabin. Then they were airborne, zipping low over the 14th Street bridge.

Carpenter turned his attention to the window and the darkened terrain below.

The Monongahela National Forest was as remote as it was inhospitable. Nine hundred and twenty-one thousand acres of lung-bursting heights and ankle-breaking valleys choked with blueberry thickets, highland bogs, and swift-running rivers.

It was the kind of place where you could walk for days and never see another soul, which made it the perfect place for the CIA's newly funded Training and Application Lab.

The helo clattered north, the rock face narrowing until the exposed granite was less than a foot from the rotor's edge. But the pilot was an old hand and expertly adjusted to the rush of thermals that battered the bird and continued climbing until they were over the towering firs that guarded the summit of the ridge.

On the far side of the tree line, their destination sat on a hill in the center of a clearing—an antebellum Classic Revival mansion—its two-story portico supported by fluted Corinthian pillars reminding him of something from *Gone with the Wind*.

The pilot flared over the front lawn and set the helo down before advising Carpenter that he was heading north, to Elkins, to refuel. Carpenter nodded, grabbed his bag, and climbed out, waiting for the Airbus to take off before starting toward the woman waiting near the front of the house.

At five-foot-four with dishwater blond hair and wide, curious green eyes, there was nothing threatening about Victoria Arno. But Carpenter had seen her file and knew that while Arno might look like a librarian, she, like all of Shaw's creations, was a predator posing as a house pet. Which was precisely the reason Carpenter had put her in charge of Site Tango.

"Well, you got me here," he said.

"And I promise you won't regret it," Arno purred, slipping past the two heavily armed guards posted on either side of the door and stepping inside.

The first time Carpenter visited Site Tango, an army of contractors were in the process of modernizing the interior, a daunting task considering the mansion was built before modern conveniences such as electricity and running water.

Anyone else would have gone broke trying to make it habitable: ripping out the rotten wood, tearing up the sagging floors, not to mention all the security upgrades that were needed before it could be certified as a Level IV secure site.

If it had been up to Carpenter, he'd have torn down the place and started from scratch—not giving a damn how it turned out as long as it was functional. Arno, on the other hand, was required to live on-site, which meant the mansion had to be both functional and livable.

Compared to the rugged, inhospitable wilds that surrounded the property, the eggshell-white walls, distressed hardwood floors, and exposed white oak rafters gave the interior a light, almost airy feel.

"Like what you did with the place," he said.

"Amazing what you can do when money is no object," she replied, leading him down the hall and into her large office.

"So, what is so damn important?"

"This," she said, taking a folder with EYES ONLY printed in blood-red letters across the front.

"Feels awful thin," Carpenter said, taking the folder from her hand.

"You might want to take a seat before you start reading."

"I've been in this game a *long* time," he smirked, "and I doubt there is anything in here that's going to blow my skirt up."

"Have it your way, sir."

Carpenter opened the file and managed to make it halfway down the first page before the realization of what he was reading turned his knees to water. "Y-you've got to be . . ." he said, hand shooting out for the desk.

"Hayes and Shaw . . . has this . . . ?"

"Been verified? Yes, sir," Arno said.

"Please tell me you got a location ping," Carpenter said, his heart pounding like a bass drum in his chest.

"He's in Grand-Bassam."

"I want a team ready to roll in the next twelve hours," he said.

"I've got just the man for the job," she replied. "But, sir, if I may . . ."

"What is it?"

"Director Shaw, he is obviously helping Hayes, and *if* he finds out what's going on . . ."

"You find me someone who can kill Adam Hayes," he said. "I'll take care of Shaw."

# 20

## KORHOGO, IVORY COAST

While the ground crew fueled up the gunships, General Dábo called the pilots and assault team leaders over and opened the envelope Cabot had sent.

"I have satellite imagery of the target area," he said, pulling out the five high-definition stills and passing them around.

While the Ivorian army didn't have their own surveillance satellites during the civil war, Dábo had been able to use his contact in France to gain access to tactical imagery. Usually the photos were weeks old, the quality of the shots so poor that they bordered on unusable.

Cabot's, on the other hand, were crystal clear, and not only had they been taken within the last twelve hours, but someone had marked every rebel position at the airfield.

"These poor bastards don't stand a chance," the lead pilot grinned.

"Good, because the president wants the airfield in our hands in two hours."

"Two hours?" Captain Koffi said. "B-but the helicopters aren't even fueled."

"You worry about coming up with an attack plan," Dábo said, pulling his gold-plated .45 from its holster. "Let me worry about the helicopters."

Fifty minutes later the gunships were ten miles south of the airfield, Dábo frowning at his watch. He'd cursed and threatened the ground team, promising to kill them all if they didn't get the gunships fueled and in the air in twenty minutes. While his strongarm tactics had worked, the pair of gunships had been forced to reduce their speed to accommodate the slower Mi-17.

Dábo glanced out the side window and found the helo still lagging in the distance.

*The hell with this,* he thought, keying up on the radio and ordering the pilots into attack formation.

"Roger that, sir."

Due to the relative flatness of the terrain and the active radar at the airfield, Dábo had instructed the pilot to fly nap-of-the-earth and reached up for the handhold hanging from the roof.

"Better follow the general's lead," the bulky sergeants shouted to the captain, "these fucki—"

But the words were muted by the banshee scream of the turbines as the pilot throttled up and shoved the stick forward.

The gunship dove toward the ground like a hawk after its prey, the pilot twisting the bird hard right, angling for the two-laned highway that would lead him to his target.

"Sissé, don't you dare fucking puke in front of the general," the sergeant yelled at a young machine gunner whose face had taken on a pale shade of green.

At fifty feet the pilot pulled up and resumed level flight, Dábo letting go of the handhold, the sergeant yelling at the assault team to lock and load.

The troop compartment was filled with the meted snaps of magazines being shoved into rifles and the *thunk* of bolts slamming rounds into chambers.

At the "five minutes out" call, Dábo gave his last-minute instructions.

"The runway and the people *inside* the tower are *not* to be harmed."

"What about the people *outside* the tower?" the captain asked.

"If it moves, it dies," Dábo grinned.

"One minute," the pilot announced.

*Here we go,* Dábo thought, glancing out the window.

The gunship pilots were trained to work in tandem, and while the trail bird stayed on the deck, Dábo's pilot pulled back on the stick, the pitch of the blades changing as the helo gained altitude.

From the satellite imagery, Dábo knew there wasn't much to the airfield—a single runway, three weather-beaten hangars, and an orange-and-white corrugated-steel building that served as the terminal. On the north side of the field sat the tower, a squat two-story building of white stucco.

The only other structures were three machine gun towers and two mortar pits the rebels had constructed in the open fields on either side of the tarmac and a row of plywood barracks hidden beneath a ratty camouflage net.

Fields of fire had been set up back at the FARP and the gunships went about their work. The conversation on the radio was one-sided: the pilots calling out targets and the gunner responding with either a burst from the four-barrel 12.7-millimeter gun beneath the nose or a salvo of 80-millimeter rockets from the pods on the wing.

Having no other responsibilities at the moment, the general simply sat there, a grin spreading across his face as he watched the symphony of death.

The lead helo was the first to draw blood, using a ripple fire of 80-millimeter rockets to turn the barracks into a cloud of splinters and then twisting toward the machine gun towers. This time the main gun spat fire.

"Falcon 1, you have troops in the open, looks like they have some kind of APC in that hangar."

"General, permission to engage with missiles."

Dábo had wanted them to avoid using their anti-armor AT2 for fear of blowing up any of the main buildings, but with the APC on the ground he didn't have a choice.

"Cleared to engage."

The pilot reduced his airspeed and dropped into a hover, keeping the helo as stable as possible so the gunner could get a lock. The missile screamed from the pylon, the burst of light from the motor illuminating the dim interior.

"Yeah, he's dead."

Ten minutes later, it was all over and the Hinds were wheeling over the airfield like iron vultures in search of carrion, pillars of black smoke rising skyward.

"Take us down," Dábo told the pilot.

"But sir," the pilot interjected, "it's not safe."

"Then make it safe," he ordered.

"Yes, sir," the pilot said, snatching the radio from his RTO. "Falcon 2, this is Falcon 1, deploy your troops."

"This is Falcon 2, understood."

The Hind circled the airfield, General Dábo watching from the troop doors as her sister ship touched down and let the troops rush down the ramp before lifting off again.

Dábo was expecting the commander to form his men up and set up a base of fire before starting toward the tower, but it never happened. Instead, the overzealous officer waved for his men to follow and rushed toward their objective.

There was a spray of automatic fire from the hangar, and then a voice screamed over the radio, "Ambush."

*I don't have time for this shit*, Dábo thought, thumbing the transmit button.

"This is Dábo to Hunter 1. Take out that fucking hangar."

"But sir, our men . . ."

"That is an order, Major."

The Hind came whirling around, rockets flickering from the pods——slamming into the hangar and exploding.

"Hit it with the guns, then get us down there," Dábo ordered, before turning to Falcon 1. "Captain, I want all those rebel scum dead and the fires out in ten minutes, do you understand?"

"Y-yes, sir."

Dábo climbed out of the helo and crossed the tarmac, his radioman at his heels.

"Where is Captain Koffi?"

"He is at the hangar with the prisoners, sir," a sergeant said, pointing to a knot of kneeling men.

Dábo nodded and stomped over. "Captain, I need these fires out, now," he shouted.

"Of course, sir, we would already have taken care of it, but these prisoners . . ."

But Dábo wasn't interested in the prisoners.

"These aren't prisoners, they are traitors," he said, stripping the gold-plated .45 from his holster and shooting both men in the head. "Now get those fires out."

Dábo barged into the control tower with five minutes to spare, the smoking .45 still in his hand, and scanned the fearful faces cowering before him.

"I am General Joseph Dábo, the commander of the Republican Guard," he announced. "Who is in charge here?"

"I-I am, sir," a middle-aged man with a graying goatee, wearing a white button-down, answered. "My name is Daniel Aké. There is no need for the gun, sir."

"I will be the one who decides that, do you understand?"

"Y-yes, sir."

"Good. I want to make myself perfectly clear. Those men outside were enemies of the state, rebel scum, and were dealt with accordingly," he said, holstering the pistol. "As long as everyone does as I ask, none of you will be harmed. Do I make myself clear?"

"Yes, sir."

"Excellent. There is a plane coming in," he said, taking the paper with the tail number and radio frequency from his pocket and handing it to the man. "You are to make sure we are ready to receive him."

The man pulled a pair of readers from his pocket and frowned at the paper. "No flight plan?"

"No."

"Do you have any idea *where* this aircraft is coming from?"

"That is all I have."

"Hmm," the man frowned. "Th-this is not an easy ask, but we will do our best."

He crossed the room, came to a halt next to the radar operator, and handed the man the paper.

"This might take some time," Aké said.

Dábo nodded and moved to the window overlooking the runway where the APC smoldered. "Tell them I want that piece of junk off the runway, *now!*" he told his RTO.

"Yes, sir."

The rush of adrenaline that had come with the assault had begun to wear off and Dábo was suddenly tired. He pulled the cigarette case from his pocket, lit up, and took a deep drag. Since getting the call from Cabot, his only focus had been taking the airfield, but it was only now that it was safely in his hands that Dábo began to consider the implications of his actions.

It was an election year, and high on President Alassane's platform was reunification—ending the fighting that had gripped the country since the civil war.

*What is he going to say when he learns what I've done here?* he wondered.

Dábo knew the answer, but he was positive that this was one situation that his wife couldn't get him out of.

"Sir, I have your aircraft on the scope, bearing zero-three-four degrees," the man said.

Daniel Aké moved over to the radar station, the general tight on his heels.

"Have you tried to make contact?" Aké asked, peering at the screen.

"Yes, sir, but I'm not getting an answer."

"Is it him?" Dábo demanded.

Both Aké and the controller ignored him.

"Sir, I think the aircraft is in trouble."

"In trouble, what does that mean?"

"The aircraft is rapidly losing altitude, that plus the fact that we cannot get the pilot on the radio is usually an indication of a problem," Aké said, pulling off his readers and grabbing a pair of binoculars from his desk.

"Someone turn up the power on the transmitter," he said, moving to the window, Dábo close on his heels.

Aké lifted the binoculars to his eyes and turned to the northeast.

Dábo was already thinking about what he was going to do with the money when the speaker on the wall came to life, the voice calm despite the message.

"Mayday . . . Mayday . . . Korho . . . tower . . . this is Pilgrim three-niner x-ray. Request . . . emergency . . . landing."

# 21

## BOBO-DIOULASSO

A irspeed was the only thing that mattered, and Hayes forced himself to block everything else out, ignoring the flashing warning lights and the urgent TERRAIN—TERRAIN—PULL UP of the Ground Proximity Warning System alerting him to what seemed an imminent collision.

Hayes waited until the last possible second to start his climb and gently pull back on the yoke. The Provider's nose tipped skyward, the airspeed indicator heading in the wrong direction as the altimeter ticked upward.

He begged and pleaded with the plane, but she wasn't going to make it. As a last-ditch effort to get over the rocks, Hayes dropped the flaps—the sudden shake of the yoke indicating that he was getting dangerously close to stall speeds.

One second they were hanging in limbo, the bottom of the plane inches from the rock face, and then they were over—nothing but clear sky and flat ground as far as the eye could see.

"Hell, yeah," Hayes yelled, slapping the yoke with his left hand and retracting the flaps with his right.

While the Provider would never win a beauty contest or a race, the old warbird could take a punch, which was the only reason Hayes had stayed with her when his gut was telling him to strap on the chute and get the hell out.

"Mayday, Mayday, this is Pilgrim," he said over the radio.

But there was no response.

According to the GPS, he was fifty miles north of Korhogo, and the fact that he couldn't get ahold of the tower was the least of his problems. While the Provider was currently holding steady at seven thousand feet, all it took was one look at the fuel gauge, its needle buried in the red, to know it wouldn't last. Even with all the maneuvering over the drop zone, the Provider should have had enough fuel to make it to Korhogo. The fact that it was in the red told Hayes that there had to be a leak.

The only thing he could do was adjust the fuel mixture and throttle back, but even with the Provider running as lean as possible, he knew he was living on borrowed time.

*Just hold on, girl,* he begged.

Without the tower, it was up to Hayes to figure out the most fuel-efficient approach, so he activated the autopilot and grabbed the chart. According to it, the runway at Korhogo ran east to west. The last weather report had the wind coming in from the west, so Hayes plotted his approach accordingly.

He plotted and replotted his route, double- and triple-checking his math until he found the most fuel-efficient trip, turned off the autopilot, and banked the plane gently to the east, leveled out, and flew straight for ten minutes before heading south.

A final turn brought him to the west and he was ten miles out from the spot he *hoped* was the airfield when he saw the smoke— three charcoal pillars rising into the sky like ancient funeral pyres.

*Yeah,* that's *not good,* he thought, beginning his descent.

According to the chart, the runway was large enough to accommodate the Provider, but at five thousand feet it looked impossibly short and barely wide enough to handle a single-engine Cessna.

*Only one way to find out.*

He'd centered the nose on the runway and was about to drop the gear when the radio came to life.

"Pilgrim three-niner x-ray, this is Korhogo tower, do you copy?" the calm voice asked in French.

The surprise of hearing his tail number over the radio was overshadowed by the realization that he was no longer alone, and he eagerly pressed the talk button.

"Tower, this is Pilgrim three-niner x-ray requesting an emergency landing," he replied in French.

"Advise nature of emergency."

"Where do you want me to start?" he asked, dropping the gear.

There was a moment of silence, the controller not sure how to answer the question, finally coming back with a "Roger that."

He was at fifteen hundred feet when the port engine began to sputter like a lawnmower with a busted carburetor and the Provider started to pull to the right. Hayes shut the engine down, aware of the fresh sheen of sweat breaking out on his forehead.

"Uh, Tower, I just lost an engine," he advised, knuckles white on the yoke.

Hayes double-checked the gear, knowing it was down, but needed to give his mind something to do when he saw the cloud of ocher dust skitter laterally across the runway.

Atop the tower, the blazing orange windsock hung limp, and Hayes was beginning to think his eyes were playing tricks on him when he saw it flutter.

*If it wasn't for bad luck, I wouldn't have any luck at all.*

By the time he reached five hundred feet, there was a full-value wind blowing in from the south, and Hayes felt the gust of air pushing the aircraft out of position.

He gave the rudder pedals a hard kick, managing to get the plane back online a second before the tires hit the runway. As soon as the wheels made solid contact, he stomped hard on the brakes and pulled the throttle into reverse thrust.

The engine groaned, the acrid stench of burnt rubber and overheated brake pads inundating the cockpit, but Hayes didn't care. He was alive and that was all that mattered.

The Provider shuddered to a halt a hundred yards from the end of the runway—the silence that followed the rush of air through the shattered glass was deafening.

He shut down the plane and unhooked the harness, the back of his shirt peeling from the seat like Saran Wrap when he got to his feet and stepped out of the cockpit. Hayes headed aft, hands shaking when he unlatched the troop door. The only thought on his mind was getting the hell out of the plane.

The door swung open and he stepped out onto the tarmac, the Ivorian sun hot as a blast furnace on his face.

*I made it*, he thought.

The relief that came with cheating death was more powerful than any narcotic. Hayes could have stood there forever, savoring the warmth of the sun on his face and the sway of the green grass in the wind.

But the moment was cut short by the unmistakable bacon fat smell of charred flesh and the squeal of tires on asphalt. He followed the sound toward the tower in time to see a pair of Toyota Hiluxes race into view—their beds overloaded with gunmen.

*This isn't good,* he thought, watching the pickups race toward him.

His first thought was to run, but with the plane shot to shit and nothing but open ground on all sides, Hayes knew he wasn't going anywhere.

*Well, this sucks.*

But this wasn't the first time he'd found himself stuck in a third-world shithole on the wrong end of an AK-47, and in his experience the best course of action was to play the dumb American redneck.

Hayes stood there, arms raised over his head, a lopsided grin stretching across his face, when the trucks screeched to a halt in front of him. The passenger-side door of the truck swung open and a tall man in starched BDUs jumped out, sunlight flashing off the stars on his collar as he came stomping across the tarmac.

He stopped next to Hayes, tore the sunglasses from his face, and stared open-mouthed at the damaged plane.

"Wh-what have you done?" the man demanded in French.

"Sorry, pal," Hayes answered with a shrug, "no parlez vous French."

He watched the anger spread across the man's face, saw the jerk of his shoulder that told him a blow was coming, but, sticking to his plan, made no move to get out of the way.

"You idiot," the general snapped, backhanding him across the face.

It was a hard blow, the force rocking Hayes back on his heels and starring his vision. He stepped back, making space, but the general wasn't through. He waded in and hit him with a sweeping right to the gut, the impact folding him like a cheap card table, blasting the air from his lungs. He bent double, gasping like a fish on the bank, but before he could go down, Dábo fired a knee at his face.

Hayes was fully committed to his role but had no interest in a broken nose. He twisted to the left, dropped his head, and took most of the blow on his shoulder before collapsing to the ground.

The force bowled him over. Hayes felt the rage rising up from the pit of his stomach, but forced it down.

He'd seen the general's type before. The man was a bully who'd made his rank by killing women and children, and as much as he wanted to beat the man's ass, show him what happened when you tangled with a real man, Hayes wasn't stupid and knew the camouflaged coward wouldn't hesitate to order his men to kill him if he felt disrespected.

Forcing yourself to take an ass kicking wasn't easy for a man of his ilk, but it was the only option that guaranteed that he'd stay alive.

He bent down and grabbed Hayes by the front of the shirt and lifted his upper body off the ground.

"Where is the Russian?" he demanded, slamming his fist into Hayes's face.

*This is going to get ugly,* the voice commented as the general hit him again.

But Hayes knew how to handle men like this. While his attacker was drawing him close for another punch, he was busy collecting a mouthful of blood.

"I don't speak fucking *French*," he spat, spraying blood across the front of the general's spotless uniform.

The man dropped Hayes like a hot coal and leapt backward, eyes dropping to his ruined tunic, his face turning white with rage, lips twisting into a feral snarl. "I-I'll fucking kill you!" he screamed, reaching for the pistol strapped to his hip.

Hayes had been hoping for a better outcome—hell, he'd even been willing to take an ass kicking, but a bullet was a different story.

*Yeah, I don't think so.*

By now the soldiers had been drawn closer by the violence, each one wanting to see the general kill the American. From the ground all Hayes could see were boots and the barrels of the soldiers' AK-47s, but it was all he needed.

His plan was simple: Roll to the right, grab the closest barrel with his left hand, and pull whoever was holding it into the general's line of fire. If it worked, Hayes estimated that he would have enough time to draw his own pistol, get to his feet, and kill a few of them before they shot him down.

If it didn't, well, at least Hayes got to die on his feet.

# 22

The closest barrel was three feet to his right and Hayes was ready to make his move when he heard a screech of tires skidding to a halt, followed by a burst of automatic rifle fire crackling through the air. He winced, expecting to feel the burn of hot lead across his chest, but instead he heard a woman yelling orders in French.

"General, put down that pistol!"

"I am in command here," the man snapped back.

For his part, Hayes wasn't sure what the hell was going on, but whatever it was, he knew he didn't want to address it from the ground.

He scrambled to his feet and found an auburn-haired woman

standing in front of the general, a scrum of heavily armed men standing menacingly on her flanks. All it took was one look and Hayes knew the men were mercs—South Africans, by the looks of the FALs and Vektor R4s in their hands. *But why are they here, and who's the chick?* he was wondering when he realized she was looking at him.

All it took was the slightest of nods and the pit bulls were moving—shouldering through the gaggle of Ivorian soldiers, rifles up and ready.

Hayes turned to face them, right hand now glued to the pistol at his waist.

"Don't even think about it," one of the mercs said in French.

"Doesn't *anyone* here speak English?" he asked, falling back into his earlier role.

"I said, don't even think about it, mate," the man repeated, this time in English.

"Hey, cool's the rule, right?" Hayes said, raising his arms above his head for the second time that day.

"On the top of your head, fingers interlaced and joined," the man said, waiting until Hayes complied before tugging the pistol from its holster. "Nice bit of kit, this," he said, nodding appreciatively at it.

"That old thing?" Hayes said. "Won it in a poker game."

"Then you won't mind if I keep it."

Hayes shrugged, knowing he didn't have a choice.

"Get him to the truck," the woman ordered, before turning back to the now-cowed general.

Hayes started toward the truck, passing close enough to the woman to hear her ask, "Any sign of the Russian?"

*The Russian? Vlad? What the hell has that idiot gotten me into now?* he wondered, letting the men drag him toward the Hilux.

It was the first time he'd thought about the Russian since landing. The realization that he'd left the man's body lying on the floor of the cockpit came with a twinge of guilt, but Hayes brushed it away, knowing he needed all of his focus if he wanted to stay alive.

"Grab some hood," the man said, and Hayes complied, leaning over the front of the truck.

The man who searched him knew his job and quickly had the contents of his pockets and the money belt with his passport and extra cash laid out on the front of the truck.

"Get his watch and belt, too."

Hayes unbuckled his belt and added it to the pile but made no move to take off the Sangin Neptune strapped to his wrist.

"Your ears full of shit or did that general blow out your eardrums, bruh?" the man asked.

"My ears work fine, but if you want this watch, I hope you packed a lunch."

"Is that a fact?" the man demanded, stepping into Hayes's face. "What if I shot you right—" but the woman cut him off before he could finish his threat.

"Wikus, get him in the truck and up to the hangar now."

"Better listen to your mama, boy," Hayes winked.

"Get your ass in the truck," Wikus said, grabbing him by the shirt and shoving him into the back of the truck.

Moments later they were speeding across the tarmac, Hayes crammed between the two men, Vlad's blood staining his fingers like henna. It was a short drive to the terminal, but long enough for his head to fill with a hundred questions.

Hayes got out of the truck, the mercs herding him up a flight of steps and through the door. The interior of the terminal was outdated—faded like a picture from an '80s travel magazine—the once-colorful mural that adorned the wall covered with antigovernment graffiti and grotesque caricatures of President Soro.

Hayes had decided there was nothing to gain by antagonizing his captors, and since getting out of the truck he'd assumed the deferential slump of a man resigned to his fate. But beneath the hunched shoulders and bowed head, his blue eyes never stopped moving. They darted back and forth across the hallway, noting every doorway and window he passed while keeping a pace count in his head.

For all he knew the two men had been ordered to take him out back and put a bullet in his head. If this was the case, the entire venture was pointless, but Hayes knew that as long as there was breath in his lungs, it was his duty to escape.

Not for his sake, but for that of his wife and son.

Twenty paces to his front, the hallway formed a T intersection. One of the mercs used the barrel of his FAL to prod Hayes to the left, and a second jab to get him through the metal door on the far wall and into one of the concrete-block detention rooms on the other side.

The room was small, maybe eight by eight, the only furnishing a stainless-steel table, two chairs, and a mirror mounted to the back wall.

"Cuff yourself," Wikus ordered, tossing Hayes a pair of handcuffs.

"Seriously?" he asked.

"Either you do it, or I'll have *him* do it," the merc said, nodding to his fellow South African, "but trust me, you don't want him putting cuffs on ya."

"Good to know," he said, snapping one of the cuffs around his wrist and the other to the length of lead pipe welded to the table.

"Make yourself comfortable, mate. You and I've got a lot to talk about," Wikus sneered before he and the other merc stepped out of the room.

*Looking forward to it.*

Like most operatives, Hayes had spent his fair share of time inside the "tank." He'd been the detainee—the man chained to the table—wondering what horrors the people on the other side of the two-way mirror had in store for him. But he'd also been the man behind the glass wondering how much pain he'd have to inflict to break the person on the other side.

Thanks to the time spent in the latter position, Hayes knew all the dirty tricks interrogators liked to use—tricks like cutting a half inch off the front legs of the detainee's chair so that he was constantly sliding off the edge.

*Nice try,* he thought, switching out the chairs before taking a seat.

Having already studied the room and finding nothing of interest, Hayes turned his attention to the only link between himself and the men who'd taken him into custody—the cuff around his wrist.

There was no doubt that the South Africans knew their job, but the fact that Wikus had used a handcuff piqued his curiosity.

Having to detain someone was one of the hazards that came with the job, which was why any time Hayes went on an op, he always packed a handful of plastic zip-ties. The reasons were obvious: they were light, durable, and strong as hell. But most important of all, they were disposable.

A handcuff, on the other hand, seemed like a pain in the ass. Not just because they were heavy and needed to be maintained, but mainly because unless you wanted to buy a shit-ton of cuffs, you had to go back and retrieve them every time you used a pair.

It seemed like an unnecessary hassle and brought up the question: *Why does Wikus carry a pair of handcuffs?*

He found the answer engraved at the base of the cuff snapped around the lead pipe, in tiny letters that read REPUBLIC ARMS MODEL 65—SAP.

*Model 65 . . . general issue for South African cops assigned to Koevoet,* Hayes thought.

*Koevoet,* or *crowbar* as it was translated in English, was the nickname of South West Africa's Police Counterinsurgency Unit. The group of specially trained men who used controversial and often brutal tactics to "pry" apartheid-era insurgents from the civilian population.

Hayes had never met any face-to-face, but he knew enough about their reputation to start thinking about using the ceramic cuff key sewn into his waistband to get the hell out of there.

But before he could let himself out, the door swung open and Wikus stepped gleefully into the room.

"Oh, mate," he said, slamming the door behind him and throwing the latch, "you and me, we've got something to talk about."

"Like what?"

"Like the naughty things I found in this," he said, tossing Hayes's bloody assault pack on the table.

# 23

BRATISLAVA, SLOVAKIA

Cyrus Vandal sat in the center of the shipping container, na-
ked except for the pair of ratty sweatpants and the black
hood his captors had pulled over his head. Using his legs,
he scooted back in the chair, the cold metal frame against his bare
skin sending goose bumps rushing across his body.

But it was a momentary discomfort, barely noticeable after
the previous twelve hours he'd spent shivering in the darkness, the
corrugated-steel prison sucking the heat from his body. He did
everything he could to stay warm while his Slovakian captors
beat on him until their arms got tired.

When he still refused to talk, one of his interrogators stepped
to the edge of the container and ordered one of the guards sitting
outside to *priniest' hadice*—bring the hose.

Before joining the CIA's Special Activities Division, Vandal had spent ten years as a Navy SEAL. Thanks to the twelve brutal days he spent at SERE, he knew what was coming when the man in the navy-blue track suit appeared with the faded green garden hose.

"We'll see how tough he is now," one of the interrogators said, taking the hose from the man in the track suit.

At SERE the cadre had taught them to shut off their mind—"go to your happy place." But at the moment all Vandal could focus on was the nozzle being shoved into his mouth and the rush of well water down his throat.

Most men would have cracked, told them the color of their mother's underwear after that, but not Vandal.

"C'mon, guys," he choked out, after vomiting a stomachful of water on the floor, "I was a SEAL, you think this is the first time someone has tried to drown me?"

"Just wait until the boss gets here," the lead interrogator said after zip-tying him to the chair. "We'll see how funny you find it then."

But Vandal had no intention of waiting. As soon as his captors closed and latched the door he went to work on the zip-ties securing his muscled arms behind his back.

Sitting in the darkness, he knew there were easier ways to make a living than working for the CIA's Special Activities Division. Jobs that *didn't* involve getting your ass beat by a handful of Slovak gangsters.

*But where's the fun in that?* he thought.

Without a watch there was no way to tell the time, but when Vandal paused to take a break, he could tell that the sun had come up from the heat radiating off the container. After catching his breath, he worked his thumb over the edge of the cuff, feeling the notch he'd cut in the plastic.

*Almost there.*

Vandal set the notch against the sliver of metal on the back side of the chair, pulled his arms apart, and was busy trying to saw through the cuffs when he heard voices outside the Conex.

He redoubled his efforts, worked at the cuffs until the sweat rolled down his face and his shoulders were hot from the lactic acid building up in his muscles. He leaned forward and pulled his arms apart, straining against his bonds.

The plastic popped but refused to give. Before Vandal could try again, the metallic jangle of the latch being thrown told him he was out of time.

With no other choice, he slumped forward in his chair and dropped his head, assuming the position of defeated prisoner seconds before the door groaned open. He sat there, ears straining in the dark, feeling the eyes on him, waiting for someone to speak.

Then he heard it, the raspy voice of Ján Malicar—leader of the Dunajská Streda underworld and one of Interpol's most wanted criminals.

"So this is the guy who's been giving you so much trouble?"

"Yes, boss."

"Bring him outside, we'll see how tough he is."

The guards stepped inside, their boots echoing off the Conex as they walked over. "We told you, asshole," one of the men said before grabbing the back of his chair.

They dragged him back the way they'd come, the metal legs scraping over the floor like nails on a chalkboard.

Before he could close his eyes, the hood was ripped free, the sunlight blinding after the hours of darkness. Vandal tried to drop his head, get away from the light, but before he had a chance, a pair of rough hands had him by the chin and were torquing his head skyward.

"So, you are the Yankee dog the Americans sent to kill me?" Malicar demanded, hand dropping to the knife strapped to his hip.

"That's right," Vandal replied in perfect Slovak.

"He speaks," the man smiled to his cronies as he ripped the blade free, the light glinting off the razored edge as he held it in front of Vandal's eyes. "Let's see what else I can get you to say . . ."

But before he had a chance to finish his threat, Vandal snapped his head forward, driving his forehead into the man's nose.

"*Aaaaagh!*" the man screamed, hand racing to his shattered nose, the blood already gushing down the front of his shirt.

Before the guards could leap into action, Vandal spread his arms as wide as he could, clenched his core tight, and whiplashed his body forward in the chair. The second the cuffs snapped free, he was on his feet, scooping the chair off the floor and flinging it at the guards.

The man with the broken nose swiped at him with the blade, but Vandal twisted left, watched the blade flash past his face, and caught the man's wrist. He twisted until he heard the snap of the bone and then, in one smooth motion, hip-tossed the man to the ground.

Still holding his arm, Vandal stomped down hard on the side of Malicar's throat. He took a second to gather his strength, and then with a sharp pull snapped the man's neck.

# 24

**N**ext door to the detention room, Theresa Mallory pulled another cigarette from the pack of Marlboro Reds and lit it off the butt of the previous. As a rule, she only allowed herself five cigarettes a day, but that had gone to shit when she arrived on the flight line, found the plane shot to hell and General Dábo seconds away from putting a bullet through the pilot's forehead.

*What would have happened if I hadn't arrived when I did? What would I have told the boss?*

She knew that she might have been able to handle the loss of one or the other, *but both?* The thought sent a shudder up her spine.

Just like everyone else who worked for Cabot, she was afraid of him. But unlike the gun thugs, fixers, and money men he used to keep DarkCloud afloat, Mallory wasn't afraid that he would kill her—though she had no doubt the Frenchman wouldn't hesitate to pull the trigger if he thought there was something to be gained by her death.

No, there was nothing he could do—no physical pain or psychological trauma—that hadn't already been inflicted on her in the charnel house of her birth, the public housing where she'd learned firsthand that there was nothing sacred about human life. It was just another commodity, a pound of flesh to be bought for a handful of quid or stolen at the point of a knife. For Mallory, physical pain was *nothing*; her fear came from the emotional coldness that Cabot used to control the women in his life.

Even now, standing there in the detention room, the cigarette smoke tumbling free of her mouth—only to be immediately inhaled through her nose—the thought of failing him was a fate worse than a thousand deaths.

She heard boots in the hallway and turned toward the door. The shadow that fell across the threshold was followed by a respectful knock.

"Come in," she said in French.

The door swung open and General Dábo stepped inside, a shorter man in gray coveralls behind him.

"I have brought the head mechanic, as requested," he said with an obsequious nod and one of his polished smiles.

Mallory had met hundreds of Dábos in her life, big men with eggshell-thin egos who used charm and guile to get what a gun could not. It was this ability to see past a man's façade and into the innermost recesses of his being that had attracted her to

Cabot in the first place—and the reason she'd risen so high in his organization.

"Thank you, General," she said.

"But of course, madam," he replied. "Is there anything else that I can—"

"You can wait in the hall," she snapped, ignoring the blaze in his eyes.

She waited until the door had closed and she heard Dábo's footfalls receding down the hall before turning her eyes to the man in the coveralls.

"What is your name?"

"Drissa . . . Drissa Zadi," he gulped.

"And you have inspected the plane?" she asked, stepping closer.

"Yes, madam."

"Can you fix it?"

"The damage to the fuselage is mostly cosmetic. I have my men patching it now . . ."

Mallory advanced on the mechanic, the ice in her eyes dropping the temperature in the room by ten degrees.

"That is *not* what I asked you!" she snapped.

Like most of Africa, Ivory Coast was deeply patriarchal, a male-centered society where women were to be seen but not heard. Mallory's sudden aggressiveness caught the mechanic off guard.

He stepped back, recoiling like a man who'd reached into a basket for a piece of wood only to find a snake. "O-of course, madam, m-my mistake," Zadi stammered, pulling an oil-stained shop rag from his coveralls and wiping it across his glistening brow.

Mallory moved to the bench next to the window, where the pilot's passport was laid out next to her bag. "I need that plane ready to fly to Grand-Bassam in four hours," she said, taking out a stack of cash and holding it up for Zadi to see, "and I am willing to make whoever does this for me a *very* rich man."

The mechanic's eyes widened at the sight of the money. He licked his lips, his earlier fear forgotten.

"Now, what I need to know is if *you* are that man, Drissa Zadi," she said, placing the cash on the bench before retrieving the suppressed Walther, "or do I need to keep looking?"

The mechanic looked from the cash to the pistol and then back to the cash, his tongue flicking across his lips.

"Think carefully before you answer," she warned.

"I am that man," he said.

"Then I suggest you get to work."

"Of course," he said, edging toward the door.

Once the mechanic was gone, Mallory scooped the pilot's passport from the table and reclaimed her spot at the mirror. She thumbed through the booklet, the feel of the paper against her fingers and the dull shine of the optically variable ink under the light telling her everything she needed to know.

*It's fake.*

The ability to spot a forged note or government document was not a skill set possessed by many of the white-collar types who worked for Cabot. And even if it was, an employee would never find himself in a position to offer it, because when the boss called it wasn't to converse. He ran his company like the military that had molded him, and direct communication was a one-way street—Cabot giving the orders and the underling listening.

But thanks to years of hard work and her unprecedented

winning streak, Mallory had set herself apart from the pack and moved through the hierarchy to become one of his chief advisers, which was why she'd been surprised when Cabot called and told her that he needed her in Korhogo.

She'd been in Paris, on the second day of a much-needed vacation, when her phone rang.

"There is a plane waiting to fly you to Crete, where you will meet up with a team and fly to Côte d'Ivoire."

"I wasn't aware we had any interests in Ivory Coast," she'd said, grabbing her suitcase from the closest.

"It's a special project," Cabot had said, "one that requires a woman with your delicate touch."

By the time he hung up, Mallory had packed up and was heading out the door.

She'd spent the four-and-a-half-hour flight to Heraklion wondering what in the hell was going on, hoping the answers were waiting for her on the ground. But when she landed and met up with Wikus and the rest of the team, all Mallory found were more questions.

Back in Korhogo, she brushed the thoughts from her mind and adjusted the volume knob on the speaker mounted to the wall. Then she turned her full attention to the man sitting at the table.

*Who are you, Mr. Hayes?*

"Looks like you got yourself into a bit of a spot, mate," Wikus said, crossing to the table. "I'm going to ask you a few questions"— leaning into Hayes's face—"and you damn well better answer them."

The South African was an imposing man, with thick arms and the barest hint of a neck. A bruiser. The kind of man who got off on inflicting pain, but instead of the fearful looks Mallory was used to seeing when the burly merc went to work on a man, Hayes appeared almost bored.

"What are you doing in the Ivory Coast?"

"I'm a reporter."

"I dated a journo once," Wikus said, unzipping the assault pack.

"What was he like?"

Getting a person to do your bidding was a subtle art, one that Mallory had mastered well before she came to work for Cabot. Which is why she had given Wikus clear instructions on how she wanted the interview handled.

"You can yell, scream, and be as menacing as you like, but do not hit him, understood?"

She'd felt confident that she'd made herself clear, but when Wikus looked up from the pack, his face red and his hand curling into a fist, she wasn't so sure.

But instead of flattening Hayes's nose he upended the assault pack and dumped the contents on the table.

"What's this, your recorder?" he asked, picking up a pair of night-vision goggles.

"What do you want?" Hayes asked.

"Well, that's simple," Wikus answered, lowering himself into the chair across from the American. "I want to know how a nice-looking lad like yourself ended up landing here with a dead man in the cockpit and a plane filled with more lead than a number two pencil."

# 25

KORHOGO, IVORY COAST

W hile Hayes was fully enjoying watching the South African fight to control his temper, the man was starting to get on his nerves.

"Listen, man, we both know you ain't running shit, so why don't you do me a favor?"

"What's that?" Wikus said, leaning forward.

"Shut the fuck up and go get your boss."

The fact that Wikus didn't immediately flatten his nose confirmed his earlier suspicion, that whoever was on the other side of the glass had the South African on a tight leash. But Hayes was tired of screwing around and the man's incessant questions were giving him a headache.

"Look, fuckface, I'm not telling you shit, so stop wasting *my* time and the world's oxygen and go get your mommy."

Wikus came out of the chair like he was strapped to a rocket. "That's it, you smart-mouthed cunt," he said, firing a meaty fist toward Hayes's face.

Even with his hand cuffed to the table, he knew he could take Wikus to the ground without breaking a sweat. Hayes also knew that while it might feel good for a few minutes, it was the fastest possible way to blow whatever cover he had left.

But there were ways to hurt a man without making it look intentional.

Hayes waited until the last second, and then, flexing his neck and bringing his shoulders up to his ears, dropped his forehead into the path of the man's punch.

He'd taken some hard hits, but Wikus punched like a mule and the blow snapped his head back, the force pushing the chair onto its back leg, and if it hadn't been for the cuff securing him to the table, Hayes knew that it would have sent him to the floor. He tried to shake it off and right his chair, but the simple task left him feeling like a drunk trying to pass a field sobriety test.

He'd untangled the cuff from the chair and had just gotten all four legs on the floor when Wikus came charging around the table. His face blood red. Eyes brimming with the promise of violence.

Hayes jumped to his feet and kicked the chair into the enraged South African's path. It was a weak counter, one he fully expected the man to avoid. But at the last instant one of the wheels hit a crack and the chair tipped onto its side, driving one of the arms into Wikus's groin.

The blow stopped him like a .357 to the skull and he dropped to his knees, mouth stretched in a silent O.

Before Hayes could press his advantage, someone in the hall booted the door and a rush of Ivorian soldiers came flooding into the room. They rushed toward the table and Hayes was preparing himself for a beatdown, but the soldiers ignored him, grabbed the sobbing South African from the floor, and dragged him out. Leaving Hayes and the woman from the tarmac alone in the room.

"I, uh . . ."

"You wanted the one in charge," she said. "Well, here I am, Mr. Hayes."

He studied the woman as she walked toward the table, wondering why she was here, what she wanted with him. Usually he found all the answers he needed in the eyes, but this woman's were blank and, behind a perfect coat of makeup, her face was unreadable.

"Lady, who are you and why are you people so interested in who I am and what I'm doing here?"

"My name is Theresa Mallory," she said.

"You're not a cop and you obviously don't work for the government, so what do you want?"

"I'm a lawyer," she answered, taking his passport from her bag and opening the front cover.

"You going to get me out of here?"

"Considering the body we found in your plane, it's not a lawyer you need, but a priest."

"Is that why you're here? To offer absolution?" Hayes asked.

"Mr. Hayes, do you know the penalty for traveling under forged papers in Ivory Coast?"

"Who says they're fake?" he asked, slipping back into the good ol' boy routine.

"*I* do," she answered, the tone of her voice cold as ice.

Back in the day, when Hayes had to operate overseas, he and the rest of the Treadstone operatives traveled under false papers—or non-official cover, as it was known in the State Department—but Hayes didn't have that option now because his passport had been confiscated before he was booted from the States.

While the loss of his papers was a pain in the ass, it wasn't a game changer and Hayes knew that all he needed to do to get new papers was visit one of the many cache sites he'd set up during his time at Treadstone.

On paper it seemed like an easy enough solution, but it wasn't until he made the first attempt at a bus station in Berlin that Hayes realized he was being watched. Once he suspected that he was being followed, he backed off the drop and set about to identify the surveillance team.

He spent ten minutes cruising the street for a car, found a sedan that was beat up enough not to need an alarm. He stopped at the driver's-side door and fished around in his pocket like he was searching for the keys, while checking the street.

*Clear.*

Using the flat-head screwdriver he carried for just these occasions, Hayes punched the door lock, climbed inside, and after snapping the steering column used the screwdriver again to bypass the ignition.

Hayes found a map in the glove box and searched for an area that would give him the advantage. He chose the Schönhauser Allee Arcaden, the three-story mall located in Pankow, a large residential center northeast of the airport.

A minute later, he pulled out onto the street and drove north, eyes glued to the mirrors anytime he made a turn, and by the time he arrived at his destination had clocked the trail car—a navy-blue BMW 550i.

He parked on the street, got out, and headed toward the mall, using the storefront windows to check the progress of his pursuers.

There were two of them—a man and a woman—and to anyone else they might have escaped notice. But not Hayes; he immediately pegged them for what they were: a pair of desk jockeys *pretending* to be operatives.

On the one hand he was relieved that Shaw didn't consider him a serious enough threat to send the best, but on the other hand, it was kind of insulting to think the director had *seriously* thought he wouldn't immediately see them for what they were.

Shaking the pair had been comically easy, but Berlin was blown, and worse than that, Hayes still didn't have his papers. He wasn't sure how long it would take them to phone in, let someone know that they had lost their target, but one thing was for certain: Shaw was going to take his dumping a surveillance team as a personal affront. And would send a more qualified team to make sure it didn't happen again.

With that thought at the forefront of his mind, Hayes boosted a second car and headed west. He drove to Frankfurt, took a train to the border, and crossed into France on foot.

In France he put on a counterintelligence clinic: He stuck close to the border, finally ending up in Strasbourg, where he made sure that the CCTV picked him up boarding a train for Zurich.

Hayes ducked into the bathroom to change clothes and used a pair of scissors and a bottle of dye to cut and color his hair. When he stepped off the train at the next stop, he was a different person.

He'd thought that he'd gotten away clean, until he went for the second drop in Marseilles, but this time Shaw had sent in the pros. While Hayes felt the heat, he never got anything close to a positive identification.

In the end, his only choice had been to buy a set of papers from a half-blind forger in Marseilles, so he wasn't surprised that Mallory was calling bullshit on his passport.

But while he still didn't know what she wanted, Hayes had no problem identifying her angle. Her approach was crystal clear. She was defining the stakes, trying to rattle him with implied threats of Vlad's body on the plane and the penalty for traveling on a bogus passport.

*But why? She's not a cop, and from the looks of those knuckle draggers she's rolling with she sure as hell ain't Mother Teresa, so what does she want?*

He realized the only way he was going to find out was to give her what she wanted—a story.

"Look, I got into some trouble a few months back," he began.

"What kind of trouble?" she asked, pressing a cigarette between her crimson lips.

There were a multitude of acceptable answers, but something about the way Mallory was staring at him over the unlit cigarette, studying him like he was some kind of science experiment, told him that she was looking for something.

*Leverage.*

"Smuggling," he said.

Mallory nodded and sparked the lighter and leaned in, keeping her eyes on him, waiting until the tip of the cigarette was an inch from the flame, before dropping her eyes and stretching the cigarette out toward it.

The move was done in silence, but to a man versed in the nuances of the game, it spoke volumes.

She was in control and not afraid to show it.

The paper caught fire, the smell of the burning tobacco muting her perfume. It wasn't until the cigarette was lit that she looked up.

"I've got a proposition for you," she said.

# 26

Hayes stood on the scaffolding in front of the Provider's engine, sweat pouring down the front of his coveralls as he pushed himself up on his toes. He angled the flashlight to get a better look inside.

Outside the hangar, the day had begun to mellow, the thunderstorm that had blown through two hours before took the teeth out of the heat but added to the humidity. Satisfied with what he found inside the engine, Hayes clicked off the flashlight, stuck it in his pocket, and took a long pull from the liter of bottled water the mechanics had given him.

The water was warm, but it was wet and that was all he cared about.

He screwed the cap on the bottle and took another long, hard look at the plane. Four hours ago, the Provider had more holes in the fuselage than a slice of Swiss cheese, but not only had the team of Ivorian mechanics patched them, they'd come damn close to matching the original paint.

But what really had him stumped was how they'd managed to get the engine back online. But they had.

Hayes cast a quick glance across the hangar, saw Mallory and the general standing on the far side—well out of earshot—and turned to the lead mechanic.

"How?" he asked the man in French.

"Well, we used Bondo to patch the—"

"Yeah, I got that, I mean how did you fix the *engine*?"

"Magic," he said.

"Well, I don't fly on magic, so I guess it's either you tell me how you pulled it off or I tell General Dábo to find another pilot."

The smile fell from the mechanic's face and he raised his hands in defeat. "Fine, fine, no problem," he said. "The fuel pump took a bullet and some of the fuel lines were nicked by the fragmentation, so I replaced them. Easy, see."

"You just happened to have spare parts for an engine that was discontinued before you were even born just lying around?"

"Easier if I show you," the mechanic said.

They climbed down the scaffolding, ducked beneath the prop, and started toward the back of the hangar.

"It hasn't always been like this," the mechanic said.

"Like what?" Hayes asked, pulling a rag from his pocket and using it to wipe the sweat from his brow.

"You know, the war, the killing," he answered, opening the

door and stepping outside. "It's hard to see it now, but there was a time when this was a fully functional airport. A place people actually *wanted* to come to. But . . ."

"But TIA," Hayes said, finishing the man's thought.

"Yep, TIA," the mechanic nodded.

*TIA—This Is Africa.*

It was a common expression, one used by Africans and non-Africans alike. A statement that was equal parts endearment and resignation—one that perfectly summed up his current condition and the agreement he'd made with Mallory back in the interrogation room.

From the tone of the conversation, the dispassionate way she'd laid out the facts, it had almost seemed like Hayes had had a choice in the matter. But if there was any confusion about his situation, the cold bite of the handcuff securing him to the table had been quick to make his position clear.

"It was a simple proposition, between my employer and your copilot," she'd said.

"Which he had no right to make," Hayes had reminded her.

"Be that as it may, the cargo still needs to be delivered to Grand-Bassam."

*Fucking Vlad,* he'd thought.

*Should have killed him when you had a chance.*

As much as it pained him to admit it, the voice had a point. His decision *not* to kill Vlad, to go against both his instincts *and* his training, had been a mistake.

"What's in it for me?" he'd asked her.

"The mechanics here have assured me they can repair your plane, make it airworthy for the trip—"

"How in the hell is that—"

"Do *not* interrupt me, Mr. Hayes," she snapped, her eyes burning hotter than the cherry at the end of her cigarette.

The rebuke had echoed off the walls and the blood had rushed to his face, leaving his skin hot, like a fuse waiting for a match.

*Just take it easy, wild man,* the voice had sighed. *Don't let the little lady get your panties in a bunch.*

It had been good advice, and Hayes knew he should take it. The only problem was, he'd run out of patience eight hours ago.

"As I was saying, the mechanics will make the necessary repairs to get you to Grand-Bassam, and once there my employer will pay for a *complete* overhaul."

"A complete overhaul, huh?" Hayes had said, not attempting to keep the incredulity out of his voice.

"That is what I said, isn't it?"

"Lady, they stopped making that bird in 1970."

"Do you have a point?"

"My *point* is that even if you *could* find the spare parts, do you have any idea how much that would cost?" he'd asked.

"You let me worry about that. Do we have a deal?"

Hayes had sunk every last dime into the Provider, and now that it was a thirty-thousand-pound paperweight, there was no way for him to recoup his investment. So of course he wanted it repaired, but following the mechanic around the hangar, Hayes knew that wasn't why he'd taken it.

He'd taken the deal because it was the only way out of the situation that *didn't* involve killing everyone else at Korhogo.

"There's your answer," the mechanic said, pointing to a concrete pad where three haggard-looking prop planes, with their faded South African Airways emblems, sat wingtip to wingtip.

*Well, I'll be a son of a bitch,* he thought.

"Is that a . . ."

"Canadair North Star," the mechanic grinned at him.

"But how?" he asked, still not believing his eyes.

"Like I said before, people *used* to want to come here, and someone had to fly them."

Before he could ask any more questions, Hayes heard the squeak of the door opening followed by the clack of Mallory's heels on the concrete.

"Well?" she asked, "are you satisfied?"

Hayes wasn't a superstitious man and had never been one to put much stock in signs or portents. But growing up in the South, he'd met plenty who did. Old men who'd turn around and go the other way if they saw a black cat crossing the walk in front of them, or his grandmother who always kept a mirror on the front porch to scare away evil spirits.

To him it was all a bunch of nonsense, but standing there staring at those old planes, he found himself wondering. Trying to figure out the odds of landing at the *one* airport that happened to have the parts he needed to get back in the air.

*If you need a sign, take it as a sign,* the voice said, *but whatever you are going to do, let's get the show on the road before this bitch changes her mind.*

"Mr. Hayes, are you flying or not?"

"Yeah, let's get this over with," he said.

**27**

After conducting an SSE—or sensitive site exploitation—of Malicar's camp, Cyrus Vandal headed east to the flat he'd rented near the Medická Záhrada—the park behind the hospital. Inside the safe house he burned the clothes he'd taken off one of the dead gangsters, and after thirty minutes in the shower almost felt clean.

While he was sure the local authorities wouldn't shed a tear over Ján Malicar's untimely demise, the same could not be said for his associates, and Vandal knew he had to get out of town.

Using a tube of concealer, he did what he could to cover the bruises and then dressed quickly in a muted gray sports coat and blue slacks, grabbed his bag, and headed for the door. Out in the street, Vandal donned a tweed newsboy hat, pulling the brim low over the pair of wraparound shades that covered his eyes.

Twenty minutes later he arrived at Petržalka station, just another face in the crowd as he crossed the platform and climbed aboard the 11:20 to Vienna. He locked the door behind him and settled into his seat—out of danger—but was unable to relax until the train crossed the border into Austria.

Vandal felt the tension easing from his muscles and was about to open the paper when he felt the persistent buzz of his phone in his jacket pocket.

*Now what?*

"Go secure," an electronically modified voice said as soon as he answered.

"Going secure," Vandal said, activating the encryption package and waiting for the green box to appear around the edge of the screen before returning the phone to his ear.

"There is a problem in Africa you need to deal with," the voice advised.

"What's the problem?"

"Someone needs to go away."

*A termination order. Okay, this could be fun.*

"Where is the target?"

"Last contact was in Morocco, but target is currently on the move."

"On the move? You mean you don't have an active location?" Vandal demanded.

"Affirmative. This is a very fluid situation, but it came from the top. All information has been uploaded to your computer and necessary assets are being moved into place. You just worry about getting there."

Vandal glanced at his watch and saw that it was almost noon. Assuming he got a flight on the first thing smoking it would be at least sixteen and a half hours before he got on the ground. Add an hour for customs and arranging transportation, then however long it took to get on the road, and the target could have a full twenty-four-hour jump on him.

"By the time I get in play, the target could be anywhere."

"Just get there," the voice said.

"Fine," Vandal said, and then as an afterthought, asked, "who is the target?"

"Adam Hayes," the voice answered, and then the line went dead.

**28**

KORHOGO, IVORY COAST

H ayes stood outside the forward entrance door, his heart hammering in his chest like the bass line of a rap song. He told himself that he was just waiting for his eyes to adjust to the gloomy interior of the plane before climbing in, but that was a lie.

The truth was, despite the patched holes and the freshly scrubbed interior, Hayes could still smell the blood beneath the pine cone reek of the disinfectants the mechanic had used to clean the plane.

According to Mallory, his passenger not only wanted to go to Grand-Bassam, she *needed* to go, and while Hayes was pretty sure she was full of shit, part of him *wanted* to believe that he was doing the right thing, to prove to Shaw—and, more important, to himself—that he was more than just a killer.

*Keep telling yourself that, pal,* the voice laughed.

The spurt of anger that followed the remark was enough to get him through the door and into the cockpit. He dropped into the pilot's chair and looked out the recently repaired cockpit window. Zadi stood in front of the aircraft, nervous as a cat over water.

The mechanic pointed to the starboard engine, raised his hand into the air, and made a motion like he was twirling a lasso. In the cockpit, Hayes leaned forward to see past the sheet of cardboard duct-taped over the shattered window, and made sure the prop was clear before turning on the engines' fuel pump.

Unlike the more common inline engines, the old radials were crotchety and getting one to start was more of an art than a science, which was the main reason most pilots hated the old birds and their finicky engines.

Hayes, on the other hand, had nothing but respect for the tough old engines and confidently began the start-up sequence. He began with the starboard engine, flipping the electric fuel pump to R and then pressing the start switch, which engaged the engine's magneto: the electric motor that started the propellor spinning. He waited until the blades had completed two full rotations before hitting the ignition switch.

The engine chugged to life and he scanned the now-immaculate gauges that dotted the control panel, watching them bounce happily into the correct positions. With the starboard engine running smooth as a sewing machine, Hayes turned his attention to the mechanic.

Zadi pointed at the port engine and repeated the lassoing motion, but this time the process wasn't quite as smooth.

Instead of jumping to life, the engine backfired and spewed black smoke from the exhaust pipe. Outside the cockpit, Zadi's face went white. His earlier nervousness gave way to genuine fear, and he immediately held up a closed fist—the signal to shut the engine down.

It was the right call, but knowing how much Zadi had riding on a clean start, Hayes ignored it, and instead of shutting the engine down made minute adjustments to the air and fuel mixture, babying the engine until he had it running smooth.

*And that, ladies and gentlemen, is how it's done,* he thought.

Outside the plane, the color had returned to Zadi's face, the consternation that had clouded the mechanic's proud visage replaced by an ear-to-ear grin.

*"Très bon!"* he shouted. Very good.

Hayes wanted to keep the engines running, and after signaling to Zadi that he was going to pull the plane out of the hangar, he disengaged the brakes and inched the throttle forward. The Provider started forward, out of the shadows and into the sunlight.

Out on the tarmac, he could see a mirage shimmering off the runway fifty yards to his front.

*Go for it,* the voice urged.

Hayes used the mirrors to check behind the plane and saw a group of soldiers lounging in the shade of the hangar, their eyes closed against the sun, weapons lying on the ground next to them.

Even if they realized what he was doing and opened fire before he made it to the runway, there was no way they could stop him. Nothing but the fact that he'd given his word. He cursed and reached for the throttles, but instead of shoving them forward, he pulled them back to idle and reengaged the brake.

Before getting out of the pilot's seat, Hayes reached under the instrument panel and retrieved the Beretta 92f from its hiding place. He got to his feet, clipped the holster to his waistband, press-checked the pistol to make sure there was a round in the chamber, and stepped out of the cockpit.

With the engines running, it wasn't safe to use the pilot's door, so with the reassuring feel of the pistol on his hip, Hayes dropped the ramp and headed back to the cargo hold.

Out on the tarmac, he saw Mallory waiting for him at the door of the hangar, his assault pack sitting on the ground next to her feet.

"Everything to your satisfaction?" she asked.

He nodded, eyes darting to the far corner of the hangar where Wikus and the rest of his goon squad held a tight perimeter around a blond-haired girl.

"Excellent," Mallory said, handing him the pack.

Hayes opened the main compartment and glanced inside, finding the gear he'd arrived with, plus a satellite phone and a thick manila envelope.

"What's this?" he asked, taking out the envelope.

"To cover any *incidentals* you might encounter along the way."

"Incidentals?" he frowned, not liking the sound of the word.

Hayes opened the flap, and when he saw the fresh one hundred-dollar bills packed inside, let out a low whistle.

"There's got to be ten grand in here," he said, running his thumb over the cash.

"Yes, there has been a slight change in plans."

*Of course,* he thought.

The deal he'd agreed to in the detention room was that he'd fly his passenger to Grand-Bassam, where an escort would meet them at the airport. Mallory had assured him that General Dábo had already spoken to the commander on the ground and that Hayes would be allowed to land, refuel, and depart without being bothered.

*So what had changed?*

Guessing his thoughts, Mallory was quick with an answer.

"The ground team has been delayed, and instead of meeting you at the airport, they will be waiting for you at the Hôtel la Commanderie."

"What about transportation?"

"A vehicle will be waiting for you when you land," she answered. "Any more questions?"

"Yeah, who is she?" he asked, nodding toward the blond-haired girl.

"A passenger, Mr. Hayes," she said, motioning for Wikus to bring the girl.

*Yeah, right,* he thought.

Wikus escorted the girl across the hangar, giving Hayes his first clear look at his passenger. She was pretty, with ash-blond hair and smooth, sun-bronzed skin that from a distance made it difficult to determine her age. But as she drew near Hayes guessed that she had to be in her early twenties.

*Old enough to know what she's getting into,* he told himself.

"One more thing," Mallory said, leaning in. "Zoe is a Type 1 diabetic."

"You're just telling me this now?" he hissed. "What if . . ."

"It won't, she has an insulin pump. The only reason I mention it is because like all girls her age, she is self-conscious about it."

"Well if she is self-conscious about it, I don't imagine she's going to like some stranger knowing about it."

"Just make sure she doesn't leave her insulin in the plane," she whispered before turning to the approaching girl. "Zoe, this is the pilot I was telling you about. His name is Adam Hayes and he is going to fly you to Grand-Bassam," Mallory said by way of introduction.

Not sure what else to say, he stuck out his hand.

"Nice to meet you."

"An American?" she asked Mallory in French, her eyes never leaving Hayes's.

"It was last-minute," the lawyer said with a Gallic shrug.

Hayes wasn't used to taking shit off someone he'd just met, but he clung to his pretense of not speaking the language and bit down on the smartass comment he wanted to hurl at the two women, figuring that if he could keep his mouth shut for a few more minutes, he might just get the hell out of here alive.

"Just pretend he is one of your dogs and you'll be fine," Wikus added in his guttural French.

*Stay cool, you can do this,* he told himself.

Mallory suppressed a smile and switched back to English.

"Well, now that you two have been introduced, I suggest you get in the air."

"Best thing I've heard all day," Hayes said, turning to the plane.

"Hey, asshole," Wikus said, stepping up behind him, "you let anything happen to her and there's not a place in the world where you're going to be able to hide. Get me?"

"You aren't going to have to look for me," Hayes said.

"Oh, yeah, and why's that?"

"Because when this is over, I'll be coming back for my property," he said, nodding to the 1911 stuck in Wikus's waistband.

Zoe was halfway to the plane, but with his anger stuck on

simmer, Hayes ended up beating her to it. He stomped into the cargo hold, went to the control box, and shoved the lever into the up position.

Seeing the ramp lift free of the ground, Zoe broke into a run, whatever names she was calling him drowned out by the engines.

"What was that?" she demanded in English, when she made it inside.

"You know how these *American* planes can be," he said.

Zoe pulled off her sunglasses and looked around the bare cargo hold, scowling at the nylon troop seats. "Where am I supposed to sit?"

"That's up to you," he said, already heading to the cockpit.

Hayes had already strapped himself in and was contacting the tower when Zoe's head appeared over his shoulder.

"Can I . . . ?"

He leaned over and grabbed the pair of headphones from the copilot's seat and handed them to her, not noticing the blood until Zoe had pulled them on.

*Oops.*

"Better take a seat," he said, waiting for her to comply and then showing her how to strap in.

"Comfortable?"

"Yes, thank you."

"Good, now let's get the hell out of here."

Hayes contacted the tower, more out of habit than anything else, and after receiving clearance, maneuvered the Provider to the end of the runway.

*Let's get the hell out of here,* he thought, shoving the throttles to full power.

# 29

## GRAND-BASSAM

Hayes leveled off at twenty thousand feet, his mind racing as he double-checked his heading. It was a little more than three hundred miles to Grand-Bassam, and while he would have preferred to spend the time in silence, he had questions—questions that needed to be answered before they landed.

He glanced over at Zoe and found her sitting with her eyes shut, arms folded tight across her chest, the iPhone she'd produced shortly after takeoff plugged into her ears. Hayes had no idea what she was listening to and was pretty sure that even if she told him he wouldn't have recognized the artist.

Her posture, on the other hand, was an entirely different story.

Like all married men, Hayes had been on the losing end of

enough arguments to know that nothing good *ever* came from disturbing a woman sitting like that.

But it was either talk or spend the next three hours in silence. *Well, here goes nothing,* he thought.

He tried clearing his throat and then faked a few deep-chested coughs, but with the engines droning like a pair of swamp fans Hayes realized that he could fire a howitzer in the cockpit and she probably wouldn't hear it.

*Guess I'm just going to have to take it up a notch,* he thought.

He hauled back on the yoke, let the Provider's nose climb skyward for a few seconds before shoving the controls forward.

Compared to the roller-coaster ride he'd taken across southern Burkina Faso, the maneuver was gentle as a summer breeze, with the only noticeable effects being the tickle in the pit of Hayes's stomach that came during the few seconds of zero gravity.

The same could not be said for his passenger.

Hayes wasn't sure if Zoe had nodded off or if she simply wasn't accustomed to flying, but whatever the case, she jumped so hard that if she hadn't been wearing the harness, he was pretty sure she would have blasted right through the windscreen.

"What in the hell was that?" she screamed, her blue eyes wide as saucers.

Knowing that Zoe would be furious if she even *suspected* he'd done it on purpose, Hayes spent a few seconds making a big show of regaining control of the aircraft, waiting until he'd leveled out before pointing to the headset over his ears.

"Can't hear you."

Zoe took a few ragged breaths and, seeing that he was in control of the plane, nodded, pulled her headset over her ears, and repeated the question.

"What was *that*?"

"Must have hit a thermal," Hayes said. "These older planes don't have the engines to climb above the weather."

"You think it will happen again?"

"Not sure, but if it does, the only way I can talk to you is if you keep your headset on."

"Okay . . . okay . . ." she panted over the radio.

"Just take a few deep breaths, in through your nose, out through your mouth," Hayes said.

Zoe followed his instructions, matching him breath for breath until she'd regained her composure.

"How *old* is this plane?" she asked, studying the interior as if seeing it for the first time.

"She was built in the late sixties, but her last official flight was in 1986."

"And it's safe to fly something this old?"

"Well, she wasn't in the best shape when I found her, but it wasn't anything a few months of hard work couldn't fix. Did most of the repairs myself."

"So, you're a mechanic?"

"Not really."

"But you've worked on planes before . . . right?"

"Uh, maybe we should talk about something else," he said, not liking where the conversation was going.

"Fine . . . so how long have you been a drug smuggler?" she asked.

The question caught him off guard and left him stammering for a reply.

"Drug smuggler . . . ? Who told you that I was a drug smuggler?"

"Mallory did," Zoe shrugged. "She said that's why you have such a big plane. But if you don't want to talk about it, that's cool."

Hayes was desperate to keep the conversation going and threw out a number at random, "It's been . . . let me see . . . five years."

"How does it work?"

"Uh . . . you know, pick up the drugs here, smuggling them there . . ."

"You're full of shit," she grinned.

So far the conversation was not going as planned and Hayes found himself wishing that he'd paid more attention during the asset recruitment class he'd attended at Harvey Point—the Agency's covert training facility located near Hertford, North Carolina.

Recruiting foreign nationals, gaining their trust, and then getting them to turn on their government was a CIA case officer's bread and butter. It was a subtle and long-studied art that revolved around MICE: an acronym that stood for Money, Ideology, Coercion, and Ego.

Knuckle draggers like Hayes, on the other hand, got a three-hour CliffsNotes version: a down-and-dirty how-to that ended with the cadre saying, "The best way to get a foreign national to *not* turn you over to the authorities is to give them something they need."

Back at Harvey Point, the concept had seemed straightforward enough, but sitting behind the controls while Zoe turned his cover story into Swiss cheese, Hayes realized it was time to change the subject—*again.*

"So . . . you ever been to Grand-Bassam?" he asked.

Real *smooth. Why don't you just ask her about the weather, dumbass?*

"Quite a few times, actually," she said with a smile.

"Seriously?"

"Yep. In fact, my father taught me to surf in Grand-Bassam . . . but that was years ago. Back when he actually wanted to spend time with me."

Hayes watched her as she spoke and noticed the change in her eyes when she mentioned her father. He wasn't sure if it was sadness or regret, but there was something there—a vulnerability to be exploited.

*Keep her talking.*

"You know, when I was a kid, I didn't get to see much of my old man."

"Really?" she asked.

"Yep."

"Why?"

"Well, we didn't have a lot of money growing up and when my mom got sick my dad had to pick up a second job. Sometimes if he got off early, I *might* see him at the breakfast table, but usually he came home and went right to bed. He was working his ass off to make sure we had everything we needed but I . . . I . . ."

He trailed off, the emotions that came with the memories making him uncomfortable.

*Why the hell am I telling her all of this?*

The last time Hayes had talked about his childhood was with the shrink in Tacoma, and even then he'd done so grudgingly. He thought by keeping the details light and his responses to her questions vague, the doc might move on.

But all his avoidance did was pique her curiosity and no matter how far he tried to steer the conversation away from those formidable years, she always found a way to steer it back.

"Let's go back to how you felt about you father *not* being around," she'd say. "Did you resent his absences?"

"Shit, lady, that was twenty-four years ago," he finally snapped. "How the hell am I supposed to remember how I felt when I was ten years old?"

It was a lie. Hayes remembered *exactly* how he'd felt, because unlike bullet holes and broken bones, the wounds passed from father to son *never* healed.

"But you what?" Zoe asked, her face showing real interest in his words.

"Well, I treated him like a real asshole," Hayes said. "Swore that if I ever had a kid, I'd never be like him."

"Do you have children?" she asked.

"Yeah." He nodded.

"And?"

"Let's just say the apple didn't fall far from the tree," he said, his voice barely audible.

Zoe frowned, but before she could follow up on his answer a tiny *beep* drew her attention to her waistband.

"Oh, crap," she said, inching up her shirt, revealing a black box the size of a deck of cards.

"Everything okay?" Hayes asked.

"Yeah, it's . . . my insulin pump. I've got to change the cartridge."

"Oh . . . uh . . . do you need some . . . some privacy?" Hayes asked, face coloring at the sight of her bare flesh.

"Why, Mr. Hayes, who knew that you were such a gentleman?" she said, grinning coyly at his obvious discomfort.

"Just saying that if you do, I can turn on the autopilot and . . . you know . . . step out."

"That won't be necessary," she said, taking a black case from her bag.

Zoe deftly made the switch, ejecting the empty ampule and exchanging it for the fresh one she took from the case.

"Before I got this, every day it was needles, needles, needles—always checking my sugar levels and injecting myself with insulin—but this takes care of it for me," she said, sliding the loaded ampule into the tray and snapping it shut. "See, all done. No more shots and no more doctors."

"Yeah, I'm not a fan of doctors myself," Hayes deadpanned. "Bunch of bloodsuckers, if you ask me."


Mallory was true to her word and the landing at Félix Houphouët-Boigny International Airport was without incident. The tower instructed Hayes to taxi to the cargo ramp on the south side of the field, where he shut down the aircraft.

"Well, we made it," he said after helping Zoe off the plane.

"And I've never been so grateful," she said, turning, the ocean breeze touseling her hair as she pulled herself into a languid stretch. "Now to find a bathroom."

"I'm sure they have one in the office," he said, pointing to the low-slung building to their front. "Let me finish up here and we'll go check."

"No, I have to go *now*," she said with a grimace that told Hayes waiting around wasn't an option.

"All right," he said, "but come straight back."

"Yeees, *Dad*," Zoe grinned.

Hayes watched her go, waiting until she stepped through the door before climbing inside the plane, retrieving the drip pans and chock blocks from their spot next to the door and tossing them out.

He set the drip pans below the engines and after kicking the chocks into place, was securing the troop door when the sound of approaching engines drew his attention to the flight line and the army-green Hilux and a Toyota Pathfinder racing toward the plane.

With the door locked, Hayes started toward the nose and was moving around the landing gear when Zoe stepped out of the building.

She crossed toward the plane, head down, eyes locked on the phone in her hand—oblivious to the vehicles until they skidded to a halt in front of her.

Zoe barely had time to react before the soldiers were leaping from the bed of the pickup and moving to block her path. She dodged around the hood and was stepping out into the road when an officer grabbed her by the shoulder.

"Get your hands off me!" she shouted.

"Be quiet!" the man snapped.

But Zoe wasn't having it.

She kicked him hard in the shin, cursing in French as she tried to twist free of his grip.

"I said, be *quiet*!" the officer ordered.

He raised his hand into the air and was about to slap Zoe across the face, when Hayes stepped in behind him.

"I wouldn't do that," he said, pressing the Beretta into the back of the officer's skull.

"You must be Adam Hayes," the officer sneered.

"And you're a dead man if you don't take your hands off her *right now*."

"Very well," he said, releasing his grip.

"Zoe, get in the truck," Hayes ordered, waiting for her to move before shoving the officer toward the Hilux.

The officer turned and studied Hayes, eyes cold as a viper's.

"You got something you want to say?" Hayes glared at him.

"A message from General Dábo," he said.

"Well, spill it, then get the hell out of here, before I revoke your birth certificate."

"The general says, 'Be careful, the streets of Grand-Bassam can be *quite* dangerous.'"

"Is that a threat?"

"Take it as you wish," the man said, pulling down his sunglasses, "but it would be a shame if something happened to Ms. *Cabot.*" The soldier grinned, turned, and strutted back to the Hilux.

Hayes watched the soldier climb into the backseat, the name bouncing around inside his skull like a flaming pinball. But he held his anger in check and waited until the truck had pulled away before he climbed inside the Pathfinder and slammed the door behind him.

"I-is everything okay?" she asked.

"Zoe Cabot, is that your name?"

"What? Who told you that?"

"Just answer the question."

"No, that is not my name," she said defiantly.

But Hayes wasn't buying it.

"Take off your sunglasses," he ordered.

"What . . . why?"

"Because I want to see your eyes."

Zoe recoiled, her face pale, lips quivering when she finally spoke.

"Y-you are sc-scaring me, Mr. Hayes."

"I'm going to do a lot worse than that if you don't do what I tell you," he said, voice cold as ice.

Zoe was shaking, but she complied, and when she pulled the sunglasses from her face, the fear in her blue eyes was palpable.

But Hayes was too pissed to care. He was tired of the lies, fed up with being moved around the board like a pawn.

*This isn't a game, it's my life.*

"I want you to listen very carefully, because I am only going to ask you this once. Either you tell me the truth or you're on your own. Do you understand?"

"Yes," she said in a tiny voice.

"Good. Now tell me, is your father Andre Cabot?"

**30**

LANGLEY, VIRGINIA

Ten hours after leaving Site Tango, Mike Carpenter was in his office, the six a.m. meeting he'd had with Senator Miles replaying in his head.

"I don't care *what* you do or *how* you do it, but I want Shaw dead by the end of the week. The man is a liability."

"Yes, sir," Carpenter had said, nodding, his head fogged in from lack of sleep.

"Now I realize that going after one of your own isn't an easy ask," Miles had added, his early aggressive tone softening. "But if you make this happen, I promise that by the end of the year, you'll be sitting in the director's chair."

"Consider it done, sir."

"That's what I like to hear."

Contrary to the senator's presumptions, Carpenter didn't have any qualms about killing Shaw. For him the man was just another speed bump—a minor obstacle to be hurdled on his way to the top of the CIA.

But while the acceptance of the order had been easy, the *execution* was proving to be a different story.

When he first came to the Directorate of Operations in the early '80s, Carpenter had a Rolodex full of former Cold Warriors. Meat eaters who'd mastered their dark arts in the back alleys and shadowy streets of Soviet Europe.

Back then he could have revoked Shaw's birth certificate with a single phone call.

But September 11 had fundamentally changed the way America prosecuted a war. If Shaw had been a Muslim extremist hiding out in the windswept mountains of Yemen, or a cave in Afghanistan, Carpenter could have sent a Hellfire down his chimney. Or sent a JSOC kill team to blow down his door and smoke him in his bed. But this was the United States and killing a man like Levi Shaw was going to require a deft touch.

The only problem was the CIA wasn't exactly known for its finesse.

*It's got to look like an accident.*

The first option was to hit him at home. Carpenter wondered how difficult it would be to hack into the smart meter outside of Shaw's Alexandria residence and fill the house full of gas—blow his ass up while he was sleeping in his La-Z-Boy.

But he abandoned the idea, knowing that no matter how skilled the hacker, it was impossible *not* to leave fingerprints.

No, he needed to do it the old-fashioned way. In public, with plenty of witnesses to describe the scene to the local police.

*But how?*

Sitting in the back of the Suburban at five-thirty that night, Carpenter still didn't have an answer.

*The hell with it,* he thought, turning his attention to the line of brake lights he saw through the windshield.

"What's going on?" he asked his driver.

"Damn DDOT, tearing up the beltway again," he said, double-checking the sideview mirror in preparation for merging to the outside lane.

As the SUV shifted left, Carpenter found himself instinctively looking over his shoulder, and he was about to tell his driver that he was clear to come over when a Porsche came racing up from behind, its driver rapidly blinking the headlights as he cut across two lanes of traffic.

"Surely this asshole isn't about to—" he began.

But before the words were out of his mouth, the German sports car was slashing past the Suburban, narrowly missing the bumper.

"Damn, that was close," he said, turning back to the front.

"It was safer driving in Iraq," his driver said, flashing him a smile in the rearview. "At least over there you could actually shoot back."

*How did I not see it before?*

Carpenter didn't know, but he immediately pulled the Moleskine notebook from his coat pocket and got to work.

He spent the rest of the ride in silence—nurturing the ember of the plan forming in the dark recesses of his mind—working out the logistics: the time of day, how many men he would need, and where to set the kill zone.

Carpenter was firing on all cylinders, and by the time he climbed out of the Suburban and started for his front door, he knew that Shaw was as good as dead.

**31**

## GRAND-BASSAM

While there were many villages along Ivory Coast's south-eastern shore with access to the ocean, it was Grand-Bassam's strategic location at the mouth of the Comoé river that led the French to choose it as their colonial capital.

Within weeks of settling the area, French engineers were busy constructing the docks. Months later, the first merchant ships begun to arrive from Europe. The goods packed into their bulging hulls were immediately transferred into canoes and transported upriver.

This never-ending flow of goods going out and cash coming in soon transformed this once sleepy fishing village into the crown jewel of French colonial Africa.

Hayes had seen the pictures of the town in its prime—the

white stucco villas the merchant princes built for themselves, the stately French Colonial government buildings, and the cobblestone promenades that lead to the town square.

But as they approached the outskirts of Grand-Bassam, it was immediately obvious that time had not been kind.

What had once been hailed as "little Paris" was gone. Its streets had been torn up, the bricks used to build houses in the northern section of town. The villas that were still standing were now cadaverous caricatures of their former selves, the shattered doorways and empty window casements yawning black as the eye sockets of a skull.

"You sure this is the place?" he asked.

"This is the old town," Zoe said. "It was abandoned in 1896 during the yellow fever epidemic."

"So, it gets better?"

"Much," she said, motioning for him to take a right at the next intersection.

The road took them south and the ruins of the old town gave way to modern buildings and sidewalks full of pink-faced tourists.

"See," Zoe said, pointing to a pair of blond-haired girls in bikinis walking arm in arm down the sidewalk. "Perfectly safe."

"For them, maybe," he muttered.

"What was that?"

"Never mind," he said.

He parked in front of the Hôtel la Commanderie and hopped out, grabbing her bag from the back of the car.

Hayes wasn't sure what it was about the girl that fired up the protector in him. Maybe it was the innocence he saw in her eyes, or the pained frown when she talked about her father, but whatever it was, he wasn't leaving until he was sure that she was safe.

"Want to join me for lunch?" Zoe asked before climbing out.

"Not sure I can afford this place," Hayes answered, eyeing the doorman.

"Daddy's paying," she said with a grin.

"In that case, lead on."

Just as they finished a delicious meal, Zoe's phone vibrated across the table, and Hayes glanced down, memorizing the number on the display before she scooped it up.

"It's Jean Luc," she said, picking up the phone.

"We are pulling up now," a voice said in French, "you need to be ready to move."

"I will meet you at the door," Zoe said in French, ending the call. "I've got to go."

Despite the previous ten years of practice, Hayes sucked at good-byes, mainly because he never knew what to say. Most of the time he went with the tried and true "have a safe trip," followed by a handshake, but for some reason this time it didn't seem to fit.

"You got everything?" he asked lamely.

"I think so," Zoe answered, sliding her phone into her back pocket and shouldering her backpack.

"Well . . . all right, then," he said, sticking out his hand.

But instead of taking his hand, Zoe stepped in and wrapped her arms around him.

"Thank you," she said.

Caught off guard by the embrace, all Hayes could think to do was give her a friendly pat on the back followed by, "Yeah, sure . . . no problem . . ."

He was wondering if he should walk her out but was saved from the decision by the arrival of three black Land Rovers.

The convoy pulled up to the front door and before the lead vehicle had come to a complete stop, a serious-looking man in a desert-tan plate carrier hopped out of the second SUV and bounded into the hotel.

"Oh, I forgot *l'addition*—the bill," she said.

"Don't worry about it."

"Are you sure?"

"Yeah, no problem."

"Zoe, let's go," the man at the door snapped.

"Better get going," Hayes said.

She turned to leave, but only made it a few steps before spinning on her heel and hurrying back.

The sudden about-face caught Hayes off guard and he was about to ask if everything was okay, but before the words could form, Zoe pushed herself up on her tiptoes and kissed him lightly on the cheek.

"Wh-what was that for?" Hayes stammered.

"For being a good man," she said.

"Zoe, we have to go now!" the man at the door barked, and then she was gone, her shoes *click-clack*ing on the floor as she scurried across the lobby and out the door.

*Good luck, kid,* he thought as the man marched her to the SUV.

Hayes paid the bill and grabbed his bag and was thinking of using some of Mallory's cash to get a room for the night when he heard the waitress's voice behind him.

"Excuse me, but the mademoiselle, she left this on the table."

*Shit, her insulin.*

Hayes snatched the case from her hand with a hurried "thank you" and shot across the lobby. He was halfway to the door when the lead Land Rover pulled away and, knowing he wasn't going to make it in time, he shouted at the doorman, "Stop that truck!"

"*Quoi?*" the puzzled doorman asked.

"The truck—*le camion*—stop the fucking truck!"

But by the time the man figured out what he wanted it was too late.

"Good job, Stevie Wonder," Hayes spat before shouldering past the doorman and blasting out into the porte cochère in time to see the convoy already halfway around the circular drive.

He hurtled the hedges and ran across the lawn, angling for the trail Land Rover ten yards away. Hayes ran straight at the driver's-side door, screaming at the top of his lungs and frantically waving the case over his head, desperate to get the man's attention.

He wasn't sure if the driver simply hadn't seen him or if he had orders not to stop. Whichever the case, the man never checked up and by the time Hayes made it to the drive all that was left of the Land Rover was a cloud of dust.

It was barely twenty yards from the front of the hotel to his current location, but the heat plus the prawns and rice he'd stuffed down his throat at lunch left him feeling sluggish. He slowed his pace, breathing heavily through his mouth.

Hayes knew that if *he* was running Zoe's protective detail, he would have made sure that each truck had extra insulin just in case something happened.

*You willing to bet her life on that?* the voice asked.

Hell, no, he thought.

Hayes shoved the case into his back pocket and forced himself into a loping run, angling for the line of shrubs that separated the hotel property from the road. He ran hard, legs pumping like pistons as he charged across the grass and dodged around the knot of spectators who'd gathered at the edge of the sand volleyball courts.

By the time he made it up the gentle incline and stopped before the hedges he was soaked in sweat and the skin around his hip was raw from the sandpaper rub of the Beretta's grip. But the physical discomforts vanished when he made it to his destination.

From the inside of the Pathfinder there'd been nothing daunting about the decorative shrubs that marked the edge of the hotel's property, but the view from the ground was a different story. What he'd thought were decorative shrubs were actually more akin to the hedgerows the allies had faced in Normandy—too tall to jump over and too thick to plow through.

*Just great,* he thought.

Hayes dropped into a crouch and scanned the bottom of the brush. He found what he was looking for a few yards to his left: a rectangular break at the bottom of the bush wide enough to accommodate a man of his size.

With no time to waste, Hayes threw himself flat and began low-crawling beneath the bush. It was easy going for the first few inches, but then the space started to narrow, and the only way Hayes could continue was by keeping his arms pressed tight against his sides.

Hampered by the tight confines, and with only his feet to propel him, Hayes was in no position to defend himself from the swarm of mosquitoes attracted to his body heat. All he could do was curse ineffectually while they bit his face and darted in and out of his mouth.

He twisted and turned his upper body, drilling through the undergrowth, the volume of his curses growing with each branch that raked his skin. The sidewalk was less than a yard to his front and Hayes knew by the slowing of the foot traffic that the pedestrians could hear him, but he was beyond giving a shit.

With a final push of his legs he wormed free of the bushes and climbed to his feet, ignoring the open-mouthed stares of the pedestrians on their way to the beach. He patted his back pocket, and after making sure he still had the case, was brushing the leaves and dirt out of his hair. He turned to his left and started down the walk, toward the intersection half a block away.

From his position on the south side of the street his view was limited by the row of budget hotels and a large white triangular building at the corner, but he had a clear view of the traffic running east and west and was almost in position when the convoy made the turn onto Route d'Azuretti, engines howling as the drivers stomped on the gas.

Hayes shot a glance over his shoulder and wasn't surprised to see a man in a floral shirt standing at the crosswalk, the toe of his sandaled foot tapping on the concrete as he waited for a break in traffic. It was perfectly normal behavior for Europe or the States. But this was Africa, where there was no such thing as a "licensed driver" and traffic laws were treated more like suggestions than rules. Hayes had spent enough time on the continent to know that waiting for a break in traffic before crossing the street could take hours.

Time Hayes *didn't* have to waste.

By the time he looked back to the west, the convoy was halfway to the intersection, and while the jury was still out about the man in the tan plate carrier, there was no doubt about the men behind the wheels. They were pros and they dissected the traffic with a surgical precision, never allowing more than three feet of separation between each vehicle as they raced toward the intersection.

After watching them drive, Hayes knew the convoy wasn't going to sit around and wait for him to cross the street. He had to go—now.

During his time in Africa, Hayes had been amazed by the ethnic and cultural barriers that spanned the country. Even with his practiced ear for language and preternatural ability to absorb the local cultures, he was constantly reminded that he was an outsider.

But at the end of the day, Hayes knew that no matter where you were in the world or what language was being spoken, there were two things that needed no translation: cash and guns.

"Well, I'm sorry it had to come to this," he said, drawing the Beretta from his hip.

Hayes stepped out into the street. Before he had a chance to level the pistol on the rusted bread truck barreling toward him, the driver had locked up the brakes. He got the same results with the rider of the red moped occupying the inside lane.

"You fucking crazy, man?" the rider demanded in French.

"No, just late," Hayes replied, checking the soldiers at the end of the block before stepping onto the concrete median that separated the four-lane road.

As a singleton operator, Hayes knew that his survivability hinged on *not* drawing attention to himself. But like all men in his position, he was a natural gambler, and while the stunt with the pistol had broken one of the cardinal rules of the profession, the gamble had paid off. Not only had the soldiers at the end of the block *not* noticed the gun, as an added bonus, the ripple effect from the bread truck had snarled the traffic.

While the Land Rovers tried to extricate themselves from the traffic, Hayes jogged across the street. He hopped onto the sidewalk and weaved through the window-shoppers milling outside the shops selling handmade souvenirs.

"You want a keychain?" one of the vendors asked.

Hayes shook his head *no* without breaking stride, and by the time he was nearing the final shop, the lead vehicle was pulling into the turn lane. He pulled the case from his back pocket and was shifting left, trying to get into the driver's line of sight, when the familiar brush of cold air up the back of his neck stopped him dead in his tracks.

In an instant he saw it all: the pedestrians streaming down the sidewalk, the Land Rover inching forward, its driver ready for the left-hand turn that would take the convoy northbound, away from Hayes and the hotel.

Then, like a scratched DVD, the scene jumped back into real time—the crash of the glass shattering followed by the banshee scream of the RPG from the window, and the chalk-white tail as it screamed across the street, slamming into the hood of the lead Land Rover.

Then he saw it—a flicker of movement, a figure standing on the roof of the building across the street, a flash of flame from the tube on his shoulder followed by the bloodcurdling wail of the RPG.

# 32

GRAND-BASSAM

The heat scalded Hayes's skin. He raised his arms to his face and was turning away, trying to get to cover, when the overpressure swatted him off his feet and sent him tumbling toward a Peugeot 504 stopped in the middle of the road.

He hit hard, the impact spiderwebbing the glass beneath him, the crack of his skull against the pillar turning the world black.

It was the pain that brought him back. The dull ache that started in his lower back and raced up his spine like a fuse. His eyes fluttered open, but instead of the earlier blue sky and bright sun, the street was on fire. Thick black smoke coiled from the burnt-out Land Rover, the air dense with the scent of comp B and the muted screams of tourists over the staccato chatter of gunfire.

Hayes twisted free of the glass, rolled across the hood, and dropped into the gutter. He shook his head, tried to clear the fog, and pushed himself up to a knee, where he conducted a functions check: inspected his body for any holes, tears, or broken bones. When he was sure there was nothing wrong that a few aspirin couldn't fix, he turned his attention to the street and the firefight unfolding twenty yards to his front.

After being hit by the RPG, the lead Land Rover had rolled across the intersection, bumped over the curb, and nosed into a building, where it sat burning like a funeral pyre. The rest of the convoy was still in the turn lane, boxed in by a pair of brown Ford Excursions and under fire from men in gas masks and black body armor.

Hayes studied the scene, noting the deployment of the Excursions and the knot of assaulters as they flowed toward the convoy—the lead shooters keeping a steady rate of fire on the vehicles while the security element fired canisters of CS gas toward the street.

It was a textbook ambush and Hayes realized that whoever had planned it knew what they were doing. But while the plan was conceptually solid, all it took was one look at the closest Excursion for Hayes to find a flaw in the execution.

For a blocking position to work, a driver must pin the target vehicle in place, either against an immovable object or by—

But the driver had stopped short, leaving a gap that the driver of the Land Rover was working to exploit.

The driver shifted into reverse, cranked the wheel hard over, and backed up.

"Keep going," Hayes urged, but the driver didn't listen and immediately shifted into gear and stomped on the gas.

Then everything went to shit.

But before he could exploit the situation, one of the security men saw him standing there and sent a gas canister skipping down the street. It hit ten feet in front of him, bounced into the air, and exploded in a chalk-white cloud.

*Looks like that's our cue,* the voice urged.

Hayes had been gassed enough times to know he didn't want anything to do with the cloud of CS coming his way, but instead of turning to leave, he dropped to a knee, eyes locked on Zoe's Land Rover.

*They're not going to make it.*

The thought had no sooner crossed his mind than the Land Rover slammed into the Excursion's front quarter panel.

*Just stay down. It's not your fight,* the voice said.

For once, Hayes had to agree.

He'd done his job. Held up his end of the agreement when he delivered Zoe to the hotel. *The rest is up to her protection team.*

The thought had no sooner crossed his mind than the right passenger-side door of the second Land Rover was flung open and the man in the tan plate carrier bailed out.

He laid his rifle against the doorpost and yelled, "Get on line," before opening up on his attackers.

The rest of the security team bailed out of the SUVs, formed up at the back of the Land Rover, and began laying down a base of fire.

"Set," one of the men yelled.

The moment the team leader heard the command, he stopped firing and tore a smoke grenade from his kit. He pulled the pin, and after flinging it toward their attackers, moved to the back door of the Land Rover and pulled Zoe out.

During his time in Afghanistan, Hayes had been forced to

break contact when his team came under fire by larger elements. When this occurred, the time-tested method for getting the hell out of Dodge was the "peel drill."

On paper the tactic was simple enough—the team was formed into a column with the number one man suppressing the enemy on full auto. Once the shooter ran out of ammo, he "peeled off" from the column, allowing the next man in line to open fire while he retreated back the way they'd come.

It was the perfect tactic for the situation and would have worked *if* the man in the tan plate carrier hadn't taken a bullet to the back of the skull.

*Shit.*

The moment the team leader went down, it was every man for himself, with the majority of the team turning west and rushing back the way they'd come. Leaving Zoe quivering in fear beside the dead man.

"You sons of bitches," he said, tugging the Beretta free.

The man with the launcher was in the process of sending another canister toward the Peugeot when Hayes burst from cover. The man hastily fired the munition and dropped the launcher, hands scrambling for the MP5 hanging from the sling around his neck. His hand was just closing around the pistol grip when Hayes hit him with a controlled pair to the chest.

The gas enveloped Hayes like artificial fog, clawing at his eyes, the particles sticking to his sweaty skin, burning his face like battery acid—robbing him of his bearings.

The visibility was shit and it only got worse as he closed in on the convoy. If that wasn't bad enough, he also had to contend with the motorists and tourists fleeing the gunfire. Every time one of the faceless, elongated silhouettes stepped into his path, the

Beretta snapped on target and Hayes had a split second to decide if they were friend or foe.

The security element, on the other hand, had no such qualms and were soon firing bursts of automatic fire into anyone dumb enough to cross the street. Hayes was running out of air, his vision darkening at the edges, feeling more than hearing the rounds zipping past his head.

A man raced in from right to left, orange tracer fire following him across the street. "Get down," Hayes yelled in French. He ran to the man, tried to grab him and wrestle him to the ground, but before his hand closed around the man's arm, a bullet found its mark and the man dropped like a marionette with cut strings.

*Just keep moving.*

Using the muzzle flashes as his guide, Hayes lurched forward, all too aware that if he ran into one of the shooters with a gas mask, he was as dead as disco.

If he wanted to escape the battery acid burn of the gas in his lungs, all he had to do was turn back the way he'd come. The fresh air would clear the chemicals from his system, but he stayed the course, the pistol in his right hand up, left arm sweeping in front of him like a blind man's cane, the only break in his stride a momentary pause to vomit.

Hayes felt the metal of the Excursion with his hand a split second before his forehead slammed into its side with a hollow *thunk*. He staggered backward, cursing, and dropped to a crouch, searching for the body of the man he'd shot.

He brushed rubber and, thinking he was back at the tire, was just about to turn around when he felt a boot, then a leg.

*Thank God.*

He ran his hand up the man's body until he reached the gas

mask. He set his pistol on the ground and ripped the mask free. Working by feel and the muscle memory etched during the hour he'd spent in the gas chamber at Fort Benning, he grabbed the elastic straps, hooked them over the protective lenses, and pressed the inner mask against his face. Holding his palm flat against the outlet valve, Hayes blew out a hard breath, clearing the contaminated air from the mask before pulling the straps tight over his head.

With the mask secured to his face, Hayes was protected from additional exposure to the gas, but he knew the only things that would reverse the effects he'd already sustained were time and clean water—both of which were currently in short supply.

Hayes stuffed the Beretta into his waistband and stripped the dead man of his rifle. He dropped the magazine and pushed his thumb down on the exposed bullet at the top of the mag, the spring tension telling him it was topped off. In one smooth motion he slammed the magazine home and slapped the charging handle. The reassuring *chunk* of the bolt told him that a bullet was in the chamber.

*Time to stack some bodies.*

He moved around the back of the van at a crouch and paused at the bumper to peek out. The fog had yet to dissipate, and even with the mask protecting his eyes, the shooters looked more like shadows—dark, body-armored blobs with disembodied heads— than men.

Any other time and he would have tried to get close enough to positively identify his targets before opening fire. But with the man before him actively firing at the Land Rover, Hayes didn't have a problem skipping a step.

He thumbed the selector to fire, centered the rifle's EOTech holographic sight on the back of the shooter's head, and fired. Thanks to the MP5's mellow recoil, Hayes was able to keep the reticle on target and was ready to send another round when he saw a puff of pink mist that told him there was no need.

*One down.*

Hayes hooked around the bumper, closing in on the flash of rifles and the muted voices shouting just out of sight. He paused at the front tire, hesitant to step out into the open until he had a better grasp on the situation, but all too aware of the ticking clock in his head to stop.

He knew he needed to move, to make something happen while he still had a chance, but what?

Hayes was considering his options when a stiff ocean breeze danced across the street. The wind cut through the cloud of gas like a straight razor.

Then he saw her standing at the rear of the SUV, screaming in fear as one of the men grabbed her by the arm.

"Nooooo," she screamed, slapping at the man's face and biting at his hands when he tried to pull a black bag over her head.

"Quiet, bitch," the man ordered, slapping her hard across the face.

The blow buckled her knees and Zoe sagged against the SUV and would have dropped to her knees if the man hadn't kept her upright.

The wet-handed smack of flesh on flesh lit the rage brewing in Hayes's heart and he stepped out, the rifle at his shoulder.

"Contact left," a voice shouted.

Before Hayes could fire on the man holding Zoe, bullets came snapping in from the flank, forcing him back behind the van.

*Shit.*

Hayes leaned out, settled the reticle on the black-clad shooter, knowing he'd rushed the shot the moment his finger touched the trigger.

He managed to fire three shots at the black-clad figure when a second shooter opened up. He ignored the bullets, steadied his aim, and dropped the man with a head shot before pivoting left, finger double-pumping the trigger as he engaged a second man.

The first shot hit the man in the chest and while the ballistic armor kept the bullet from finding flesh, the impact punched him backward into the van. Instead of adjusting his aim, Hayes thumbed the selector to full auto and held the trigger down, let the muzzle rise do the work for him.

The second shot hit an inch higher than the first, and was once again stopped by the plate carrier, but the third found flesh, blowing out the man's throat and leaving a crimson stain on the skin of the bus.

The shooter sagged against the Land Rover, dropping his rifle, fingers clawing at his ruined throat. He held on tight, but Hayes knew from the spurts of arterial spray through his interlocked fingers that he wasn't long for this world.

The crunch of gravel beneath boots drew his attention and he turned to find a third figure charging through the smoke. Hayes swung to engage, but the man was fast and on him and, in an instant, clubbed him in the head with the stock of the rifle. It was a staggering blow that sent him reeling, cracked the seal on his mask, and flooded his lungs with a fresh dose of gas.

Hayes tried to step back, make space, but the man was all over him, slamming the buttstock into his kidney, ripping the MP5 from his grasp, and then grabbing him by the throat.

The fight was up close and personal, all elbows and knees,

close enough for Hayes to feel the man's breath on his face. But, blind and choking on the smoke, there was little he could do but absorb the beating the man was laying on him and wait for an opening.

Finally, the man tried for the knockout blow, firing a loping fist at his head, but Hayes ducked below it, reached up, and ripped the mask from his attacker's face.

"Fucker," the man cursed, breaking off the attack to try and reseal his mask.

Hayes, on the other hand, had no intention of letting up and grabbed the man by the shoulders, pulled him close, and drove his forehead into the man's nose. The cartilage exploded with the crunch of fresh wood and the hot spray of blood over his face.

He bellowed in pain and took a lurching step backward, giving Hayes the space he needed to tear the Beretta from its holster.

Hayes fired two shots into the man's chest, the slap of the 9-millimeter to his chest plate shoving the man backward, giving Hayes the time to line up the head shot. He'd just pulled the trigger, the bullet snapping his target's head back, when he heard the roar of an engine.

He glanced right in time to see the Excursion blast through the smoke, its grille guard big as a billboard.

Hayes threw himself clear, the rush of the passing SUV tearing at his clothes. He ducked his head and, rolling over his shoulder, came up in a crouch, the Beretta bucking in his hand.

It was an impotent gesture and he knew it. Knew that any damage the 9-millimeter did to the truck was cosmetic, but he didn't care. Hayes was pissed. The rage that had begun as a flicker of flame had grown to a raging inferno, the heat and pressure building inside of him, leaving Hayes at critical mass.

The bullets shattered the back glass, but the driver kept the accelerator pinned to the floor and swung the Excursion into a screeching left turn, Hayes dropping the empty magazine, stripping the spare from his belt and slamming it into the pistol.

But by the time he dropped the slide and got back on target, the Excursion was racing north—well out of range of the pistol.

Hayes slammed the pistol into its holster. The silence that followed the gunfight was deafening, broken only by the ringing in his ears and the wounded cries of the innocents scattered around the street.

His heart went out to them, but the distant wail of sirens told Hayes that medical personnel were on their way—Zoe, on the other hand, was on her own.

He needed to go now, before it was too late, before the police made the scene and threw him in cuffs. But instead of heading back to the hotel, jumping into the Pathfinder, and driving like a bat out of hell to the airport, Hayes bent down, snatched the submachine gun from one of the dead, and started toward the dark-green motorcycle lying abandoned in the roadway.

*What the hell are you doing?* the voice demanded. *This is* not *your fight.*

"It is now."

# 33

GRAND-BASSAM

Hayes slung the submachine gun and squatted beside the downed Ducati Multistrada, pressed his back against the seat, and got his feet set beneath him. He took a breath and pushed off with his legs, the skin on his forearm sizzling like bacon against the exhaust pipe as he worked to get the five-hundred-pound Ducati onto its wheels.

*Of all the motorcycles in Africa, how is it I've got to find the heaviest son of a bitch on the road?*

Finally, he got it upright, and after swinging the sub gun around to the small of his back, Hayes reached across and thumbed the starter.

It cranked right up, and Hayes hopped on, spun the bike north, and twisted hard on the throttle. The Ducati shot forward,

Hayes working through the gears, hoping whoever owned the bike had full coverage, as he raced after the fleeing Excursion.

The Ducati Multistrada was designed as a dual-purpose bike, a hybrid that combined the performance of a sport bike and the long-distance capability of a touring model. Thanks to its 1200cc liquid-cooled engine, by the time Hayes hit the bridge the needle was already sweeping past sixty miles per hour.

From the peak he glimpsed the road ahead—the Excursion weaving in and out of traffic. The solid-steel brush guard, combined with the driver's aggressive tactics, left the motorists in its path two choices—get out of the way or get run over.

Hayes had grown up riding motorcycles. He'd started with dirt bikes, 250cc Yamahas that were great for cruising the back roads of his native Tennessee, but too slow—and illegal—to ride on the street.

Hayes would have to wait until he turned sixteen and got a driver's license before graduating to the much bigger and faster street bikes. The rush that came with being on the open road, the wind in his hair, warm sun on his face, was exhilarating.

It was also dangerous as hell, and even though he'd never been in an accident, all he could think about as he started down the hill was what his father had told him when he first got that street bike: "Son, there are two types of bikers in this world—those who have wrecked and those who will wreck."

Hayes wasn't sure where the memory came from, if it was a portent of his impending doom or just his subconscious screwing with him. Either way, the time for thinking had passed. He was committed, and it was either focus on the cars ahead or end up feeding the vultures perched atop the power lines.

He shifted into sixth gear, leaned low over the handlebars,

and blanked his mind. At lower speeds Hayes had felt every bump, every defect in the road, but at eighty miles an hour the Ducati settled in and all it took was the slightest shift of his weight to send the bike cutting to the left.

Hayes centered the front tire on the white dotted line and shot the gap, the engine echoing off the line of cars on either side. At this speed he knew all it would take was for one driver to open his door or veer out of his lane and he was done. Finished. But with a mile between him and the target vehicle, it was a risk Hayes had to take.

In the distance, the driver of the Excursion swerved into the right lane, and knowing that he had to get over, Hayes downshifted, slowing the bike while searching the line of cars for a break in the vehicles. He squeezed the brake and dropped into fourth gear, knowing that if the truck turned while he was boxed in it was game over.

But the line of cars remained unbroken, the traffic bumper to bumper for as far as he could see.

The Excursion's brake lights flashed; it was about to turn, and Hayes was still stuck in the center lane and unable to get over.

He was about ready to start shooting out tires when the engine gave out on an overloaded work truck twenty-five yards in front of him. The driver of the injured truck hit the brakes and the moment Hayes saw the hole in the traffic, he was back on the throttle.

Hayes let the RPMs rise, waiting until the engine was screaming beneath him before shifting gears, and then he was leaning left, slicing around the work truck and into the right-hand lane, rushing after the Excursion.

He pushed the Ducati hard, careful to keep the tires to the left of the seam that demarcated the roadway from the shoulder and rocketed after the massive SUV as it made the right-hand turn off the highway.

*Don't lose them.*

As Hayes neared the turn, he let off the gas and downshifted, using the transmission to slow the bike.

*You're too fast,* the voice warned, but Hayes was already committed.

He leaned into the turn, shoving hard on the inner bar, knee hovering dangerously close to the asphalt. With his eyes locked on the spot he wanted the bike to go, all he had left to do was hold on.

There was nothing natural about taking a turn at a high rate of speed, and while Hayes knew the laws of physics were on his side, his brain screamed at him to slam on the brakes. But he resisted the urge, all too aware that this far into the turn, even the slightest touch of the brakes could send him flying off the bike.

Hayes held his line, carving the Ducati around the apex of the turn, waiting until the road straightened out before shifting his weight back to the center and rolling the throttle.

Two hundred yards ahead, the Excursion chugged sluggishly down the road. The heavy SUV was still trying to regain the speed it had lost negotiating the turn.

*Got you.*

Up to that point his only concern was catching up with his prey, and now that he'd done it, Hayes realized he had another problem.

*How the hell am I going to stop that thing?*

The easiest and most effective way to stop a car in motion was to kill the driver, but with Zoe unsecured in the backseat, he couldn't take the risk. Shooting out the tires posed the same risk, and Hayes realized the only option that didn't end up with Zoe in the morgue was to get inside the truck.

*But how in the hell am I going to pull that one off?*

Then he saw it, the gaping black maw that had once been the Excursion's back window.

*You're not really going to . . . ?* the voice began.

"Oh, yeah," he answered, twisting the throttle.

In Hayes's experience, the key to pulling off a high-risk maneuver had nothing to do with the plan and everything to do with his ability to execute before his brain caught up with his balls.

Wishing he had a helmet, Hayes set the cruise control and brought his feet up to the seat. The bike wobbled beneath him, but he got his balance and inched up into a crouch. Still holding on to the handlebars, Hayes cleared his mind.

He blocked out the road racing beneath him and the buffeting crosswind threatening to swat him off the bike, focusing on nothing but the impossibly small rectangle of shattered glass that was his target.

Timing was everything, and at the last instant, Hayes shifted his gaze to the Ducati's front tire and the rapidly diminishing space that separated it from the Excursion's back bumper. Knowing that if he didn't get the jump right, instead of sailing into the SUV, the collision would pile-drive him into the rear end.

Wait for it . . . wait for it . . . *now!*

Using the handlebars as an anchor, Hayes catapulted himself over the windscreen a split second before the Ducati slammed into the back of the SUV. And then he was airborne, the added force of the collision slingshotting him through the shattered window and into the back of the Excursion.

At fifty miles an hour, he had barely enough time to brace for impact. He turtled his head into his shoulders and brought his hands up to cover his face before slamming into the pair of kitted-up goons who were trying to get a zip-tie around Zoe's wrist.

Hayes bowled them over and went pinballing through the gap between the driver and passenger seat, thumping hard against the dash. The only thing that saved him from a broken back was the bulging assault pack strapped to his shoulders.

"Shit . . . that . . . hurt . . ." he grunted.

The sudden arrival of the bloodied man in their midst threw the Excursion into an uproar and Hayes took advantage of the confusion, bringing his leg up to his chest and slamming a size twelve hiking boot into the passenger's face. He ricocheted the man's head off the window hard enough to shatter the glass.

"Adam . . . help me!"

"Get to the door!" Hayes yelled.

He crunched up into a sitting position and was reaching for the wheel when the driver hit him with a backhand to the face that laid him flat. The blow starred his vision, but he was quick to recover. While the driver went for the pistol holstered on the front of his kit, Hayes snatched the Microtech Troodon from his pocket.

"Too slow," he said, pressing the thumb release on the spine of the knife.

The blade deployed with a snap, and Hayes spun the handle, flipped it into an underhand grip, and buried the blade in the driver's thigh. The driver's first reaction was to pull away from the blade, and he let off the gas, hand still going for the pistol.

Hayes yanked the knife free with a hard twist, brought it up to center, and spiked it through the man's forearm with enough force to bury the tip of the blade into the PMAG on the man's chest.

"That'll hold ya for a second," Hayes said, reaching down between the man's legs and grabbing the seat adjustment bar.

He yanked up and, using his shoulder, pushed the seat toward the rear, feeling the Excursion slow as the pressure on the accelerator was relieved. He was reaching across the floorboard, trying to engage the emergency brake, desperate to stop the SUV, when Zoe's captors recovered.

"Come here, you bastard," one of the men shouted, grabbing Hayes by the legs and yanking him into the backseat, power-slamming him onto the floorboards, Zoe screaming in his ear.

"Heeelp meeee!"

Then the man was all over him, holding him by the throat with one hand and trying to beat his face in with the other.

Hayes ate the first punch, but when the man reared back for a second one, Hayes shrimped onto his side and coiled a leg around his torso. Grabbing the man's forearm with his hand and pushing with his leg, he was able to shove him off balance. The move created just enough space for Hayes to hit him with an elbow to the temple.

The man sagged, and Hayes shoved him into his dazed teammate, turned onto his stomach, and scrambled for the door handle.

"Zoe, we have to jump!" he yelled, shoving the door open.

"I—I can't!" she screamed.

She was terrified, the fear in her eyes palpable, but it was the only way.

"You can do it," he said, grabbing her by the shoulder and inching her toward the door.

"Noooo . . . I—I can't . . ." she wailed.

"Yes, you can," he said, turning her to the open door.

For a moment he thought he had her, but then she looked down, saw the blurring asphalt outside the Excursion, and in the next instant she was clawing at his face, twisting against his grip like a cat over running water.

*Just hit her and throw her ass out,* the voice snapped.

He knew it was the right call, but growing up in the South, Hayes had been taught from an early age that there was nothing worse than a man who put his hands on a woman. And even now, with both of their lives hanging in the balance, he found himself unable to do what needed to be done.

"Just close your eyes and—"

The words were cut off by the slam of something hard against the back of his skull, followed by a pair of rough hands grabbing him by the belt. A man kicked him in the arm, breaking Hayes's grip on Zoe's shoulders, and then lifted him off the floor.

"You want to jump . . . then have at it," the voice said, and then he flung Hayes out the open door.

# 34

I t was hot on the tarmac and Cyrus Vandal was sweating, the clothes he wore beneath the insulated flight suit wet against his skin. He dug out the tube of amphetamines he'd been issued before leaving the States thirteen hours before and popped the orange pill into his mouth, chasing it with a long gulp from the bottle of water. Only then did he start walking toward the MC-130 Talon that was idling in the darkness.

Vandal waddled up the ramp, weighed down by the rucksack hanging upside down between his legs and the bulky cargo bag in his hand.

Inside the Talon's cargo hold, the Special Operations jump-master assigned to the insertion double-checked the connections on the MC-4 Ram Air parachute strapped to his back and the gear strapped to his body. It was a job he'd done thousands of times. He worked in silence, tapping each connector, tugging on each strap, his face blank in the muted glow of the red light that illuminated the cargo hold.

When he was satisfied, the jumpmaster disconnected the hose connected to the bail-out bottle on his hip and clipped the end into the Talon's onboard $O_2$. Vandal tested the flow and gave him a thumbs-up before lowering himself onto the nylon bench.

"Good to go. We'll be airborne shortly," the jumpmaster yelled over the roar of the engines.

Vandal nodded, and while the crew chief closed and secured the ramp, he leaned back and rested his helmet against the bulkhead, staring up at the exposed wires and cables that ran the length of the cargo hold.

Thirty seconds after the crew chief buckled in, the Talon was rolling, shaking like a washing machine on meth as it raced down the runway and leapt into the air.

Vandal had been up for twenty-four hours and was exhausted. His eyes were hot from lack of sleep and his throat dry as a bone from the combination of dehydration that accompanied the long flight and the flow of pure oxygen from his mask.

*Just going to close my eyes for a second.*

The relief was immediate, and while he waited for the chem to kick in, his mind worked to play catchup—digest the flurry of information that had consumed the previous day.

As a Marine Raider, Vandal was well aware of Special Operation Command's long reach. Their ability to find the nation's enemies, fix them in place, and then send in teams to finish them was unparalleled. But he was still marveling at how the techs at the Signals Intercept and Analysis Lab had been able to not only locate his target but track him during the fifteen hundred miles to Luanda.

But they had, and now the rest was up to him.

The chems kicked in shortly after takeoff and the initial dump of amphetamines hit his flagging nervous system like kerosene to a fire. One second Vandal could barely open his eyes and in the next instant he was wide awake and focused—ready to take on the world.

Fifty minutes later he was standing at the open ramp, watching the horizon pitch through the night-vision goggles attached to his helmet as the pilot rolled the Talon into its final approach. Vandal braced himself against the strut, the weight of his gear threatening to bend him double, the wind cutting at him like an icy flail.

At thirty thousand feet the air was negative forty degrees and even with the insulated jumpsuit and the speed rushing through his blood, Vandal was shivering. His hands were numb inside his Gore-Tex gloves.

He pushed all the discomfort from his mind and turned his attention to the red jump light and began counting the seconds in his head until it was go time.

*One one thousand. Two one thousand. Three one thousand. Now.*

Right on time, the light blinked green and Vandal took three steps forward and flung himself into the abyss. He locked his body into position—arched his back, held his arms and legs tight while ducking his head, and was soon falling at one hundred and twenty miles an hour. Rocketing through the slate-gray clouds like a demon cast down from heaven.

Four seconds after exiting the aircraft, his chute deployed and caught air, jerking him to a halt. He looked up, checked the canopy for holes, and grabbed the steering toggles, before checking the compass on his tac board.

Seeing that he was off his azimuth, Vandal pulled down on the toggle, steered back on course, and after using the GPS strapped to his wrist to check his ground speed, settled in for the ride.

At four thousand feet he came out of the clouds and got his first glimpse of the ground: the Bondo-gray earth to his front and the India ink shimmer of the Atlantic Ocean off to his right. He activated the remote infrared beacon that had been inserted before him and spent the next twenty seconds searching the mass of green ahead.

Then he saw it, a persistent yellow blink from a clearing five degrees to his right. Vandal gave the toggle a gentle tug, centering up on the beacon.

At higher altitudes it had been impossible to judge exactly how fast he was falling, but as he broke a hundred feet the ground came rushing up at him, forcing him to yank down hard on the toggles to slow his descent.

Then he was down, the canopy collapsing around him as his feet touched the ground.

He worked fast, disconnecting the riser straps and releasing the gear clips—the canopy billowing like a dying jellyfish as he ripped the suppressed H&K MP7 from his gear bag and scanned his surroundings.

But the only sign of life was the yellow blinking of the infrared strobe attached to the roof of the Toyota 4Runner waiting for him in the tree line.

When he was sure that he was alone, Vandal pulled off his gloves and stepped out of the insulated suit. Using a collapsible shovel, he buried his chute and jump gear, and after loading his pack and gear bag into the back of the SUV, it was time to go hunting.

# 35

## GRAND-BASSAM

An hour after being thrown from the Excursion, Hayes parked in the shadows at the edge of the convenience store lot and cut the engine. He climbed out of the Mitsubishi SUV he'd carjacked on the highway and gingerly shifted some of his weight onto his left.

*Son of a bitch,* he thought, biting down on the pain that rolled up from his damaged knee.

When he was sure the leg would hold, Hayes started across the parking lot, the sole of his shredded boot *slap-slapping* against the pavement as he angled toward the phone booth sitting outside the store. He was almost there when he noticed the pair of thugs drinking beer on the curb.

*You've got to be shitting me.*

After being shot at, blown up, and thrown from a moving vehicle, the *last* thing Hayes wanted to deal with was a pair of thugs trying to roll him up.

Determined to avoid an altercation, Hayes kept his eyes forward and prayed that they would leave him alone. But the predatory smiles that slid across their faces when they got to their feet told him that it wasn't going to happen.

"Need to use the phone, do ya?" the first thug asked after posting up in front of the booth.

"That's right," Hayes answered.

"Gonna cost ya."

"How much?" he asked, reaching for his wallet—then remembering he'd lost that, too. "Great."

"What, lost your wallet?"

"Yeah, something like that," he said.

The second man leaned in and whispered something into the leader's ear, gesturing toward his wrist with a machete he had just pulled from behind his back.

"You're right, that is a *nice* watch," he grinned. "I think it will go perfect with the others."

"The others?" Hayes asked.

"You see, this here is our phone, and anyone wants to use it has to pay a toll," he said, nudging a plastic sack that sat on the ground.

Hayes glanced down at it. The phones, wallets, and watches packed inside told him that it had been a busy night. Hayes could tell where this was going but he wasn't sure he had the energy to try and stop it.

"So, what's it gonna be?" The man took a swig from his half-empty beer bottle.

"Listen, junior, you're not getting my watch, so why don't you and your buddy grab your loot and fuck off before someone gets hurt."

"What the fuck ya say to me?" the tough demanded, upending the bottle.

"You heard me."

The kid was fast, Hayes had to give him that. Before the words were out of his mouth the punk was swinging the bottle at his head, but Hayes was ready for it. He ducked beneath the blow and slammed a left hook into the kid's gut.

The punch blasted the air from his attacker's lungs. He folded in half, his mouth open wide in a silent scream. Before Hayes could finish him off, Machete Man waded in, the blade hissing through the air.

Hayes stepped inside, got a two-handed grip on the man's wrist. He pulled his arm straight, torquing the wrist around until the elbow was pointing up—the skin over the joint stretched white as wax paper.

Machete Man grunted in pain and tried to spin out, but Hayes stomped down on the side of his knee, the joint exploding with the pop of wet celery.

The man screamed in agony, the machete clattering to the ground as Hayes swung him around and slammed his head through the side of the phone booth, turning in time to see the man's partner yank a blade from his waistband.

He came in hard and fast, the blade glinting in the light as he slashed and stabbed at Hayes's face.

Hayes danced back, the only weapon at his disposal the Texas Silencer Outrider in his back pocket. He yanked the suppressor free and, holding it against his forearm like a nightstick, parried the thrust aimed for his liver—thankful that the Outrider was made of Grade 9 titanium instead of aluminum.

The fight was silent, the only sound the scrape of blade against suppressor and the hiss of the punk's breath as he feinted, slashed, and stabbed at him, trying anything to get inside of his guard—relentlessly pushing the fight.

While his attacker had yet to break a sweat, Hayes was gassed. His knee was throbbing, threatening to give out every time he put too much weight on it. On top of that, the gash on his forehead had cracked and fresh blood was leaking into his eye, obscuring his vision.

*All right, I've had about enough of this,* he thought.

He circled left, the pain that came with each step rolling up his leg like fire.

"Should have paid the toll when ya had a chance, old man," the punk taunted, inching closer, bouncing the knife back and forth between his left and right hand.

"Well, c'mon then, before my beer gets warm," Hayes said, coming to a halt.

"What beer?"

"The one you have in that sack—the one I'm going to be drinking in"—he paused and glanced at his watch—"let's say ten seconds, if you'd stop dancing around like a little bitch."

"I've got your bitch right here," the punk said, resuming the attack.

He leapt forward and dropped his shoulder, feinting a slash to get Hayes off balance before launching a kick toward his damaged knee.

Hayes saw the kick and checked it with a kick of his own, the impact sending a lightning bolt of pain up his leg. He bit down on the pain and pivoted, clubbing the suppressor down on the punk's wrist.

The blow shattered the bone, but before his attacker could scream, Hayes reversed the Outrider and slammed it hard across his throat—crushing his windpipe and sending him tumbling to the ground.

Hayes kicked the blade into the weeds and limped to the phone booth, snatched the beer from the bag, and twisted the cap free. He raised it to his lips and took a long pull.

The beer was lukewarm from its time out of the cooler, but even so, as Hayes stepped into the phone booth he couldn't remember anything ever tasting that good.

He lifted the phone from the cradle and dialed the number Mallory had given him.

# 36

Even with the sun buried deep below the horizon and the gentle easterly wind blowing in off the ocean, it was hot inside the phone booth. The humidity added an oppressive thickness to the air.

Hayes was tired and, standing there, the hypnotic double beep of the line ringing in his ear, the only thing keeping him from passing out on his feet was the pain cascading through his body.

He drained the rest of the beer in one long pull and set the empty bottle atop the housing when the line connected and Mallory's voice came over the line.

"Who is this?" she demanded.

"Your errand boy," Hayes answered.

"This line is *not* secure, you need to call me back on the phone I gave you, right now," she said, her voice sharp as a whip.

"Believe me, I would if I could, but . . ."

"But *what?*" she demanded.

"Well, it got thrown out of a truck," he said.

There was silence on the other end of the line and for a second Hayes thought Mallory had hung up on him.

"Hello?" he asked. "You still there?"

"Oh, I'm here," she huffed. "I was just trying to gather my thoughts, figure out what kind of an *idiot* allows someone to throw an eleven-hundred-dollar Iridium satphone out of a truck. I mean, how does that even happen?"

Hayes bit down on his anger, wishing he had another beer. This time it was Mallory's turn to break the silence.

"*Hello*, are you there?"

"Yeah, I'm here."

"Good, now back to my question. How . . . did . . . *your phone* . . . get . . . thrown from a truck?" she asked, breaking each word down like she was talking to a child.

"Because," Hayes answered, his voice hard as iron, "it was in my pocket."

"Wait, what?"

"You heard me," he said.

"What . . . what happened . . . where . . . where's Zoe?"

"They took her."

"Wh-who took her?"

Ten seconds ago, he'd been ready to give Mallory both barrels. Tell her that he knew about Zoe's real identity and what she thought Andre Cabot would do when he learned that Mallory had hired a bunch of cowards to protect his daughter. Sheep in wolves' clothing who had cut and run when they found themselves toe to toe with a team of pipe-hitting motherfuckers.

But Hayes resisted the urge, knowing there was more to be gained if he stayed in character. Let her think that he was just another dumb American in way over his head.

"I don't know who they were, but they had big guns and knew how to use them."

"Tell me exactly what happened."

Hayes started at the airport, told her about the altercation with Dábo's men and their arrival at the hotel. He told her about Zoe leaving her insulin on the table and was just getting to the ambush when the man lying on the bottom of the booth came to with a pained groan.

"What was that noise? Is someone else there?"

"No, it's just . . . hold on a second," he said, covering the mouthpiece and toeing the man in the side with his ruined boot. "Hey, man, can't you see I'm on the phone?"

The man grunted and rolled onto his stomach with a "F-fuck you."

"Do yourself a favor and stay down."

But instead of heeding the warning, the man pushed himself into a sitting position, and after steadying himself took a swipe at Hayes's leg. "I-I'm gonna bust you up . . ."

*Is this guy serious?*

"Knock it off," Hayes said, pushing the man off balance.

"Are you there? Who are you talking to?" she demanded in an aggravated voice.

"Just some bum hassling me for cash," he said.

"Well, get rid of him."

"Yeah, just give me a second," he said, setting the phone atop the housing and grabbing the empty beer bottle.

By the time he turned around the man was holding on to the edge of the phone booth, trying to pull himself to his feet.

"I told you to stay down," he said, clubbing the man across the back of the neck with the bottle.

The blow had the desired effect and sent the man tumbling to the ground, but Hayes made sure that he was down for the count before retrieving the phone.

"Sorry about that," he said.

"I don't like talking about this over an open line, but I think I know who took Zoe."

"How?"

"Listen, I can protect you, but you need to get out of Grand-Bassam."

"*Protect* me? From who?"

"These men who attacked you, they know your face, do you *really* think they are going to let you leave?"

"They've got to find me first."

"You are a white guy in Africa flying a vintage American plane, how hard do you think it is going to be for them to track you down?" she asked.

*She's done this before.*

"Fine, tell me where to go."

# 37

GRAND-BASSAM

Hayes stood outside the stolen Mitsubishi studying the map he'd spread across the hood. The light of the Streamlight Micro clutched between his lips formed a golden halo around Angola.

He shook his head, marveling at his continued streak of bad luck and the fact that out of *all* the cities in Africa, all the hell-holes she *could* have sent him to, of course it had to be Luanda.

Hayes had tried to beg off, telling her it was too far, but Mallory wasn't having it.

"That's almost fifteen hundred miles away," he'd said.

"Something wrong with your plane?"

Once again he found himself trapped by his cover, unable to tell her that the problem with his plane was that it was parked at an airfield about an hour's drive from where he'd left a stack of dead bodies.

*Dammit.*

"No, I just figured . . ."

"I think it is time we got one thing clear. You aren't paid to think. You are paid to do what the hell I tell you, when I tell you to do it," she'd snapped. "You got that?"

"Yeah."

"Good, now get your ass to Luanda," she'd said before hanging up.

"Might as well get this over with," he said now, killing the light and climbing back into the SUV.

He started the engine and drove east, knowing the first order of business was to ditch the stolen Mitsubishi. Usually he'd park it on the street near his destination, leave the keys in the ignition, and let the local underworld handle the issue of getting rid of the car. But one look at the interior, the seats, and door handle stained rust red from his blood, and Hayes knew this time, that wasn't an option.

*Going to have to find a place to ditch it. Someplace close to the airport.*

He found an abandoned cannery a quarter mile from his destination, pulled the SUV inside, and cut the engine. Grabbing the remnants of his shredded assault pack off the passenger seat, Hayes eased out of the vehicle, taking his time so that he didn't drop any of his meager belongings, when the rotten fish guts smell sent the contents of his stomach racing into the back of his throat.

"The hell with this," he said, pushing himself into a hobbled jog.

By the time he made it to the airfield he was drenched in sweat and beyond giving a shit. He approached the gatehouse, brushed past the guards at the gate with a hard look that dared them to try and stop him, and limped across the tarmac—the only thought on his mind getting the hell out of Grand-Bassam.

Hayes unlocked the troop door, yanked the chock blocks and drip pans and threw them inside the cargo hold with his ruined assault pack, and then climbed up after them, slamming the door shut behind him before scrambling up to the cockpit.

He sped through the startup sequence, and when the engines were running smoothly, he grabbed the radio and tuned the dial to the tower frequency. "Tower, this is Pilgrim three-niner x-ray ready to taxi from cargo ramp."

"Pilgrim three-niner x-ray," the voice answered, "cleared to taxi. Advise hold short of runway zero-three."

Hayes repeated the transmission and swung the nose toward the taxiway, head swiveling left to right, searching for traffic and obstructions. Once he was sure it was clear he eased off the brake and guided the Provider down the taxiway, slowing as he approached the double yellow lines that marked the runway holding position, knowing that if Dábo or his men were going to make a move this is where they would do it.

"Tower, this is Pilgrim three-niner x-ray, holding short," he said. "Request clearance to take off runway one-one."

"Negative, Pilgrim three-niner x-ray—hold for incoming aircraft."

*Incoming aircraft?*

The night was clear, and with the moon shining bright overhead, Hayes had a clear view of both the runway and the sky, and there wasn't a cloud *or* an approaching aircraft in sight.

"Tower, this is Pilgrim three-niner x-ray, say again your last."

Silence.

He leaned forward in his seat and twisted his neck back the way he'd come in time to see a pair of army Jeeps closing in fast on his tail.

In all his years of flying, Hayes had never even *considered* disregarding the tower, but that changed when he saw the finger of yellow flame emerge from the muzzle of the M60 machine gun mounted to the roll bar of the lead Jeep.

"The hell with this," he said, letting off the brakes and advancing the throttles, ignoring the controller's angry voice in his ear.

"Pilgrim three-niner x-ray, you are instructed to *hold*. You are *not* cleared—"

"Yeah, yeah," Hayes said, leaning forward and killing the radio, waiting until the nose was centered on the runway before shoving the throttles to full power.

But the troops in the Jeeps weren't giving up that easily.

While the drivers bounced across the grass median, desperate to cut the aircraft off before it reached takeoff speed, the gunners kept their triggers locked to the rear.

Hayes watched the coil of green tracers arcing past the nose, knowing it was just a matter of time before one of the gunners found their range, sending a hail of bullets through the glass, or worse, one of the engines.

He hadn't even reached the halfway point of the runway and one look at the airspeed indicator told him that she wasn't going to make it—not on her own, at least.

But luckily the old warbird had one final trick up her sleeve.

Hayes leaned forward, finger extended over the red safety cover marked JATO. He paused and double-checked the airspeed

JOSHUA HOOD

indicator. Realizing it was the only way he was getting out of Grand-Bassam alive, he disengaged the safety and flipped the toggle switch—igniting the eight external rocket bottles mounted below the rear landing gears.

The rocket motors screamed to life; the sudden acceleration of the jet-assisted take-off system shoved Hayes back in his seat. "Later, fellas," he hooted, holding on for dear life as the Provider hurtled down the runway. The white cloud from the rockets inundated his pursuers, obscuring their view.

At ninety knots, he pulled back on the yoke, and the moment he was airborne retracted the landing gear. He leveled off at eight hundred feet and banked hard to the southwest, flying fast and low over the Gulf of Guinea.

Hayes waited until he was six miles over international waters and well out of the Ivorian Air Force's reach before climbing to twenty thousand feet. He adjusted his course, banked east, and then reduced the throttles to cruising speed. After checking the gauges, he let out the breath he hadn't realized he'd been holding.

But despite the relief that came with making it out of Grand-Bassam alive, Hayes couldn't shake the feeling that all he'd accomplished was to jump out of the frying pan and into the fire.

Three hours later, Hayes landed on a dusty airstrip fifty miles north of Luanda. After he shut down the engines, he grabbed his travel bag and the envelope of cash Mallory had given him and climbed out onto the tarmac, limping to the hangar.

The man at the counter saw him coming and his eyes went wide, hand dropping below the desk for the pistol Hayes assumed he had stashed there.

"I just need fuel and a place to clean up," he said. "How much?"

"First I need to see your passport," the man said.

"No problem," Hayes replied, slapping a thousand dollars on the counter.

The man glanced down at the stack of cash, frowned, and then looked back up at his bloodied and beaten customer.

"I am afraid that—"

"Oh, yeah, and no police," Hayes said, adding a second stack of fresh one-hundred-dollar bills to the first.

"Of course, sir," the man grinned, scooping up the cash before handing Hayes the key to the washroom.

*That's what I thought.*

The washroom was about what he'd expected, a dingy rectangle of tile with a sink, toilet, and rusted metal bench in front of an open shower. It was filthy, but Hayes had made do with worse.

His clothes and hiking boots were little more than rags after being thrown from the truck. He stripped off his shirt and dropped it on the floor. He sat down on the bench and was about to tug the hiking boots off his feet when he felt something hard sitting low in his back pocket.

"What the hell is that?" he asked.

Then he remembered.

Zoe's insulin. Had it survived?

He pulled the case from his pocket and studied the scuff marks across the lid and the dents that came from where his body had slammed into the street. The hinges creaked when he opened it. The undamaged vials inside took him back to the ambush. How small she looked when the men tugged the black bag over her head and rag-dolled her into the back of the Excursion.

The fear in her eyes when he'd tried to get her to jump.

*You need to forget the girl, get the hell out of here while you still can,* the voice urged.

There was a part of Hayes that wished it were that easy, but he knew that quitting wasn't an option.

Hayes had his mission and, live or die, he was going to see it through.

He kicked off his boots, stepped out of his pants, grabbed the pile of ruined clothes off the floor, and dumped them into the trash before taking the bar of soap into the shower.

Even with the knob turned wide open, the water wasn't more than a dribble, but as Hayes lathered up he knew that nothing short of a pressure washer and a new set of skin would have made a dent in his appearance.

After ten minutes of scrubbing, he gave up, and dressed quickly in a pair of tan Carhartts, a faded denim button-down, and a pair of Ariat Ropers.

He was still tired when he stepped out of the washroom, but the shower and the change of clothes had their effect and there was new life in his step when he returned to the counter.

"I need a truck, nothing special, it just has to run," he told the man behind the counter.

Hayes knew the moment the words were out of his mouth that the man was going to try and screw him, but he didn't care. All he wanted was to get on the road and get to Luanda before the sun came up.

Twenty minutes later he climbed into a beat-up Land Cruiser, the envelope of cash considerably lighter than it had been when he walked into the hangar, but at least he was moving.

It was an easy drive from the airfield to the capital and, as he'd hoped, Hayes arrived just as the sun was coming up.

After the languid decay of Grand-Bassam, the scene waiting for him in Luanda was a breath of fresh air. The towering glass skyscrapers sparkled like diamonds in the morning sun, the well-paved streets and luxury sedans cruising the waterfront a far cry from how it had looked in the early 2000s when the country was still locked in a vicious civil war.

As Hayes continued south along the coast, the glitz and glamour of Luanda faded away as he entered the working-class municipality of Belas. Here the residents were too busy trying to make a living to bother with hiding the scars of war, and there was evidence of the fighting on the buildings that lined the Lar do Patriota.

But Hayes wasn't complaining. In fact, he found the pockmarked walls and chipped concrete façades oddly comforting.

*Yeah, I'm pretty sure that's not normal,* he thought as he arrived at his destination.

Instead of pulling up to the hotel, he circled the block before pulling the SUV into an alley across the street. He cut the engine, pointed the binoculars across the street, and thumbed the focus knob, trying to negate the mirage dancing like a dervish across the blacktop.

Despite the end of the hostilities and the economic growth that followed, Angola was by no means safe. And while the heavy police presence around the city center kept the thieves and kidnappers at bay, those tourists brave enough to venture into the surrounding municipality found themselves easy prey.

To combat the ever-growing threat and to ensure the continued safety of their guests, the proprietors of the working-class hotels began upgrading their security. Some hired armed guards, while others constructed eight-foot walls around their property.

Not to be outdone by his competition, the owner of the Hotel Sunshine turned his lodging into a miniature fortress, adding an eight-foot wall and concrete-reinforced gatehouse manned by round-the-clock guards in tactical gear.

While the proprietor was sure the guests saw the AK-wielding gate guards and the razor wire stretched atop the wall as proof that the Hotel Sunshine was the most secure venue in Belas, Hayes saw a prison.

*Yeah, I'm not going in there without some serious hardware.*

He returned the binos to their spot on the passenger seat and threw the Land Cruiser into gear. He pulled out onto the street and turned north, the SUV's asthmatic A/C blowing lukewarm air in his face.

Hayes's reputation as a loner was well earned, but it was not because he liked being alone so much as he disliked most of the people he'd run across during his time at Treadstone. Like most male-dominated professions, it had an overabundance of assholes. Alpha males with testosterone-inflated egos and quick trigger fingers.

But despite the effort he'd expended in his war of self-sufficiency—and against his better judgment—Hayes realized that he needed help.

## WASHINGTON, D.C.

evi Shaw was sitting at his desk, staring blankly at the laptop before him, when there was a knock at the door.

"Come in."

The door swung open and a plain-faced woman with short black hair stuck her head through the crack. "Director, your car is here."

"Thank you, Linda," he said.

Shaw closed the laptop and shoved it into his battered attaché case, grabbing the holstered Walther PPK from the drawer before getting to his feet. He clipped the pistol to his waist and retrieved a worn Donegal tweed coat from the wicker rack by the door before stepping out.

"You work too much, Linda," he said, pulling on the jacket.

"Almost done, sir," she smiled up at him.

"Fine, but make sure someone walks you out to your car," he said, heading for the door.

"Yes, sir."

With the sun heading down, the temperature had dropped, and Shaw pulled up his collar before starting down the steps to the Lincoln Town Car waiting for him at the curb.

He climbed inside with a weary sigh and set the attaché case on the floorboard.

"Carter, put the game on, will ya?" he asked.

"Roger that," his driver said, fiddling with the radio knob as he pulled away from the curb.

"And if you put on the Yankees again, you're fired."

"Understood, sir," Carter laughed.

They drove east, Shaw half listening to the game as they turned onto Wisconsin Avenue and headed south across the Key Bridge. His mind drifted back to Hayes and their conversation the night before.

That Hayes *wasn't* coming back was a foregone conclusion; Shaw had known that *before* the call. And while he didn't blame the man, having to relay the news to the Senate Intelligence Committee had not been the highlight of his day.

Senator Miles had taken the news surprisingly well. In fact, instead of the ass-chewing he'd expected, the man barely raised his voice. But instead of finding relief in the senator's mellow response, it left Shaw with a growing unease.

*He's up to something. But what?*

Shaw looked out the window and stared down at the gunmetal-gray waters of the Potomac flowing beneath the bridge, knowing the answer to the question and wishing like hell he could do something about it.

Fifteen minutes after merging onto George Washington Parkway, he felt the Town Car slow. Shaw looked up, frowning at the line of brake lights ahead of him.

"You've got to be kidding me," Carter said, toeing the brake.

"I thought they were done tearing up the roads for the year."

"They are," Carter answered, "or at least that's what they said."

"Looks like they lied," Shaw said, seeing the flashing DDOT sign ahead and a signalman waving the cars toward the off-ramp.

"Why the hell are they diverting us here?" Carter wondered as he reached for his GPS.

"Apparently wanting to watch the game in the comfort of my own living room is too much to ask," Shaw said.

"Sir, I hate to be the one to tell you this," Carter said, merging onto the off-ramp, "but they don't have a chance."

"Is that a fact?" he asked, looking out the window.

"Afraid so," Carter said, following the road as it twisted to the right. "The problem with your Mets is you've got no offense."

"Oh, here we go," Shaw said.

"I'm serious, sir . . ."

But Shaw was too focused on the solitary figure standing on the side of the road, a bare signpost five feet to his rear. The way the man casually lifted his hand to his mouth when the Town Car passed reminded him of Iraq and the insurgents who stood on the side of the road watching the convoys.

The memory sparked a long-forgotten scratching at the base

of Shaw's skull. A ragged itch that put him instantly on guard—and sent his hand dropping down to the 9-millimeter Walther PPK.

*Who was he, and was that a sign?*

Before he could shout a warning, the road hooked hard left, the blind turn catching both Shaw and his driver off guard.

"Hold on, sir," Carter said, his knuckles bone-white on the steering wheel.

He let off the gas and cranked the wheel hard over, cursing, fighting against the centrifugal force trying to shove the Town Car off the road.

In the backseat, Shaw braced himself against the door and was reaching for his seatbelt when a flash of movement drew his attention to the tree line ten yards ahead.

*What in the hell?*

He leaned forward and was squinting through the darkness when a pair of spotlights came to life. The blaze of white light through the passenger window hit like a flashbang and Shaw raised his hand to his face. He blinked away the stars in time to see a jacked-up pickup with a solid-steel bumper cannonballing down the firebreak.

"Carter, watch—"

But before the words were off his lips the truck slammed into the Town Car's front right quarter panel, the impact blasting the glass from the passenger-side window and sending the vehicle spinning across the road.

Shaw threw himself to the floorboards a split second before the tires hit the curb and then the Town Car was airborne, pinballing off trees, glass shattering, metal crumpling as it tumbled down the embankment and slammed nose-first into an ancient oak.

———————

Shaw's senses came online like a computer after a hard reboot. His hearing came back with the high-pitched hum and the cotton feel that came from shooting a rifle without earplugs.

He tried to sit up, but the lance of fire in his head left him dizzy and panting in the darkness. Shaw collapsed back into his seat, hacked against the residual powder from the airbag, tasting the copper tang of blood on his lips when he spit.

*Where am I? What happened?*

Slowly the details of the accident came back and he remembered the signalman diverting them off the expressway. The missing signpost and the truck barreling down the firebreak.

*Ambush.*

The word blinked on and off in his mind like a neon sign, and lying there in the backseat, Shaw knew this wasn't over.

*They're coming back. You need to move.*

"C-Carter," he grunted. "We have to move. You hear me, son?"

Silence.

The door was jammed, and Shaw was forced to kick out the window, the shattered glass cutting at his legs when he climbed out. He grabbed the door handle and hauled himself upright—the shooting pain radiating from his knee almost sending him to the ground.

He limped to the front of the vehicle, one look at the blood sprayed across the window and his driver's caved-in skull telling him everything he needed to know.

The dump of adrenaline that had come with the collision was wearing off, and Shaw found himself rocked by a sudden wave of dizziness. He sagged against the car, knowing from his ragged breathing and the cold, clammy feel of his skin that he was going into shock.

He was on the verge of passing out when the *snap-crack* of dried branches drew his attention to the crest of the hill. Shaw looked up, a pair of red-lensed flashlights bobbing down the incline sending his hand dropping to his hip.

But instead of the cold steel of the Walther, Shaw found nothing but air.

*Shit.*

Knowing there was no time to look for the lost pistol, he grabbed the door handle and, using the last of his strength, wrenched it open, the creak of the hinges loud as a rifle shot in the still night air.

Carter's body lolled, and Shaw leaned across him, glass cutting his fingers as he pawed at the SIG 229 holstered at the man's hip. He got a hand around the grip, but when he tried to pull the pistol free from the holster it wouldn't budge.

He could hear the assassins off to his left, the muted footfalls through the undergrowth and the crimson throw of their lights off the crumpled hood telling him they were closing in fast.

He gave the pistol an angry jerk, but still the holster refused to turn loose of the SIG.

*Why the fuck won't this come out?*

Shaw was panicking now, the awareness of his encroaching death coiling around his heart like an icy snake.

*You need to calm down. Figure this out before it's too late.*

He studied the holster strapped to his driver's hip, fully expecting to feel the white-hot burn of a bullet at any second. Instead, he felt a plastic thumb break on the inside of the holster. The plastic tab reminded him that while *he* still carried old school leather holsters, Carter and pretty much everyone else on the payroll had shifted to Kydex—plastic holsters that came with built-in Level II retention.

He thumbed the retention latch to the rear and this time the SIG came out like greased lightning. Pistol in hand, Shaw stumbled backward, his leg buckling beneath him as he rolled free of the door.

He tumbled to the dirt, falling across a jagged strip of metal that sliced his face, the rush of pain and the spurt of hot blood down his cheek forgotten the second he heard the voice from the rear of the car.

"We've got a live one."

Shaw rolled onto his back and shifted his body until he had a clear line of sight through the shattered glass of the back door. He brought the SIG up in a two-handed grip, centered the sights on the figure he saw through the back glass, and fired three quick shots.

Thinking the shots had come from *inside* the car, the second shooter opened up—hosing the interior of the Town Car with lead.

Still on the ground, Shaw flipped onto his stomach, laid the front sight on the pair of legs standing on the other side of the vehicle, and sent a 9-millimeter hollow point through the man's kneecap.

The joint exploded like a ripe melon and the shooter screamed in pain, managing a half step back before tumbling to the ground.

Shaw grunted to his feet and limped around the back of the Town Car. He paused at the hood and looked down at the man sprawled out on the ground. Too tired to bend down and check his pulse, he put a bullet though the top of his skull.

On the other side of the car he found the second shooter busy trying to secure a tourniquet around his thigh—his H&K MP7 still lying in the dirt where he'd dropped it.

Shaw kicked the submachine gun into the weeds and limped over to the man, gun smoke still coiling from the barrel of the SIG. He stopped in front of the shooter, eyes void of any emotion as he studied him over the pistol sights.

"H-help me and . . . and I'll tell you everything," the man begged.

"Thanks, but I've got this one all figured out," Shaw said before pulling the trigger.

# 39

After leaving the Hotel Sunshine, Hayes drove back to the beach, found a shaded alley close to the Fortress São Miguel, and parked. He rolled down the windows and studied the beach bar two hundred yards to his south through the binoculars.

From the exterior the Rusted Nail was warm and bright. Everything from the neon-yellow awning that covered the back deck to the tables overlooking the ocean exactly as it should be.

But it was the tanned woman in the white tank top cleaning the windows who held Hayes's attention. He thumbed the focus knob and zoomed in on her face as a pair of early risers stepped into view. The woman stopped what she was doing and turned to greet them, an easy smile spreading across her face.

She seemed perfectly at ease standing there in the sunlight, not a care in the world, but Hayes saw past the façade, noting the out-line of the pistol at the small of her back and the faded scar on her chest when she reached up to tuck a strand of hair behind her ear.

The conversation lasted all of thirty seconds and then the woman was alone, the smile falling from her face as she scanned the street. Her green eyes darted like hummingbirds in flight, searching for something she *sensed* more than saw. She scanned left to right, taking in the movement closest to her before jumping across the street.

Then she was looking directly at him.

*Hello, Charli.*

Her gaze lingered on the alley for less than a second, and while Hayes knew there was no way she could have seen him parked deep in the shadows, for an instant he could have sworn there was a hint of recognition in her eyes, a glint that left him feeling exposed. But he brushed it off, returned the binoculars to the passenger seat, and pulled the faded baseball cap over his eyes.

*Well, this ought to be fun.*

Hayes woke up at noon, sweating from the sun beating down on him like a bully with a magnifying glass. The scene before him had changed; the plaza that had been empty before was now full of tourists taking pictures of the ancient fort and eyeing the wares the local craftsmen displayed on linen sheets.

He wiped the sweat from his brow, the savory scent of roasted meat and vegetables wafting from the grills of the sidewalk ven-dors reminding him that he hadn't eaten in twelve hours. But it was the sight of the blue-coated police patrolling the plaza that told him it was time to move.

Hayes started the engine and pulled out of the alley, in search of a phone to call Mallory and food to assuage his hunger.

He found both three miles to the east at an open-air market, where he ate two bowls of calulu, a traditional fish and vegetable stew, downed a liter of bottled water, and then paid the shop owner twenty bucks to use the man's phone.

Hayes dialed the number, adjusted the Beretta at his hip, and waited for the call to connect.

This time it was Wikus who answered.

"Thought you were told to come to the hotel, errand boy. What happened, you get lost?"

"If you think that I'm coming anywhere near that place, you're dumber than you look," he answered, glancing down at his watch.

In Grand-Bassam he hadn't cared if they'd tracked the call, but now that he was in the same city as Mallory and her merry band of pirates, Hayes wasn't taking any chances.

"So you need to figure out another spot, someplace nice and open where I can see you and you can see me. Got it?"

"Listen here—"

But Hayes was done taking orders.

"You've got fifteen seconds. Yes or no?" he demanded.

"I will let Mallory know," Wikus growled.

"Good. I'll be in touch," he said, ending the call.

Hayes pulled on his shades, tugged the brim of the ball cap down over his eyes, and stepped out into the street. He needed to buy a phone and a few other items before heading back to the Rusted Nail.

He climbed into the Land Cruiser and, wanting to stay away from both the city center and the Hotel Sunshine, drove north— a hint of a plan forming at the edge of his mind.

His first stop was the AngoMart on the Estrada Zango, where he bought a brace of burner phones to communicate with Mallory, a baby monitor, and bandages and iodine for his wounds. On the way out, he paused at the bank of pay phones outside. Incredibly, one still had an ancient phone book attached. Hayes ripped it from the chain and hurried to the SUV.

He spent five minutes conducting countersurveillance, making sure that he hadn't picked up a tail before pulling into a parking lot. Hayes's Portuguese was rusty, but thanks to the ads inside the phone book, he was able to find the section for hardware stores. After consulting the map the man at the airfield had given him, he located one five miles from his current position.

Anywhere else in the world Hayes could have covered the distance in fifteen minutes max, but like the rest of Africa, traffic in Luanda was a bitch, the streets packed with cars and vendors darting in and out of traffic selling everything from yellow jugs of gasoline to bushels of fruit.

*Good thing I'm not in a rush.*

During his time in the 82nd Airborne, Hayes's knowledge of explosives was limited to pulling the pin on a grenade and throwing it before it exploded in his hand. Everything else was handled by chemists—trained professionals—who worked in military armament facilities.

It wasn't until he went to the Special Forces Qualification course at Fort Bragg, North Carolina, that Hayes learned that everything he needed to make something go boom could be found at a hardware store.

By the time he arrived at his destination, the ancient A/C had given out and the clutch and brakes were hot from the constant stop-and-go of the street.

But Hayes made the most of his commute, using the drive to compile a list of what he needed, so that when he finally stepped inside the store and grabbed one of the rickety carts, he was ready to go.

Most of the items, like the sections of lead pipe, dry cell batteries, road flares, and the household cleaners, were easy to find. The more esoteric components, on the other hand, taxed both Hayes's imagination and his limited knowledge of basic chemistry, but he made it work and, three hundred dollars later, had what he needed.

After everything was loaded up, all that was left to do was find a base of operations—somewhere he could work undisturbed until it was time to head back to the Rusty Nail.

# 40

I t was noon when Cyrus Vandal pulled into the parking lot of the Hotel Epic and parked beneath the shade of a coconut palm. He climbed into the backseat of the 4Runner, stripped out of his travel clothes, and dressed quickly in a pair of khaki chinos, a white silk button-down, and a pair of leather deck shoes.

After clipping the SIG 365 onto his belt, he shrugged into a light-blue sports coat and climbed out. He moved to the rear of the SUV, paused to check his surroundings, and when he was sure that he was clear, opened the hatch.

One of the first rules he'd been taught at Site Tango was how to blend in—avoid drawing unnecessary attention. Most of the tactics and techniques were obvious, like *don't walk into a five-star hotel carrying a bulky cargo bag and the olive drab ruck-*

*sack*, which was why he'd requested the cooler-sized Pelican case and the nondescript backpack that were sitting in the back of the SUV.

With all the gear packed into the case, it weighed well over a hundred pounds, but Vandal effortlessly lifted it out, set it lightly on the ground. He grabbed the pack, slung it over his shoulder, and closed the hatch.

He extended the Pelican case's telescoping carrying handle, slipped a pair of Ray-Bans over his eyes, and started toward the entrance.

At three hundred and forty-one feet, the glass-fronted hotel was one of the tallest buildings in the city, and from the balcony of the three-thousand-dollars-a-night Presidential Suite, Vandal knew he'd have a commanding view of the capital.

The only problem was that the current guests, a Mr. and Mrs. Alistair Chadwick from Virginia Water, Surrey, had the room booked for the rest of the week.

But that wasn't Vandal's problem.

He was halfway to the door when the Bluetooth rang in his ear.

"Yes?" he answered.

"It's done," Skyler advised, her voice tiny in his ear.

"Good. Call me back in fifteen."

Vandal ended the call and stepped up on the curb, followed the walkway beneath the awning, offering a nod to the man in the gray suit holding the door.

He stepped inside, pulled his sunglasses off, and, after slipping them into his coat pocket, scanned the interior.

Despite himself, Vandal was struck by the understated elegance of the lobby. The white marbled floor, chromium staircase, and the teardrop chandeliers that hung from the ice cube–white ceiling seemed to reflect Luanda's commitment to atone for its violent past. While he, on the other hand, was just getting started.

With that thought in mind, Vandal started across the lobby, where a red-faced man was shouting at the manager.

"Do you know what this is?" the man demanded, waving a credit card in the man's face. "It's a bloody Amex Black."

"Mr. Chadwick, if you could please calm down," the manager begged.

"Calm down? Calm *down*?" the man bellowed. "First you tell me that my credit card has been canceled and now you want me to calm down?"

*Sucks for you, mate.*

Cyrus brushed past the man and sidled up to the front desk, where an openmouthed clerk stood watching the proceedings.

"Problem?" Vandal asked the man in Portuguese.

"An issue with the gentleman's card, it seems," the man answered with a strained smile. "How may I help you?"

"Is the Presidential Suite available?"

"As a matter of fact, the maids are cleaning it *now*," the man said, nodding to the red-faced Englishman.

"Oh . . . I see," he said, doing his best to maintain a straight face. "Well, if that's the case I'd like to book it for the rest of the week."

"Of course, sir."

Vandal took the key and shot Mr. Chadwick an unapologetic wink on his way to the bank of elevators around the corner. Following the deskman's instruction, he stepped into the first car on the right, inserted his key into the slot, and pressed the only button on the panel.

The elevator arrived at the forty-second floor with a polite *ding* and he stepped out into the hall, the Pelican case rolling silent behind him. He stopped at the mahogany door at the end of the hall, swiped his key over the reader, and stepped inside.

Leaving the Pelican case in the sitting room, Vandal peeled off the coat and kicked out of his shoes. He grabbed a beer from the fridge and, knowing that this was the first and last time he'd ever stay in such a room, took his time soaking it in.

The Presidential Suite was a flawless match of form and function, its white oak hardwood floors and the flaxen rug serving as the perfect complement to the russet-brown couches and the chestnut rafters.

But the pièce de résistance—the very soul of the room—was the floor-to-ceiling windows that made up the south wall.

Vandal padded to the door and stepped out onto the balcony, the tile warm on his bare feet as he crossed to the railing.

After getting used to the monochrome gray sky and sooty white snow of Slovakia, the sights and sounds of Luanda threatened sensory overload. From the liquid gold blush of the sun off the Atlantic to the verdant green of the hillsides far to the north, the city was awash in color.

For anyone else, finding one man in a city of two and a half million people would have been like searching for a needle in a stack of needles. An impossible task, even for someone with Vandal's training.

But for the techs back at Site Tango, it was just another day in the office.

Leaving the beer on the balcony, he went inside and squatted down in front of the Pelican case. He worked the latches and after opening the lid revealed the tools of his trade: the suppressed

H&K MP7, pair of SIG 226s, and the Accuracy International AX308 Covert with its Nightforce 5-25x56mm scope.

"Hey, there, good lookin'," Vandal said, grabbing the straps embedded into the foam and lifting the entire shelf free.

After gently setting the weapons aside, he retrieved a laptop and a black cylinder from the case and stepped back onto the balcony.

Vandal set the laptop on one of the wicker chairs. While he waited for it to boot up, he opened the cylinder and pulled out a miniature S-band antenna—an object that looked like a corkscrew on steroids—and connected the coax cable that trailed from the end to the computer's USB drive.

He carried the antenna to the railing and, sighting down the coil that protruded from the metallic dish, centered it on the city. He checked to make sure that it could move equidistant from left to right and was just clamping the antenna to the railing when his phone rang in his ear.

"Code in," a flat, electronic voice ordered.

Vandal lifted the phone to his eye and held it there, waiting for the click of the shutter and the "authentication complete" that followed before returning the phone to his pocket.

A second later, Skyler was back on the line.

"Are you in position?" she asked.

"Yes, I'm set up and ready to rock and roll," he answered.

"Okay. I am going to set up the uplink. Stand by."

Vandal retrieved his beer from the table and took a drink, watched the flicker of the computer as Skyler took control. The rapid-fire opening and closing of the programs on the screen gave the impression that the laptop was possessed.

*Fucking spooky.*

A red light appeared at the base of the antenna, followed a second later by the whir of the motor in the base. "We are live and . . . tracking," Skyler said, as the antenna began oscillating from left to right.

Now all that was left to do was wait for Hayes to make a call.

# 41

## ROCHA PINTO, LUANDA

Sandwiched between the airport to the east and the highway to the west, the barrio of Rocha Pinto was a country unto itself. A neighborhood that both the police and the military avoided, where the rule of law was that of the RPG and AK-47.

Which made it the perfect spot for Hayes to lie low.

He'd found the hotel in the phone book, but knowing the locals' propensity for burning down buildings, he called ahead, just to make sure it was still standing.

The woman who answered the phone confirmed that they were open and seemed genuinely excited at the thought of having a guest.

"Do you need directions?" she asked.

"I think I can find it," he replied. "See you soon."

He drove northwest on the Estrada de Catete, then turned onto the Avenue de 21 Janeiro, which he followed south past the airport.

He was making good time, everything going according to plan until he made the right-hand turn at the Toyota plant and found himself surrounded by a warren of streets without any street signs.

*You've got to be kidding me.*

Hayes spent the next ten minutes burning gas, before pulling over next to an open field inhabited by a fleet of junked-out cars and a mob of barefoot kids kicking around a soccer ball. He pulled the Beretta out of its holster and shoved it under his thigh, then grabbed the map from the visor, ignoring the rattle of gunfire in the distance while he searched for his position.

He'd already marked the hotel on the map, and after finding the field was working on a route when the bass-rattling thump of a car stereo on full blast drew his attention to the road.

Hayes looked up, a frown stretching across his face as he studied the vehicle rolling toward him.

*What in the holy hell is that?*

At first glance he'd thought it was a van, but as it drew near, he saw that someone had used some kind of torch to cut the body off behind the cab, turning what had once been a functional vehicle into something straight out of the Thunderdome, complete with the spike-haired gun thugs holding rusted AKs and drinking beer in the back.

*Don't stop . . . don't stop . . . and* shit. *They're stopping.*

The vehicle came to a rusted halt next to him, the driver motioning for Hayes to roll down the window.

There were literally hundreds of ways to say hello in Portuguese, from the formal "good afternoon" to the informal "how's it going?"

But this wasn't Hayes's first time in a nonpermissive environment. He'd been here before and knew the key to avoiding unnecessary gunplay was to make sure the boys realized he was not the kind of prey they were looking for.

With that in mind, he rolled down the window and, looking the boy full in the eyes, said, *"Qual é cara?"* What's up, bitch?

The driver did a double take, the sound of the gringo spitting street slang at him catching him off guard. While Hayes waited for him to regain his composure, he dropped his hand to the butt of the pistol.

"You lost, bro?" the man-child finally asked.

"Why? Are you with Triple A?" Hayes answered.

"Tri-pol-Eh?" the boy frowned, his hand snaking out of the window as he reached down for the door latch. "You a funny guy, eh, gringo?"

"What's your name, kid?" Hayes asked, letting the smile fall from his face.

"They call me Razor," the boy answered, fingers inches from the handle.

"You don't want to open that door, Razor," he said.

There was a kinship among predators, a sixth sense that told the jackal it was best to keep clear of the lion, and it was instinct that caused the boy to pause, reevaluate the gringo with the hard eyes.

"Oh, no?" he asked, his pack silent behind him. "And why is that?"

"I think you know," he answered.

"He's bluffing," one of the passengers hissed. "Let's take him."

"You die first," Hayes said, the Beretta appearing in his hand like a magic trick. "Got me?"

"Yeah, yeah, we . . . we got ya," they nodded in unison.

"Cool," Hayes said. "Now if you can tell me where to find the Hotel Claro, I'll be out of your hair."

Five minutes later he was pulling up to his destination.

Compared to the monoliths of glass and steel that towered over the Bay of Luanda, the three-story coral-pink Hotel Claro was a dump. But Hayes could tell from the freshly swept porch and the sparkle of the windows that Senhora Marta ran a tight ship.

The interior confirmed his first impressions. While the décor was dated, everything from the cowbell that hung over the door to the vinyl floor peeling from the sun was spick and span.

At the jingle of the bell, a pleasant-faced woman in a hand-spun cotton top emerged from behind the beaded curtain, a bright smile spreading across her caramel skin. *"Ah, Senhor Hayes,"* she said, *"boa tardes."* Good afternoon.

Senhora Marta's smile was infectious. As he strode to the burnished wood counter, Hayes was immediately at ease.

"You didn't have any trouble finding the place, did you?"

"Not at all," he lied.

"As you see," she said, turning to the pegboard laden with keys, "you have your choice of rooms. What would you like?"

"Something on the third floor, facing the street, if you don't mind," he said, taking a mental picture of the pegboard.

"Room 306 has a very nice view."

Hayes took the key, went out to the truck, and grabbed the items he'd picked up. He carried them back to his room, surreptitiously clocking the exits—compiling a mental list of escape routes on his way up the stairs.

The room was small but neatly furnished with a queen-sized bed, small closet, and a mini-fridge that hummed contentedly in the corner. He stepped inside, left the door cracked behind him, and carried the bags to the table by the window.

After double-checking the parking lot, he unboxed the baby monitor, grabbed the camera, and carried it back into the hallway. He used the adhesive square on the bottom to stick it to the exit sign that hung from the ceiling and headed back to the room.

Once inside, Hayes locked the door and threw the bolt, making sure it was secure before returning to the monitor on the table. Compared to the ultra-high-definition micro cams he'd used during his time with Treadstone, the camera stuck to the back side of the exit sign was a piece of shit. Both the quality and clarity of the image beamed back to the base station left much to be desired.

But as he remotely adjusted the camera's angle, panned it to the right so he could see most of the hall and part of the stairwell, Hayes realized that it was better than nothing.

Leaving the monitor charging on the table, he carried the remaining sacks into the bathroom. He set them on the sink and cracked the window over the toilet, ensuring the room was properly ventilated before pulling on a pair of rubber gloves and getting to work.

Using the box cutter he'd purchased from the hardware store, Hayes cut the tops off the road flares and used a sieve to separate the magnesium from the filler. After separating the contents into two jars, he pulled off his shirt, tied it over his mouth and nose, and carried the bottle of ammonia and the weed killer to the tub.

Hayes had never been good at chemistry; in fact, he'd slept through most of the science classes he'd been forced to take in college. But kneeling over the bathtub—the chemicals bubbling in their jars as he mixed and strained them together—he stayed focused, all too aware that he was one wrong pour away from being turned into pink mist.

He finished around eight-thirty p.m., rinsed out the bathtub, and took a shower. Before leaving the room, he moved the bed, pried up one of the boards, and wedged the munitions into the space beneath.

Replacing the boards and moving the bed back into place, Hayes grabbed the book of matches from the ashtray on the table and stepped out into the hall. He closed and locked the door and then dropped to a knee, tore one of the matches from the book, and wedged it between the door and the frame.

*Just in case Senhora Marta has any shitbag relatives lurking around.*

It was almost nine when Hayes backed the Land Cruiser into the alley he'd used early that day and cut the engine. He stayed behind the wheel, letting his eyes adjust to the dark. Once they were acclimated, he tore the cellophane from the pack of SLs he'd bought on the way in.

Hayes had never been much of a smoker, but knew that in a bar they were a valuable prop—something that could be used to mask the fact that you weren't getting shitfaced with the rest of the patrons. After rapping the pack against the flat of his hand, he stuffed them into the front pocket of his button-down and pulled out one of the burner phones.

Considering the late hour, Hayes thought it unlikely that the meeting would be going down tonight, but wanting to get the call out of the way before he went inside, he dialed Mallory's number.

It was a nice night, cooler than it had been in Grand-Bassam and not nearly as muggy. As he waited for the call to connect, Hayes scanned the street, shaking his head at the handful of tourists strolling across the plaza, wondering if they were too drunk or too dumb to realize that Angola was *not* the kind of place you went for a walk after the sun went down.

Before he could come up with an answer, Wikus was on the line, his voice tense and lacking its usual bluster.

"Tomorrow, eight a.m."

"Where?"

"The Museu da Moeda, you know it?"

"Yeah," Hayes said.

"Nice and public, just like you wanted," Wikus jeered.

"Fine. See you there, and bring my pistol," Hayes said, ending the call and climbing out of the Land Cruiser.

He crossed the street and paused at the door, telling himself that he was using the darkened glass to check his backtrail, but knowing it was a lie. The truth was, he was stalling, willing to use any excuse to prolong the inevitability that lay inside.

*Just man up and get it over with,* the voice suggested.

"Easy for you to say," Hayes muttered, reaching out for the doorknob, "*you're* not the one she wants to kill."

*Yeah, that's a good point.*

**42**

C yrus Vandal sat on the balcony, watching the right-to-left sweep of the S-band antenna as it siphoned the cell phone, microwave, and radio signals emanating from the city. After each pass the data was shot to the laptop, which recorded the relative location of each voice and converted the audio into a chain of ones and zeros before feeding them into the computer's voice analysis software.

For the first few hours he'd sat enrapt before the laptop, watching the scroll of data as it passed through the voice analyzer, waiting for the *ding* in his ears to tell him the computer had found a lock—found Adam Hayes.

But after watching the endless blink of the NO MATCH icon across the top of the screen, Vandal found his attention beginning to wander as the frantic pace of the previous twenty-four hours finally caught up with him and he closed his eyes. He savored the gentle breeze that scampered across the balcony and the soothing hiss of the scanning S-band through the headphones pressed over his ears.

He felt himself drifting off and was almost asleep when there was an electronic *ding* in the headphone. In an instant he was wide awake, eyes snapping to the laptop on the table beside him and the blinking VOICE MATCH—PROBABILITY HIT 99.9%.

*Hayes. I found him.*

Using the trackpad, Vandal brought up the audio clip and pressed the play button, the beep in his ears replaced by the acid hiss of the recording.

*"Tomorrow, eight a.m."*

*"Where?"*

*"The Museu da Moeda, you know it?"*

*"Yeah,"* Hayes said.

*"Nice and public, just like you wanted."*

*"Fine. See you there, and bring my pistol."*

He played it again, focusing on the voices. The first man had sounded Australian, maybe South African. Vandal couldn't be sure, but there was no confusion about the second voice.

It was Hayes, no doubt about it.

He ripped the headphone from his ear and leapt to his feet, phone in his hand, dialing as he stepped into the room. He held the phone in front of his face. *C'mon, c'mon, hurry the fuck up.*

The instant he heard the camera shutter click, he set the phone on the table, grabbed the Bluetooth, and pressed it into his ear. He stripped out of the clothes he'd been wearing since arriving at the hotel, dressing quickly in a pair of black cargo pants, a micro-thin Kevlar vest, and a graphite shirt.

Vandal was stuffing his feet into the pair of Asolo hiking boots when a voice came on the line.

"Go ahead."

"Do you have the lock?"

"Stand by . . . yes, we have the lock."

"What do we have in the area?"

"Closest ISR asset is a JSOC Reaper operating out of Senegal . . ."

"Anything closer?"

"Negative."

*Shit.*

"Fine, I'll do it myself."

Vandal ended the call, and after shoving the phone into his back pocket, grabbed one of the SIGs from the case. He clipped the holster to his belt, tugged the H&K MP7 from the case, and dropped it and two extra magazines into his assault pack.

Then he was moving to the door, heart hammering in his chest with the thought of drawing first blood.

# 43

## RUSTED NAIL, LUANDA

Hayes stepped inside the Rusted Nail and tugged the faded ball cap down over his eyes, nodding at the group of hard-looking men gathered near the door on his way to the end of the bar. He pressed his back to the wall and lit a cigarette, pretending to smoke while taking stock of his surroundings.

Before coming inside Hayes had done his homework—marked the doors and the windows on the exterior of the building. So he knew that the door ten steps to his right would take him out to the patio and from there down to the beach.

The hall to his left matched up with the two windows on the east side of the building and he assumed they were bathrooms. But he had no idea about the door behind the bar.

*Doesn't matter. Pay attention.*

He turned his attention to the woman behind the bar, watched as she poured the men standing before her a round from a bottle of Patrón.

"C'mon, Charli, take one with us," the tallest one begged in Portuguese.

"Nito, you know I can't afford this stuff."

"It's on me."

"You sure?"

"Yeees, just have a drink with me."

"Well, if you're paying," she said, grabbing the bottle and reaching below the bar for a glass.

Instead of the shot glass the man had expected, Charli came up with a tumbler, poured herself a man-sized drink, smiling as she held it up.

Before the man could recover, she downed the drink, slammed the glass facedown on the bar, and was moving toward Hayes, a huge smile on her face.

"What'll it be?" she asked.

"Johnnie Walker. Black if you've got it," he said, looking up.

The blood drained from her face, leaving her skin white as the scar on her chest. "I—I always knew they'd send you," she said.

Hayes reached out, grabbed her wrist as it flashed toward the rear of the bar.

"Get rid of them," he said, nodding to patrons at the end of the bar.

She tried to jerk her arm away, but Hayes held it firm, careful to use only as much pressure as necessary.

"Get rid of them, Charli, and don't do anything stupid," he said, letting her go.

She jerked her hand free, the fear that had clouded her eyes receding like the surf at low tide as she massaged her wrist. "And if I do? What are you going to do, shoot me in the back? Doesn't seem like your style."

"Do you really want to find out?" Hayes asked, hand falling to his waist.

"Fuck you, Adam," she snarled, whirling away from him and stomping back to the far side of the bar to tell the men it was time to leave.

"Leave? But it's not even eight," one of the men complained, "and I haven't finished my drink."

"Come back tomorrow," she said, "and I'll make it up to you."

The men might have been tipsy, but they weren't stupid, and quickly figured out the reason that they were being cut off. "Is this because of him?" the tallest of the group asked.

"No, Nito, I'm just tired."

But the man wasn't having it.

"What did you say to her, *gringo*?" he demanded. Charli's easy smile faltered as the man started toward the end of the bar. "Hey, I'm talking to you."

Hayes watched him.

"*Cuidado*"—careful—"big man," he said, "nothing down here but trouble for you."

"*Nito,*" Charli said, her voice sharp as a whip, "if you ever want to drink in here again, you'll leave, now!"

Her tone caught the man off guard, froze him in place, and he looked back at his mates for reassurance.

"Let's get out of here, *mané,*" one of the men said, his hand already on the knob.

"Fine," he nodded, "but you better watch yourself, *cabrão.*"

"Yes, yes, now go," Charli said, shooing them from the bar.

"Nice guys," Hayes said.

"Luanda is a rough place and the locals don't take to foreigners," she answered, throwing the deadbolt and extinguishing the light over the door. "But once you gain their trust and they finally accept you . . ."

The last of her sentence trailed off as Charli spun on her heel, a silver automatic in her hand, the safety already snicking free as she snapped the pistol on target, eyes wide over the sights when she found herself aiming at an empty chair.

Hayes came in fast, his hands around the pistol before she even knew he was there. At this range he knew a hundred ways to kill, but instead he used a simple wrist toss to send her to the floor, waiting until she was on the ground before gently pulling the pistol from her grip.

"You done?" he asked.

"Go ahead, finish what you started," she snarled, pulling down her shirt, exposing the mass of scar tissue.

Hayes stepped back and dropped the magazine from the pistol, and cleared the round from the chamber before dropping it on the table.

"Kinda figured you'd still be holding a grudge."

"You tried to kill me," she said, "so yeah, you can say I'm still holding a grudge."

"Word on the street was that if the bullet had been an inch to the left you'd be in the ground right now."

"Yeah . . . so?"

"You know how hard it is to miss by an inch at seven hundred yards?"

"Wait . . . what?" she demanded, the anger falling from her face.

"Charli, I've never missed a shot in my life," he said, heading back to the bar.

By the time she got to her feet and came to join him, he'd selected a bottle of kapuka, the homemade vodka favored by the Angolans, and was filling a second shot glass. He watched her sidle up to the bar, eyes as suspicious as ever.

"Let's say I believe you. Believe that you missed me on purpose," she said, taking one of the glasses. "Why would you do that?"

"Because I only kill people who *deserve* it," he said, downing the shot, the white liquor hot as fire on the way down.

She looked down at the scar and then up at him, her face suddenly somber.

"I remember coming out of surgery, the doctors telling me how lucky I was. The police wanting to know what happened, who shot me, and why."

"Did you tell them it was because you were selling guns to the Libyans?"

"Yeah," she snorted, "that's exactly what I told the Egyptian secret police." Then her face went serious. "No, I told them . . ."

"Told them that you got hit by a stray bullet while filming the protests in Cairo," he finished for her.

"How did you . . . ?"

*Who do you think took you to the hospital, Charli?*

"Word gets around."

"So, if you're not here to kill me," she said, grabbing the bottle and refilling their glasses, "what the fuck do you want?"

"I need your help," he answered.

"Friends don't ask for favors."

"Yeah, well, we aren't friends," Hayes replied. "Besides, you owe me."

"Fine. What do you want?"

"Guns, Charli, I need guns."

"I don't do that anymore," she said.

"Really?" Hayes said, taking a step back and giving the iron-bound door to his rear a sharp kick of his heel. "So, this must be where you keep the champagne?"

"You're a bastard, you know that, right?" Charli asked, digging a ring of keys from her pocket on her way around the bar.

"Takes all kinds."

She unlocked the door and reached past Hayes to flick a switch on the wall, the single bulb hanging from the bare ceiling revealing a flight of metal stairs.

"Ladies first," Hayes said, stepping out of the way.

"Do *not* tell anyone about this room," she snapped.

"Scout's honor," he said, letting her get a few steps ahead before falling in behind her. His hand curled around the butt of the Beretta.

At the bottom of the stairs, she typed a code into the keypad on the wall and the overhead lights blinked to life. Hayes offered an appreciative whistle as she unlocked the floor-to-ceiling weapons lockers that lined the wall.

"Damn, girl, for someone who's out of the game, you sure have a lot of toys," he said.

"After you shot me I decided to give up the quantity and step up the quality," she answered.

"So, no more Russian surface-to-air missiles and crates of Italian land mines?" Hayes asked, moving to the lockers.

"I don't sell junk," she said.

The first three lockers contained nothing but battle rifles, the weapons hanging on the racks reflecting Charli's commitment to quality. The Belgian FN SCARs, Austrian Steyrs, and Israeli-made Tavors left Hayes feeling like a kid in a toy store.

"You got a bag?" he asked, taking an H&K 416 with a 40-millimeter grenade launcher mounted beneath the barrel from the rack.

"Sure do," she said.

Fifteen minutes later, Hayes stood at the workbench working the blade of the Cold Steel trench knife over a sharpening stone. He tested the edge against his thumb and slid the blade into its sheath.

He dropped the knife into the bag. Charli was at his elbow as he studied the contents.

Besides the H&K, Hayes had selected a Knight's Armament PDW, B&T APC 9-millimeter submachine gun, Remington 12-gauge TAC-14 shotgun, plus a bandolier of 40-millimeter high-explosive grenades, and two fully automatic Glock 18Cs.

"Sure you didn't forget anything?" she asked wryly.

"You don't happen to have a gunship lyin' around, do ya?"

"No," she said.

"Then I guess this will work."

"So, does this make us even?" she asked.

"Yeah, Charli," he said, hefting the bag onto his shoulder. "We're square."

"Good, now get the hell out."

"I'm going, I'm going," he said, starting up the stairs.

He was almost to the top when Charli yelled up from the bottom, "Hey, Adam?"

"Yo," he said, turning around.

"Think fast," she said, tossing him an olive drab pouch.

He snatched it out of the air and flipped it over, frowning at the red cross sewn on the front. "A trauma kit? What's this for?"

"Because, no matter what you keep telling yourself," she said, flashing a lopsided frown, "you're not the man you used to be."

"You take care of yourself, Charli," he said—and then he was gone.

# 44

RUSTED NAIL, LUANDA

B y the time Vandal arrived at the grid coordinates, the chem
had kicked in and his heart was pounding against his breast-
bone like a sledgehammer on an anvil. He killed the engine
and cracked the window, letting his senses acclimate to the darkness before climbing out.

He stuck to the shadows, moving along the east side of the
road, the urgent beep of the GPS in his ear telling him that he was
getting close to the signal's point of origin.

*Where the hell are you?*

Vandal stepped off the curb, continuing south, the slowing of
the tone in his ear telling him that he was moving *away* from
the POI.

He retraced his steps to the mouth of the alley, knowing that

if it hadn't been for the GPS he would have missed the dented
SUV backed into the shadows.

*You need to slow down,* the voice commanded. *Get your head
out of your ass if you don't want to go home in a box.*

The first time Vandal heard the voice he was in one of Site
Tango's operating theaters—one second he was dancing with Mi-
chael Jackson on a propofol cloud and in the next instant he was
wide awake, a scrum of men and women in light-blue scrubs
hovering over him.

*What in the hell?*

Vandal had tried to lift his arms but found they were secured
to the bed—the helplessness sending his heart rate skyrocketing.

"Doctor, he's awake," one of the nurses had said, "blood pressure 140 over 90 and rising."

"Shit," a second voice had said. "Can somebody dose this guy
before he tears these sutures?"

Vandal had opened his mouth, tried to scream, to ask what
they were doing to him, but they'd put a tube down his throat and
all that came out was a muffled groan. He'd shaken the bed, trying
to rip free, the clang of the metal competing with the flashing red
lights and blaring alarms on the monitors that surrounded his bed.

Then he'd heard it—*You need to relax. Everything is fine.*

He'd turned his head, searching for the source of the voice, but
all he'd seen was a blur of scrub tops rushing around him.

*Relax, I'm here now,* the voice had instructed.

Then everything had gone black.

From that moment on, the voice was his constant companion.
Always chattering in his head, offering suggestions, telling him
where he'd screwed up. Reminding Vandal that the days of being
alone inside his own head were gone for good.

"Enough to make a man want to clean out his mouth with buckshot," he muttered.

Before the voice had a chance to reply, there was Hayes, walking out of a bar, bulging bag over his shoulder.

*Holy shit, there he is.*

The sight of his quarry sent a shot of adrenaline rushing through his veins and Vandal's hand inside his jacket for the suppressed H&K MP7 strapped below his left arm.

*Are you out of your mind?* the voice demanded. *This isn't Compton. You're a professional, for God's sake. Get in close and do it right.*

"Fine," he said.

For an instant it looked as if Hayes was going for the alley, but instead he stayed on the sidewalk, heading toward Fortress São Miguel.

Vandal stepped out of the shadows and fell in silently behind him.

*You're too close. Back off,* the voice warned.

But Vandal could see that Hayes was heading for one of the many alleyways that lined the street, and instead of listening to the voice and backing off, he sped up.

*What the hell are you doing?*

*Will you shut the hell up and let me work?* Vandal demanded, wishing the voice had come with an off switch.

He slowed at the alley, the H&K out and up as he panned wide, the Aimpoint Micro mounted to the rail clearing the edge of the brick in time for Vandal to see his prey turn into a second alley.

He knew he should be patient, but the thrill of the hunt combined with the amphetamines coursing through his system was too heady a mixture to resist. Vandal stepped off in pursuit.

Keeping the buttstock pressed against his shoulder, he lowered the muzzle and slipped down the alley, cheating to the left as he approached the intersection.

He leaned out, the submachine gun coming up, his thumb already pressing the selector from safe to fire, but the alley was empty.

Vandal moved forward at a crouch, his senses straining to the max, head and eyes on a swivel. *Where the hell did he go?*

He was a quarter of the way inside the alley when he saw the low gate, and the fresh boot print pressed into the damp earth.

Reaching out, he grabbed the top of the gate and, easing it to him, slipped silently through. The prints continued straight, toward a chest-high brick wall. Vandal was moving to follow when he felt the cold press of a barrel against the back of his head.

Hayes was about to step off the curb when he saw the figure waiting in the shadows. At first he thought it was Nito, waiting to tune him up after being forced out of the bar, but then the man reached into his jacket and Hayes saw the glint of a suppressor in the moonlight.

*Yeah, that ain't Nito.*

He seamlessly changed directions and, staying on the sidewalk, started toward the fortress and the maze of alleyways that lined the surrounding neighborhood.

Hayes took his time, each step measured and sure as he followed the snaking shadow of the sidewalk. The purpose of his leisurely pace was twofold. First and foremost, it kept whoever was on his tail from realizing they'd been made, but more important, it allowed Hayes to take maximum advantage of his environment. Use the glass-fronted shops and the mirrors of the vehicles parked on the street to watch the watcher.

From first contact, the moment he saw the bulbous tube of the suppressor attached to the end of what looked like an MP7, Hayes knew the man was a pro.

While he had a laundry list of enemies who'd love to see him dead, the fact that the man on his tail was all by his lonesome meant one of two things—he was either extremely sure of himself, or he was from Treadstone.

Hayes was tired and all he really wanted to do was head back to the hotel and get some sleep, but at the moment, that didn't appear to be in the cards.

He ducked into the first alley, forcing himself to maintain his pace, staying at a determined walk, waiting until he was into the second alley before breaking into a jog, taking a hard right toward the gate. Stomping his foot down hard in the dirt before blasting through.

Hayes stayed in the sprint for another few yards, making sure to scuff the ground, before circling back to the gate, ducking into the shadows, and waiting to see if the man would follow.

He lowered the duffel to the ground and pulled out the Beretta, threaded the suppressor he'd taken from Charli onto the barrel. He was snugging it tight when he heard it—the gentle creak of the gate being pulled open.

The shadow came in slow, the H&K up and ready to fire, the man's eyes locked on the fresh print on the ground. Hayes let him pass and then moved in behind him, jammed the suppressor hard into the back of his skull.

"You do anything but breathe and I'll burn you down. You hear me?"

"Yeah, I hear you."

"Good, now, on your knees."

"I'm not—"

"Wrong answer," he said, clipping the man hard across the back of the neck, the blow sending him and the MP7 in his hand clattering to the ground.

But before he had a chance to press the advantage, his attacker spun and tried to sweep Hayes's leg.

He stepped back to avoid the sweep, and then his attacker was on his feet, firing a meaty hook toward the side of his head.

Hayes sidestepped the blow and brought the pistol up to fire, but before he could pull the trigger, the man hit him with a wicked backfist to the side of the head that sent the Beretta spinning from his hand.

During Hayes's career he'd been hit by every size of man on planet earth. From skinny brawlers to barrel-chested heavyweights, he'd been rocked by them all. But the crash of the man's fist against the side of his face left him feeling like he'd just been hit by a train.

The blow starred his vision and he stepped back, desperate for space to recover, but his attacker offered no quarter.

"Let's see what you've got, old man."

He came in hard and fast and hit him with a sweeping right to the gut that blasted the breath from his lungs. Hayes doubled over, somehow managing to get his arm up and block the man's knee before it crushed his face.

"Shit, I thought this was going to be a fight," the man taunted, before firing a lightning jab that smashed Hayes in the nose and sent a tidal wave of blood flooding into his mouth.

*Who the hell is this guy?*

Hayes feigned a right cross that sent the man bouncing directly into the chopping leg kick that smashed into the outside of his attacker's thigh.

It was a solid blow, one that would have broken the leg of a smaller man, but the man brushed it off with a smile and countered with a head kick of his own.

Hayes managed to get his arm up and brace for impact before the man's shin slammed into his biceps, the force shoving him off balance and turning his arm instantly numb. Seeing that he was hurt, his attacker tried to end the fight with a flurry of punches, but Hayes was done fighting fair.

Ducking beneath the first punch, he reached down, scooped up a handful of dirt, and flung it in the man's eyes. His attacker cursed, and while he was trying to clear the grit from his eyes, Hayes drove his knee into the man's groin, followed by snapping a forearm to the face that sent his attacker staggering backward.

The man let out an angry war cry and sent a looping hand slicing through the air, but Hayes threw himself under it, ducked into a roll, and came up with the Beretta.

"Playtime's over, junior," he said, double-tapping the man in the chest.

# 45

By the time Hayes got back to the hotel it was midnight and he barely had the strength to make it upstairs. After the beating he'd taken earlier he was already well past the point where a normal man would have given in to the pain. Part of him wanted to lie down and die, but quitting wasn't an option.

Not because he didn't want to, but because he didn't know how.

He walked into his room, fingers leaving a streak of crimson on the handle, and dumped the bag of guns on the bed before limping into the bathroom and turning on the shower. He stripped out of his clothes and stepped beneath the ice-cold water.

After the shower, he toweled off, used the second box of bandages on his face and the iodine on his busted knuckles, and then shuffled back into the bedroom. Barely enough gas in the tanks to strip the sheets from the bed and make a pallet on the floor.

Finally, he grabbed the baby monitor connected to the camera he'd set in the hall, made sure it was working, and after setting it on the floor beside him, laid his head on the pillow.

Then he was out.

Hayes lay on the floor, one second dead to the world and in the next instant wide awake, rolling free of the pallet, the suppressed Knight's Armament PDW cradled in his hand, senses straining for the sound that had woken him up.

Then he saw it, the flash of the phone vibrating on the floor next to his pallet.

"Charli?" he asked, answering the phone. "What's going—"

"You're burned."

*Burned? What the hell? No one even knows that I'm here.*

The rush of adrenaline that came with the words cut through his fogged mind like the early morning sun, and he instinctively moved to the window.

"What are you talking about?"

"I'm talking about the hit team that just broke into my bar," Charli said.

*Oh, no.*

"Are you . . . ?"

"I'm fine," she said, "they came in after I'd locked up and gone home. Wouldn't have known what was going down if my security camera hadn't been linked to my phone."

"Still the luckiest girl I've ever met," he said.

"Yeah, and you're still a shit magnet."

"Seems that no good deed goes unpunished these days," he said.

"You'll never balance the scale. You know that, right?" Charli asked.

"Thanks for the heads-up," Hayes said, ending the call.

He got dressed in the dark and was putting on his shoes when he saw a van pull to a stop outside the hotel, the cargo door sliding open and men with guns climbing out onto the street. Hayes took in the proceedings with the detached eye of a predator—the questions rapid-firing through his brain. There was no doubt about the men's intent: They were there for him.

*But how did they find me?*

He'd done everything right, dumped his phone, spent an hour running countersurveillance, making sure no one was following him before coming back to the hotel.

He dismissed the question as irrelevant. The why and the how would come later; right now, the only thing that mattered was what he did in the next few minutes.

That his attackers had lost the element of surprise gave him the advantage, but, turning away from the window and taking stock of his gear, Hayes knew that whatever edge he had was time sensitive.

Holding the baby monitor, Hayes moved to the door, eyes locked on the screen. He'd been here before: alone and outgunned, heart hammering in his chest like a runaway jackhammer, every sound—every creak of a guest shifting in their bed or knock of the aged pipes—amplified a thousand percent.

He worked on his breathing, took a deep breath through his nose and held it in his lungs for a five count before exhaling. It was a simple exercise, one designed to reset the body's natural fight-or-flight reaction, and his pulse had almost returned to normal when he saw the first man step out of the stairwell.

*Here they come.*

# 46

Hayes set the monitor on the floor, the Knight's Armament in his hand feeling like an extension of his body, watching the six-man kill team slip down the hall, the emerald halos pooling from their night-vision goggles giving them the appearance of green-eyed ghouls.

Two doors short of Hayes's room, the point man raised a fist into the air and the stack stopped on a dime. The man tapped the flat of his hand to the top of his helmet and then he was moving, two shooters tucked into his hip pocket while the rest of the team stayed put.

He carried the cell past the door, dropping the number three man on the knob side and carrying the number two man across the threshold. Once on the other side of the door, the point man covered the hall, while the number two man turned to face his mate on the other side of the door.

When he was set, he lifted his rifle to high ready—the signal that the number three man had the door.

Inside the room, Hayes watched the breacher reach for the knob, ready to rock and roll—yank open the door and engage the second the charge laid him flat. But before he had, a low *pssst* cut through the silence and the breacher froze. The fingers of his bare hand hovering inches from the knob.

Hayes followed the sound to its source and had just turned his head to the left when a seventh man stepped into view. The greenish-yellow glow emanating from the device strapped to the man's wrist provided the answer to how the kill team had found him.

The moment he saw the light, Hayes turned away from the door and rushed to his bag. He ripped the front zipper open and retrieved Zoe's insulin case. Everything suddenly made sense. Mallory canceling the meeting—the kill team finding it at the hotel.

*You stupid, gullible asshole.*

He carried the case to the mini-fridge and tossed it inside, but when he moved back to the door and pressed his eye to the peephole, he realized it was too late.

Out in the hall, the man was still studying the device on his wrist, but it was obvious from the way he kept turning his body from left to right that the fridge's lead lining had blocked the signal.

Hayes knew it didn't matter—they knew he was there, and it was only a matter of time before they found him.

*You can run,* the voice suggested.

Hayes considered it, but realized if the fall didn't kill him, whatever security element the assault team had downstairs would.

No, he was going to have to fight.

Having already retrieved his makeshift flashbangs from the spot beneath the floorboards, he retrieved one from the pack Charli had given him and studied the fuse as he moved to the door.

The majority of off-the-shelf flashbangs used a time-delay fuse that gave the user four to five seconds between the time he pulled the ring and detonation. Hayes, on the other hand, had been forced to make his own fuse, and considering how much magnesium he'd stuffed into the makeshift munition, he hoped that he'd gotten the calculations correct.

*Only one way to find out.*

He slung the rifle across his chest, grabbed the doorknob, and twisted it open—wincing inwardly at the creak of the spring. *Damn, Marta, you ever heard of oil?*

With the door prepped, Hayes hooked the ring over his thumb and took a deep breath, clearing his mind of everything but the actions he'd planned to take on contact, knowing that all it was going to take was one stray bullet—one misstep on his part and it was game over.

"Here goes nothing," he said.

In an instant everything slowed, and Hayes was aware of every detail: The tug of the pin ripping free. The door yawning wide, revealing the assaulter in the hall, his eyes locked to his wrist. Followed by the muted bang of the knob slamming into the wall. The assaulter's head jerking at the sound, eyes wide when he saw Hayes standing there, a smoking IED in his left hand, rifle coming up in his right.

"Oh, shit."

"You got that right," he said, firing a three-round burst into the center of the man's chest plate.

The impact of the rounds sent his target stumbling backward, and before he'd hit the opposing wall Hayes had hooked the flashbang at the stack of assaulters and ducked back into the room.

The bang detonated with the roar of a howitzer, the explosion shaking the walls, sending plaster falling from the ceiling.

When Hayes stepped back out into the hall, he found the carpet on fire and the assault team stumbling blindly through the dense cloud of white smoke. He was about to open fire on the men when the assaulter he'd shot before tossing the bang pushed off the wall and tried to swing his rifle onto target.

Hayes hit him with a buttstock to the side of the helmet and a thrust-kick to the chest, but neither blow put the man down, and before he had a chance to fire a shot, his teammates had recovered from the blast.

"Kill him," one of the men yelled, spraying a burst down the hall.

*Get to cover.*

Hayes ducked beneath the bullets, drove his shoulder into his attacker's gut, and looped his nonfiring hand around the back of the man's legs. Without breaking stride, he lifted the man off his feet and drove him through the door on the other side of the hall.

Inside the room, Hayes dumped him headfirst onto the floor, the impact knocking the man unconscious.

"Don't go anywhere," he said, yanking a fragmentation grenade from the man's belt.

Hayes let the spoon fly and moved to the door, counting in his head while he cooked off the grenade.

"You assholes picked the wrong hotel," he shouted, leaning out and underhanding the frag down the hall.

"*Grenade!*" one of the assaulters shouted—and then he was gone. Lost in the thunderous explosion.

. Hayes stepped out of the room, the dust kicked up by the explosions scalding the back of his throat. He scanned the hall, taking in the damage to the walls, the blown-in doors, and the blood pooling from the crumpled figures lying on the floor.

*Man, ol' Marta is going to be pissed in the morning.*

He was about to head back to the room when a muffled groan signaled that one of his attackers had survived.

*Looks like we've got a live one.*

Hayes pulled a Streamlight Micro from his pocket before toeing the assaulter onto his back. With a click of the pressure pad, he activated the flashlight and shined it into the man's face.

"Wikus," he hissed.

"D-don't kill me . . ." he begged.

"Oh, I'm not going to kill you," Hayes said, returning the light to his pocket and lifting Wikus from the ground. "Not when we've got so much catching up to do."

# 47

MAYOTTE

Gone? What the hell do you mean she's gone?" Cabot demanded.

"Sir, we . . . I mean . . ." Mallory stuttered. "*I* don't know."

"Well, what the fuck *do* you know?"

"Sir, if I may," Beck said, nodding at the phone. "Ms. Mallory," the big German began, "tell us what happened."

"We . . . the team followed the tracker to the hotel in Angola. They had a lock. They never got positive ID on Zoe, but the man . . . Adam Hayes . . . he was there."

"And?"

"The team went in and he"—Beck hooked a thumb at the closed door—"was the only one who came out."

*Six men. Six of my best men go in and only one comes out. How? How does something like that happen?*

Cabot was no stranger to violence—to violent men. He'd seen enough of them during his time at the DGSE, shark-eyed men who could kill you with something as innocuous as a pencil. But that was their job, their *raison d'être*—reason for being—but this Hayes, he was just a smuggler. A pilot.

*No, something about this isn't right. Something is not adding up. But what?*

Cabot knew there was only one way to find out.

"Bring him in," he said.

The German nodded, slipped across the room, and opened the door.

"You, inside," he said, leaning out.

Cabot finished his drink and, leaving the empty lowball at the window, returned to his desk. He took a seat, but instead of looking at the man, he turned his attention to the monitor on his desk and studied the personnel file on the screen.

While Cabot had ultimate say when it came to the hiring and firing of DarkCloud personnel, he didn't meddle with Beck's security teams. The towering German had free rein when it came to hiring *specialists*: the shooters and spies who handled aspects outside of the company's normal purview.

Unlike the techs, programmers, and managers whom Cabot saw on a day-to-day basis, his dealings with these men were limited to signing their paychecks and reading their personnel files.

Before the September 11 terrorist attacks on the United States, these men were harder to find, but two decades of war had created a seemingly bottomless talent pool, a lethal flesh market where with the right introductions and a fat enough wallet you could find men willing and able to kill your boss, guard your yacht, or even invade a foreign country.

Cabot scanned the file, getting a snapshot of the man in front of him. *Tyler King, another fucking American from some no-name town in Texas.* According to the file, he'd done ten years with the Navy SEALs before going to work for the CIA's Special Operations Group. The entry and exit stamps that adorned the photocopied pages of his passport read like the U.S. Consulate's no travel list: Syria, Yemen, Iraq, Indonesia, and Afghanistan— he had them all.

Cabot leaned back in his chair and studied the man standing in front of his desk.

Tyler King was of medium height with wide shoulders, powerful hands, and close-cropped blond hair. Of his facial features the only thing Cabot could be sure of was that he had blue eyes; everything else was a one giant bruise.

"Your résumé reads like a Gray Man novel," he said, "which is why I'm having a hard time understanding how you couldn't kill one man."

"I don't know who that man was, but—"

Cabot cut him off with a wave of his hand and turned his attention back to the screen. "It says here that you have a wife and two daughters back in Texas. Is that true?"

"Yes, sir, Mr. Cabot," Tyler said, the confusion on his face evident.

"Normally they would already be dead, but as a father with a daughter of my own, I've decided to give you the chance to redeem yourself," Cabot said, opening the desk drawer and pulling out a snub-nosed .38.

"What do you mean?" Tyler asked.

"Simple," Cabot said, placing the revolver on the desk. "Take this pistol, put it in your mouth, and pull the trigger. Do that and your family lives."

"And if I say no?"

"If you say no, I will send Beck to your house and he will bring your family back here and I will kill them in front of you."

Tyler looked at him, face hard as he studied Cabot's eyes. "You'd do that? K-kill my little girls?"

"And I wouldn't lose a wink of sleep."

Tyler nodded and picked up the pistol. He checked the cylinder to make sure that it was loaded before putting it to his temple. "I always knew you were a son of a bitch," he said, and then he pulled the trigger.

"Didn't think he had it in him," Cabot said, looking down at the body.

"Tough men, those Texans," Beck said. "Now, what do you want to do?"

"Get the helicopter ready, I want to be airborne in an hour."

"Where are we going, sir?"

"To get my money."

# 48

Hayes mashed the accelerator to the floor and blew through the intersection, the needle sweeping toward sixty when he cut the wheel hard, sending the top-heavy SUV drifting around the corner.

He kept the lights off and the pedal down, pushing the Land Cruiser hard to clear the city, not letting off the gas until there was nothing but black in his rearview mirror.

Hayes had no idea where he was, but quickly realized that it didn't matter. He was alive and if he wanted to stay that way, he needed to find out what in the hell was going on.

Fifteen minutes later, he pulled the Land Cruiser off the road, the headlights casting long shadows across the bare earth before him. He climbed out and did a quick recon of the area before returning to the truck, opening the back door, and looking down at the bleeding man on the floorboards.

"You and me got some unfinished business we need to attend to," he said, grabbing Wikus by the hair and dragging him out of the truck.

Hayes kicked the South African's legs out from under him and slammed him to the dirt, then reached down and yanked the pistol from the holster on Wikus's hip.

"You miss me, girl?" he asked.

The South African's eyes were hard and angry even through the swelling. He tried to scream at Hayes, but with the duct tape covering his mouth all that emerged were random vowel sounds.

"What was that?" he asked, tearing the tape from the man's lips, trying to take as much skin as possible.

"I *said,* fuck you!" the man spat.

"You know, Wikus, I've been looking forward to this day since we first met," he said, shoving the pistol into the back of his pants and limping back to the truck.

"Just get it over with, then. Take that pretty pistol of yours and put a bullet in the back of my skull."

"Let's not get ahead of ourselves," Hayes said, opening the back hatch and pulling out a five-gallon jerrican of gasoline.

"Wait . . . now just wait a bloody minute," the South African said.

"Oh, now you want me to wait?" Hayes asked, unscrewing the cap. "What happened to getting it over with?"

"Look . . . I'll tell you everything I know . . . just give me a—"

"Oh, I'll give you something, all right," Hayes said, upending the can over the man's head.

Wikus tried to scream, to beg, but the fumes choked him, stole his breath, and with his hands zip-tied behind him, he was help-less to do anything but squirm as Hayes doused him with gaso-line.

When the can was empty, he flung it into the darkness and pulled the pack of cigarettes from his pocket. He pressed one between his lips and lowered himself into a crouch.

"D-don't do this . . ." Wikus begged.

"I thought you had something to say," Hayes said, the book of matches he'd taken from the hotel in his hand. "If that's the case, you might want to start talking."

"Zoe . . ." he began.

"What about her?" Hayes demanded, tearing a match from the book.

"I know where she is."

Hayes scraped the match against the striker, the flare of the flame dancing in his cold eyes. He lit the cigarette before extin-guishing the match with a shake of his hand and then settled the weight of his gaze on Wikus.

"And how the hell do you know that?"

# 49

## USS *BATAAN*

After one hundred and eighty-two days at sea, the sailors and Marines aboard the USS *Bataan* were ready to go home. But while the rest of the Amphibious Ready Group galloped west across the Atlantic Ocean, ready to make up for the anniversaries and birthdays they'd missed during their six-month tour, the *Bataan* was still on station, the crew forced to loiter seventy-five miles off the coast of Angola until their unexpected guest cut them loose.

Levi Shaw stood on the signals bridge, the burn of the salt air across his freshly sutured cheek cold as a knife. He looked down at the pair of V-22 Ospreys sitting on the flight line, knowing how bad they wanted to go home and hating himself for being the one standing in their way.

But it couldn't be helped.

After the wreck Shaw knew he had to move fast, make something happen before Carpenter and Senator Miles learned that he was still alive, knowing that the moment they found out they would cut him off at the knees. Shut him out of both the CIA and Treadstone.

Out of options and running short on time, Shaw played the only card he had left—he went to the DoD.

Getting a meeting with the chairman of the Joint Chiefs had cost him every favor that he'd collected during his thirty years with government, and even then all the man would give him was five minutes.

"Better talk fast, Levi. I'm flying out to Camp David in twenty."

"Sir, what do you know about Operation Treadstone?" he began.

That got his attention.

"Go on," the general said.

Shaw knew the next words out of his mouth could very easily end him up in a black site, but he didn't care. The Department of Defense was the only organization left that could protect him— keep men like Miles and Carpenter from using Treadstone as their personal kill team.

In the next few minutes, Shaw told him everything, stripping back the curtains on thirty-plus years of secrecy.

"Jesus," the general said when he was finished.

"I realize it's a lot to take in."

"Like trying to drink from a firehose," the man said. "But I'm still not exactly sure what it is you want."

"It's simple, sir. I turn Treadstone over to the DoD, give you the labs, the training, the assets, everything you need get the program back on track."

"And what do you want in exchange?"

"One of my men is in trouble and I need your help to get him out before the CIA kills him."

Shaw was still thinking about the general's face when the door swung open and the *Bataan*'s commanding officer stepped out—steam billowing from the coffee mugs clutched in his pawlike hands.

"Thought you could use one of these," he said, offering one of the mugs.

"Appreciate it, skipper," Shaw replied, following the captain back to the railing.

He took a sip, the strong black coffee warming him from the inside out.

"You get any sleep, or did you spend all night in the signals room?"

"I managed a few hours," Shaw said.

"Liar," the captain smiled.

"How far would you go to save one of your men?" Shaw asked.

The captain sipped his coffee in silence, his brown eyes darting over the deck, taking in the pilots checking over the Ospreys and the team of Marine Raiders collected around the ramp.

"To the ends of the earth, if I had to," he said.

Shaw was about to tell him he'd do the same when the door slammed open behind him and one of the sailors from the signals room stepped out.

"Sir, we just intercepted a call. I . . . I think we found him."

# 50

The Antonov An-12 flew west over Angola, the sound of its flaps and the pitch of its Ivchenko AI-20 turboprops signaling its final approach into Quatro de Fevereiro Airport. In the cargo hold, Andre Cabot watched as Beck and the rest of his security detail busily donned their body armor and checked their rifles before turning his attention to the window.

The first lesson he'd learned at the DGSE was the importance of a simple plan. "People around here believe that for an intelligence operation to work it had to be as complicated as a Swiss watch," his first training officer had told him. "It's bullshit, Andre. Total nonsense, just keep it simple and you will be fine."

It was a lesson Cabot had taken to heart.

One that had guided his rise through the ranks of the

intelligence apparatus, and later allowed him to take DarkCloud from a small startup of five employees to a multibillion-dollar empire.

By the time he met President Edward Obote, the "lesson" had become a rule, the centerpiece of the strategy that guided his every action, which was why Cabot had initially declined to help the Ugandan strongman shore up his sham of a government by spying on his opposition.

*But you didn't, did you?*

There was no need to answer.

The fact that Cabot was risking everything by coming back to Angola with his Russian transport packed full of mercenaries was answer enough.

While other men in his position would have been lured to take the job by the handsome paycheck waiting at the end, it wasn't the money, but the unprecedented access to President Obote's Internal Security Organization and the files the Ugandan intelligence service had been collecting on its African neighbors since 1986 that proved impossible to resist.

It was from these files that Cabot learned of Lars Gunderson, the Senior VP of Angola's Banco Angolano de Investimentos, and the two hundred million dollars of aid money just waiting to be transferred from the bank's wire room.

Before Uganda he wouldn't have even gotten out of bed for two hundred million dollars, but now, with his empire crashing around him and the French government stealing everything that wasn't nailed down, the money was everything.

It was the perfect plan: simple in its design, elegant in its execution. Cabot could have pulled it off without ever leaving his office if it hadn't been for that fat fuck Nigel Pritchard screwing him in Mahé, holding back the codes that would have allowed him to remotely transfer the money from BAI's wire room to the bank accounts he had spread across the globe.

The chirp of the wheels on the tarmac snapped him from his reverie and he turned to find Beck already standing at the tail of the aircraft.

"On your feet," the fierce German yelled, throwing the ramp lever.

The heavily armed mercs collected their gear and weapons, and when the Antonov rolled into the open hangar, followed Beck down the ramp.

By the time the pilots cut the engines and Cabot stepped off the aircraft, the pair of six-wheeled Ural 4320 utility trucks were already running, the mercs packed beneath the vinyl tarps that hung over the cargo beds.

"Are we ready?" he asked.

"Yes, sir," Beck answered.

# 51

## ILHA DE LUANDA, ANGOLA

Hayes drove west on Avenida 4 de Fevereiro, the sight of the Museu da Moeda reminding him how much things had changed in the past hour. Just as he'd suspected, Wikus and Mallory had been planning to kill him at the meeting in the morning.

But now Wikus was gone and if Hayes had his way, Mallory and whoever else was waiting for him across the bridge on the Ilha de Luanda were soon to follow.

A half mile ahead, the road split, the signs planted on the median advising drivers to veer left to stay on the highway. Hayes stayed straight, following the road up the hill, the Land Cruiser's thirty-year-old engine whining in protest as it climbed to the top of the rise.

From the apex, he had a clear view of Luanda Bay, the blinking red lights from the port to his north followed by the strobing marquees and yellow stream of traffic coiling through the city center, and the lengthening blackness of his destination directly ahead.

Hayes drove until the road came to a dead end and turned right onto Avenida Murtala Mohammed, the five-mile thoroughfare that ran the length of Ilha de Luanda. A glance at the map told him that he was nearing his destination. Hayes doused the headlights, cut the wheel to the left, and eased the Land Cruiser off the roadway.

The tires bounced over the curb and Hayes guided the SUV down the back side of the hill. He guided the Land Cruiser into the trees until he was sure it couldn't be seen from the road.

Having already disabled the dome light, Hayes eased the door shut behind him and stepped to the rear of the truck. He opened the hatch and threw back the dusty blanket spread across the floor—the moonlight glinting off the weapons arrayed before him.

The plate carrier he'd taken from Wikus was a size too small and even after letting out the straps, it left a portion of his lower abdomen exposed. But this late in the game, Hayes was just happy to have *any* body armor at all.

He secured the straps over his torso, threw an extra thirty-round mag for the Glock 18C into his assault pack, and grabbed the H&K 416. Closing the hatch behind him, Hayes slipped a 40-millimeter HE round from the pouch on the front of his kit, fed it into the grenade launcher mounted to the bottom of the barrel, and closed the breech.

Then it was time to move.

Hayes ducked into the trees and started east, using the Silva compass he'd taped to the buttstock of the rifle to guide him back toward the road.

Five minutes later, he dropped to a knee at the edge of the tree line—the tiger-striped BDUs and the black-and-green greasepaint smeared across his face rendering him invisible to anyone who might be watching.

He pulled out a pair of night-vision binoculars that he used to study the compound across the street, the sight of the target area taking him back to the darkened stretch of coastal lowland and the fear he saw in Wikus's eyes when he scraped the match against the striker and lit the cigarette.

*"Zoe . . . I know where she is."*

*"And how the hell do you know that?" Hayes demanded.*

*"B-because, I . . . I . . ." he stammered.*

*"You what?"*

*"Listen, if I tell you . . . you've got to—"*

*"No," Hayes said, cutting him off.*

*"If I tell you, he is going to kill me. You have to—"*

*This time, instead of words, he backhanded Wikus hard across the face.*

*The blow snapped the South African's head to the side, spraying droplets of gasoline across the dirt as he fell.*

*"This isn't a negotiation," he said, grabbing Wikus by the shirt and hauling him back onto his knees. "You either tell me the truth or I'm going to turn you into a human tiki torch."*

*"It was Cabot's idea," the South African blubbered. "He took a job working for the president of Uganda, something to do with*

*elections, and it went south. The press found out about it and he got jammed up with the French government. They were seizing his assets and . . ."*

"What the hell does this have to do with Zoe?"

*"I don't know all the details. All Mallory told me was that his passport had been revoked. He couldn't travel to Africa, so he sent Zoe, she was some kind of collateral."*

"Collateral for what?"

*"For the two hundred million dollars of aid money that BAI is holding in their wire room."*

Hayes had seen some evil shit in his life, things that would make Ted Bundy look like a choirboy, but nothing as twisted as Andre Cabot using his own flesh and blood to get his hands on two hundred million dollars.

*What kind of man does that?*

Hayes didn't know, but of one thing he was certain: *I'm not going to get any answers standing out here.*

He was about to start across the road when he heard the distant rumble of heavy vehicles coming his way. He ducked back into the trees, threw himself flat seconds before a wash of white light bloomed over his position.

Hayes hazarded a quick glance at the road, which only added to his confusion. A line of massive Russian 6x6s were lumbering toward him.

*Who the hell are these clowns?*

He watched the cargo trucks turn into the drive, the lead vehicle's brake lights flashing red as it stopped short of the gate. The passenger door swung open and a tall man with a suppressed rifle climbed down and started toward the wrought-iron gates with what looked like an explosive charge in his hand.

The man bent to study the lock, but instead of placing the charge as Hayes had expected, he grabbed the iron bars and simply shoved them open. He waved the first truck through but stopped the second with an open hand, then moved around to the back of the truck and banged on the tailgate.

A gloved hand reached out, pulling the flap free, revealing a cargo compartment full of heavily armed men.

Hayes was too far away to hear what the man was saying, but as soon as he moved to the front of the truck, two men climbed down from the back, and trotted to the guard shack while the vehicle pulled away.

*Well, that's great.*

He turned and moved north about fifty yards, making sure he was out of the line of sight of the men in the guard shack before darting from cover. He dashed across the street and ducked into the trees that surrounded the target area.

While waiting for his heart rate to settle, Hayes studied the wall and was considering going over, bypassing the guard shack altogether, when he saw a pinprick of red light.

*Camera, shit.*

With going over the wall now out of play, Hayes turned south and started back toward the guard shack. He crept soundlessly through the trees, taking his time, each step slow and silent as a jungle cat stalking its prey. The journey seemed to take an eternity, but he knew that it was probably less than ten minutes later when he stopped short of his target and dropped to a knee—senses straining in the darkness for any sign of the men.

But the night was silent.

Hayes slung his rifle onto his back and drew the trench knife Charli had given him before lowering himself flat. He practically buried his face in the ground and slithered his way forward, the steel of the brass knuckles cold on his fingers.

He took his time, measuring his progress in inches, not feet, silently creeping closer. At five feet he could smell them—the scent of gun oil and the onion stench of their body odor—and hear the muted hisses of their whispers. He knew that even the slightest sound would give him away.

*Nice and easy.*

He slipped to the door, the scrape of metal over concrete freezing him in place.

"Jameson, will you hurry the hell up?" a voice hissed. "This bloody thing isn't exactly light."

"I'm bloody working on it, aren't I?"

Hayes leaned to his right, slowly eased an eye around the doorjamb until he could see inside the shack. He found both guards on the left wall, the one closest to him busy positioning a table near the window while the second struggled under the weight of the belt-fed FN MAG 58 in his hands.

*About time I got a break.*

He stood at the doorway, heart hammering in his chest as he watched the men, forcing himself to wait for the perfect moment to strike. The seconds seemed to stretch into hours but finally the table was in just the right position.

"There," one man said, standing upright.

"About bloody time," the gunner said, reaching for the MAG 58's bipod legs.

Before the gunner had the legs snapped into place, Hayes was inside the shack.

He slipped up behind the closest guard, clamping tight over his mouth, and then in one quick motion he torqued the man's neck to the side, burying the blade in his neck. Hayes felt the man sag in his grip and jerked the blade free, shoving the dying man across the room.

The second man had just set the machine gun on the table when he heard the wet smack of his mate slapping into the wall.

"Jameson, what the hell?" he demanded, turning.

The gunner took a step forward and stopped, and while his mind struggled to process what he was seeing, Hayes was all over him.

He grabbed the man by the back of the hair, and after slamming his face hard into the brick wall, sunk the knife into the base of his spine.

It was instant paralysis. The man dropped like a stone, Hayes waiting until he was laid out on the ground before driving the heel of his boot into the man's throat.

Hayes bent over the dead man. After he'd cleaned the blade, he returned the knife to its sheath and snatched the man's radio off his kit. After turning the volume down and clipping the radio to his belt, he collected the men's grenades, stuffed them into his pockets, and unslung his rifle.

With the rifle pressed tight to his shoulder, Hayes moved to the door, checked to make sure it was clear, and stepped into the night. He darted behind one of the palm trees that lined the drive and pulled the night-vision binos from his cargo pocket.

Hayes dropped to a knee and studied the parking lot, making a note of the three empty vehicles parked short of the building— a bank—before turning his full attention to the men deploying from the back of the Russian 6x6s.

While he watched the mercs ready their weapons, the radio clipped to his hip hissed to life, and a man with a French accent began barking orders over the net.

At the sound of the voice, Hayes shifted away from the men massed behind the 6x6 to the fuzzy silhouettes standing next to the open passenger-side door. He thumbed the focus knob and made minute adjustments until he had a clear view of the men.

The first was tall and broad-shouldered with a scar across his face that looked bone-white in the ambient light. But it was the man with the radio that held his attention.

*Cabot.*

Hayes activated the binos' internal range finder, the red 400 YDS that flashed across the screen telling him the distance from the palm to Cabot's position in front of the truck.

At that distance he'd be hard pressed to hit the man with one of the 40-millimeter grenades. The rifle, on the other hand, was a different story.

But before he had a chance to even *think* about taking the shot, the thump of boots across the asphalt told him that the containment team was on the move.

He dropped the binos to the dirt, cursing himself for his lack of focus, knowing that the men were wearing night vision—if even one of them had been paying attention to the range finder's infrared laser, he was already given away.

*You dumb shit,* the voice chided. *What were you thinking?*

Hayes brought the rifle up to his shoulder and watched the

darkened shapes fanning out across the parking lot. The realization that they might be maneuvering on him left him feeling exposed. But while his instincts screamed for him to move—find a new position—Hayes resisted. Knowing while they might have missed the laser, even Ray Charles couldn't miss a man running across the lawn.

*No, hold fast.*

Hunkered down behind the palm tree, Hayes was starting to think that he'd gotten away with it—that the men hadn't seen him—when he heard "light him up" followed by the opening burp of a machine gun.

*Well, that answers that.*

Keeping his body behind the tree, Hayes managed to fire off a grenade before the first line tracers came whipsawing overhead. Still on one knee, he snapped open the breech, ejecting the spent casing and shoving a second 40-millimeter round inside when the grenade detonated with a flash of orange and a resounding *cruuump*.

The machine gun fell silent and Hayes was on his feet, angling toward the cover of a parked pickup to his front. He was almost to cover when a second shooter opened up from his right, close enough that he saw the gunner's face backlit by the muzzle flash.

With no time to aim, and his index finger still curled around the trigger of the 416, Hayes pointed the rifle in the general direction of the shooter's feet and fired.

The grenade hit the ground five feet in front of the man and detonated, the blast blowing the man off his feet, and Hayes was almost to the back of the pickup when a second shooter arced in, the AK in his hands strobing as he fired.

Hayes brought the EOTech up on target and was pulling the

trigger when a bullet slammed into his chest, the impact cracking a rib and sending him staggering off balance.

*Shit, already?*

Pushing away the pain, he managed to bring the rifle to his shoulder and stitch a burst across the shooter's chest before throwing himself to cover behind the vehicle.

"He's behind the truck!" a voice shouted.

Hayes dug a frag from his pocket, pulled the pin, and lobbed the frag at his attackers, the bullets hammering the bed of the truck telling him it was time to move.

*But where?*

The grenade exploded and Hayes leaned out and opened fire on three men rushing toward him, managing to drop two of them before a hail of return fire sent him scrambling back to cover.

*Got to move,* he thought, inching to the front tire.

# 52

## ILHA DE LUANDA, ANGOLA

Andre Cabot was out of the 6x6 the second it stopped in front of the building, barking orders into the radio clutched in his hand.

"Alpha, I want this building secured. Bravo, get a perimeter set. *No one* in or out, do you understand?"

"Alpha copies."

"Bravo copies."

"Good. Now fucking *move*!"

"You heard Mr. Cabot!" the team leaders yelled over the banging of the tailgates and the scuffle of boots and muted curses as the men leapt from the back of the trucks.

The men hit the ground en masse and then, like liquid mercury, instantly separated into smaller units—Bravo breaking into gun teams before racing off into the darkness, Alpha already stacked up and moving toward the door.

The team leader stopped the men short of the door with a closed fist, his voice little more than a whisper when he keyed up over the radio.

"Breachers up."

Three men from the rear of the stack peeled off and dashed to the door, two of them pulling cover while the third slapped a charge on the door. He worked fast, clipping the det-cord into the blasting cap, and then he moved backward, unspooling the wire from the pouch.

"Set," the breacher said as soon as they reached the minimum safe distance.

"Blow it," the team leader responded.

Cabot watched the breacher hook his finger through the ring at the top of the firing device and instinctively turn away a split second before the door exploded in a reverberating boom. By the time he turned around, the first three men were stepping through the breach, the number one man turning left, digging his hard corner, the number two man tight on his tail, when Cabot saw the firefly blink of muzzle flashes through the smoke, followed by the staccato chatter of a rifle opening up.

The number two man stumbled, but before he could fall, the next in line shoved him out of the way.

"Alpha Two, frag out," the assistant team leader said, his voice cool as a fan despite the chaos unfolding inside the house.

The grenade detonated in a roar of orange, the concussion blowing out the windows in the room to the left of the door, the rolling thunder of the explosion followed by the distinctive *thwap, thwap—thwap, thwap* of the assault team's suppressed rifles.

"Alpha Two, Tango down."

"Alpha Three, Tango down."

Cabot moved to the bank, sidled up to one of the shattered windows, and peered inside. Through the smoke he could see two bodies splayed out on the floor near the front door, their lack of faces telling him that they'd been caught by the breaching charge. Farther in, one of his men sat slumped against a wall—his killer lying facedown a few feet to his front.

But Cabot didn't care about the dead, all he wanted was his money.

"Alpha, what is taking so damn long?" he demanded over the radio.

Silence.

"Alpha team, come in."

*Dammit.*

"Beck!" he yelled, turning away from the window, his anger burning in his guts hot as a blast furnace.

"Yes, sir?"

"Get in there and find out what in the hell is taking them so long," he ordered.

"Of course," the big German said, before turning to the Bravo team. "You two, come with me."

They rushed inside, the gun smoke in the building closing around them like a charcoal curtain, and then Cabot was alone, helpless to do anything but pace back and forth in front of the shattered window. Painfully aware that the money he so desperately needed was somewhere on the other side of the wall.

*What is taking them so long?*

He was about to ask Beck for an update when a shout from the Bravo team leader drew Cabot's attention to the rear.

The sharp "contact front," followed by the staccato chatter *brrrraaaaaaaap* of one of the belt-fed FN MAG 58s opened up behind him.

Cabot turned in time to see a line of orange tracers zip across the parking lot toward one of the pickups that had been sitting there when he arrived. The bullets slammed into the vehicle, tracers hitting the engine block and bouncing skyward.

"What now?" he demanded, lifting the night-vision monocular to his eye, focusing on the pickup in time to have it whited out by the flash of an exploding grenade. Cabot cursed as he waited for the night vision to recover from the overload of ambient light, and when it did he saw a lone figure leaning out behind the pickup, firing at his men.

*You have got to be joking.*

"Bravo Two, suppressing fire," the team leader ordered over the radio. "Bravo Three and Four, flank left."

Cabot watched in disbelief as the one-man army tore into his men, silenced one of the machine guns with his first grenade, then stopped a fire team's advance with the second.

"Can anyone kill *this motherfucker*?" he yelled into the radio.

"We're on it, sir," the Bravo team leader responded.

Turning his back on the firefight unfolding behind him, Cabot tried to raise the Alpha team leader on the radio, but once again there was no response.

"Beck . . . Beck, what the hell is going on in there?"

Silence.

"Fuck it!" Cabot yelled, slamming the radio to the ground and yanking the Glock 19 from its holster. "I'll do it myself."

He moved to the door, paused to retrieve the flashlight from the assaulter lying facedown in the threshold, pressed the thumb switch, and stepped inside.

The explosive residue and gun smoke hung thick in the air, the particulate catching in the back of his throat, choking him as he crossed the lobby. Cabot pulled an Hermès handkerchief from his coat pocket and, holding it to his nose, started to the back staircase.

He was almost there when the house lights flashed to life. The sudden blaze of yellow against his dilated pupils left him temporarily blinded.

"What the hell?" he growled, raising his hands against the glare.

He blinked away the spots, unaware of the figures arrayed on the balcony above him until one of them spoke.

"Hello, Daddy."

# 53

ILHA DE LUANDA, ANGOLA

Hayes was in the fight of his life, and with more men pouring in, all he could do was aim and fire, aim and fire, until he ran the rifle dry and the bolt locked to the rear. He dumped the mag and dropped to a knee, shoved a fresh magazine into the magwell, and slapped the bolt release.

The reload had taken less than three seconds, but his attackers had taken advantage of the lull in fire and were closing in.

*Shit.*

But it was either that or get cut down in the open.

He kept his finger on the trigger, managing to make it to cover before running the rifle dry again. While he wasn't happy about the ammo, the expended thirty rounds had done their job, left bodies scattered across their line of advance. The second wave faltered—went to ground and began firing indiscriminately across the parking lot.

He prepped another frag and sent it wobbling in the air, waiting for the explosion before darting from cover and throwing himself toward the dead gunners draped over their MAG 58.

Hayes had been in enough gunfights to know that a bullet didn't care about a man's sentiment—or the delicate sensibilities that governed society. A bullet's job was to kill and his was to stay alive and if he had to use a pair of dead bodies to accomplish that task—then so be it.

While his attackers shook off the effects of the grenade, Hayes ripped the machine gun from the dead gunner's hand, and then wrestled the man's body on top of his mates, dropping flat just as the attackers opened fire.

Lying flat, Hayes grabbed the fresh belt of ammo from the ground and worked on reloading the machine gun, doing his best to ignore the meaty *thunk* of the rounds slapping into the dead men's flesh.

He got the gun up, shoved the buttstock into his shoulder, but held his fire, wanting as much meat in the grinder as possible before opening up. He waited, his finger resting on the trigger, as the men rushed toward him—and then let them have it.

The MAG 58 bucked like a bronco, unleashing a wall of lead into the rushing masses. Hayes held the trigger down, working the machine gun back and forth, the bullets cutting the men down like wheat on harvest day.

He ran through the first belt and quickly loaded a second, kept hammering away at the men until the barrel was sunburst red—then it was over.

Hayes stayed behind his makeshift sandbag until he was sure

all the men were dead, then he got to his feet and trotted toward the front of the bank—half deaf from his dance with the MAG 58.

He never heard the vehicle racing across the parking lot.

One second Hayes was running to the front door of the bank and in the next instant he was airborne, his body skipping off the windshield, the impact tearing the rifle from his hands, sending it cartwheeling into the darkness.

He hit the roof, but instead of crumpling beneath his body weight, the thin aluminum flexed like a trampoline and sent him bouncing over the vehicle. As he sailed through the air, Hayes was all too aware of the ground rushing up at him and desperately twisted his body, vainly trying to get his legs beneath him.

But instead of the feline landing he'd been hoping for, Hayes hit like a bag of shit. The impact of his body splattering across the pavement knocked the breath from his lungs and blasted the magazines from the pouches on the front of his kit.

The pain cascaded across his body like a sheet of lightning and he lay there, flat on his face, dimly aware of the magazines skittering across the asphalt and the approaching footfalls that stopped in front of his face.

Hayes lifted his head with a pained grunt, vision swimming as he looked up at the figure standing over him.

"You don't look so good," the man said.

"Didn't I . . . already kill you?" Hayes asked.

"Kevlar," Vandal said, giving the front of his chest an affectionate tap. "Never leave home without it."

"So, I guess," Hayes began, wincing from the effort of pushing himself to his feet, "this means you're ready for round two?"

"If you don't have it in ya, I can always shoot you in the face," Vandal suggested.

"Thanks, but I'll take my chances."

"Well, let's do this," Vandal said, producing a Ka-Bar from the sheath on his hip.

Hayes reached down and drew from his boot the trench knife he'd picked up at Charli's.

The two men circled each other, a grin spreading across Vandal's face. "You pick that up in Flanders, back when you were fighting the Huns?" he asked.

"I've got shit to do," Hayes said. "So, can we get this over with?"

"Fine with me," Vandal said, feinting a slash, while he danced to the right.

Unlike his opponent, who appeared to have all the energy in the world, Hayes was too beat up to take the bait.

Vandal's second slash was the real deal, and the blade came in hard and fast. The speed caught Hayes off guard, forcing him to retreat.

"Have you always been this slow, old man?" Vandal asked.

"Keep talki—" he began, but before he could finish Vandal was darting forward, the knife held low.

Hayes went to parry, but Vandal pulled the blade back and fired a punishing left jab over his guard. The man's knuckles slamming against his face were followed by the white-hot rack of the Ka-Bar across his thigh.

*Shit, he's fast.*

He tried a leg kick, but Vandal avoided it, pivoting out of the way before firing one of his own, the solid thump of the blow tripping Hayes's sciatic nerve and buckling his leg.

"Damn, that looked like it hurt," he taunted.

Hayes was breathing hard, the fight starting to remind him of the one he'd had in Grand-Bassam—the only discernable difference was that this time he wasn't sure he'd be able to finish his opponent.

Vandal continued to toy with him, landing punches and slicing him with the Ka-Bar at will. But after a few minutes of Hayes not mounting a serious defense, he began to tire of the game.

"All right, old man, playtime's over. You got any last words?" Vandal taunted.

Hayes had been waiting for him to stop his amphetamine-fueled bouncing and the moment his feet came to a halt, he hit him with a stiff jab to the mouth. The smash of the knuckleduster against his attacker's jaw sent a pair of molars blasting from his lips.

The blow knocked Vandal on his heels, and he stutter-stepped backward, caught his balance. "Lucky shot," he said, spitting blood.

"You think so?"

Vandal exploded forward, the Ka-Bar hissing through the air as it carved toward his face. But Hayes stepped inside, hit him with two quick lefts, trying to duck beneath the blade, when Vandal slammed the pommel down on the back of his neck.

There was a starburst of pain and Hayes went down on one knee, never seeing the blow that sent him bowling across the asphalt.

He went down hard and immediately rolled to his right, Vandal standing above him, trying to stomp on his face.

"C'mere, you little shit," the man barked, booting him in the side, Hayes knowing from the dry snap and instant firebrand of pain that he'd broken a rib. Then Vandal had him by the hair, lifting his torso off the ground, the Ka-Bar rushing toward his throat.

"I've got you now," Vandal said.

"I don't think so," he said, punching the trench knife through the side of his knee.

The results were immediate. Vandal's leg buckled and he screamed in agony. He released the death grip he had on Hayes's hair and stepped back, staring in horror at the blood spurting from the gash in his pants.

His eyes were off the fight for less than a second, but it was all Hayes needed.

He rolled left and bounced to his feet, the blade slashing up, severing the tendons in Vandal's right arm, the Ka-Bar clattering to the ground as Hayes drove the heel of his boot into the side of the man's damaged knee.

The joint exploded, and the assassin went down, his eyes confused, mouth hinged open in a yawning scream.

Hayes grabbed him by the throat, the rage in his eyes hot as a blowtorch. "You gonna beg?" he demanded, his voice echoing like the drum of a war god.

"Would you?"

"Not a chance," Hayes said, spiking the blade through the top of his skull.

# 54

ILHA DE LUANDA, ANGOLA

Cabot stood rooted in place, the sight of his daughter and Mallory flanked by armed henchmen hitting him like a Taser shot. Panic rushed through his body, paralyzing his brain, leaving his mouth instantly dry.

*Who are these people? Where are my men?*

"Either say something, or close your mouth, Daddy," Zoe said.

"I . . . I don't understand," he stammered, looking from Mallory to his daughter. "What is going on? Wh-who are these people?"

"Two hundred million dollars buys a *lot* of new friends, Daddy. You taught me that, remember?"

The mention of the money sent a torrent of rage tumbling through his body. Its heat burned through the panic that gripped his brain, blotting out the fear of the guns trained on his head.

"That's *my* money!" he yelled, the Glock 19 trembling in his hand.

"*Was* your money." She grinned at him.

All Cabot could think of was killing her right there. Raising the Glock and unloading the magazine, consequences be damned.

*Rather die on my feet than go out on my knees.*

He was about to raise the pistol and take his chances when he caught a flutter of movement out of his peripheral. Cabot's eyes darted left and lingered there for a fraction of a second, just long enough to see Beck and three other men standing just out of sight, before bouncing back to his daughter.

From the brief glance it was obvious the men were in bad shape, their faces and the front of their body armor drenched in blood. But they were alive, which meant Cabot still had a chance.

*Stall her.*

"Zoe, why are you doing this?"

"Why?" she laughed. "Are you serious?"

"Yes, I don't understand why you would do this to me."

"Are you really so self-absorbed, so *full* of your own bullshit that you don't know?"

"I have no idea," Cabot lied.

"Because I fucking *hate* you," she screamed. "I've always hated you, and when I found out why you sent me to Grand-Bassam, when I realized how badly you needed this money to save your stupid company, I promised myself that I would do whatever it took to make sure you never got it."

"Zoe, wh-what have you done?"

"I got rid of it. It's all *gone*."

"You . . . you . . . spoiled little . . . *bitch*!" he screamed, the Glock sweeping up and onto target.

The moment his finger pulled the trigger, time slowed to a crawl and Cabot saw it all—Beck and his men bursting from the doorway, rifles blazing. The man to Zoe's right, grabbing her by the shoulder, throwing her to the ground. A second man jostled Mallory, sending her stumbling into the path of his bullet, which snapped her head back and sent her dropping to the floor.

Hayes was staggering toward the front door, the shotgun he'd stripped from one of the dead men cradled in his hand. He was fifty feet away when the screaming started, much too far to make out the words, but close enough to identify one of the voices.

*Zoe.*

He picked up the pace, forced his battered body into a stumbling shuffle, angling for the side of the open doorway. He was almost there when the gunfire erupted from within the building.

Hayes pressed his shoulder to the brick, feeling the high-caliber rounds slamming into the walls. He had one frag left, but with Zoe inside, he was hesitant to use it.

With no other option, he dug one of the makeshift flashbangs from his assault pack, tugged on the ignitor, and lobbed it inside.

Just like the one at the hotel, the bang detonated with a resounding *boooom*—the concussion blowing out whatever windows were left inside the bank, and when Hayes rolled in, he was immediately overcome by the caustic white cloud of burning magnesium.

But Hayes pushed through, shot toward the hard corner and, seeing most of the shooting was taking place on the second floor, started for the stairs.

He made it to the landing and turned, following the gunfire to the hallway. He was about to pan across when a man with a sub-machine opened up on him, one of the bullets catching him high in the shoulder before he could use his shotgun to drop the man. The pain rolled down his arm, red-hot and scalding, but Hayes pushed it away. Racking the pump, he turned back to the hall. When he panned the opening, he noticed a second shooter posted up in a bathroom to his right. Hayes fired, the spread of 12-gauge buck catching the man in the side, blowing him off his feet.

Because of the low ceilings the gun smoke had nowhere to go and hung in the hall like smog on a summer's afternoon, distorting the outlines of the men blazing away before him.

Not wanting to accidentally hit Zoe with a wayward pellet, Hayes dumped the shotgun and stripped the STI from the holster. He fired on the move, finger dancing on the trigger as he worked the hall, engaging the targets as they appeared in front of him. No time to see if the men went down, only time to point and shoot.

He was halfway through the magazine when he saw a doorway. Hayes cheated to the far side of the hall, and came at the room from an angle. When he crossed the threshold, he collided with a massive man with a blood-spattered face.

His attacker tried to muzzle-punch him in the chest, but Hayes twisted out of the way and chopped the STI across the back of the man's neck. It was a hard blow that would have sent most men to the floor, but the man shook it off. Grabbing him by the front of the plate carrier, the man flung him into the room.

"You little shit," the man cursed in German.

Hayes slammed a hard elbow into his adversary's face, felt the grate of broken teeth and the pop of his jaw before the man bull-dozed him into a desk. He tried to get a shot off, but the big German grabbed his arm and began banging his hand against the desk in a desperate bid to tear the pistol free.

Hayes felt his grip weakening and, knowing that he was a second away from losing control of the pistol, sent his arm raking across the desk, his fingers closing around the handle of a letter opener an instant before the STI went cartwheeling from his hand.

Before the pistol hit the ground, the German had him around the throat and was lifting his head forward, ready to bang the back of his skull into the desk, when Hayes buried the letter opener in the man's eye.

He immediately let go of Hayes's throat and backpedaled across the room, his bloodcurdling shrieks echoing off the walls. The newly freed Hayes managed to stagger from the desk and dropped to his knees beside the STI.

His left arm was numb from the shoulder down, but he managed to get the pistol on target and put a bullet in the center of the man's forehead before collapsing.

Hayes lay on the floor, the now-empty pistol in his right hand—blood pouring from the bullet wounds in his legs and shoulders, soaking the carpet beneath him. He was running on fumes, his body broken and battered, already well past the point where a normal man would have laid down and died.

But Hayes kept moving, following Zoe's screams to the end of the hall.

He reloaded the pistol and, using the desk for support, clawed his way to his feet and staggered out into the hall.

*Hold on, Zoe. I'm coming.*

# 55

ILHA DE LUANDA, ANGOLA

Hayes moved down the hall, his shoulder leaving a trail of blood on the wall. The doorway was only ten feet in front of him, but in his condition it may as well have been a mile.

*Just one foot in front of the next.*

But it was easier said than done.

Hayes stepped off, blood squishing inside his boot with every step.

*You need to put a tourniquet on that leg before you bleed out,* the voice urged. *Can't help anyone if you're dead.*

It was good advice that Hayes knew he should follow, but from the anger in the man's voice at the end of the hall, he wasn't sure if Zoe would last that long.

"Where is my money?" the man shouted. "Give it to me!" The

enraged order was followed by the wet smack of an open hand finding flesh.

"I'm done taking orders from you!" she shouted back.

"You're done taking orders?" the man laughed. "Then how about a bullet?"

Hayes pushed through the door, half stumbled, half fell into the room, just as the man was lifting a Glock 19 toward Zoe's cowering figure.

"Put it down," he ordered, over the sights of the 1911.

"Who the hell are you?" the man demanded, turning to face him.

"Drop it."

"Adam, just kill him!" Zoe shouted.

Usually Hayes wouldn't have hesitated, but there was something familiar about the man, something that kept him from pulling the trigger.

*But what?*

Hayes tried to think, but he'd lost too much blood, and that combined with the multiple shots to the head left his mind swimming.

"Last warning," he said. "Drop it or die."

"You must be the pilot," the man said, tossing the pistol on the table that separated him from Zoe.

"Pilot?"

"Yes, the one who flew my daughter to Grand-Bassam."

"And you're Andre Cabot, Zoe's father."

"That's right," he nodded, "and if you—"

"*No*," Zoe shouted, darting for the table. "You are *not* talking your way out of this one."

The sudden flurry of movement caught Hayes by surprise, and

his head snapped to the left, the arc of the 1911 in his hand slow as molasses.

Zoe, on the other hand, was fast as lightning, and in the blink of an eye had the Glock in a two-handed grip, finger closing around the trigger as she spun toward Hayes. She fired two shots that sent him dropping to the floor.

"I'm sorry, Adam," she said, turning the pistol on Cabot, "but like I said, I'm done taking orders from him."

"Zoe . . . don't . . ."

But it was too late, the Glock was already bucking in her hand, the first shot catching Cabot in the neck, spinning him through the plate glass window and out onto the terrace—the metal railing the only thing keeping him from tumbling over the edge.

He slid to the ground, hand clutched tight over the bullet hole, the bright-red blood spurting through his fingers telling Hayes that he wasn't long for this world.

"Good-bye, Daddy," she said, ending him with a bullet between the eyes.

Then she was moving back to Hayes, the pistol smoking in her hand.

"I bet there are a ton of questions in that tiny brain of yours," she taunted.

"Not really." Hayes winced, right hand pressing hard against the bullet wound, left resting on the floor near his pocket.

"Oh? You have it all figured out?"

"Yeah, I'm a sucker and you're a spoiled rich girl with daddy issues."

"How very American," she sneered, leveling the pistol at his head.

"But you forgot one thing," he said, taking his hand off the bullet wound and reaching over to his left side.

"What's that?"

"I've got a grenade," he said.

Zoe stepped closer and leveled the Glock at his face, a tight smile spreading across her lips.

"Guess I'm just going to have to blow your head off then," she said.

"See that?" Hayes asked, nodding at the spoon lying on the floor next to his leg.

"Yeah . . . what about it?" she asked, her face wrinkling into a frown.

"A couple of seconds ago, that was *on* the grenade," Hayes said, flashing her a bloody smile.

The triumphant smile fell from Zoe's face. She backed up, desperately scrambling for an avenue of escape.

"Might want to run."

She dropped the pistol and took off for the door, Hayes falling onto his side as she rushed past him. He used the last of his strength to send the grenade bouncing after her.

Zoe screamed, her anguished "Noooooo!" cut short by the deep *whuump* of the grenade detonating in the hall.

Then there was silence.

# 56

ILHA DE LUANDA, ANGOLA

All he could think about was getting outside, stopping the bleeding before he lost consciousness.

He got the door open and stepped inside, his blood-filled boot squishing as he stumbled across the room.

*Just keep going,* the voice urged. *You can make it.*

But Hayes wasn't so sure—he was leaking like a sieve. The pain whited out his vision before receding back into his guts, where it clawed at his insides like a rat trying to escape a burning building.

Hayes staggered down the hall, hand pressed tight over the bullet wound, blood seeping through his fingers like a bottle of spilled claret. He was fading fast, his vision tunneling at the edges, the pressure in his chest building, each step on his damaged leg sending a thunderclap of agony reverberating through his body.

There was nothing subtle about the crash: One second he was moving forward, dragging his damaged leg behind him, and in the next instant he was sprawled out on the floor, wondering how in the hell things had gone to shit so fast.

*Get the fuck up.*

But his body refused to listen. It had reached its limit, the beating it had taken over the previous days, the lack of sleep and loss of blood finally catching up to him.

Even the voice had given in, resigned itself to the fact that this was the end.

*It's over.*

"No, not yet," he said, ripping the trauma kit Charli had given him off the front of his plate carrier.

One look at the blood pooling across the tile floor, the crimson stain spreading out beneath his armor, told him what he already knew—he was dying and nothing in the kit was going to change that.

But while saving his life wasn't an option, looking down at the medical supplies he'd dumped between his legs, Hayes realized that if he worked fast enough, he might be able to extend it long enough to say good-bye.

With that in mind, he shrugged out of the plate carrier and took stock of his wounds.

While the bullet wound to the leg was the easiest fix, it was the hole beneath his armpit that needed immediate attention. Hayes cut the assault shirt with the medical shears from the trauma kit, and got his first look at the wound.

It was small, not much larger than a pencil eraser, but he knew from the weight on his chest, and the wet rattle that came with each breath, that the bullet from Zoe's Glock 19 had done its job. It had punched through his ribs and torn a hole in his lung, leaving him with an infantryman's nightmare—the sucking chest wound.

Hayes had treated enough of them to know that the pressure building in his chest was from the fluid filling his collapsed lung, and that if he didn't treat it soon, he would drown in his own blood.

He lifted an object that looked like a tan Sharpie from the floor and tore off the cap, revealing a 10-gauge decompression needle the length of his index finger. Holding it in his left hand, Hayes probed along his ribs with his right, found the intercostal space, and used his thumbnail to make a mark.

Switching the needle to his right hand, he picked up the empty casing and put it in his mouth. He placed the tip of the needle over the indentation, bit down on the plastic, and in one sure stroke, drove the needle deep into his chest.

His world exploded in a mushroom cloud of pain and Hayes bit the plastic casing hard enough to crush it between his teeth— but he could breathe, and that was all that mattered.

The act of stabbing a needle into his chest had sapped the last of his reserve and sent his blood pressure dropping like an elevator with a cut cable. Knowing that he was seconds from passing out, Hayes scrambled for the auto-injector, managed to tear the cap free and press his thumb against the trigger, firing the needle into his thigh.

The five milligrams of epinephrine hit his central nervous system like a shot of ether, the double dose of synthetic adrenaline racing through his veins.

*Now get the hell up.*

Hayes lurched to his feet, eyes locked on the Land Cruiser across the street. He staggered across the parking lot, the blood running from the knife wound, coiling over the front sight of the STI in his hand and splatting like raindrops on the asphalt.

After ten feet, Hayes knew he didn't have the strength to make it in one shot and cheated left, angling for the hood of the closest bullet-riddled pickup. He was almost there when he caught movement a foot to his right, saw one of the wounded men reaching for a rifle.

"*Seriously?*" he asked, as the man grabbed the pistol grip of his AK.

The man flipped onto his back, grunting from the effort of leveling the rifle at Hayes's chest.

"I'll fucking kill you," he hissed.

"Not without clearing that jam," Hayes said, firing a shot through the center of the man's skull without breaking stride.

He shuffled to one of the vehicles and leaned against it, the blood dripping from the barrel of the STI. But he knew he wasn't going to make it to the Land Cruiser.

*Just need to sit down for a second.*

He slumped against the 6x6 and dug the burner phone from his pocket.

*What the hell are you doing?* the voice demanded. *They'll find you.*

But Hayes didn't care. He was dying.

Gritting his teeth against the pain, he dialed the number and leaned his head back against the tire.

*Please pick up*, he begged.

Hayes was about to give up, let the darkness take him, when

the line connected, and Annabelle's sleepy voice came through the headset.

"Hello?"

He tried to speak, to answer, but the sound of her voice was like a shot of morphine, rendering him speechless.

"Adam . . . is that you?"

"Y-yeah, baby," he croaked, "sorry for waking you up . . . but . . ."

The pain rolled up his body like a river of fire, its all-encompassing heat taking his breath away, threatening to consume him from the inside out.

"What's wrong? Are you hurt? Adam, talk to me."

Hayes was panting now, the sweat bucketing down his face, the beat of his heart erratic.

"Annabelle . . . I'm not going to make it . . . I want you to know that I'm s-sorry . . ." He paused to catch his breath, the tears burning his eyes, rolling down his cheeks. "Sorry I wasn't a better man."

"No, Adam! You listen to me . . . I don't care what you have to do, you come home to us. Your son needs you . . . I need you."

Before he could reply, Hayes heard the unmistakable *thump-thump* of approaching helos. He tracked the sound east, to the rosy-fingered dawn spreading across the horizon, watched the two black specks racing toward him.

*You're too late.*

She was screaming now, her voice sharp as shattered glass. "Adam . . . Adam, are you there?"

"Yeah . . . I'm here."

"You listen to me," she sobbed, "you have to come home. Your son needs you . . . I need you."

"You tell Jack that I love him."

"You are going to tell him yourself, do you hear me?"

"Not this time, baby," he said, his voice barely a whisper.

The stabbing pain in his heart sucked the breath out of him and he was aware of the phone falling from his hand, plastic clattering against the asphalt, Anabelle's tiny voice screaming through the speaker.

*So tired.*

Hayes's breath caught in his throat and his heartbeat slowed to an erratic thump, the downdraft of the lead Osprey touching down on the far side of the parking lot pushing him over. He lay on his side, vision narrowing as the squad of camouflaged men came bounding down the ramp, eyes determined beneath the black-and-green greasepaint smeared across their faces as they rushed to him.

Then there was darkness.

# 57

Levi Shaw sat in the back of the lead Osprey, the expressions of the Marine Raiders packed in around him unreadable beneath the greasepaint. They were a battle-hardened team, combat-seasoned from multiple deployments running ops in some of the roughest corners of the world.

Shaw, on the other hand, was an outsider and could sense that his mere presence on the op made the men nervous.

"Feet dry," the pilot announced over the radio.

While the team leader barked last-minute instructions to his operators and the medical team triple-checked their aid bags, Shaw tugged a thirty-round magazine from his plate carrier and slapped it into the magwell of the CAR-15 resting barrel-down between his legs.

He grabbed the charging handle and was pulling it to the rear when he heard the team leader's voice over the radio.

The Raider captain inched closer to Shaw.

"Sir, what are our ROE?"

"ROE?" Shaw asked.

"Yes, sir, our rules of engagement?"

"I wouldn't worry too much about that, young captain," Shaw said over the *chunk* of the bolt slamming a seventy-gram TSX boat-tailed hollow-point into the chamber.

"Why is that, sir?" the man asked, the confusion on his face evident.

"Because that man down there," Shaw said, nodding toward the window, "doesn't tend to leave many survivors."

"But if there are any survivors . . . if he missed any?"

"Well, if that's the case, you boys feel free to send 'em to hell for me."

Before he could answer, the pilot was back on the radio, his voice hesitant as he held the massive tilt-rotor in a hover.

"Pretty tight down there, sir. We are going to have to find an—"

But Shaw had already ripped the headphones from his ears and was rushing to the flight deck.

"Put it down," he ordered.

"Sir, it's too tight," the pilot said. "It's not safe."

"Either you put this bird down, or I will," he said, aiming the CAR-15 at the controls.

All it took was one look into Shaw's eyes and the pilot's hesitation evaporated. "You better hold on," he said, nosing the Osprey over the wall.

Shaw stayed in the cockpit, any questions he'd been harboring about if Hayes had lost his edge since leaving Treadstone evaporating when he saw the bodies and the piles of expended brass that dotted the parking lot.

"Holy shit," the copilot said, "who the hell *is* this guy?"

"That's classified," Shaw said, turning back to the cargo hold.

A minute later the Osprey was on the ground, the Marine Raiders bounding down the ramp—Shaw tight on their heels.

"Sir, it's not secure," the team leader advised at the bottom of the ramp, but Shaw brushed him off and sprinted after the trauma team.

By the time he caught up with the medics, they had Hayes laid out on the sidewalk—one medic already doing chest compressions while a second took a pair of surgical shears to his bloody pant leg.

"This guy needs a priest, not a medic," one of the men said.

Shaw wanted to threaten, to beg them to save Hayes's life, but before he could figure out which one to pick, Captain Fox was pulling him away.

"Sir, these guys are the best in the business. Let them do their job."

Shaw nodded, helpless to do anything but watch as the trauma lead barked out an order.

"Jonesy, get a bag of O positive started. Eric, tell the crew we are wheels up in five. I want the crash cart charged and the norepinephrine ready the second we hit the ramp."

"Roger that, boss," the medic said.

While Eric keyed up on the radio and advised the surgical team on board the second Osprey, the team leader opened his aid bag, pulled out what looked like a toy drill, and snapped a large-bore needle to the end.

"Jonesy, you got my blood?" he asked, pressing the needle to Hayes's shin.

"Right here, boss," the medic answered.

"All right, here we go."

He pulled the trigger, the electric motor barely audible over the thump of the rotors as he drilled the needle into the bone.

"All right, I'm in," he said, disconnecting the drill from the needle, taking the tube running from the bag of O positive that Jonesy handed him and snapping it into the base of the needle.

Then they were moving, Hayes bobbing on the stretcher as they rushed back to the Osprey.

# EPILOGUE

## UNDISCLOSED LOCATION

One minute Hayes was gone, floating through the endless black that separated the living from the dead, and then there was a distant spark on the horizon, the murmur of voices, and invisible hands dragging him toward the light.

He fought against the tide, tried to pull free, but it was too late.

The pain came back with a vengeance, hard and fast like a punch to the gut. He opened his eyes and saw the masked faces hovering over him.

"Wh-what are you . . ."

"Doctor, he's awake. Blood pressure 140 over 90 and rising."

"That's impossible," a man said.

The instant he stepped into view, Hayes reached up and

grabbed the man by the front of his scrubs. "What are you doing to me?" he demanded, pulling him close.

"Shit, someone dose this guy before he tears the sutures."

Hayes shoved him away and was reaching for the IVs stuck in his arm, ready to tear them free, when Shaw stepped into view.

"Adam, calm down," he said, grabbing his hand. "It's okay. You're safe now."

"Safe?"

"Yes, you're safe. Just relax, I've got you."

Then the drugs kicked in and it was back to the black.

Hayes wasn't sure how long he'd been out, but when he finally came to, his mouth was dry and his mind was fogged from the drugs.

He tried to sit up but had barely lifted his head from the pillow when the vertigo and rush of nausea told him it was a bad idea.

"Easy, son," Shaw said, stepping into his line of sight.

"W-water," he croaked, nodding to the pitcher sitting on the bedside table.

"The doc didn't think you were going to pull through," Shaw said, filling one of the Styrofoam cups with water, "but I guess you showed him."

Hayes took the cup, water spilling over his chin as he gulped it down. "More," he said, handing the cup back to Shaw, studying him as he refilled it. Noting the fresh sutures on his cheek, the cuts that crisscrossed the man's hands.

"You look like shit," he said.

"Yeah, well, you're no spring daisy yourself."

This time he savored the water, his mind filling with a thousand questions as Shaw walked to the window and pulled back the shade.

"Why?" Hayes asked, squinting against the onslaught of sunlight that filled the room.

"Why what?"

"Why'd you come for me?" Hayes asked.

"Old and sentimental, I guess," Shaw answered with a sly smile.

"Funny. What happened to your face?"

"Carpenter tried to kill me," Shaw said. "Slick son of a bitch sent a couple of his hitters to ambush me on my way home."

"Because of me?" Hayes asked.

"Because of *us*," Shaw answered, returning to his bed. "When I let you go off on your little crusade it made certain senators think that I'd gone soft. And let's face it, with you gone, Treadstone's nothing but a paper tiger."

"Killing senators is what got me into this mess in the first place, Levi," Hayes said.

"I'll handle Miles and Carpenter," Shaw said, patting him on the hand. "You just get healthy. I've got big plans for you when you get back."

"Who said I'm back?" Hayes asked.

"Well, I *did* save your life," Shaw grinned, "so it's either come back to work or spend the rest of your life owing me one."

"Still a devious son of a bitch, I see," Hayes said.

"I'll take that as a yes," Shaw said, getting to his feet. "Now get some rest, son."

## About the Author

JOSHUA HOOD is the author of Robert Ludlum's *The Treadstone Resurrection, Warning Order* and *Clear by Fire.* He graduated from the University of Memphis before joining the military and spending five years in the 82nd Airborne Division. On his return to civilian life he became a sniper team leader on a full-time SWAT team in Memphis, where he was awarded the lifesaving medal. He is currently a full-time author living in Collierville, TN.

---

ROBERT LUDLUM was the author of twenty-seven novels, each one a *New York Times* bestseller. There are more than 225 million of his books in print, and they have been translated into thirty-two languages. He is the author of the Jason Bourne series: *The Bourne Identity, The Bourne Supremacy,* and *The Bourne Ultimatum* – among other novels. Mr Ludlum passed away in March 2001.